ANNE DOUGHTY was born in Armagh, Northern Ireland. She is the author of twelve novels including *A Few Late Roses* which was longlisted for the *Irish Times* fiction prize. After many years living in England she returned to Belfast in 1998 and wrote the first of the novels that make up the Hamiltons series.

a&b

Beyond the Green Hills

ANNE DOUGHTY

Allison & Busby Limited
12 Fitzroy Mews
London W1T 6DW
allisonandbusby.com

First published in Great Britain in 2002.
This paperback edition published by Allison & Busby in 2015.

A CIP catalogue record for this book is available from
the British Library.

10 9 8 7 6 5 4 3 2 1

ISBN 978-0-7490-1981-5

Typeset in 10.25/14.45 pt Sabon by
Allison & Busby Ltd.

The paper used for this Allison & Busby publication
has been produced from trees that have been legally sourced
from well-managed and credibly certified forests.

Printed and bound by
CPI Group (UK) Ltd, Croydon, CR0 4YY

For Rosemary,
who has always shared her experience

PROLOGUE

They stood in the shadow of the great stone pillar and studied every detail of the fields and orchards that covered the little humpy hills all around them. The old cottages, long and low, white painted, were tucked into their hollows on the south-facing slopes, sheltered from the north and west by plantings of trees. There was the odd new farm building, and a few two-storey houses, edging the little lanes that turned and twisted, dipped into valleys and climbed over their smooth, well-rounded shapes.

The blue tractor finished its work. The driver unhitched the plough and drove off down the lane below them. Gleaming in the sunlight, the newly ploughed field was left to the gulls, which hunted up and down the straight, newly turned furrows.

'You love this place, Clare, don't you?'

'Yes, I do,' she said firmly. 'I'd be heartbroken if I thought I'd never stand here again.'

She paused, remembering a summer Sunday

long ago when she'd climbed up to the obelisk for the first time. Uncle Jack had been there and various aunts and uncles she couldn't quite sort out. She was nine years old. She'd looked all around her and made up her mind that she was going to stay with Granda Scott, even if Auntie Polly wanted to take her with them to Canada.

'I think I do belong here, Andrew, like you do. But I'd be sad all my life if I never saw anything of the world out there, beyond the green hills.'

CHAPTER ONE

'Do you ever wish you could make time stand still?' Clare asked, as she rolled over and sat up on the short, springy turf of the sunny hollow where they'd lain down to rest.

They'd been so lucky. Day after day, all through this miraculous week, the sun had poured down on them out of a flawless blue sky. Beyond their sitting place, the flower-studded grass gave way to powder-fine sand. The tide was far out, the brilliant blue-green mass of the Atlantic a good half mile away. So soft and distant the ripple of minute waves, it was entirely overlain by the whisper of a tiny breeze and the devoted murmurings of the insects which swung in the globes of sea campion and nuzzled the pink heads of thrift that bloomed all around them.

A mile of shimmering white sand away, the fishermen's cottages in Port Bradon stood around their small harbour. The only inhabitants of the beach were cows, a dozen of them, settled happily on the warm sand, a short distance from the grassy slopes that ran down to the shore.

'Hm?' he said sleepily, an arm thrown across his eyes as he turned towards her, the sunlight catching a hint of red in his fair hair.

She pulled his hair, laughing as a trickle of sand slid down his face.

'Deaf ears! I asked if you ever wished you could make time stand still.'

He smiled up at her.

'If, perhaps, this fortnight could go on for ever?' She nodded.

'But think what we might miss. What joys might be stored up in the weeks which would come after.'

His voice was light and teasing, his blue eyes full of a tenderness that still amazed her.

'I keep thinking I'll wake up and find it's all a dream,' she said, half seriously.

'Why should it be?' he asked easily. 'We knew we wanted to be together. We knew we wanted to be lovers. Why shouldn't it be wonderful now we've finally managed it?'

His smile faded as he watched her face grow thoughtful and rather sad.

'Perhaps I think it's too good to be true. All this and you too,' she said, with an attempt at lightness.

She threw out a hand to embrace the sky and the sea, the dazzling white gulls gliding overhead, the golden splashes of tormentil dotting the hollow where they sat.

Suddenly Clare shivered, as if the warmth and light of the June day had been switched off.

It was November, and she was looking down through the leafless tree beyond her window to the pavements of Elmwood Avenue below. The last of the leaves lay saturated and brown, tramped into the wet surface below the dark, dripping branches. Although it was midday, the room behind her was dark but for a single point of light, the glow of her gas fire.

In her hand, she held a letter from Andrew. He was trying to comfort her. She had lost her grandfather and her home. She had friends, she had her grant to live on, she had her work, but it seemed to her then that she had lost all that she loved. Except Andrew. He was the only one who grasped what it meant not to be able to go back to the place where you grew up, where you knew every stone and tree, every detail of a house and garden. However tedious and hard her life had so often been in the house by the forge, in those first awful months she had felt sure that she would never heal the loss of all that had been so familiar.

'Perhaps this all seems unreal,' she said slowly.

'But why should what is beautiful and happy be any less real than what is sad, or dark, or painful?' He sat up and reached out for her hand, his eyes moving over her face, usually so mobile, now so still, sombre and downcast. He had never seen her look like this before. Her shoulders drooped as if she were burdened by cares, her eyes focused on a tiny fragment of golden flower she had picked and now held between finger and thumb. She rubbed its short stem so that it twirled round and round, the tiny red speckles on the base of its petals now invisible in the blur of gold. 'Was last night unreal?' he asked urgently. To her own surprise, Clare blushed. 'No, my love, it wasn't,' she said softly.

She glanced up at him and caught his look of anxious concern just as it softened.

'There's nothing of the phantom lover about you,' she added, smiling weakly.

Making love to Andrew for the first time had been no more difficult than kissing him for the first time, all those years ago on their first outing to Cannon Hill.

A week ago, they'd arrived at the old fisherman's cottage, tucked in under the cliffs beyond the harbour at Ballintoy, a bag of food in the boot of their borrowed car. They'd found a bottle of wine waiting for them and a note from Clare's old friend Jessie, explaining the peculiarities of the cottage. Andrew had pushed open the door into the tiny bedroom. The high bed was so large it filled almost all the space. They looked at each other and laughed.

'We'd better have supper first or we won't get

any,' Andrew said as he turned her round and propelled her back into the other room.

They'd eaten the food in the bag, drunk the wine, and made love in the moonlight, eagerly and joyously. They drifted into a blissful doze, woke up and made love again, the roar of the incoming tide loud in their ears. And again, as fingers of light reached across the patchwork quilt and a blackbird tuned up for its morning song. Exhausted at last, they'd fallen asleep and not opened their eyes till the middle of the morning.

'No wonder football teams are locked up when they're in training,' Andrew said, as he peered into the kitchen cupboard, in search of bowls for their cornflakes.

She looked at him blankly as she turned from the larder, a jug of milk in her hand.

'Passion can be quite debilitating, don't you think?' he asked, with a perfectly straight face.

She laughed till the contents of the milk jug rocked like a stormy sea.

They'd just managed to eat breakfast before going back to their crumpled bed.

It had all been so easy. Easy to make love, easy to cope with the primitive arrangements at the cottage, where water came from the spring under a bush near the back door and the loo was a rickety wooden plank over a hole in the ground. Easy to be together hour after hour.

That first week, they'd worked their way all along the north coast. They'd tramped the length of the Giant's Causeway, taken it in turns to sit in the Wishing Chair, promised not to tell each other their wish. They'd looked down into the chill waters below the Minstrel's Window at Dunluce Castle and imagined the sheer rage of the storm that had brought it crashing into the sea, one fearful winter's night, long ago. They drove to Ballycastle, walked along the beach to Marconi's cottage. Staring out across the wide ocean he'd been the first to span with radio waves, they wondered if they'd ever visit America themselves.

They had talked, hour upon hour, as if to make up for all the years of silent letters and frustrating phone calls. At night, they made love with the same urgency, trying to satisfy their deep longing in the sheer passion of the moment, only to discover that such longing grew by what it fed on.

'You're quite right, you know,' she said, coming back to the present. She squeezed his hand. 'Sometimes the dark things, the sad things, seem more real than the good things. I wonder why. Is black more real than white?'

'Perhaps we've been encouraged to see the dark as more real. Sin-soaked religion with hellfire at the end of it is supposed to concentrate the mind on our follies and failures rather than our joys and successes.'

'But I don't even go to church now,' she protested.

'You don't have to. It gets into the bloodstream. You pick it up from other people, from how they behave, what they say. *Ach, shure ye never know the day. Just when he was on the pig's back, shure didn't the good Lord call him in and he fell off the muck spreader. Dead and buried an' him that pleased he'd just got his pension.*'

Clare laughed. She'd forgotten just how well Andrew could still mimic the local Grange accent. And he'd got the uncompromising tone so right. So often in the days when she'd sat on the settle by the stove listening to the men who visited her grandfather of an evening she'd heard them speak in such a way that even the mildest disagreement seemed impossible. She'd even felt there was real enjoyment in telling the tale of a well-known figure suddenly struck down, someone seen or talked to only a day or two previously. It wasn't that they weren't sorry at the loss of a neighbour, but their enthusiasm for telling a story of death and disaster had always puzzled her.

'It could be good old Calvinism, Clare. Never let yourself be happy or you'll be struck down. Happiness is not for the likes of us mortals.'

She nodded thoughtfully and then smiled. 'Are you happy, Andrew?'

'Yes. I am. Happier than I've ever been in all

my life,' he said firmly. 'And what about you?' he added more hesitantly.

'Yes,' she said, nodding vigorously. 'I'm happy too. So happy I get the wobbles,' she added, laughing, as she moved into his arms.

They lay entwined until they grew too hot in the strong sun.

'How would it be, my best beloved, if I drove us into the nearest metropolis and bought us an ice cream?'

She laughed as he extended his tongue and licked a large, imaginary cone. What a silly she'd been, having such dark thoughts when life was all they'd ever hoped for. The years of separation were over. The summer lay ahead. Andrew would be in Belfast and so would she. For the next three months, while she was working with Jessie and her husband, Harry, they'd actually be in the very same street. They'd see each other every day. And this time next year, with Finals behind her, they'd be married. They'd be properly together at last, never to part, free to shape their future the way they wanted it to be.

'Where *is* the nearest metropolis?'

'I really don't know,' he said honestly. 'But there's an Antrim map in the car. Fairly ancient, judging by the colour of the cover. But things don't change that much around here. If we can find somewhere with a church, a chapel and at least three pubs, it'll be big enough to have a shop with a fridge and Walls choc ices.'

He paused, looked at her very seriously, and then continued.

'On the other hand, Your Honour, I have to say, on the evidence accumulated over the years, it is an established fact that watering places such as Portrush support a superfluity of establishments wherein the delicacy in question may be consumed, suitably seated, from a silver receptacle.' He paused for effect. 'Furthermore, in such establishments, I have it on good report, it is the custom to offer a wide choice of this particular consumable – and you don't get your fingers sticky either.'

He stood up, pulled her to her feet and into his arms. After a short delay, they set off through the dunes, back to the car.

CHAPTER TWO

Clare opened her eyes and gazed round the broad terrace of The Lodge. Beside her, Andrew lay in a sun-bleached deckchair, his eyes closed, minute specks of cream emulsion paint dotting the bridge of his nose and the pale triangle of skin revealed by one of his cousin Edward's oldest shirts.

At that moment, Teddy opened his eyes. He sat up, glanced at his watch, considered Andrew's recumbent figure and looked down at the stretched-out figure of his sister, Ginny, her cotton shirt tucked up, her long legs already a gleaming, honey gold.

'Five minutes more and then back to work,' he announced firmly.

Ginny's eyes flicked open.

'Edward,' she began, a look of outrage on her face. 'Not only do you waylay us into participating in your *grand summer manoeuvre* when we are *all* supposed to be *on holiday*, but now you treat us like minions. Well, it won't do. This minion is on strike.'

Clare laughed aloud as Ginny spread herself out more comfortably, folded her hands across her stomach and closed her eyes again.

'I didn't waylay you,' he protested. 'I explained my difficulties to Clare and Andrew when they got back from Ballintoy, and they offered of their own free will.'

'I'm not here, I've gone away,' Ginny murmured. 'I'm on holiday on a tropical island, lying on a pure white beach, with blue water lapping the palm trees. Goodness, what's that?'

A shot shattered the stillness. A cloud of rooks rose flapping and protesting from a clump of trees beyond the paddock. The detonation was rapidly followed by others of diminishing magnitude.

'It's only the breadman, Ginny,' Edward said patiently. 'His exhaust is exhausted,' he explained. 'Mum said to tell you she'd left a list on the kitchen table. And we owe him for the Armagh papers.'

Clare watched Ginny get to her feet, pull his ear and head for the kitchen. How lovely it would be to have a brother you could tease, she thought sadly, someone you could be really fond of, make jokes with, not like her own brother. Since their parents died, she'd tried so hard to be a proper sister, visited him whenever she could, brought him what small presents she could afford, but the older he got the more surly and unsmiling he became.

'Sure, yer Granda's done his best, I'll say that

fer him, since the day yer Auntie Polly brought him here,' Granny Hamilton had said on her last visit to the farm. 'An' he admits there's no improvement at all. William's just one of those people with no time for anyone but himself.'

The contrast with Edward was almost too painful to bear. Although he was only just nineteen, Edward had already shouldered many of the responsibilities his father's death had landed on him, but he hadn't lost his capacity to make them laugh. There was an openness about Edward, a warmth and a good-naturedness she found totally appealing.

'Well then, Boss, shall we get back to it?' said Andrew, soberly.

As he got to his feet, he put a hand down to Clare's cheek and touched it gently.

'It really is awfully good of you and Clare to help me out like this,' said Edward sheepishly. 'It was a far bigger job than I thought. It didn't look so bad till I got started.'

'Don't worry about it, Edward,' said Clare warmly. 'I'll add it to my curriculum vitae. Picture rail painted by the yard, to professional standards. Besides, I like my outfit,' she added.

She flapped the long sleeves of the smock he'd found for her, the one his mother wore when she painted in oils. Daubed with patches of brilliant colour, it looked like a work of art itself.

'Are you sure you don't mind being up that ladder, Clare?'

'No, truly, Edward. Heights don't seem to bother me.'

The breadman's van started up again. Edward paused, listening.

'Back in a tick,' he said over his shoulder, as he ran down the steps from the terrace. 'Must give Ginny a hand. There's enough bread on Mum's list to feed the five thousand.'

Andrew dropped his arm lightly round Clare's shoulders and kissed her cheek.

'You don't mind, do you?'

'No, not a bit,' she said honestly. 'I've discovered I like painting. I'd never done any before,' she added, as they walked slowly along the terrace.

The French windows of the large, airy sitting room stood open wide, the stacked furniture beyond looming up like silent, white-clad watchers.

'It'll look lovely when it's finished,' she said, as they took their brushes from the jar of white spirit and dried them off.

'Yes, it's a super room. I've always loved it,' Andrew replied. 'Aunt Helen knows just where to put things for the best effect and how to make it welcoming. The furniture isn't nearly as good as the stuff at Drumsollen, but it always looks much better.'

Clare laughed wryly. There was a time she'd

known the furniture at Drumsollen only too well. As the housekeeper's Saturday girl, she'd polished it regularly. She'd cursed the assorted objects that had to be moved from every surface before she could begin, but the smooth, mellow wood was lovely to touch. Even dusting the carving and the delicate inlay work had been a pleasure.

As she went to place her ladder below the next unpainted section of picture rail, she caught sight of Andrew's face, sad and anxious, his lips pressed together, a sure sign he was uneasy.

'Will you be going over to Drumsollen this week?' she asked cautiously.

'I suppose I should.'

Without looking at her, he prised the lid off a new tin of paint and stirred the contents. She waited patiently, knowing there was more to come.

'Edward says he got a cool reception when he went to make sure the roof repairs had been done properly,' he began. 'If she couldn't be nice to her caring landlord, she'll hardly be very keen to see me. Now Grandfather's gone she doesn't even have to be civil.'

'Maybe she's lonely, Andrew.'

'Hard to imagine her missing anyone. She must have loved him once, I suppose. But then, showing your feelings wasn't the done thing in their day, was it? Could we ever get like that, Clare?'

He looked so utterly miserable Clare abandoned

her ladder, took the tin of paint out of his hands and put her arms round him.

'Maybe age takes love away,' she said, sadly. 'I don't know any old, married people who even seem to like each other any more. Granny Hamilton only speaks to Granda now when there's some bit of everyday business she has to mention, yet she gave up going to America to marry him.'

'Will you come with me?' he asked suddenly, holding her so tightly she could hardly breathe.

'Where to?'

'Drumsollen.'

'Oh, Andrew, don't you think that might make it worse? I'm not sure she's ever forgiven me for tackling her at your Uncle Edward's funeral.'

To her complete amazement, Andrew threw back his head and laughed.

'What's so funny?'

'That cap you wore,' he said, still laughing. 'I'll never forget it I can still see you standing there, telling her what you thought of her. It must he the only time in human history the Missus has apologised to anyone. It ought to be recorded in the Annals of the Richardsons,' he said, pausing and kissing her. 'Please, Clare. Come with me. She's going to have to know sooner or later. Let's get it over with.'

'All right, I'll come,' she said quickly, as she

caught sight of Edward and Ginny walking along the terrace towards them.

'Thank you, love. That'll help,' he said, a look of profound relief on his face.

When they emerged from the shadow of the long line of trees beyond the mental hospital, they saw the gates of Drumsollen standing open. As Andrew swung the bonnet of Aunt Helen's car between the stone pillars, Clare glanced across at the low wall beyond them. In another life, she and Jessie used to park their bicycles there while they nipped across the road, down to their secret sitting place by the small, deeply entrenched stream.

'Well, here we are,' said Andrew flatly, as he stopped the car and glanced up at the worn stone frontage of the three-storeyed mansion.

Clare squeezed his arm encouragingly.

'We're a right pair, aren't we? You'd think we were going for an interview.'

To her surprise, he didn't smile. He didn't even seem to hear her. She watched him straighten his tie in the driving mirror and brush non-existent hairs from his shoulders before he got out. He was wearing his best trousers, a clean shirt, his college tie and blazer. Apart from Uncle Edward's funeral, she'd never seen him dressed so formally before.

'Are my seams straight?'

He studied her legs minutely and nodded before

he realised she was trying to make him laugh. He pressed his lips together again and smiled bleakly.

'She can't eat us, Andrew. Why are you so bothered?'

'I don't know. Honestly, Clare, I don't know.'

He reached for her hand and they walked up the stone steps towards the heavy front door. It too stood open, the entrance hall in shadow beyond.

'My goodness,' Clare said, in a whisper, as they stepped across the threshold, leaving the afternoon sunlight behind.

'What is it?'

'Everything,' she said, stopping dead before the polished table with its long out of date copies of *Country Life* and *Shooting Times*.

She looked up at the chandelier above her head, its cut-glass drops tinkling minutely in the movement of air from the open door. 'I'd forgotten how big this hall is. And the way the ancestors stare down at you. I must have got used to it the year I worked here. Don't you feel it pressing down on you?'

'I don't know what I feel,' he replied, looking round him as if he was hoping to find some way of escape. 'Let's go down to the kitchen and tell June we're here.'

'Ach, there's ye's are, the pair of you.'

Before they'd time to move, they caught the echo of footsteps on the wooden stairs from the kitchen. Breathless from hurrying, June Wiley, once

Andrew's devoted nursemaid, then housekeeper, now the sole remaining pair of hands in this huge house, crossed the threadbare carpet and threw her arms around them both.

'I was listenin' fer the car. My, yer both doin' powerful well,' she said, looking them up and down. 'Aren't ye glad to be home, Andrew? An' I'm sure Clarey's glad to see ye back. Ach, Clare dear, I shoulden call you that these days.'

'Call away, June,' said Clare quickly, her eyes misting with tears. No one had called her Clarey since Granda Scott died.

'It's great to see you, June' she said, returning the hug. 'Can we come home with you and visit John and the girls when you finish?'

'Deed aye. Sure they're expectin' ye both. We'll want to hear all yer news. But I'd best not keep ye's now. She's waitin' fer ye.'

She nodded significantly. Putting an arm round each of them, she walked them across the hall to the foot of the broad, carpeted stairway.

'Ye'll see her badly failed, Andrew, since the Senator went. She can hardly walk at all, but don't let on I told you. I'll see ye's later.'

Their feet made no sound on the wide, and shallow stairs, the once-red carpet now faded by the sun that flooded through the tall windows and made patterns on the walls. The air in the broad first-floor corridor struck chill. Clare shivered and felt goose pimples rise on her bare arms. She squeezed Andrew's hand as they approached the one room in Drumsollen she had never been permitted to enter.

'It'll be all right, love,' she whispered, as they paused at the door.

'Come in.'

The voice that responded to Andrew's knock had lost nothing of its imperiousness. Madeline Richardson, the Missus to her one-time servants, her family, friends and acquaintances, sat in a high carved wooden chair that was well padded with cushions. She wore a silk blouse and pearls, a pleated tweed skirt and matching cardigan, heavy stockings and stout walking shoes – just what she would have worn in the long past days when she would go out to instruct the gardeners, or to pick the flowers she always arranged herself for the guest bedrooms.

Now the garments hung on her emaciated body. Her face was gaunt, her cheeks hollow, her rouge an unconvincing area of colour on skin the colour of parchment. Her hands, bony and blue-veined, gripped the arms of her chair. Remaining upright was clearly an effort of will.

'Andrew, bring that low chair for Clare, over here beside me, if you will,' she said, before there was any question of kiss, or handshake. 'What a splendid day for your visit. I'm sure you had a pleasant drive from Caledon,' she went on, without looking at either of them.

Clare seated herself on the low chair, her eyes almost level with the small undulations in the pleated skirt that marked the position of the Missus's knees. Not having been invited to sit down, Andrew stood waiting awkwardly.

'I've ordered tea for four-thirty. Perhaps, Andrew, you would help Mrs Wiley with the trays. I know you always like to chat to her. And I shall have a word with Clare.'

It was not yet four o'clock. Andrew departed without a word. Whether he felt relieved at having been dismissed, or angry that his grandmother had managed to avoid greeting him, in any way, Clare would have to find out later.

'Eh bien, Clare, I hear you have been in Paris. Did your studies go well?'

The voice was quite firm, its intentions clear. Perhaps it was to be an interview after all. Clare looked up at the haggard face. There were creases of pale eye shadow on the drooping lids and carefully pencilled eyebrows above the large, over-bright eyes. They watched her closely, waiting.

'I didn't go to study. Not directly. But I did learn a great deal. My professor found me a family in Paris who wanted an au pair. Actually, I spent more time in Deauville than in Paris.'

A smile of pleasure, of longing almost, lit up the old woman's face, filling it with an animation Clare had never seen before.

'Deauville! Oh, que j'aime Deauville.'

Clare was more taken aback by the softness of her tone than by the sudden move to French. She'd heard her speak the language before, but this was not how it sounded when she'd reprimanded Andrew for speaking to a servant.

Madeline Richardson asked a stream of questions without pausing for any reply: questions about places, particular buildings, a hotel where she'd once stayed, a small cafe where they'd had second breakfast after swimming. At last, she paused and looked at Clare expectantly.

'Bien sur, Deauville est très agréable,' she began. 'My friend, Marie-Claude, used to go there as a child. She still visits the old woman who looked after her in those days. She says Deauville has changed remarkably little. Many of the places you've mentioned, I recognise at once. Some of the hotels have changed their names, but Marie-Claude says they haven't changed their style. And people still promenade.'

The old woman pressed her hands together and cast her eyes towards the ceiling.

'Oh, so. We had such *fun* in Deauville. Of course, we were chaperoned, but there were ways of communicating with young men that everyone knew. If a young man wished to meet you, he would find out where you were staying and send you a bouquet. There were always two cards with a bouquet, one that you handed to your chaperone with some suitable message and another concealed in the flowers. That one you read later.'

She paused and looked at Clare meaningfully, as if to make sure she understood. When Clare smiled broadly, she continued.

'My cousin and I were taken to the Royal Hotel by my great-aunt. She was a very strict lady, but even she was charmed when we came back from a morning walk and found the room full of flowers.'

She paused, considered, and then went on.

'My cousin was very beautiful, you see. She also had the advantage of being rich.'

She smiled at Clare, confident she would appreciate the point.

'I was never beautiful, but I was thought handsome by some. We both had our little adventures in Deauville.'

She paused once more, longer this time, as if she were still absorbed in the world she had known in another century, when she was young and her life opened before her, full of possibility and promise.

'And will you go again this year, to Deauville, with your French family?'

'No, I'm staying in Belfast this summer. I have a holiday job working at the gallery with my friend Jessie and her husband. His father has retired now and he's expanding into new areas. It's really very interesting.'

'Ah, I see.'

Clare was not sure what it was she saw, but her next question made it clear.

'I suppose you're going to marry Andrew when you get your degree?'

'Yes, I am.'

Clare was rather pleased at the coolness, the steadiness of her reply, but she was taken completely by surprise by the old woman's next words.

'What a pity. You really could do so much better for yourself. I'm sure he loves you, he always was such a loving child, but he's got no money and no ambition. Love isn't everything, you know. It wears badly with the rub of the years, especially when there's no money. It's women who pay the price for lack of means.'

Clare could hardly believe her ears. The irony was just too much for her. Four years ago, she'd first come to this house simply to earn twelve and sixpence extra a week, because her grandfather's new landlord had doubled the rent of their house and forge. Now, she was being told by the lady of the house herself that her nephew wasn't good enough for her.

Something in her words brought Clare up short, however. She wouldn't listen to any criticism of Andrew, certainly not from this woman who had excluded him from her life as far as possible, but her final words echoed and re-echoed round the elegant room.

It's women who pay the price for lack of means.

Clare saw herself, a little girl of nine, sitting at Granny Hamilton's kitchen table. Auntie Polly was going back to Canada and wanted her to go with them, but she wanted to stay behind and live with Granda Scott at the forge.

She couldn't recall Granny Hamilton's exact words, but she'd warned her what a hard life it was for a girl, living in the country. Things might improve when bread was off the ration and when the electric came, but, even then, she should think twice before saying no to Canada. She'd need to make up her mind on a clear day, Granny Hamilton had ended.

Clare glanced across the room to the four-poster bed with its draped velvet curtains, a matching velvet-covered couch at its foot. The rich colours might have faded, but the wallpaper and hangings, the curtains and carpets still had great elegance. The furniture was lighter in style and much more delicate than in the big rooms downstairs. Decorated in gold, it reminded her of what she'd seen in the salons of Versailles. Such a contrast with Granny's stone-floored kitchen, its stove and scrubbed wood table.

Two lives, two women, so very different, yet they were saying the same things about the quality of life available to a woman, unless she marry a man of adequate means.

However much she might want to, Clare couldn't dismiss the warning. After all, had she not had some experience of her own? Even when there was work available, Granda Scott had been too old to make much money at the forge, so they lived mainly on his pension, a struggle all the time to make ends meet. When her parents died, no one had provided an income for her, as Ginny's grandfather had, for both Ginny and her mother, when her father died. Her life had been much harder than Jessie's, for even after Jessie lost her father, there was an uncle who paid for her to go to secretarial college.

It s women who pay the price for lack of means.

There was something more to it than that, but what it was she'd have to work out for herself.

'And did you go to Châtelet, or the Opéra, when you were in Paris? What did you see?'

Clare realised she'd fallen silent. The older woman was deploying her well-practised skill in directing the conversation. The subject was being changed, firmly and positively.

'*Swan Lake* at Châtelet, Serge Lifar at the Opéra.'

As the question had been put to her in French, she replied in French. To Clare's great surprise, she found herself overcome with compassion for this

33

crippled, old woman who had tried to shape the world the way she wanted it and ended up alone and unloved.

Clare took a deep breath and told her exactly what it was like to see ballet for the first time. To step into a new world known only from books and music on the radio, to mingle with the crowds of Parisians in the theatre bar, watch the rich and famous and enjoy performances she had only dreamt of. She spared no detail, even when the Missus closed her eyes and sat so still Clare thought she must surely be asleep.

But she was not.

'Remind me, Clare, to make a note before you go,' she said abruptly, continuing to speak French as the door opened. 'I have a gift for you. I do not have it here, but I am dispersing my remaining personal possessions. I need to make a note of my intentions, in case we do not meet again,' she added firmly. 'A souvenir from my days in Paris and Deauville,' she ended, dropping her voice to a whisper.

'Thank you, Mrs Wiley. I'm sure Andrew will appreciate your efforts on his behalf,' she said, in a voice so far removed from her previous tone that Clare was almost startled.

As June and Andrew collected up small tables from other parts of the room to accommodate the plates of scones and cake for a most sumptuous tea, Clare felt herself go pale, drained by some emotional effort she could neither grasp nor understand. It was all she could do to take the cup June handed her without spilling it. Deciding which of the sandwiches and savouries to begin with was quite beyond her.

But Madeline Richardson was undaunted. She dismissed June Wiley courteously, placed Andrew in charge of the teapot, directed his attention to the brownies made especially for his coming and proceeded to enquire about the health and activities of his uncle and family, his surviving aunt, her husband and daughters, and his great-aunt in Norfolk.

Clare was relieved to find that Andrew seemed perfectly relaxed, able to do justice to June's tea while giving a proper account of his relatives. On one occasion, he even managed to make his grandmother laugh.

'Poor old Julia, she got very nervous when they arrived at the Palace and were being lined up to be presented. She was convinced her knickers were going to fall down. So she asked for the loo. They told her to be terribly quick and sent her off with a footman in attendance. She says she walked miles! When they arrive, he throws open the door and ushers her in and there's the loo, on a raised dais with three steps up. She insists it was at least another fifty yards away.'

When the topic of Andrew's relatives on his

mother's side had been exhausted, Mrs Richardson moved on to the family at Caledon, eliciting a detailed account of Aunt Helen's new husband, the progress of Edward's studies at Trinity and the latest developments in Virginia's plan for setting up her own riding stables.

Of Andrew's own activities, his plans, hopes and dreams, nothing whatever was asked. They said their goodbyes just after five and went down to the basement to help June Wiley with the washing up. Madeline Richardson remained in her large room, a sandwich and a glass of milk under a cloth on a side table. Until nine o'clock the next morning, she would be there alone, unable to walk further than her radio, or her commode. She had refused Edward's offer of a telephone in her room. If she needed a phone, she declared, she would use the one in the study.

When at last they left the house, with June in the back seat, all Clare wanted was Andrew, the comfort of his arms and the relief of tears, but first there was the visit to the Wiley family. She'd been so looking forward to seeing John and the three girls. She couldn't possibly let them down, but how she was going to get through the next few hours she had no idea whatever.

CHAPTER THREE

As they bumped their way along the narrow track, Clare noticed the grass growing up the middle became progressively much taller and more luxuriant. The potholes were much deeper too. Edward was trying to avoid the worst of them by swinging the car from side to side. Each time they swung to the left, she was able to look down into the clumps of yellow flag iris blooming on the bank of a deep, narrow river full of swift-flowing brown water. When they swung to the right, fresh green fronds of willow trailed the roof of the car and spilled through Ginny's open window.

'Do either of you two young gentlemen have the *slightest* idea where you're going?' Ginny demanded, as the car splashed across a broad wet area, a spring flowing from the steep hedge bank below the willows, a low green cliff, rich with the lush growth of high summer.

'No, not the slightest,' said Andrew cheerfully, as he folded up the one-inch map. 'Terra Incognita, white on the map except for the drawings of sea beasts. You are now on a Richardson's Mystery Tour. Right here by the oak tree, Edward.'

'Clare, have *you* any idea where these idiots might be taking us?' Ginny went on. 'I thought we had agreed to a picnic, not a cross-country rally.'

Clare laughed. 'I might,' she said slowly, not wanting to spoil the surprise. 'But I don't think we came this way last time.'

'*Last time!* You mean you survived?'

'Clare and I *almost* came here for our first date,' said Andrew, leaning round from the front passenger seat to enjoy Ginny's amazement. 'But there were some difficulties.'

Clare gigged.

'Difficulties!' exclaimed Ginny. 'Putting it mildly, I'd have thought. So, tell me, dear cousin, about your difficulties,' she went on.

'Well, I plucked up courage and asked Clare to go for a ride,' Andrew began agreeably, 'but she said no, she was sorry, she hadn't got a horse. Then, next day, she told Jessie she was going for a ride with me, so Jessie gave her directions for a nice, quiet place about ten miles from Drumsollen. But unfortunately I hadn't got a car.'

Edward began to chuckle, then to shake with laughter. As the car wobbled and bounced even more fiercely than before, Clare lay back in her seat laughing. It wasn't just the memory of that first date, it was the look on Ginny's face.

'Teddy,' Ginny remonstrated, 'the only mystery about this tour is that we are still in one piece. Why don't you let *me* drive?'

'I need the practice,' he gasped, when he could manage to stop laughing.

'You can say *that* again.'

'I need the practice,' he repeated obligingly.

Ginny groaned and looked at Clare for solidarity, but she was laughing helplessly.

At that precise moment the car ran smoothly forward on to a broad, sandy ridge, green with new grass and dotted with daisies and tufts of purple and white clover. Edward chose the highest point of the site and stopped the car.

'Now say you're sorry, sister dear,' he said triumphantly, waving his hand at the gleaming mass of Lough Neagh, blue and sparkling in the afternoon sun, the minute wavelets at its edge lapping on the fine, white sand only twenty yards away from where the car had come to rest.

They climbed out and stood looking around them, the sun warm on their shoulders and bare arms. To the east, a small wooden jetty, its irregular structure bleached white by sun and rain, projected into the waters of the lake. A couple of rowing boats were moored to a large, orange buoy. At the landward end of the jetty, a curtain of fishing nets hung suspended from an arrangement of poles, the twisted fibres dividing the brilliant sky into small, interlocking squares. All was quiet but for the hum of bees in the clover. There wasn't a soul in sight.

'How lovely,' said Clare, her eyes gleaming with pleasure as she scanned the prospect before her, from the hazy hills of Tyrone to the wooded inlets of the Antrim shore. She'd seen the lough many times from various low hills around the Hamiltons' farm, as well as from Cannon Hill, but she had never before stood on its shore.

'Look,' she said urgently, pointing towards the reedy sandbanks where the river they'd followed fanned out and poured its brown water into the lake only a short distance away.

A heron was fishing in the shallow water. At the sound of their voices it had taken off. They followed its leisurely flight across the sandy beach, shading their eyes as it headed out over the still water, its reflection a perfect mirror image. It landed on the edge of a small, tree-covered outcrop not far from the shore, a dazzling white mark against the dark background, its long bill dipped towards the gleaming water at its feet.

'In view of your success, I withdraw my comments on your driving skills unreservedly, Teddy,' Ginny said. 'But I'm not sure you ought to make a habit of driving Harry's car cross country,' she went on more seriously. 'I don't think the suspension's up to it.'

'Whose car?' retorted Edward.

'Sorry, sorry, sorry. *Your* car, I mean. It *was* Harry's for a very long time though, wasn't it?'

'I gather he didn't want to sell it to you,' said Andrew, turning to Edward as he opened the boot and began handing out the picnic things.

'No, he said it was a liability. It would only cost me money.'

'So how did you persuade him to let you have it?' Clare asked, as she collected a basket and a rug.

She remembered Harry, a wiry, dungareed figure with a tool bag, usually engaged in fixing something. If there was no other transport available at The Lodge, Andrew would collect her from the forge in the battered, blue Austin. Harry's car had been elderly then, and that was three years ago.

Edward shrugged his shoulders.

'I said it was all I could afford. I needed to get to the Bishop's Library in Armagh for some work I'm doing. So he gave it to me on condition I let his brother-in-law do the repairs for me on the cheap.'

Clare smiled to herself. She wasn't surprised. Harry had known the Richardsons since Edward was old enough to want to carry his nails and stand watching him work.

'Would you like me to get the Primus going, Edward?' Clare asked, as he took the box from the boot and stood looking at it doubtfully.

'Oh, yes please. It always pops at me and goes out.'

'It'll be easy today, there's no wind,' she said, taking it from him.

'Clare, it's not just wind. I can't even get the wretched thing to work on the kitchen table when there's a power cut!'

'My goodness, these smell good. What are they?' demanded Ginny, who was opening greaseproof packets and laying out sandwiches and cake on faded willow-pattern plates.

'Brownies,' said Andrew over his shoulder, as he brought the teapot to Clare. 'June made them for tea at Drumsollen and slipped us the rest in a doggy bag. The chocolate cake in the tin is hers as well.'

'Aren't brownies American?'

'Mm. Mother got the recipe from an American girl she was at school with in Switzerland. I've always loved them.'

'I didn't know your mother went to a finishing school,' Clare said, as she poured boiling water into the teapot.

'Oh yes, all nice gels went to finishing school. Ask Ginny about it.'

Ginny groaned.

'You cannot possibly want to know anything about it, Clare.'

'Yes, I do. Where did you go? What did they teach you?' she asked, suddenly aware of a whole piece of Ginny's life she knew nothing about.

'Ghastly. Unspeakable. Boring. Mum couldn't afford Switzerland so I went to this decaying mansion in the Wicklow Hills. The only good thing about it was the stables. That's where I met Conker's mother. Queen of Tara, by Pegasus, out of Pride of Kilkenny. She was lovely.'

'But what did you do apart from ride, Ginny?'

'We learnt to walk properly, how to pick up a handkerchief, how to arrange flowers for a dinner table. Really useful things like how to clean grease spots off silk and freshen your diamond necklace. How to talk to boring people who won't say anything to help you.'

'You're pulling my leg, Ginny,' said Clare, laughing, as she poured four cups of tea and handed one across to her.

'No, I'm not. Truly.'

Ginny put down her half-eaten sandwich, sat up straight and folded her hands neatly in her lap. 'Oh, you live in Scunthorpe, do you? How interesting. I haven't managed to visit Scunthorpe myself. Do you find the weather pleasant there? I expect it's just as irritating as it is here, invariably fine when one is at work and horribly wet when one wants to be outdoors . . .'

Edward helped himself to a sandwich and passed the plate to Ginny, who took it daintily and offered it coyly to Andrew.

'And did you have a pleasant stay in Caledon, Mr Richardson?' she continued, her total attention focused upon him. 'I hope your cousins were entertaining company and showed you something of the neighbourhood. I understand the countryside is rather varied and, of course, Armagh is quite historic, isn't it?'

She smiled sweetly at him and then scowled.

'I'd never have stuck it if it hadn't been for Conker,' she said with a huge sigh.

'But you said you met Conker's mother,' said Clare, puzzled.

'Mm. She was in foal. Mum promised if I stuck it out, they'd buy me the foal, providing he or she was all right. But it was ghastly. A complete waste of time if it hadn't been for her.'

'But don't you find it useful, knowing how to freshen up your diamonds?'

'My dear Clare, I'm so glad you reminded me about that. I had quite forgotten, and mine do need doing. They get so dusty at all these balls I'm obliged to attend.'

Ginny threw out her hands in an elegant gesture. 'I did also learn how to cut a chocolate cake. I take it you've brought the silver cake knife, Teddy.'

Edward dug his hand into his trouser pocket and offered her his penknife. She sighed dramatically and proceeded to cut four equally sized pieces without creating so much as a crumb.

Tea might not have been as sumptuous as June Wiley's effort at Drumsollen, but there was plenty of it and they all ate heartily. There was much laughter and teasing. Afterwards, Ginny stretched out on the picnic rug while Edward brought his father's binoculars from the car and trained them on Coney Island. Clare and Andrew took the chance to follow a thread of path that led them through a willow copse and into another small, sandy bay.

They found a tree trunk worn smooth by long immersion in the lake and sat side by side, their arms around each other.

'I think I've fallen in love with your family as well,' said Clare softly, as they disentangled themselves from a long, passionate kiss.

'The feeling appears to be mutual,' Andrew replied. 'I've never known Ginny call Teddy "Teddybear" in front of anyone except Aunt Helen and Uncle Edward, but she often does in fron of you! She certainly doesn't do it in front of Barney. Have you noticed?'

'Yes, I have. I asked her about Barney one night when we sat up talking for ages. She said he's all right, but she can't get used to him being with her mother all the time. She admitted she'd been really annoyed when they first started going out together, but Edward told her she was being selfish. Anyone who made their mother happy again was a good idea, even if they couldn't stand him, was what he'd said.'

'Good old Edward, that's just like him. You're fond of him, Clare, aren't you?'

'Yes, I am. If I could choose a brother, I'd choose Edward.'

'What about me?'

'No, no use as a brother,' she said shaking her head vigorously. 'But there are other possibilities.'

He raised an eyebrow and she laughed. They were silent for a little, watching the sunlight on the water, the dipping and bobbing of wagtails along the shore.

'What are you thinking, Clare? A penny for your thoughts.'

'I was wondering if we'd remember today when we're old, and say to each other, "D'you remember that day we went for a picnic with Ginny and Edward?" And I was thinking of where we might be and what might have happened in the meantime, whether Edward will become an eminent historian, and Ginny breed horses and.'

'And Clare and Andrew? What about them?'

'I hadn't got that far,' she admitted. 'But I think I shall always remember today because it feels as if I have a family again. Do you understand, Andrew?'

'Yes, my love, I do. It's been a great week and we still have one more evening. Shall we take

Ginny and Edward to Cannon Hill and plan our futures up by the obelisk as the light goes?'

'Oh Andrew, what a lovely idea. It's going to be such a beautiful clear evening. I've only been to Cannon Hill once since the day we went together. I'd so love to go again.'

CHAPTER FOUR

'Come on, Clare, stop dreaming. This isn't going to get that essay written,' she said aloud, as she turned away from her window.

She'd been standing by her table, her coat and scarf still on, her cheeks cold from the crispness of the air, watching the sunny afternoon fade to a pale yellow sunset streaked with wisps of red and purple cloud.

'There'll be frost tonight,' she added, as she bent to light the gas fire.

This late in the year, she sorted her books, tidied her room and made a mug of tea before she even thought of taking her coat off. She stood drinking it as the room grew dimmer.

The summer had melted away so quickly. She could hardly believe how much of term had passed already. She wasn't sure whether to be glad or sorry. Sometimes she worried that time moved so fast when she needed all the time there was to get through the work for Finals. At others, she was grateful. She'd become impatient. She'd spent so much of her life, preparing, waiting, hoping. Revision and exams, essays and class tests stretched back through the years to the time when she'd worked on the old washstand in the empty 'boys' room' next to her own small bedroom. She often thought of how she'd come out to breathe the evening air under the canopy of roses at the front door, so reluctant to return to the stuffiness of the small room, the smell of damp and peeling wallpaper, the notes and the dictionaries.

Warming her hands round her mug of tea, her mind reached back again to the pleasures of the summer. It had been such a happy time, despite the fact that Andrew's new job had been no great joy to him. He said he found it boring rather than demanding. The dreary lodgings the senior partner had thought suitable sounded even more genteel than those where Jessie had once been faced with a list of rules on the back of her bedroom door. But Andrew didn't seem to mind at all. Nothing could be that bad, he said, when they could laugh about it together and make their plans for the future.

For her own part, the work in the gallery had been a real pleasure. She so enjoyed having beautiful things around her, oil paintings and watercolours, antique glass and silver, fine pieces of furniture, Victorian jewellery and carving. It was lovely to be with Jessie. She'd never lost her capacity to say the outrageous thing. Her only concession was to save her comments for Clare's ear alone. Sometimes her mimicry of the more self-regarding of their customers was so sharp and so accurate, they had to retire to the stock room until they could manage to stop laughing.

As she checked out invoices or talked to customers, sharing their pleasure, wrapping precious objects in swathes of newspaper, the excitement that bubbled up whenever she thought of Andrew was her greatest joy of all. 'He isn't *away* any more – he's *here*, I'll see him at lunchtime, or this evening, or tomorrow.' She'd go on with what she was doing, smiling quietly to herself, feeling a wonderful sense of ease and pleasure.

They'd spent every possible moment together until term began. They'd walked the deserted city streets on summer evenings, peering into shop windows, entertaining themselves with the highest of high fashion, cheerfully choosing the furniture, the crockery and the casseroles for their first home, even though they could afford none of it.

When Andrew found he was expected to have a car for the job, they made the best of it. A loan was provided by his bosses, but the rate of repayment left him nearly as short of money as he'd been while doing his articles. But together they could afford petrol and picnic suppers. On the best summer evenings, they drove up into the hills and watched the sky grow pale and the lights begin to flower in the shadowy city below them. When it rained, the elderly Austin provided shelter. 'Our portable viewing station', Andrew called it, when they parked at Shaw's Bridge in drifting mizzle and sat watching the swans pass under the old stone arches that once carried the main road to Dublin.

Jessie and Harry had bought a large, handsome house on the Malone Road with a huge overgrown garden full of rhododendron. Though it had been badly neglected and now needed to be completely redecorated and modernised, Jessie and Harry were thrilled to have it. They had wonderful plans for restoring its elegant, high-ceilinged rooms and making it a family home.

As soon as the gallery closed on Saturday afternoon they'd go off, armed with wallpaper stripper and paintbrushes. They camped in one of the less awful bedrooms, where the only furniture was the huge new bed they'd bought with the first of their wedding present money. At night, they had to go and fetch fish and chips, or cook supper on a Primus stove, because the ancient electrical wiring was so doubtful they daren't use any of the power points.

When Jessie and Harry slept at the new house, Clare and Andrew had the use of the flat over the gallery, the poky rooms reminding them of the fisherman's cottage at Ballintoy. For a few brief hours they too could behave as if they were married, cooking a meal together, sharing the chores, planning what they would do if the flat were actually theirs.

'Come *on*, Clare,' she said crossly, as she caught herself staring out of the window once again. The street lights were flickering into life in the gathering dusk, winking at her like the Christmas decorations in the windows of the big stores.

It was not so much that the work itself had become wearisome, but that she seemed to be so aware how long it had been going on, and now she just longed to escape. Working in the gallery all through the summer and having Andrew's company most evenings and every Sunday; had only made it worse. She'd had enough of her own company and the need to discipline herself hour by hour, week by week.

She thought of Jessie's infectious laughter and Harry's good-natured teasing, of Andrew's arm around her shoulders as they walked in town or the Botanic Gardens. She thought of the small bedroom high above the traffic in Linenhall Street.

She sighed, peeled off her coat, hung it up, and pulled on a heavy sweater. She made sure she had everything she needed laid out on her table, switched on her lamp and wrapped a rug round her waist before settling in Robert's chair.

She stared at the blank sheet of lined A4 in

front of her, took the cap off her fountain pen and put her hands over her face.

'It will all be over by the beginning of next June,' she encouraged herself. 'Let's just get through the winter. It's bound to be better in the spring.'

March blew in with furious storms and high winds that broke small branches from the trees, even on the sheltered pavements of Elmwood Avenue. Before they had fully subsided, Andrew had to have some days off work to attend the funeral of his Great-aunt Beatrice, the formidable lady who lived on the Norfolk coast.

Clare always remembered the story of her adventures in the 1953 floods, how she'd retreated to the first floor when the water started pouring under her kitchen door, then, as the waters rose higher, to the gable window of the attic. As the sea defences gave way and the waters rose higher, she'd stood there, calmly flashing her lantern till she was picked up by a passing coastguard cutter.

Alone in her room, darkness stretching beyond the fragile circle of her lamp, each time the wind roared in the chimney and set the branches outside her window threshing madly, she was filled with foreboding, as she thought of Andrew's sea crossing to Liverpool. She could not get the fate of the *Princess Victoria* out of her mind, running into difficulties in weather just like this, going down within sight of the Ulster coast. Nothing would take away her sense of dread that she would lose Andrew just when they were together at last.

Every hour of the four days of his absence, she held him in her thoughts, as if she could ward off disaster, so long as he was never out of her mind. She left her room only to go to lectures, hurrying back as soon as possible. If disaster were to burst upon her, only there would she be able to face it.

Totally unable to concentrate, she tried to do useful jobs, but every time Mrs McGregor's telephone rang, she would go rigid with fear. At the very first ring, she'd creep out on to the landing and lean over the banisters, listening for any clue to the tone of the call. When her name failed to echo up the stairwell she'd sigh with relief, slip silently back into her room and make yet one more effort to be sensible and go on with her work.

In the event, Andrew's journey was as unexceptional as her cousin Ronnie's had been that January when the *Princess Victoria* was lost. When he was safely back, Clare was so cross with herself, she made up her mind not to tell him what an idiot she'd been. Indeed, she tried hard to forget the whole horrible experience. But it was not until March was nearly over and the earliest signs of spring appeared that she began to feel her spirits rise and the shadow of her panic finally faded away.

'Could you manage the whole day on Saturday,

Clare?' Andrew asked, as he walked her back to Elmwood from the Library, where he now had a reader's ticket to consult the Law collection.

'Yes, if I can finish this essay tomorrow. It's got to be in on Monday,' she explained wearily. 'Why, what were you thinking of?'

'Richardson's Mystery Tour,' he said, grinning. 'If you could do a picnic for lunch, we could have something out in the evening. Poisson et pommes frites, peut-être?'

She laughed and felt the weariness of the evening dissolve. It wasn't just the thought of an outing, nor even the 'fish and chips', it was Andrew's fluent Breton French. She hated to admit it, but the Missus had had a point when she'd once made such disparaging remarks about his accent.

'Why the mystery?' she asked, as she arrived at the front door and scuffled in her bag for her key.

He pulled a face, indicated that his lips were sealed, and kissed her gently.

'We can stay at the flat on Saturday night,' he reminded her. 'Don't forget to bring your own toothbrush.' She giggled.

'What time Saturday morning?'

'Ten?'

'I'll be ready. Take care.'

Friday was a long, hard day for Clare, with an early morning lecture, a seminar to follow and the second half of an essay in French to complete: 'The Image of the City in the Poetry of Baudelaire'. Even with her gas fire full on and her rug round her knees, she still felt cold as she sat writing and rewriting the most difficult passages, hour after hour. By three o'clock in the afternoon, the sky was so grey she'd had to switch on her reading lamp.

As time passed, it got even darker. Suddenly, she glanced up and saw a swirling mass of snowflakes driving towards her window as if they were bent on covering the piles of books and papers spread out in front of her.

'Oh no, not snow. Not for tomorrow.'

Almost in tears, she stood up, unwrapped her rug, drew the curtains and switched on more lamps. But even this gesture had no effect on the growing darkness of her mood. She felt utterly dispirited. Weary of work, of living in this one room, of the chill of winter, of the grey of wet streets. She went and stood with her back to the mantelpiece, warming her frozen legs. As she looked down the length of her room she remembered how she had stood waiting for Andrew, Virginia and Edward. Ten months ago they had set off for Caledon to collect Edward's car for that miraculous fortnight at Ballintoy.

She closed her eyes and for a moment saw the brilliant summer sun, the line of the sea ruled straight across the horizon, the seabirds swooping and riding the air currents. She wished she could fly, up into the blue sky, out over the sea to that far horizon that beckoned so enticingly.

'It's like a mirage,' she said, unable to bear the oppressive silence of the empty room a moment longer. 'To be out in the light, walking, moving, breathing the scented air of a summer evening, or the smell of the sea.'

She sniffed, and realised she'd been standing so close to the gas fire, she was in danger of singeing her best wool trousers, a gift from Auntie Polly. Designed for the rigours of the Canadian winter, they were beautifully warm when you were out and about, but much less comfortable when you were indoors and sitting still. But neither trousers, nor colourful rainwear, nor anything else she possessed, was any antidote to the grey chill she'd felt since the snow had come upon her.

She tried to shut out its menace, but even her heavy curtains couldn't erase the memory of it, beating down upon her, covering her with its insidious carpet of silence.

'Stop it, Clare, stop it. That way lies madness.'

She did some deep-breathing exercises to ease the ache in her shoulders, then picked up the discarded rug and wound it round her again. She sat down, focused on the pad in the circle of light before her and worked on through the afternoon and evening, allowing herself only a few short breaks. By ten o'clock, she had a full draft. It would need fair copying, but that would have to wait till Sunday. She pulled the cover and cushions from her narrow, single bed, stripped off her clothes and crawled in, so weary she just left the whole lot lying on the floor.

She could hardly believe it when she woke next morning and saw a single beam of sunlight projecting a tiny circle on to the threadbare carpet. By the time she was dressed, there were blue patches between ragged streaks of cloud. As they set off, the roads were wet with thawing snow and the air had lost its bitter edge.

As they turned out of the avenue, she looked up to the Antrim hills. Dark shadows lay in the deep gullies, bare rock gleamed in the morning sun, but higher up in the colder air, yesterday's snow still lay, a white dusting, like icing on a baker's bun.

They crossed the city and took the Newtownards Road. The Castlereagh hills to the east were lower, but were still iced with a whiteness that sparkled and shimmered but showed no signs of melting.

'Aren't you taking me dancing at the Stormont Palais?' she asked, as they passed its grand gates.

Andrew grinned and glanced at her briefly.

'I've heard that they don't go in for dancing much, these days,' he said lightly. 'More a matter of marking time, waiting to see how the wind blows. Remember the old adage? "Whatever you do, do nothing."'

'So Ronnie says,' she agreed. 'He knows more about what's going on here than I do. Hardly surprising, is it, when the only newspaper I ever read is *Le Monde*.'

'What *does* Ronnie think is going on? He's always very well informed and very sharp.'

'Plus ça change, plus c'est la même chose,' she said abruptly.

'Where I learned my French, they had a saying rather like that,' he replied. 'Though not quite as delicate. A rough translation would be, "Whatever the weather, they always pee behind the same tree."'

She grinned and looked towards the low hills of North Down ahead, still snow-sprinkled in the morning sun.

'I think we're going to be lucky. It's going to be a clear day.'

'Oh dear, you've guessed,' he said, feigning disappointment. 'I had thought of a circular route via Downpatrick, but I wasn't taking any chances with the weather. This may not last.'

But the weather didn't let them down. The sky simply went on clearing as they turned off the main road and headed south for Scrabo Tower. By the time Andrew parked the Austin at the foot of the hill where once he'd parked Senator Richardson's well-cared for Rover, the sky was almost clear.

'Not quite so hot today,' he said, grinning, as they paused to rest on the steep climb up, their breath swirling round them like clouds of steam.

'And a lot easier in winter boots,' Clare replied, recalling the ache in her legs and back from her best high-heeled shoes on that last ascent.

'Are we getting old or are we out of training?' he muttered, panting gently as they climbed the last few steps of the tower's spiral staircase and stepped out on to the parapet.

'Well, we are nearly five years older,' she said. 'And I spend most of my time sitting on my bottom,' she added, laughing, as she leaned gratefully against the battlements. 'What about you? Does appearing in court give you much exercise? There are lots of steps outside the Law Courts. Do you run up and down between cases?'

'No,' he said gently, as he took her in his arms. 'I sit and think about you. That's what keeps me sane.'

They stood in silence, their arms round each other, and looked out over the quiet, sunlit countryside. There was snow on the higher ground. Under the north-facing hedgerows, the frost lay so heavy it too looked like drifted snow. Every small field was outlined by its leafless hedgerow, its bare trees and the long shadows they cast in the low sun. Beyond the fields, the lough lay like a sheet of polished pewter. The air was so still, the smoke from the nearby cottages rose without billow or curl, straight up above each whitewashed gable.

'The Mournes are even clearer than last time,' she whispered, not wanting the sound of her voice to break the spell.

For a moment, Andrew said nothing. Then he spoke, his voice seeming to come from a long way away.

'I always remember what your Granny Hamilton said about making up your mind on a clear day.'

She moved closer within the circle of his arm, touched that he so often recalled things she'd told him. No matter who it was she might mention, however casually, Andrew placed them, remembered what they'd said or done. Sometimes she felt he knew more about her life in the house beyond the forge than Jessie had ever done.

'What made you think of that?' she asked.

'I want to ask you something, Clare,' he said quietly. 'I know we said we wouldn't worry about an engagement ring, we'd just get married as soon as we could manage it. But I've had a lovely surprise. Dear old Auntie Bee hadn't much money, but she left me fifty pounds. She also left me a ring she'd once given to my mother. I knew my mother had taken her jewellery box with her to London and the box didn't survive, but that afternoon, she'd left this ring in a jeweller's in Bond Street to have a stone replaced. So it wasn't lost with the rest. It's only got a very small diamond and some garnets and it might not fit. If you don't like it, we've got fifty pounds. We could go back into Belfast right now and choose something different.'

For a moment, Clare was so surprised she couldn't think what to say.

'Oh, Andrew,' she burst out finally. 'I'd far rather have your mother's ring than any ring we went and bought, even if we had five hundred pounds. If it doesn't fit, I know it can be altered. Harry's always having antique rings done for customers. Have you brought it?'

'Yes, of course, I have. Here it is,' he said simply. 'In its very own box.'

He fumbled in his pocket and brought out a dark red, leather box. He opened it. The ring sparkled in the sunlight between them.

'Oh dear,' said Clare, 'I think I'm going to cry

'Oh, my love, my dear, dear love, why tears?'

'It's just . . . it's just . . .' she sniffed, 'well, they weren't as lucky as we are, were they? We haven't got a war to live with . . . or be killed by.'

She collected herself and took the delicate ring from where it nestled against the red silk lining. The garnets flashed as the sun caught them and she slipped the ring on her finger. She held out her hand to him.

'Perfect fit,' he whispered.

He put his lips to the ring. 'You're sure it's what you want?'

'As sure as I am that I want you.'

She slipped the empty box into her pocket, reached up, put her arms round his neck and kissed him.

CHAPTER FIVE

'Makes a change from fish and chips, Andrew,' said Jessie, grinning broadly, as he tucked in to the beef casserole.

'Mmm,' he agreed, his mouth full.

'It's lovely, Jessie,' said Clare. 'I can tell you it doesn't taste like this in the Students' Union.'

'And they don't serve Côte du Rhône with it either,' added Andrew, as Harry filled up his glass.

Amid the laughter, Clare glanced around the table. Until Jessie had started to serve, the room had still smelt of paint. This was the first evening they'd had a table and proper chairs to sit on, but it felt as if they'd been dining in this room together for years. Her eyes suddenly misted. Sometimes real happiness was almost too much to bear.

'Ah don't know what we'd 'ave done wi' out ye last weekend. Ye were great, the both of youse. Weren't they, Harry?'

'Just great,' he agreed. Looking from one to the other, he lifted his wine glass. 'Here's to you,

Clare and Andrew, the best movers and unpackers in Belfast. If you're ever out of a job, let me know.'

Laughter spilled out again. Set in the deep bay window of the only habitable downstairs room, the gleaming surface of a restored eighteenth-century table reflected back the flickering images of the candlesticks, the glass and china they'd unpacked the previous weekend, wedding presents stored away for more than a year in Harry's parents' home. Now, Harry himself, tall, dark-haired and distinctly good-looking, stood, wine bottle in hand, beaming down on the friends who'd come to share the first celebration meal Jessie had cooked in their new home.

'Come on, eat up, there's plenty more.'

Jessie waved a hand at the dish of crisp roast potatoes, the fresh vegetables and the Yorkshire puddings, which had turned out lopsided but tasted so good.

'What about yourself?' said Harry slyly. 'Should you not be eating for two?'

'Oh, shut up,' she said, giggling, as she dished out second helpings.

Clare exchanged glances with Andrew. Harry had been ecstatic when Jessie told him she was pregnant, but Jessie herself hadn't yet got used to the idea. She'd confessed she wasn't entirely enthusiastic.

'Ah don't fancy lookin' like a watermelon,'

she'd confided to Clare, over a mug of tea in the stock room. 'I'll maybe have to give up work if I get too big. There's not much room behind thon counter. An' shure Harry's always buyin' in more stuff. Ah don't know how we fit in the half of it.'

Tonight, Clare could only think how lovely she looked. How easily she'd stepped into the new life Harry had given her, a country girl like herself. She'd always had good skin and soft, wavy brown hair, but tonight there was a radiance about her she'd never seen before.

'And here's to you two,' said Andrew, raising his glass. 'Or should I say three? "May all your troubles be little ones", as the saying is.'

Clare lifted her glass and toasted them, intensely aware of their bright, happy faces glowing with reflected light and the effects of food and wine. Her eyes moved round the table. Like a magic circle. So full of love and laughter. Suddenly, she had an image of another circle, a scrubbed wooden table, Ginny and Edward in the kitchen at Caledon, sharing out the sausage and chips Edward had cooked for them after a day by Lough Neagh, and a long summer evening amid the little green hills nearby. Within one of these magic circles, no harm could ever reach her. Exposed to the light and the laughter, the anxieties that crept up on her when she was alone would just dissolve.

'Have you got a date yet, Jessie?' Clare asked, as she put down her empty glass.

'I'll tell you mine when you tell me yours,' said Jessie crisply. Clare laughed and shook her head.

'There's no use keeping on at me, Jessie. We can't get married till Andrew knows when he can have his holiday. And he can't have his holiday till the partners say so. And the partners are not exactly being helpful, are they, love?' she added, turning to him, as Harry began to collect up the empty plates.

'Well, for goodness' sake, hurry up,' replied Jessie impatiently. 'Or I'll have nothing to wear. If I go on at this rate, I'll have to hire a tent.'

'Never worry, Jessie. You'd look good in anything,' said Andrew reassuringly. 'Now come on, tell us when Junior is due.'

'October. So they say. But I can't for the life o' me see how they figure it out . . .'

Jessie went on talking as she cut deftly into a crisp circle of meringue filled with tinned fruit and topped with whipped cream. As well as her talent for watercolour and the eye-catching displays she produced in the gallery, Jessie was proving to be a good cook. Like her skill with a pencil, or brush, cooking just seemed to have come to her without any effort at all the moment she had her own cooker. Clare wondered if it would be the same with motherhood.

It seemed strange to think of her bringing up her children in this lovely house full of the fine old furniture and pictures that Harry had stored away for the rooms still to be decorated. They would play in the garden that ran down to the thick shrubbery and the steep retaining wall, beyond which the buses and cars moved in and out of the city. They would go to school in the city itself, a far cry from the lanes where she and Jessie had cycled on summer evenings, the quiet road they'd travelled together going into and out of Armagh, year after year, to school, church, doing the shopping, fetching the papers.

'Well then, what d'ye say?'

She'd heard Jessie's question all right, but it took her so much by surprise, she didn't know what to say. It was Andrew who spoke first.

'I should be extremely honoured, Mrs Burrows, to be the god-father of your child,' he said, without the slightest hesitation.

The tone was light, and the little bow he made to her was very Andrew, but the look on his face said much more than his words. Perhaps he felt something of the security and well-being she felt herself. Two couples bound by all they'd shared of each other's lives.

Clare felt his eyes upon her, waiting, as she looked from Jessie to Harry and then back again to Jessie.

'Well, I might not be much good on the God bit,' she said apologetically.

'Ach, never worry about that, Clare. Shure they can make up their own minds about that sort of thing. But wou'd ye stan' by them? Him or her, or whatever?'

Clare nodded quickly, her eyes filling with tears so unexpectedly she couldn't disguise them.

'That's just great, Clare,' said Harry warmly, jumping to his feet and pouring white wine into fresh glasses. 'And one of these days we hope we can do the same for you. Shall we drink to that? The Burrows and the Richardsons. May their dynasties reign for ever!'

Spring sunshine cast long shadows on the pavements below, as Clare drew back her curtains and gazed down into Linenhall Street. Now that term had ended, she'd moved into the empty flat above the gallery. Sadly, she'd made the move by herself. Andrew had been despatched by the partners for three days of executor work on one of the big estates in Fermanagh. It would be Friday night before he could come and join her.

Each day, she began work on her own, for Jessie had begun to have morning sickness and the effort of getting into the city centre for nine o'clock was more than she could manage. Dressed in her smartest clothes, Clare unlocked the silent rooms, dusted the gold frames, the porcelain figurines and the antique furniture. As she polished the plate glass showcases, she'd make herself familiar with each piece of antique jewellery, and all the small, beautiful objects in silver, china and glass, too fragile, or too valuable, to be put on open view, and hope that no one would ring with a complicated query before Jessie and Harry arrived.

She loved the gallery's large, airy spaces, the tall windows and carefully concealed lighting. She enjoyed observing the customers as they looked round, answering their questions, dealing with the details of their purchases, a wonderful change from the unbroken solitude of her room. Sometimes, she enjoyed her days so much, she imagined herself doing a job like this permanently. Something that would let her out into the real world.

At the end of the day, she was usually the last to leave. Suddenly, Harry would notice that Jessie looked pale and tired. He'd ask Clare if she'd mind locking up. It never ceased to amaze her how quickly the relaxed and leisurely Harry could move, once she'd said she didn't mind at all.

Tired herself by then, she'd put the day's takings in the safe, check that the showcases were locked and make her way round the empty rooms doing whatever had had to wait till the customers were gone. As the rest of the building grew silent, she'd run a dust mop over the stained and polished floors and think of Andrew. Back upstairs in the flat, she'd listen for the sound of his feet running up the bare staircase. He'd throw open the door, breathless, loaded briefcase in one hand, something for supper in a paper bag in the other. She seldom saw him before seven, but it didn't trouble her. He didn't have to go back to his digs. There was a whole night ahead of them and breakfast together in the morning.

At first, they were very happy. Andrew had found the work in Fermanagh interesting. He'd made time to go and see an elderly cousin of his grandfather who he hadn't visited since his teens. Being made welcome in Uncle Hector's rambling old house by the lake shore reminded him of happy summer holidays with his parents before the war; before the blitz had killed them and broken his links with Drumsollen. He'd loved the lakes, he said. Especially when one of his three aunts had trusted him with the tiller lines while she rowed them out to a small, uninhabited island in the midst of the tranquil waters. Uncle Hector had been delighted to see him, wanted him to bring Clare down to Inishbane as soon as her exams were over. Love to have some young people about the place, he'd said.

That first Saturday, Clare worked all day in the gallery. Andrew did the shopping and had a meal ready in the evening. On Sunday, they cooked bacon and egg long after the church bells had stopped pealing. They were just so excited to be together in their own place, with time to talk, to make love, they didn't even manage to go for the walk they'd planned.

Monday morning was difficult. They fell over each other, because neither of them had noticed the bedroom was so small they couldn't possibly get dressed at the same time. Fitting in breakfast before leaving at eight-thirty turned out to be a real challenge. There was no longer a fridge, so the milk bottle stood in a bucket of water. Wherever they put it, it managed to trip them up. The teapot too had gone to the new house, so Clare had to make tea in an old kettle. The cornflakes almost defeated them. Jessie had left cups, saucers and plates, but she had forgotten about bowls. They ended up taking it in turns to eat them from the sugar bowl.

Halfway through their first whole week together, Andrew arrived home later than usual. He looked worn and tired and carried a box of papers as well as his heavy briefcase. The senior partner had named him as his junior for a dispute involving the Fermanagh estate where he'd just completed the executor work.

Although she asked all sorts of questions, Andrew seemed reluctant to talk about the case or what it would involve, though it was clear, it would be a lengthy affair, probably tedious. As the days passed, Andrew became more and more withdrawn. Something more than mere tedium had to be involved.

'Now don't jump to confusions, Clare,' she said to herself one evening, as she moved quietly around the empty rooms of the gallery. 'Maybe he's just tired out. Think how exhausted you were by the end of term. It's still his first job. It's with a new firm. And he's told you Belfast does things differently from Winchester. It'll take him far longer to adjust than if he'd done his articles here.'

But she wasn't convinced. And the days that followed did nothing to reassure her. Andrew spent more and more time in court and in the Law Library. When he did get back to the flat, he was weighed down with papers for the following day. She had never known him so silent or so humourless. When they finally reached the comfort of their bed, he made love to her with a kind of desperation, then promptly fell fast asleep.

She was sure there was nothing to be done till the case ended. It dragged on and on, as he had warned her it might, until the very last Friday of her holiday, leaving them only the Sunday to spend together before she went back to Elmwood Avenue to begin the last hard pull up the slope to Finals.

When Andrew came back that evening, as tired and dispirited as usual, even though the judgement had been given and the case really was ended, she had a quiet smile on her face. As she put the kettle on to make coffee, she turned and said: 'Come on, my love, it's over at last. Let's celebrate. Let's have a day out tomorrow.'

'But it's Saturday. You're working, aren't you?'

'Oh no, I'm not. I've got time off for good behaviour. I told Harry we'd not had a single day out for a month and he said he'd do Saturday himself. Jessie's mother's coming up for the weekend. He said it'd give them a chance to talk, with him out of the way.'

'Good old Harry,' said Andrew, wearily. 'We're very lucky to have such good friends.'

Clare waited hopefully for him to say something more, but he stayed silent, even after she'd made the coffee and they'd carried it into the sitting room.

'I have a little present for Granny Hamilton's birthday,' she began at last, as lightly as she could. 'I'd like to drop it off at Liskeyborough. We could have lunch in Armagh. I think I've found somewhere nice to take you. My treat. We can do the poisson and pommes frites on the way home, so we don't have to go shopping tomorrow morning. How about it?'

He finished his coffee, took her empty cup away and put his arms round her.

'Clare, I'm sorry. I'm *so* sorry. I know I've been rotten company for the last couple of weeks.

I don't know how you put up with me,' he said, grinning weakly.

'Simple,' she said. 'I have a lover in while I'm waiting for you to come home from work.'

For a moment, he looked quite startled. Then he laughed. It was the first time he'd laughed since the wretched Fermanagh case had begun. She held him tight and kissed him.

'If we're going up to Armagh tomorrow, don't you think we'd better get a *very* early night?'

CHAPTER SIX

As they drove up the Lisburn Road, Clare realised with a shock it would soon be a whole year since they'd taken the road to Armagh together, the evening Ginny and Edward had collected her from Elmwood Avenue. She'd been up on her own, of course, to visit the farm at Liskeyborough. She'd been to her cousin Sam's wedding in Richhill. But she could hardly believe they had not visited Armagh, or driven over to Caledon since last June.

'Aren't the trees glorious?' she said, looking out at the burgeoning canopies, the branches almost fully clothed but the individual leaves still soft and translucent in the bright light.

The very last time she'd seen these familiar trees was early March. Sam was the first of her cousins to get married. She smiled to herself as she remembered how he'd been too shy to cross the floor to her, at her very first dance, the night Uncle Jack's lodge unfurled its new banner.

According to Granny Hamilton, there were a whole set of weddings coming up among the cousins. At least now we're engaged, she thought, we can go together. On your own, weddings could be very lonely affairs.

'What did you say?' asked Andrew, lost in his own thoughts.

'I said the trees are glorious. I love them like this, when the leaves are still young, before they mature and darken.'

'I hope we don't lose too many of them when they start on the motorway.'

'What motorway?'

He smiled and put aside whatever he'd been thinking about.

'Don't tell me it hasn't reached *Le Monde*?' he said, grinning. 'Ulster's very own motorway, Belfast to Dungannon. It's actually been started. Some of the bridges and flyovers are underway, but the first bit won't be open for ages. There'll be plenty of fun and games up ahead with the compulsory purchase of the land they need, especially beyond Portadown. We'll have a real spot of "No surrender, not an inch". Not unless you pay me a small fortune, that is.'

She looked at him quickly, alarmed by the bitter sharpness in his voice. She was hearing it more and more often and it worried her for she'd heard that tone before. That was how Ronnie talked, just

77

before he gave up trying to find a job as a journalist in Belfast and went to Canada.

Her friend, Keith Harvey, had a sister who worked in Toronto. She said Ronnie was building up quite a reputation for himself as a political commentator through his columns for Canadian newspapers with large Scottish or Ulster readerships. Andrew himself said how very well informed he was.

'Could we go round by Loughgall?' she said quickly, as they crossed the Bann and began to negotiate the Saturday morning traffic in the centre of Portadown. 'I haven't been that way since Jessie's wedding.'

'Yes, of course,' he said, signalling right as they came out of the town.

'I'm so sorry I missed Jessie and Harry's wedding,' he went on, as they took the minor road. 'I'd love to go to a real country wedding, and that little church up on the hill would be just the place for it.' He hesitated. 'Do you think, maybe, we could be married there?'

'I don't see why not,' she responded promptly, delighted by his sudden enthusiasm. 'I think there's a residence qualification or something, but I could leave a suitcase with Jessie's mother. I think that's what you do. Anyway, I've a whole family grave full of residents. That must qualify me for something. The Rector's still the one that buried Granda Scott.'

'We could go and see him, couldn't we? I think the Richardsons once paid for a new roof in the days when they had money,' he added cheerfully.

There was no traffic on the road, so he was able to slow right down as they reached Scott's Corner. They continued up the hill towards the point where the lane from the forge met the road.

'I can't stop opposite the lane,' he said, knowing she'd want a good look at the house beyond the forge, 'but I'll park in the field entrance a bit further on, so we can take as long as we want.'

He put out his indicator as they came over the brow of the hill, but before he could pull in, a mere fifty yards beyond the lane end, Clare had seen enough to make her gasp.

'Oh no, Andrew. It's gone. The forge has gone.'

She fumbled with the handle of the door, and was still trying to remember which way it turned when he came round and opened it for her. They stood together in the field entrance in front of one of Robert's gates and looked across the road at the old house, now entirely visible, its enfolding shelter of trees and shrubs all gone. Where once the forge had stood, a young pear tree at its south gable, all they could see was an open space of roughly levelled rubble. A battered van and an enormous pile of empty apple crates were parked on it. Of the gable wall of the old ruined house opposite, and the enclosed garden in its shadow, there was not the slightest remnant. The forge house itself sat empty and dilapidated, its uncurtained windows staring blankly over an open space entirely devoid of grass, or wildflowers, and liberally scattered with rubbish.

'The arch over the door has gone,' she burst out. 'They've even stripped off the rose and taken away the flowerbeds. Oh, why did they have to do that?'

She burst into tears and wept helplessly. He held her till the sobbing subsided, a look of desolation on his own face.

'Come on, my darling,' he said, releasing her and offering her his handkerchief. 'We can't do a damn thing about it, but we can go and have that lunch you promised me. How about it?'

'Yes, let's do that,' she said firmly, blowing her nose. 'If we turn right at Riley's Rocks and go by Ballyard, we can cut across to the Moy Road. It'll be easier than going into Armagh and out again.'

'That takes us past Jessie's house, doesn't it?'

'That's right. The main road's about a mile beyond that. We turn left towards Armagh. The hotel's on the left, only a little way further on,' she explained, making a huge effort to collect herself. 'It was June Wiley told me about it that evening after we'd been to Drumsollen. Helen's got a job there washing dishes, Saturday and Sunday evenings. Drumsill House, it's called. Nice name, isn't it? I must ask Charlie what it means.'

'Hill of the sallows, sallies or osiers, as a first thought,' he said, as they turned into the lane opposite Charlie Running's house, where the first clumps of primroses were unfolding in the pale sun shine that had broken through the morning's pearly grey cloud. 'Drumsollen *may* come from the same source. But no one seems to know. Pronunciation is the key, I'm told. But it's three generations since a Richardson spoke Irish.'

Drumsill House was warm and welcoming, a huge wood fire scenting the air in the entrance hall. Family portraits hung alongside watercolours and engravings of the surrounding countryside. The fireplace wall itself was decorated with a collection of well-polished firearms and weapons, more varied than anything Clare had ever seen before. She sniffed appreciatively at the mixed odours of wood smoke and roasting meat, and ran her eye round the gleaming furniture in the comfortable reception area as they waited for the menu to be brought to them.

'What d'you reckon Harry'd offer them for that grandfather clock?' asked Andrew, teasingly, as he watched her note the finer pieces among the more homely items.

'Rather a lot, I expect,' she said abstractedly, her eye moving back to a row of tall wooden objects with metal points attached to the fireplace wall.

'Andrew, are those pikes?'

He nodded, as the waiter appeared with enormous menus, the covers decorated with an etching of the house as it was in the early nineteenth century.

'How did you know they were pikes?' she asked, after they'd placed their order.

'There used to be some at Drumsollen,' he said, matter-of-factly. 'Just like those. I can remember finding them once when I was little, down in the cellar, but I don't know what happened to them.'

Clare looked at him closely. He was sitting easily in a large old chair by the handsome fireplace, very like those in Drumsollen itself, except that this fireplace was alive, with the crackle of wood and the flicker of flames, and all around there was life going on, people coming and going, greeting each other, talking, or moving in twos and threes into the dining room beyond.

'Don't you wish you could go to Drumsollen, Andrew? Not to visit the Missus. Just to look at it. To go round all the rooms and see the things that you used to know so well.'

'I try not to think about it,' he said ruefully. 'Grandmother never wanted me at Drumsollen after my parents died. Grandfather did his best to keep in touch and have me there when he could persuade her to have me, but now he's gone, I doubt if I'll ever be invited again. Even for *your* sake.' He smiled across at her. 'Grandmother seems to like you a lot more than ever she liked me. Though fairly I ought to say she doesn't seem to like Edward any more than she likes me. He told me she wouldn't even see him when he went over to make sure the roof repairs had been done properly. He'll probably sell the place as soon as she dies. It's only hers for her lifetime. So there really is no point me thinking about going there.'

'Any more than me thinking about the forge and that poor, sad house where I grew up,' she said quietly. 'Charlie Running told me that the forge is there on the 1835 maps and may be even older. How old is Drumsollen?'

'It says 1771 over the front door, but there was an older house on the site before the present one was built. There was a Richardson in Bagnell's army at the Battle of the Yellow Ford. He may have got a grant of land in lieu of pay. Officers often did.'

'So that takes your family back to 1595?' she said thoughtfully, as the waiter led them to their table in an elegant dining room with tall windows overlooking the garden.

Lunch was a great success. The food was good and the comfort of the surroundings made them feel Monday morning had receded into the far distance. For the present at least, they were together. They were happy. The burdens that pressed upon them would have to wait.

'Think, Andrew. Just for today, no one can find us,' Clare said, as she sipped her coffee. 'We're invisible. No one knows we're here. We can do whatever we want. What shall we do next?'

'What I'd really like to do is climb Cannon Hill,' he said abruptly.

Clare smiled. She wasn't entirely surprised. Cannon Hill had always been such a happy place for them.

'Why not?' she said, easily. 'We can go back by Ballybrannan and drop into Granny Hamilton on our way home. I'd love to see those twisty lanes again. All right?'

'All right,' he said, as they stepped out into the reception area. Clare went over to look more closely at the pikes.

'But I think perhaps we should pay the bill before we go,' he added with a smile.

At the entrance to the steeply sloping field that led up to the grey finger of the obelisk, there was a new notice saying that trespassers would be prosecuted.

'Do we really risk prosecution?' she asked lightly.

'Down in Fermanagh they take an even harder line. "Trespassers will be persecuted." It's fairly dubious law. I think we could risk it.'

They climbed over the chained and locked

field-gate and moved up the steep slope of the hill in silence, the sunlight bright on the fresh grass. Clare walked with her head down, scanning the turf at her feet for any sight of a wildflower that had learnt to survive on this heavily grazed, exposed site. As she'd hoped, she found the first minute pink flowers of centaury, growing close to the ground, a scatter of bright-eyed celandines and a flourishing crop of daisies. She looked up at Andrew, ready to share her delight. He was scanning the nearby hill slopes. All thought of the flowers vanished as she caught the look of pain and despair on his face.

'Andrew, my love, why so sad?' she said gently, as they reached the foot of the monument and stood leaning against it to get their breath.

'Sad? Who me?'

'Yes, you. Something's not right. It's not been right for a good while now and I want to know what it is,' she said firmly. 'And I also want to know why you're looking around those hill slopes as if everything belonging to you was lost. You did it last time too. The evening we came up here with Ginny and Edward.'

'Clare, I don't know how to tell you this,' he began, hesitantly.

For one awful moment she thought he was going to say he'd stopped loving her, that he wanted to end their engagement. One look at him told her not to be so silly.

He put his arms round her and held her so tight against him, she knew how desperate he must be, torn between telling her what was wrong and keeping his upper lip stiff, just as he'd been taught to do, all through his years at public school.

Since he was seven, he'd had to learn to hide his feelings, better not to have them in the first place. No matter what happened, he'd been expected to show a steady, even temper to the world. They'd talked about it often enough, but simply understanding the problem wasn't going to help just now.

'You must tell me, you must,' she insisted. 'I'm pretty sure I know what it is, but you must say the words yourself. For your own sake, you must say them. I know you must.'

'Yes, I must, mustn't I?'

She waited patiently as he ran his eyes over the flower-sprinkled grass, his face bleak, his body tense.

'Let's sit down,' he said at last. 'The grass is perfectly dry.'

It was dry, soft and tender, with the sun warm on her face as they settled themselves. Above their heads, the rapidly moving clumpy, white clouds added subtle texture to the blue of a lovely spring day.

'It's the job, Clare. I hate it,' he said flatly. 'I can't stand the partners. I can't stand their attitudes. It's all about power and privilege. Who you know. Who knows you. Who's done you a favour. Who you owe a favour to. And all the time, underneath, an unspoken sense of us against them. The privileged against the rest. There's not much room for justice. None at all for equality before the law. I'm compromised at every turn.'

He dropped his head in his hands and for a moment Clare thought he might be crying. But Andrew never cried. 'You must be a brave boy, Andrew.' That was what the Housemaster had said, to the seven year old who'd just travelled four hundred miles from Ulster to a new school in Dorset and had been told, after his first night in a dormitory, that both his parents and his London grandparents were dead, killed in the massive raid that began the Blitz. She'd always wondered if it was the same man who'd supervised the writing of the weekly letter home the following Sunday afternoon, when Andrew had sat, blank and near to tears, mesmerised by the sheets of blue writing paper he was supposed to fill for parents who were no longer there.

'It's all right, my love. It's all right,' she said, kissing his cheek and taking his icy cold hands in hers. 'If you hate the job, you must give it up and do something else. Or, give the job another try, far away from "the dead hand of Ulster", as Ronnie calls it. You don't have to stick it out because there's no alternative.'

'No stiff upper lip?' he said, a small, bleak smile touching the corner of his mouth.

'Definitely not. You can't kiss properly if your upper lip is as stiff as a board,' she said tenderly, stroking the back of his head. 'Now come on, Andrew, tell me what you'd really like. Pretend you're really rich and you can do whatever you like. What would you choose?'

To her surprise, he pointed across the valley. A small blue tractor was moving steadily up the slope of a field, turning the green sward into rich, chestnut-brown furrows. At the top of the field it paused, and with a deft, practised movement the driver brought the plough round in line to begin the next, dead straight furrow. As it came back down again, the rich brown earth curled away from the coulter like the bow wave of a trim, swift vessel.

'That's what I'd do. I'd farm. Dairy cattle in particular,' he said, with an assurance totally out of keeping with his normally diffident approach to practical matters.

'You know about dairy cattle?' she asked, wondering if there could possibly be some part of his life she'd missed out on.

'No,' he said, cheerfully. 'I don't. But I'd learn.'
She sat silent, amazed at his confidence. The

implications began to break in on her. Questions poured into her mind, but she held back. The change in his appearance, his whole manner, told her all she needed to know for the moment. Suddenly an image came back into her mind. A wet afternoon during her first visit to Caledon, four years ago now. They were playing Monopoly and talking. While Ginny stacked up more and more money, she'd asked each of the three what they'd do if they were rich. Andrew had made them laugh. 'I'd buy cows.' It was his unexpected promptness that amused them, not just the cows. It seemed so unlikely a wish for a man about to spend the next three years articled to a firm of solicitors in Winchester.

'Where would you farm, Andrew?' she asked as steadily as she could.

'Anywhere I could afford to buy land.'

'Canada?' she said, before she had even considered it.

He paused, looked out again at the opposite hillside, where the elderly blue tractor was now making its steady way back up to the top of the field. A smile played over his features.

'Mm. Why not? Why not Canada?'

He paused once more and the smile faded as quickly as the light goes when a cloud crosses the sun. When he spoke again his voice was dull and heavy.

'Canada. Or Australia. Anywhere. If it's dreams we're dreaming, what does it matter? It's not real. Dreams never are, are they?' he said bitterly.

'If I hadn't asked you what you'd do if you were rich, would you have told me you wanted to farm?' she asked coolly.

'No, I don't think so.'

'Well then, we're that much further on. If you want to farm, I need a job to keep us fed until the farm can support us, so I can't be a million miles from a town with a school,' she began. 'Would you have to buy land or can it be rented?'

'Depends where. In Canada and Australia it's still easy to get started, or I think it is. I've a cousin in Saskatchewan who went off with nothing about twenty years ago. They've got two hundred head now.'

'Saskatchewan, Manitoba, Alberta,' she murmured, a sudden memory filling her mind. Ox-eyed daisies and an old reaping machine outside the forge, herself in the high seat, driving her horses across the prairie.

'If we went to Canada, Ronnie would help us. He seems to know everything that's going on. When I wrote and told him we were engaged he wrote back and asked where we were going, once we were married. He simply assumed we weren't going to stay here.'

'I couldn't ask you to take the risk, Clare,' he

said, shaking his head. 'It could be pretty rough for you. To begin with at least.'

'I'm not exactly made of Dresden china,' she retorted. 'Besides, a teaching post in Belfast isn't exactly an exciting prospect. To be honest, I hadn't thought of what I would do, except be with you.'

'Nor had I,' he confessed sheepishly. 'I just reckoned, after all these years, I was stuck with law, whether I liked it or not.'

'Well, let's not get stuck with anything. Let's see what we can think up.'

He gave her his hand, drew her to her feet and kissed her tenderly.

'What would I do without you, my love? What would I do without you?'

They stood in the shadow of the great stone pillar and studied every detail of the fields and orchards that covered the little humpy hills all around them. The old cottages, long and low, white painted, were tucked into their hollows on the south-facing slopes, sheltered from the north and west by plantings of trees. There was the odd new farm building, and a few two-storey houses, edging the little lanes that turned and twisted, dipped into valleys and climbed over their smooth, well-rounded shapes.

The blue tractor finished its work. The driver unhitched the plough and drove off down the lane below them. Gleaming in the sunlight, the newly ploughed field was left to the gulls, which hunted up and down the straight, newly turned furrows.

'You love this place, Clare, don't you?'

'Yes, I do,' she said firmly. 'I'd be heartbroken if I thought I'd never stand here again.'

She paused, remembering a summer Sunday long ago when she'd climbed up to the obelisk for the first time. Uncle Jack had been there and various aunts and uncles she couldn't quite sort out. She was nine years old. She'd looked all around her and made up her mind that she was going to stay with Granda Scott, even if Auntie Polly wanted to take her with them to Canada.

'I think I do belong here, Andrew, like you do. But I'd be sad all my life if I never saw anything of the world out there, beyond the green hills.'

CHAPTER SEVEN

'Ladies and gentlemen, you have five minutes left. May I remind you to ensure that you have numbered all loose sheets and that they are enclosed within the folder provided . . .'

Clare didn't listen to the remainder of the announcement. She knew it by heart. She went on reading the last of the four essays she'd written in the preceding three hours, added missed-out commas, sharpened a wobbly acute or grave accent, clarified the odd word where sheer speed had run the letters together. As the gowned figure began to collect scripts at the back of the room, she checked her loose sheets, sealed the pink flap of her folder and had her paper ready to hand over while the invigilator was still three desks away. Five minutes later, the examination hall broke into uproar as the tensions of the afternoon exploded in an outburst of scraping chairs, squeals of laughter, and hurrying feet.

'Fancy a coffee, Clare?' said Keith Harvey,

classmate and friend, as she turned round and grinned at him.

By virtue of his surname, Keith had sat behind her in every class test and exam they'd done in the four years of the Honours French course. Long ago, they'd made a pact never to discuss a paper afterwards, just get away as quickly as possible before anyone could waylay them.

'Love one, Keith, but Andrew's probably waiting for me. He's not in court today,' she said, as she zipped her pencil case and caught up her cardigan from the back of her chair.

'Are you coming to the party tonight?'

'No, not tonight. We're heading for the hills. I told him the other day I felt like a troglodyte, only coming out of my small cave to scuttle across the road to a large one.'

'Well, it's all over now,' Keith said, laughing, as they worked their way slowly towards the crowded foyer of the Whitla Hall. 'Really over, Clare,' he went on, as they caught the first glimpse of sunlit lawns and the red brick front of the main building beyond. 'So when shall we two meet again?'

'Graduation Day, if not before,' she shouted, over the rising crescendo of sound. 'I'll be working at the gallery till we get the wedding organised and our passages booked. We've got our passports but that's about all we've managed.'

'Not surprised,' he said. 'God, it's been a sweat, hasn't it? I'll pop into the gallery and see you next week. I want to give you my sister's address in Toronto. She says she'd love to see you. She's a real fan of your cousin Ronnie. Apparently he signs himself "Ron" in Canada.'

'Ron McGillvray. Sounds right for a columnist, doesn't it? I'll remember that. See you sometime next week then, Keith. Enjoy the party,' she said happily, as they emerged from the crowd milling around on the steps and he headed off towards the bicycle sheds.

She looked for Andrew, but saw no sign of him. All around her, couples were greeting each other, going off hand in hand or with arms twined round each other. For those taking languages, this was the very last paper. Parties and celebrations had been planned for weeks now. They'd be welcome at several of them, she knew, but what she really wanted was to get away. They were going to drive up into the Craigantlet Hills, walk among the hayfields, look out over the lough and watch the lights come on in the city below. Just the two of them. To make up for all the lovely summer evenings they'd had to miss.

Clare sat down on the low wall opposite the examination hall and watched the remaining clusters of people finish their post-mortems, say their goodbyes and head off in different directions.

She looked all around her. No sign of a dark-suited figure with fair hair anywhere.

Of course, she told herself, one of the senior partners could have descended on Andrew just as he was leaving. It happened often, but seldom on Fridays. Unless they'd been in court, the partners tended to begin their weekend after lunch, leaving Andrew and his colleague in sole possession of the elegant chambers.

She tried to imagine Andrew bending over his desk amid the boxes and bundles of documents. She wondered if he ever noticed the portraits of former partners and prime ministers looking down at him so solemnly, the etchings of nineteenth-century Belfast and the paintings of the SS *Titanic* leaving the lough on her sea trials.

'Not for much longer now, love,' she said softly.

The three elderly partners had been very hard to work with. So arrogantly self-confident, so sure of their own judgement, alternative views were not required. However hard Andrew worked, only doing what they wanted done in the way they wanted it done was acceptable. Worse, what they wanted paid little attention to the ethics involved in a case. What they did was no doubt legal, but seldom what Andrew would judge right.

'I'll be a good boy. Not say a word. Not tell them what I think. Just keep my nose clean and work for a good reference,' he'd said, as they sat one evening, large scale maps of Southwest Saskatchewan spread out before them. Even if they were leaving Ulster, a good reference would still be very useful. Clare was grateful she already had hers, a letter from Henri Lavalle that made her blush every time she read it.

'Canada,' she said, quite firmly, looking around her once again.

Though crowds of people streamed past on the nearby pavements and there was a long queue at the bus stop, there was no one left on this side of the entrance gates to hear anything she said.

Over the last weeks, the thought of Canada had kept her going. Whenever washing and ironing simply had to be done, or when she tidied her room, her mind would fly off. Beyond broad expanses of wheatfield, she saw mountains rising into clear air, great white clouds piled up in a blue sky. She felt so heartened by the unlimited possibilities of moving freely in so vast an expanse of space, over the mountains themselves, or across the great plains that rolled towards their feet. All that empty country, and with it the chance to do new things. To live a real life in the real world.

When she and Andrew were together, they talked of nothing else. They perused the catalogue in the Library, took out whatever they could lay their hands on: geographical monographs, historical writings, exploration. They'd had great encouragement from Ronnie himself and also from Andrew's much older cousin, Crossley.

Crossley had thrown up his London bank job in the thirties and settled in a little-known part of Saskatchewan, the Palliser Triangle. He'd read about it by pure chance when he picked up a book in a junk shop, a survey of Southern Saskatchewan by an Irish army officer, Sir John Palliser. He'd been sent out by the British in 1857 to size up its potential for agriculture.

Palliser had had his reservations about the suitability of the area, but Crossley decided to go and see for himself nevertheless. What he'd found was a remarkable country, harsh but very beautiful, sparsely peopled, demanding to be farmed. He'd been willing to work hard and he'd done well. In his long, warm letter to Andrew, he said things were very little changed since he himself had come out. With the same hard work, Andrew would do as well. He'd be very pleased indeed to help him get started.

'A quarter to six,' she said, with a sigh. A pity Andrew should get held up today of all days.

She tried to visualise what a school might look like in the Palliser Triangle, with a population so spread out. Crossley said the ranches varied in size, but even the smaller were hundreds of acres and the larger extended to thousands.

Within a few months, she'd set out on the longest

journey she'd ever made in her life. Sometimes she felt quite nervous, but the moment she thought of the two of them together, her anxieties vanished. Together, they'd share the problems and laugh over the difficulties. They would get through. Beyond everything else, they would have choice. No one would be telling them what to do and how to do it. No one standing over them expecting them to do it their way, without question.

She looked at her watch. She'd give him another five minutes. When he still didn't appear by six o'clock, she walked quickly back to Elmwood Avenue. The phone was ringing as she went into the house. She paused anxiously in the hall and then relaxed. Mrs McGregor's voice sailed through the house.

'Jean dear, it's your maither.'

She went to her room, put her things away, looked out of the window. She felt so restless she began pacing up and down, indifferent to the squeaks and protests of the floorboards. A couple of minutes later there was a knock on her door. She ran to open it. Mrs McGregor was standing there, a piece of paper in her hand.

'Clare dear, I'm sorry, I didnae hear ye come in,' she said apologetically, passing over the old envelope on which a number was written. 'I was just sittin' doun to a cup o' tea when I heard your foot upstairs. Andrew phoned. It must a been a call box. It was terrable noisy. I cou'd hardly hear him. Ah cou'den make out what he was sayin' so he asked me to get you to ring this number. He was awful upset he couldnae meet ye. I think he hopes he might see ye later.'

Clare looked at the number, then at Mrs McGregor. She was puzzled. 'I don't recognise it at all, but I'll ring right away.'

'Awa doun an' use my phone, Clare,' she said promptly, as Clare picked up her purse. 'Jean'll be on the hall one God knows how long once her maither gets started,' she said matter-of-factly. 'If there's anythin' awry ye'll not get cut off so easy. Away on, ye know I'm slow on the stairs.'

Clare flew downstairs and into Mrs McGregor's small, crowded sitting room at the front of the house. Her hands shook as she dialled the unfamiliar number.

'Hello.'

The voice that answered was sharp, female, but otherwise unknown.

'My name's Clare Hamilton, my fiancé, Andrew Richardson, asked me to ring this number. Who's speaking please?'

There was a moment of complete silence at the other end of the line.

'Ach, Clare, it's me, Elsie Clarke. Did Andrew not tell you what's happened?'

Clare heard the voice falter and break. Elsie, the

dear lady who had once been Ginny and Edward's nanny, now the housekeeper at The Lodge, was in tears. Clare waited for the blow to fall.

'There's been an accident,' Elsie went on, managing now to sound quite calm. 'One o' them damn lorries from the quarry. They shoulden be allowed on these wee lanes. Sure there's no room at all an' the speed them boyos drive at. Virginia's face is all cut an' she's broken her arm. She's in the Infirmary in Armagh. But Edward is hurted bad. Real bad, they say. They took him in an ambulance to Belfast. That's where Andrew'll be now, I'm thinkin'. I phoned him at his work about an hour ago.'

She ended abruptly, as she burst into tears again.

'Do you know which hospital, Elsie?'

'Royal Victoria,' she mumbled, through her tears.

'Elsie, I'm so very sorry. All I can do is go up there. I promise I'll ring you as soon as I can. Where's Mrs Richardson? Mrs Moore, I mean.'

'Sure we don't know. Didn't they go down to Dublin, the two of them, to see about a mare that Virginia wants to buy and we can't get hold of them. The police has the number of their car. The poor things don't even know yet.'

For Clare that was the last straw. The thought of Helen and Barney coming back to find Edward in hospital when he'd only just arrived home for the summer was too much for her. She said a hasty goodbye to Elsie, broke down and sobbed in the empty room.

Unlike Virginia, who was severely lacerated about the face and arms, Edward was quite unmarked. He lay, pale and still, tubes and drips attached to his bare arms in a small alcove of the Intensive Care Unit. Beyond the window, the evening sunshine poured down over the city, warm enough for women to bring chairs to the doorways and sun themselves in the street below. She and Andrew sat in silence, one on either side of the bed, each holding one of Edward's hands.

The doctor had shaken his head. No, they were not sure of the extent of his internal injuries. There was no question of operating unless his condition stabilised. They were doing all they could. Had the parents been sent for?

In the stillness of the small room, Clare's mind filled with images of the long summer days she had spent at The Lodge. The first summer, Edward began by being so shy with her. But gradually he'd relaxed. He'd ended up making her laugh so with his stream of one-liners.

Last summer, there'd been no shyness at all. He'd greeted her as an old friend. They'd talked together a great deal and become very close. Often, they'd leave the tennis court to Andrew and Ginny and sit in the shade, talking about Irish history. Edward was excited about doing his own research. Already he'd found his way into the Trinity College archives and was comparing the common view of events found in most history books with the evidence of the reports he'd found, all properly catalogued, but clearly seldom consulted. It seemed to him as if the story most people knew was more important to them than knowing what had actually happened. What he'd really like to do was retell the story making proper use of the facts, however much it upset people.

She'd been so touched by his relationship with Ginny, so teasing on the surface, so deeply affectionate. She'd admitted to Andrew how much she envied Virginia her Edward, so different from her own sullen, unwelcoming brother.

Looking down at the still, pale face, she couldn't imagine how she could bear to lose the liveliness, the animation, the sudden laughter of this young man from whom she had learnt so much in such a little time.

A nurse put her head round the screen and whispered in Clare's ear: 'Mr and Mrs Moore have arrived.'

'Helen and Barney,' Clare mouthed to Andrew, as she released Edward's limp hand and got up.

Out in the corridor, Helen put her arms round

Clare and clung to her, weeping, while Andrew and Barney stood awkwardly by, waiting till she could collect herself enough to go in and look at her son, pale and motionless on the high white bed.

Edward never regained consciousness. Later, the doctor said the impact of the crash had ruptured his spleen. He died in the early hours of the morning.

CHAPTER EIGHT

The days that followed Edward's death were the bleakest and longest that Clare had ever known. Clinging to her in the hospital corridor, Helen Moore had begged her to come to Caledon with Andrew. Even if she had remotely wanted to, she could not possibly have refused her heartfelt plea.

After a few hours of exhausted sleep at the flat, they left the city very early. Slanting through the trees, the low sunlight caught the dew on the grass by the roadside. The air was fresh and the road empty of traffic. All the way to Armagh, it was so beautiful she could hardly bear to look at the familiar landscape.

They arrived in Caledon just as the village was beginning to stir. The milkman was turning out of the drive. He waved cheerily to Andrew. Ahead of them the long, low building, with its graceful pillars and elegant, tall windows lay bathed in morning sun. It had never looked so tranquil, so welcoming. The sweep of the garden was a joy. Helen and

Barney had worked so hard last autumn reshaping the herbaceous borders, improving the lawns and planting new young trees. Now, the early summer warmth of these last weeks had rewarded them, setting sweeps of vibrant colour against the fresh green of the well-trimmed lawns.

Barney was on the steps to greet them. Without a word, he hugged them both, took them through the house, sat them down in the kitchen and insisted on cooking them a proper breakfast.

The house felt as empty and desolate as if it were derelict. He'd persuaded Helen to take a sleeping pill as soon as they got back from Belfast. She was still in bed. Ginny was in hospital in Armagh. And Edward was gone, she added to herself. As she tried to eat the bacon and egg Barney put in front of her, all she could think of was his speciality of the house, sausage and chips. Tears trickled down her face and dropped unheeded on her skirt.

'I don't think Helen will be able to help us much with the funeral arrangements,' Barney said quietly, as he poured more coffee for them. 'We'll just have to make a start. It can't be for a few days anyway, because of the post-mortem.'

Clare looked across at Andrew, his face pale with tiredness and stiff with grief. Barney was being so gentle with them, but she realised immediately that the burden of making all the decisions would fall on Andrew. Her experience of country wakes,

106

her own grandfather's funeral, would hardly be much use in the context of The Lodge.

'Do you know if Edward has made a will?'

The voice was so flat and featureless, it hardly sounded like Andrew, and it seemed such a strange question to ask. She couldn't possibly imagine Edward making a will. What Edward made were games to play, bizarre tests of skill, like driving golf balls up ramps and into buckets. Edward painted ceilings and drove Harry's car down potholed tracks on picnics. Edward mended things and cooked for them. Made them laugh at his jokes and groan at his awful puns.

Today, he wasn't going to be late for breakfast. He wouldn't appear yawning, tousled and apologetic. Edward was dead. Gone away. Not coming back.

Clare stopped herself. Forced herself to concentrate on what Barney was saying. No, Edward hadn't made a will.

'It will have to be Grange Church, then,' Andrew said, looking from one to the other, his coffee untouched. 'If he hasn't made a will, the Richardson rule applies. I'll have to contact the Rector about opening the vault. When do you think the funeral might be?'

Barney pressed his lips together and shook his head.

'What do you think Helen *might* say?' Clare

asked, remembering how distraught she'd been when Edward's father had died, a bare six years before.

He shook his head again.

'I'm afraid it's going to be up to us, Clare. If we leave it a few days, Ginny should be well enough to go. It might be important for her later.'

Clare nodded, not trusting herself to speak.

When are they going to let her out, Barney?' asked Andrew.

'This afternoon. They did say to phone before we came, just to make sure. She doesn't know yet about Edward. No one knows except Elsie Clarke. She sat up last night till we got back. She heard the car pass her house and phoned us as soon as she saw the lights go on.'

Andrew covered his face with his hands. There was a long pause. He looked up at last and said bleakly: 'We'll need a list of people to be told. A preliminary announcement in the *Belfast Telegraph* and the *Newsletter* tonight. And the local papers, of course. I'll have to go into Armagh now and tell Ginny in case any of the nurses hear before they go to work.'

'Do you want me to come with you?' Clare asked.

'No,' he said abruptly. 'Barney will need you here when Helen wakes up. You could phone June Wiley for me and ask her to tell Grandmother. See if you can find Edward's address book. He has three special friends. Can you remember their names?'

'Yes, I can.'

'I'll get back as soon as I can,' he said, standing up and striding out of the kitchen without even a glance at her. She felt it like a sudden chill of rejection and burst into tears. Barney came and put his arms round her. He held her close while she sobbed as if her heart would break.

Edward had been right about Barney. He had indeed disposed of a small fortune through excessive generosity and ill-advised business ventures, but, whatever his failings, he was warm, open-hearted and kind. He let her cry, and only when she struggled to collect herself did he let himself say quietly, 'Edward thought the world of you.'

She took the large clean handkerchief he offered her. It was silk and edged with a pattern of racehorses going at full gallop.

'Edward was the brother I'd always wanted. We only had two bits of two summers together, but I feel he's been there all my life. Silly, isn't it?'

'No, not silly at all, Clare. Some people in your life really matter, however long or short the time you have them. They're the ones that make you different for having known them.'

She nodded vigorously, wiping her face and blowing her nose.

'I'm all right now, Barney. Thank you,' she said, squeezing his hand. 'What should we do next? What about the washing up?'

'Good girl. I think we'll have Elsie Clarke here shortly. She was in a bad way last night.'

Clare took a deep breath. The hardest part of all would be meeting people like Elsie and Harry who'd known Edward all his life.

Just at that moment, she heard a door close. Footsteps approached. As the clock struck nine, Elsie Clarke came into the kitchen, her usually cheerful face red and swollen with weeping.

Clare went up to her and put her arms round her. She sensed Barney slip away. As she stood holding Elsie, she felt the day had already been going on for ever. But it had only just begun.

'There'll have to be refreshments afterwards,' Andrew said decisively, as they sat round the table eating the sandwiches Elsie had produced for lunch. 'Some people are coming a long way. Edward's Trinity friends may need to stay over. Johnny Keane is coming up from Limerick.'

He looked doubtfully towards Clare.

She took a deep breath. It had all happened before. Only six years ago when Edward's father had died of a heart attack. She still remembered how angry she'd been when she'd heard the Missus complaining to June Wiley that her daughter-in-law couldn't cope. They would have to have the overnight guests at Drumsollen. Clare hadn't known Helen then, she'd just been sad for her, a woman who'd lost her husband, without any warning. Now she knew what a loving but vulnerable person Helen was, it made the Missus's complaints appear even more unfeeling.

Helen had been so happy the last few years. Barney was an old friend from childhood, long widowed and as lonely as she was. They'd met up again, begun to share their interest in horses, in gardens, in entertaining friends. Slowly, she'd come back to life. She'd even taken out the 'smock of Monet colours', and begun to paint again. Now Edward was gone, her world had collapsed around her yet again.

'I think Elsie and Olive can manage two or three bedrooms here,' Clare replied, as levelly as she could. 'But there's the problem of being so far away from the church when it comes to the refreshments. You probably remember last time.' She looked at Andrew steadily.

'Drumsollen?'

'It might make it easier.'

Barney looked puzzled. Andrew explained that they had used Drumsollen when Teddy's father died. It was less than two miles from Grange Church, while Caledon was more like ten. And it meant that people wouldn't have to go through

Armagh to find their way back to The Lodge.

'Sounds very sensible,' said Barney, 'but surely old Mrs Richardson won't want it. She doesn't seem a very approachable sort of lady.'

'I think we should at least ask her,' Andrew replied. 'Otherwise we'd have to use a hotel in Armagh.'

'I'm sure that would be even worse for Helen than having it here,' said Clare firmly. 'I think we should ask Virginia what she thinks. She and Helen are the two that matter most.'

Andrew nodded briefly.

'I know Ginny won't want it here. She asked this morning if his body had to be brought back to The Lodge. She said she couldn't bear the thought of that. She wants to remember Edward as he was, alive and happy.'

Without another word he went out into the hall and picked up the telephone.

'June, it's Andrew.'

Clare heard his voice soften momentarily as he spoke to her. Then he asked for his grandmother and stood waiting. And waiting. At last, she heard him speak. The conversation was brief and to the point.

'Thank you. I'll do as you ask. With Mrs Wiley's help, I'm sure we can manage so that we don't disturb you at all.'

* * *

112

Three days later, on a sultry, overcast afternoon, Clare walked up the stone steps of Drumsollen, hand in hand with Virginia, who just couldn't stop crying. As she stepped into the familiar hall and coaxed her towards the dining room, where Elsie Clark and June Wiley were already serving tea, Clare was sharply aware that she had passed through the elegant front door for the first time as a member of the Richardson family. It was a strange feeling that brought no joy. Would anything ever bring her joy again, she wondered.

'Come on, Ginny dear, drink up,' she said, as encouragingly as she could manage. Clare took Ginny's saturated hanky, tucked it into her sling and put a china mug into her good hand. 'Only another hour, love,' she whispered. 'Then we can cry all we want to. Please, please stop or you'll start me off again.'

Ginny looked down at her and smiled weakly, the stitched wounds on her forehead and cheeks livid against the pallor of her skin. Clare had forced herself to look and look again at Ginny's face, until she could manage it without flinching at the cruel lines, seamed with black stitches, but when she was alone with Barney she wept again. 'Every time Ginny looks in a mirror she'll think of Edward.'

'Miss Hamilton.'

Clare turned away from the tea table to see an

113

elderly man in mourning dress inclining his head towards her. His face was mottled, the loose skin flaked and dry, his nose red and bulbous. From beneath huge unkempt eyebrows, his watery eyes stared at her.

'I think I *do* remember you from poor Edward's funeral,' he said jovially. 'You brought me a second cup of tea. And now, I understand I must *congratulate* you.'

He made a gesture of bright surprise, as if to say, 'How jolly. What a jape.'

Clare took an instant dislike to him. Beneath his apparently charming manner, he was looking her up and down as if she were a filly in the show ring. He'd made no attempt at all to greet Ginny, who was standing right beside her.

'Mrs Richardson is an old friend of mine, a very "old" friend,' he went on, nodding his head in amusement at his own joke. 'She's in the drawing room and wants to speak to you, so I'd better let you run along, hadn't I?'

Without a word, Clare turned her back on him and made for the door, her face flushed with anger. She paused in the empty hall and took several deep breaths. 'I'd better let you run along,' she repeated in a whisper. 'No, Clare, don't get angry. Today is not a day to feel, just a day to be survived.'

At the entrance to the drawing room, she caught a glimpse of Andrew, talking to three young men she recognised immediately as Edward's closest friends from Trinity. Dark-suited and stiffly formal, only the youthful outlines of their faces marked them out from the collection of their seniors who appeared not to have changed at all in the six years since they last stood here, after Uncle Edward's funeral; enjoying June Wiley's home baking and Clare's own carefully cut sandwiches.

'Thank God we're going to Canada,' she murmured, as she stood in the doorway, wondering where she would find the strength to cross it. The dark figures rocked on their heels and boomed at each other. Suddenly, a gap opened in the press of bodies. Beyond, she saw the wispy, snow-white hair of the Missus, barely visible above the black leather of her wheelchair. She took a deep breath, straightened her back, and stepped into the room.

'Ah, there you are, Clare. Do sit down here, I can't possibly hear you if you stand.'

Clare recognised the chair from her last visit and lowered herself cautiously, only too aware of the damage her high heels would do to her nylons if she didn't concentrate.

'You look very well,' she said approvingly.

'Thank you.' Clare almost managed to smile. Of course the Missus would think she looked very well. Dressed in Ginny's beautifully cut black suit, tailored for her when she was at finishing school, how could she fail to look like one of them.

'You can't possibly go into Armagh and buy a suit, Clare,' Ginny had protested, when she'd said she'd have to go shopping for something suitable. 'It'll cost you pounds. You can wear mine. It really doesn't matter what I wear under all this bandaging. I certainly can't get into a jacket.'

Ginny insisted Clare try on the suit. They'd even managed to laugh at the length of the skirt on Clare's shorter figure.

'You look like Mother Hubbard. But apart from that, it fits beautifully. Stay there and I'll get Elsie to pin it up for you. Edward would be furious if I let you spend money on a boring old black suit.'

'Eh bien, I hear Andrew is taking you off to Canada. And what will become of your delightful accent there?' Mrs Richardson began, speaking in French.

'As I shall probably be teaching French, I'm sure I can manage to keep it up,' Clare replied, quite amazed that the old woman should revert once again to the language of her youth. For decades, she'd used it only when there were things to be said that servants must not hear.

'Well, I hope he makes a better job of farming than he has of law. I don't hear great reports from Belfast,' she said, matter-of-factly. 'But then, Andrew always did favour his mother's side. Charming girl, Adeline, just as pretty as you are. Full of ideas. Loved animals. My son William simply adored her. I expect that's where Andrew gets it from, this farming business. His father was more realistic, always did what was required of him. But that's not the fashion any more. Young people do as they please these days.'

'And what about Deauville?'

Clare was surprised at herself. The words seemed to have popped out entirely unbidden.

'Touché, Clare, touché,' she replied, her worn and lined face breaking into an unexpected smile. 'What you lack in experience, you've always made up for in courage. But I doubt if you'll do much with Andrew. He has no ambition. Just like his father.'

She paused, and signalled with her hand to a middle-aged man hovering nearby, clearly the next occupant of the low chair.

'Will you be married in the parish church?'

'Yes. As soon as we can arrange our passages.'

'You will be welcome to use Drumsollen afterwards, whether I'm fit to come downstairs or not. Is that clear?'

'Thank you. That's very kind.'

To her surprise, the Missus offered her a bony hand and smiled warmly when she took it gently.

'Make sure you come and see me before you leave for Canada. That little gift I spoke of last year is now with my solicitors. I shall send for it tomorrow.'

* * *

At last, the large rooms were empty. The Missus had retired to bed, Barney had taken Helen and Ginny back to Caledon. Andrew and John Wiley were working together, packing up the trestle tables used for serving tea and restoring the rooms to their normal state. They replaced the heavy dustcovers over the furniture, the light fabric that covered the portraits and paintings, the plastic sheeting that protected the carpets. When all was as it should be, they pulled across the heavy wooden shutters and slotted in the iron bars which held them firmly in place, a defence against insurgents, as potent in troubled times as the iron grilles on the windows of the basement rooms.

Down there, in the friendly company of June Wiley and Elsie Clark, Clare had changed into flat shoes, donned a large apron and was helping with the washing up. They talked as they worked, three women so practised, they could proceed with only a fraction of their minds upon it.

'The Missus is powerful failed since last I saw her,' said Elsie Clark, as she stacked dirty cups on the draining board within June's reach.

'It's a brave while since ye saw her now, isn't it?' replied June. 'Shure it's six years come October since Mr Edward died.'

'Ach, I suppose it is. The time goes that quick. Sure, here's Clare was only a schoolgirl when we came the day of his funeral. D'ye mind you hurt your ankle? D'ye have any bother with it?'

'No, not a bit, thank goodness, but then I got a charm from an' oul fella over Cabragh way. Did ye know Johnsie George, Clare?' asked June, looking sideways at her.

'Is he the one that ran away to sea when he was a boy?'

'The very one. Fancy you mindin' that.'

Clare smiled and took a tray of clean cups to the cupboard. 'The forge was a great place for hearing life stories,' she said, as she put the cups back in their places.

As June washed and Elsie dried, Clare smiled to herself. With this team at work, feeding the five thousand might still be a problem, but washing up afterwards would be no trouble at all.

'Have ye been past the forge recently, Clare?' asked June cautiously.

'I have, indeed,' she replied sadly. 'Andrew and I were up in April. I could hardly believe it.'

'Why, what's happened?' asked Elsie.

'Ach, it's this new landlord, Elsie,' June began. 'Hutchinson, his name is. He's a great man for makin' money. He has the forge knocked down that was there fer generations. All the good trees down an' away too. They say he plans to build a house where the forge was an' a couple more forby. Ach, it's a disgrace an' a shame.'

'Ah, dear a dear, isn't that desperate,' said Elsie

sympathetically. 'An' sure aren't your plans all upset again with poor Master Edward dying,' she said, looking mournfully at Clare, as she brought another trayful of dirty cups from table to sink.

'How do you mean, Elsie?'

'Well, yer weddin' and goin' off to Canada an' so on.'

'Oh, we're not delaying the wedding,' said Clare, relieved. 'Mrs Moore and Virginia want us to go ahead. It'll be a very quiet wedding anyway.'

'Aye, I'm sure they wouden stan' in yer way, nor woud young Edward either, God rest him,' Elsie replied agreeably. 'But I'm thinkin' there'll be no Canada for Andrew now. Sure how could he go, an' all the property at Caledon and Drumsollen his now to see after?'

Clare never knew how she got through the hours that followed, the goodbyes to June Wiley and John, the drive back to Caledon with Elsie chattering away in the back seat, the changing of clothes, the making of plans. Even more goodbyes as they prepared to go back to Belfast.

'I'd never have managed without you, Clare,' Ginny said, tears springing to her eyes, as they walked out together to the car. 'I shall miss you so.'

Clare put her arms round her, careful not to press on her heavily bandaged arm. She'd always liked Ginny, enjoyed her company, appreciated her elegance and humour, but in these last few days, talking together, sharing the loss of Edward, weeping together, some quite new bond had been forged between them.

'I'll miss you too, Ginny,' she said sadly. 'We managed it together. Edward would have been proud of us.'

'Get in the car, Clare. Go quickly. I'm about to bawl again,' said Ginny urgently. 'Andrew doesn't know how lucky he is to have you.'

She kissed Clare's cheek and ran indoors, just as a rattle of thunder echoed away in the west. Large, warm spots of rain the size of sixpences spattered down.

Barney opened the car door for Clare. 'Thanks for everything,' he said, bending to kiss her cheek. 'Helen and I couldn't have done without you. We'll come up and see you before the wedding, when she's a bit steadier.'

He went round to Andrew's side. 'Drive carefully now,' he said. 'The roads will be greasy enough once this rain gets on them, after all the heat and dryness.'

They made their way slowly down the drive, the rain already streaming across the windscreen, turning their parting view of the lawns and herbaceous border into an impressionist blur of brilliant colours.

Before they reached Armagh, it was lashing

down so fiercely that they had to pull in and stop, because the wipers just couldn't cope. There was a sudden blinding flash and a shattering crash of thunder right overhead. However anxious she might be, this was not the moment to speak about Canada or anything else. Just getting back to Belfast was going to be an achievement.

When they were able to go on again, lightning still lit up the sky; the noise of thunder and the swish of the tyres through the water now lying on the road was enough to make talk impossible anyway. Only as they approached Belfast itself did the storm move away and even the rain had eased when, at last, they stopped in Elmwood Avenue.

She looked at Andrew. In the lamplight, his face was drawn and white with exhaustion.

'You must go home and go straight to bed. You've got to go to work tomorrow,' she said, managing a firmness she certainly didn't feel. 'And don't get out to help me. I can manage.'

Thankfully, he leaned his head and arms on the steering wheel while she got her suitcase out of the boot and shut it firmly.

'I'll come up tomorrow, as soon as I can get away,' he said wearily. 'Thanks for being so wonderful. I don't deserve it.'

She watched him drive off and turned towards the house, grateful to see it was in darkness. The kind enquiries of Mrs McGregor were more than she could bear tonight. She tiptoed quietly upstairs in the glow from the street lamp, dropped her suitcase inside her door, peeled off her jacket and went straight across to light the gas fire. She sat and held out her hands to the glow, though the room was warm and muggy.

'It's not going to work after all,' she said, surprised to find her voice quite steady and matter-of-fact. 'I knew it was too good to be true. Every time I'm happy, every time I have someone to love and a home of my own, it's taken away. First there was Mummy and Daddy, then there was Granda Scott. Now it's Andrew.'

She thought of the roomfuls of Richardsons, all doing what they had to do, what they'd always done. The way Andrew had simply stepped into the place appointed without question, shouldered all the arrangements. Then she thought of what the Missus had said about him. Now she knew why Andrew wasn't welcome at Drumsollen. He was like his mother. Full of ideas. Yet it was she, city born as she was, who had run the farm and cared for the animals, while husband and father-in-law did what they had to do at Stormont and at Westminster.

But hadn't the Missus got it wrong? She'd said Andrew wasn't like his father. 'His father was more realistic. Always did what had to be done.' Those were her words. But wasn't that precisely what Andrew *had* done, the moment Edward died?

She sat on the edge of her chair, unaware of the pain in her back or the ache in her head. She went through it all again. Andrew was now the head of the family, heir to the bankrupt estate of Drumsollen and whatever additional burden had fallen upon Edward. It was really all so simple. A one-way choice. Was he going to marry her and go to Canada and make a home with her? Or was he going to follow the tradition, now and forever more, doing what was expected of him by anyone who could make the remotest claim upon him?

She looked down at her pretty ring with its tiny diamond and winking red stones. Thought again of the joyous moment when it slipped on to her finger, a perfect fit.

'The ball is over, Cinderella,' she said to the empty room. 'Unless the Prince carries you off to a new life and a new world, you'll have to start all over again.'

She turned out the fire, pulled off her clothes, tossed away the cushions on her bed, crawled under the bedclothes and cried herself to sleep.

CHAPTER NINE

Morning came, grey and sodden. The trees dripped heavily on the pavements, though the rain itself had stopped. Oppressed by the aqueous gloom which surrounded her, she switched on the red-shaded lamps that Ronnie had made out of old wine bottles. They glowed dimly and made no impression at all upon the room itself. In the even dimmer kitchen she made tea and toast, put it on a tray, brought it back up to her table by the window and sat down in Robert's chair.

The house was so quiet. In the week since Edward died, all the other students had gone away, off to holiday jobs, to travel abroad, or back home to the country to help on the farm. It was a relief. The less goodbyes to say the better. All she wanted to do now was to slip away. Leave behind the remains of a life Edward's death had taken from her.

She'd no appetite for her toast, but she was very thirsty. She sat drinking tea and trying to decide how best to fill the hours before Andrew came, when she would know for sure if she were right. She ran her eye around the room, paused at the large calendar produced by the engineering firm Uncle Jack now worked for. Bright with flags and bunting, the white-hulled ship had been an encouragement all through these last weeks. With a shock, she registered the red stars marking the days of her exams. Then it was May and now it was June.

She got up, tore off the weeks already consigned to history and stared at the pattern of squares revealed. Below the picture of a Viscount flying in a clear, blue sky, three entries were written in.

'See Rector about wedding,' she read aloud. 'Pack up books for store. Move out into flat.'

She went on staring at the numbered squares, searching for the one that marked the day when Edward died, an unexceptional square, no different from its companions, the square after which her life had fallen to pieces, yet once more – just like the day Granda Scott slipped down beside his anvil and lay there in the silent forge till Jamsey came looking for him.

'All things pass, however pleasant or unpleasant,' she reminded herself, smiling a little, hearing the echo of Aunt Sarah's voice; words which had proved their truth, time and time again.

She took a deep breath, got up and carried her

breakfast tray back to the kitchen. She washed up, left everything tidy, went upstairs again and began to sort her books into piles, some to be sold in the Union shop, some to go to charity, and some to be stored against a future which was now entirely open.

It seemed to take a very long time but she kept at it, bagging up the ones for the Union shop and walking over with them. Books were not just inanimate objects. Books were your history. The wearying record of exams to be passed or the reminder of past joys and present loves. Stories that once opened new worlds. Poetry which stayed on in the mind. The books you acquired told you something about who you were, who you once had been.

It was early evening and she was standing by the window when Andrew appeared, unexpectedly early and on foot. For a moment, she hardly recognised him. She peered out and watched him stride along the damp pavement, his raincoat open over his dark suit, his face pale and shadowed. Only when he rang the bell did she collect herself and run downstairs to let him in.

'You've been busy,' he said, as she held out her hand for his coat.

He stood in front of the gas fire while she hung the coat on the back of the door and came back to the fireplace to sit down. It wasn't the first time he'd appeared in the dark suit the firm insisted upon, but tonight it was hard to bear. He looked as if he'd come straight out of the roomful of Richardsons in their funeral weeds. As out of place here in her room as she had felt when she donned Ginny's black costume in a room full of patterned fabrics and much-loved soft toys.

'Time has moved on while we've been away,' she said matter-of-factly, doing her best to keep her voice steady, to speak of what was ordinary. 'Mrs McGregor has a new tenant coming at the end of next week. She was lucky to get a summer let.'

But nothing was ordinary anymore. Anything they talked about raised questions that couldn't be answered till she had the answer to the one big question.

'Andrew, I think there's something you have to tell me. I think I know, but I need you to tell me.'

The words struck a chord. They sounded so familiar. Surely she must have said them before. Suddenly, it came to her. The day they sat in the sunshine on Cannon Hill and he confessed he hated the job. The day they decided to go to Canada.

Andrew smiled bleakly and looked down at his very well-polished shoes.

'Edward's affairs are in rather a mess,' he began, as if reluctant to have to speak Edward's name. 'There's a massive bill for death duties still outstanding since Uncle Edward died and now there'll be more, unless something can be arranged. The Lodge might have to go . . .'

He broke off as if he hoped he needn't say more, but Clare was determined he should. She sat silent, waiting.

'Clare, I know you'll be so disappointed, but I can't possibly go to Canada in the circumstances. We might be able to manage it, given a year or two, but not now.'

She nodded silently. As she had known in her heart, the Prince was not going to carry her off to live happily ever after.

'Yes, I *am* disappointed, Andrew.'

To her amazement, she heard the words shape themselves quite fluently, as if they had been so long practised she couldn't possibly stumble.

'I could face making a life with you in Canada, whatever hardship that might bring, but I can't do it here. If you won't come with me, I can't marry you. I'm sure you'll be disappointed too, Andrew, that I can't stay to help.'

There. It was spoken. No more blows to fall.

'But, Clare.'

'But what?' she said wearily, smitten by the look of despair on his face as he turned towards her.

'We don't have to throw it *all* up, surely, all that we've had. Don't you love me any more?'

'Yes, probably I do, but that's not the really

important question. Not now. You've said "yes" to a life I can't share. Canada, yes, however tough, but not the Richardson circus. Ronnie's right. He said we should get out of Ulster. Get out into the fresh air. But you want to go back into the old, tight airless box, don't you?'

'It's not like that. Clare. It's not like that at all. You've got it all wrong,' he retorted, stung by her words. 'I've no more time for that crowd than you have. But there are things that have to be seen to. Do you want Helen and Ginny to be homeless, like you were? Do you think it's any easier being chucked out of a "gentleman's residence" than out of the house by the forge? Have you thought about June and John Wiley, if Drumsollen goes. Elsie and Olive Clark and the other folk at Caledon, if The Lodge goes? Or are you only thinking of yourself?'

'Sometimes one has to think only of one's self, Andrew. Especially when other people let you down. When they make you promises they feel free to break. Is there a hierarchy of promises in your code? Who comes at the top? Who gets priority? Not the wee blacksmith's granddaughter from the Grange, I'm sure,' she ended, unable to control the bitterness in her voice.

'Clare, you're not thinking straight,' he said harshly. 'What about *your* promise to me? Our engagement? Have I changed into someone you can't love, because I accept obligations that no one else can deal with? Must you always come first, no matter what's at issue?'

'No, not always, Andrew. I'm not as selfish as you're trying to make me out. But there's a limit to what anyone can cope with and I've reached it. No more waiting. No more hoping. No more struggling. No more depending on anyone else. I've had enough of being let down. I want a life that's not made out of someone else's expectations. It's a life I want to share with you. But if I can't have it with you, then I'll have to make it on my own.'

By the time she gasped out the last words, her whole body was shaking with fury.

'Then there's no more to be said.'

He stood up, walked across the room and unhooked his raincoat from the back of the door. For a moment, she thought he would go without another word. She wondered if she would have the strength not to run after him. But he turned and came back to the fireplace and stood looking down at her. 'I think something's wrong between us, Clare, and it needs sorting out, but this isn't the way to do it.'

'Will you go to Canada with me?' she said, as lightly as if she were saying, 'Shall we have a day out tomorrow?'

'No, Clare, I won't. I'm not free to go to Canada or anywhere else.'

She put her hand to her mouth and moistened her engagement ring. It was such a good fit that it took her a few moments to twist it off. She held it out to him.

'I'm sorry, Andrew. It was such a lovely dream.'

'No it wasn't,' he said, sharply. 'We were friends for five years and lovers for a year now. Doesn't that count for anything?'

'I could ask you the same.'

'Put your ring back on, Clare, and let's see what we can do to make things better,' he said quietly, his eyes on the tiny glinting stones that were catching the light from the fire, his hands firmly in his pockets.

'Will you take me to Canada?'

He stood, looking at her in amazement, and then his face crumpled into despair.

'I can't do what you want, Clare,' he said, his voice choking on the words. 'I just can't.'

She looked up at him, his face drawn, his eyes dark-circled, and wondered if this was really happening. She decided it was. That she'd always known it would.

'And I can't do what you want either,' she said firmly, standing up and holding out the ring towards him.

For a moment he looked at her blankly, then he turned on his heel and walked to the door.

'Keep it, or throw it away. No one else will ever

wear it. You know where to find me if you change your mind.'

The door shut behind him. She heard his feet running down the stairs and the bang of the front door. She didn't go to the window. She just sat on in the growing darkness, weeping, wondering if she would ever see him again.

The week that followed was a busy one. She made a long list of all she had to do and worked her way steadily down it. Each day, she made a point of writing some letters, packing some of the books she wanted to keep, making some more arrangements. The variation was designed to keep her mind alert, but despite all her efforts she felt her progress was painfully slow. She was tired all the time, couldn't shake herself from sleep in the mornings, found she was only wide awake during the small hours of the night.

The first thing she did was go and see Harry. She had to tell him why she couldn't come back to work in the gallery as she'd promised.

He'd been so kind, looked so sad when she told him about Andrew. He listened so attentively when she explained what she was planning to do. When she came to the end, there was a moment's silence, then he said: 'What would you like me to do with the rings, then?'

She was flustered and confused by his

words. The only ring she could think of was her engagement ring.

'What rings, Harry? I haven't got any rings.'

'Oh yes you have,' he replied gently. 'Don't you remember? The ones you found when you cleared out the forge house.'

She shook her head and laughed at herself.

'I'm all through myself, Harry. I knew there was something I had to ask you about.'

She'd hadn't really forgotten them, the two gold rings she'd found under the old settle when she and Jack had pulled it out from the wall. They'd lain secure in Harry's safe for the last four years. Now she knew exactly what she was going to do with them.

'I thought for a minute you must mean this one,' she said awkwardly, as she fished out the small box from her handbag and gave it to him. 'Would you give it to Andrew when you see him?'

He nodded abruptly and put it in his pocket.

'I wondered if you could offer me a price for the gold rings, Harry,' she began shyly. 'They're not quite your sort of thing, but they're fairly old, aren't they?'

'Hold on a minute an' I'll tell you,' he said quickly, as he pulled out files from his desk drawer. 'I sent them to old Fienstein at Kaitcer's ages ago and I kept meaning to tell you what he said. He's the man for marks on gold.'

He scuffled through a whole folder of papers, pulled out a single sheet, muttered about Troy weight and then read aloud. 'Two rings, both clearly marked from the same source. We suggest a date of 1790.'

'As old as that?' she said, surprised. 'Things were very troubled in Armagh in the nineties. That's when the United Irishmen were active. I always wondered if they'd been lost, or whether that was their hiding place and the owners never came back. We'll probably never know.'

'The antique business is full of mysteries, Clare. Sometimes I can hardly credit what turns up in places you'd never expect,' he said abstractedly. 'Would a hundred pounds do?'

'A hundred?' she gasped. 'They're never worth that, Harry,' she protested, shocked he should make such an excessive offer.

'No, they're not,' he agreed. 'Not yet. But you need the money now. If you want them in a year or two, you can pay me back. If you don't, I'll bide my time and sell them at a profit. In this trade, it's just a matter of biding one's time. You know that as well as I do.'

Yes, she did. She'd been very willing to learn, and Harry was a good teacher. One of the first things he'd taught her was the way fashion ebbed and flowed continuously. The successful dealer was the one who could predict the way the tide was running or spread his activities wide enough to cover whichever way it ran.

Harry was very good at the job, but even he made mistakes. 'If you don't make mistakes, you don't make anything,' he often said, philosophically. 'It's all part of life.'

Jessie wasn't at all philosophical when Clare went up to Braeside later that day to tell her all that had happened. She was even more distressed and upset than Clare had expected.

'Yer mad, Clare. Absolutely mad. Sure Andrew's dying about you,' she protested. 'What are ye thinkin' about? Sure Canada isn't the be all an' end all of things? Isn't Andrew more important than that? Could ye not wait a year or two an' then go?'

She did her best to explain, but she soon saw that nothing she could say would make any difference. It was as if Jessie couldn't get beyond the fact that it had all gone wrong. She was so distraught, in the end, Clare had to put aside her own distress and use all her energy to try and comfort her. As the tears subsided and Jessie grew calmer, Clare did begin to wonder if perhaps being pregnant had made her more emotional. She'd not been well in the last weeks and not able to go to the gallery at all on some days. Harry had said she'd been very distressed about Edward despite the fact she'd never even met him.

Walking back down the drive to the Malone

Road, the carefully pruned shrubberies already showing the signs of Harry's work, Clare knew she was very upset herself about the visit she'd just made. Unconsciously, she'd expected understanding and comfort from her oldest friend, but all she'd had was distress and sharp criticism of the most painful decision she'd ever had to make.

As she strode out gratefully along the Malone Road on her way back to Elmwood, she remembered that she and Andrew were to have been godparents to Jessie's child. Jessie hadn't mentioned it. She wasn't sure whether to be glad or sorry.

It was such a sad parting, Clare decided not to say any more personal goodbyes. When she found herself wide awake at three o'clock in the morning, she spent the time writing notes to friends and the few relatives who might just be aware of her absence.

She wasn't surprised, though, when Mrs McGregor invited her in for a cup of tea the next time they met on the stairs. She'd been such a good friend all through Clare's time at Queen's. She'd always wanted to make certain Clare was all right. When Andrew failed to turn up on her doorstep as usual, Clare knew she'd guess something was wrong. Having settled them in her comfortable, well-scrubbed kitchen she listened to Clare's brief, well-rehearsed explanation. She nodded sadly.

'If it's to be, Clare, it's to be. These things has a way o' bein' taken out o' our han's. There's maybe someone else waitin' out there fer ye. Or ye may find yer path crosses wi' Andrew again. Dinnae fret yersel. Ye did what seemed right to you, an' that's all any o' us can do. Tell me anythin' ye need, or any help I can be t' you. An' make sure ye let me know how ye fare.

'I'll miss ye,' she added, abruptly, as Clare stood up, leaving her rent book and keys and a small, prettily wrapped parcel on the kitchen table.

A week after Edward's funeral, Clare took out her one suitcase and began to pack it. She took only her very best clothes, leaving the rest, with her bed linen and kitchen equipment, for Mrs McGregor to use in her charity work. In the zip pocket of the leather travel bag Jessie and Harry had given her for her twenty-first birthday, she placed a folder of documents from which she could construct a curriculum vitae. In another pocket, she put all the money she could lay her hands on. The small remnants of her last grant cheque, a few pounds from the sale of her books and the savings from her Post Office account. It didn't amount to very much, once you took away Harry's hundred pounds.

She realised she was doing the very opposite of what Granny Hamilton had done at her age. Granny had saved up the money for her ticket to Canada then bought a wedding dress when Granda suddenly stepped into her life. Clare had saved up for her wedding dress and now she'd used the money to buy her escape.

With her case packed and the house quiet, she sorted out small change and went down to the phone. She made three phone calls. To the Secretary's office at Queen's, to say that she would like to receive her degree in absentia. To Keith Harvey, to ask him if he would have her results for her, if she phoned him the following week. To a taxi firm, to order a cab for seven-thirty to take her to the Liverpool boat.

When she'd made her calls, she couldn't face going back up to the emptiness of the clean and tidy room. She was impatient to be on her way, but there were hours still to be lived through before the boat sailed. She took up her travel bag with the paperbacks she'd chosen for the journey and headed for Botanic Avenue.

She had lunch at a window table in Queen's Espresso. One last coffee from the bright coloured cups she'd loved so much. Then she walked back up to Botanic Gardens.

Through the long, sunny afternoon she revisited all the familiar paths, watched the children play, walked through the tropical ravine, and sat and read, or just sat, taking in the sunlight, the smell of flowers, her eyes closed, her mind empty.

As the heat of the afternoon began to fade, she went back to her room and waited, by the window, one last time, till the solid shape of the large black taxi appeared, just as it had for Ronnie, six long years ago. Her suitcase already waiting in the hall, she picked up her jacket and bag and ran lightly down the stairs. She was glad to be on her way at last.

CHAPTER TEN

The taxi dropped her outside a gloomy, high-roofed shed. 'Liverpool', it said in huge, red letters. Through the open doors, across the oil-stained concrete floor, rose the side of the berthed vessel, a dark cliff face pierced by a small entrance, around which passengers and stewards, porters and delivery men came and went, dwarfed by the scale of the ship and the departure shed.

She smiled at the taxi driver as she counted out shillings and sixpences. He'd been so friendly, said the sunshine was great and what a pity we didn't get more of it and asked if she'd seen *Island in the Sun* when it was at the Astoria. That's what he'd like, a nice tropical island. Harry Belafonte he could take or leave.

'Here y'are, miss,' he said, swinging her case off the luggage platform as if it were a handbag. 'See ye enjoy yer holiday. Ah hope ye get good weather.'

'Thank you very much. I enjoyed the ride

down,' she said warmly, as she picked up her case and turned away.

No need to tell him she was not going on holiday. No need to say she might never come back. She walked slowly. Her suitcase was not very heavy, but she found carrying a case awkward. It made her feel clumsy and her back always ached after only a short distance.

Halfway across the shed, she put it down. For a moment she stood watching the birds which came and went in the dimness high above her head. Then she changed hands and went on, thinking of Ronnie, his tall figure striding across this same empty space, all by himself, just as she was. He'd said he didn't want any fond farewells and neither did she.

The gangplank was ridged and too springy for comfort; the bright lights of the reception area dazzled her. She was grateful when a steward took her case and led her down narrow, airless corridors to her tiny, single cabin.

She shut the door, dumped her travel bag on her bunk and dropped down beside it. Harry had been right. He'd insisted she book a cabin. Last time she'd travelled, two summers ago, she'd shared the lower decks with fellow students, sleeping on a shiny green couch beneath a single grey blanket. She hadn't got much sleep. In the morning, she'd had to queue up to wash in a hand basin jammed into the small space which led to the only lavatory. She still remembered how fiercely hot the water was.

The evening air was warm, with only the slightest breeze coming off the calm water when she made her way back up on deck and stood leaning on the rail, looking back to the heart of the city, only a stone's throw away. Across the channel, in the shipyards, the skeleton of a new passenger liner dominated the working vessels that unloaded coal or great wooden containers, swung up and out of their deep, dark holds in great rope meshes by tall cranes that looked like huge yellow birds.

Below her, there was a sudden outbreak of noise as a party of school children appeared, shepherded by two teachers. They chattered excitedly, asked questions, tripped awkwardly, as they manoeuvred their luggage on the vibrating gangplank before disappearing into the bowels of the ship.

She smiled, feeling suddenly very distant from the schoolgirl she had once been. Was it simply the passage of the years, or was it the experiences they'd brought her that made the life she'd once had in the house by the forge seem so very far away?

Ronnie would most certainly have stood here, where he could take in everything that was going on. He'd have noted the ships and their cargoes, watched the men who worked the pulleys and wires, calling to each other in sharp, undecipherable code. Being Ronnie, he'd have been thinking about rates of pay and working conditions, all the social and economic concerns that were now the basis of his work.

She could see his dark eyes and the gaunt lines of his face. Suddenly, she was back in the room in Elmwood Avenue when it was still his. He was singing to her. 'Fair thee well my own dear love, Fare thee well a while . . .'

She'd always thought 'The Leaving of Liverpool' one of the most moving of the emigrant songs. She'd heard it a hundred times, for it was a favourite with Jamsey when he came to play the gramophone in the big kitchen, but never before had it reduced her to tears.

Tonight, the song conjured up for her the pain of all those women who had ever stood weeping on a quay, knowing their men must leave, whether to find work, or to escape from eviction, or poverty, imprisonment or the gallows. Not knowing if they would ever come back, or even survive the journey and the harsh conditions at the end of it, make good and send passage money, or turn their back on the past and forget them. The enormity of their loss overwhelmed her.

She was completely taken aback by her feelings. It was not that she hadn't known. With a teacher like Charlie Running, a man so angered by the injustices he saw all around him that he joined the

IRA and risked his life in the 1920s, how could she fail to know? But knowing about something was not the same thing as standing on the deck of a ship yourself, saying goodbye to all that was familiar and not knowing what fate the future had in store for you.

She blew her nose and wiped her eyes surreptitiously as some other passengers came and leaned on the rail nearby. She'd written to Ronnie and told him what she planned to do. But he couldn't write back. She had no address to give him. For the first time in the six years since he left, she was out of touch, beyond the encouragement and sharp comment he'd always offered her.

Even without looking at her watch, she recognised the urgent activity below her on the quayside meant departure was imminent. The last ropes and hawsers were cast off. When she had lain awake in the last week, in the few dark hours of the short night, she'd thought often of what it would feel like to be cast adrift, launched into one's own life without sheltering arms, without someone to share the problems and celebrate the successes. Now she was about to find out.

To her surprise, she felt nothing at all. Indeed, nothing seemed any different. The view across the channel did not change, the towering bulk of the departure sheds did not diminish. Not to begin with. Then she noticed texturing appear in the still, grey water, a deeper note of the engine. And then, quite suddenly, a space appeared, a distinct gap, no longer bridged by rope or gangway, cutting off those who stood waving still on the quay from those who'd already begun their journey.

She waved a farewell herself, a kind of courtesy to the city that had been her home for the last four years, crossed the vibrating deck and stood watching the channel broaden and the low hills of the Down shore rise, smooth and green, into the paling evening sky.

Over there, hidden by some nearer ripple of the landscape, stood Scrabo Tower. She could still call to mind the pattern of little fields, green with summer growth, or iced with frost and the remnants of snow. A special place. One that had played its part in her life and in her first love. What did one do with such memories? Treasure them like letters tied with pink ribbon, moments of joy too precious to lose? Or put them away in the attic of the mind, like broken objects to be disposed of when next you had time and opportunity?

She had no answers to her questions, so she walked around the deck, studied the features of the darker Antrim shore, looked back at the wake streaming from the stern and up at the escort of gulls still following the ship. Suddenly tired, she sat down and watched the low, green hills grow misty in the light of the low sun. In what seemed no time at all, the land was gone, the ship setting course southwards for the calmest of night crossings.

The long, winding train reduced speed, clattered and rattled, as it moved crabwise across broad acres of track. The occupants of the crowded carriage stirred minutely. At first, no more than a movement of hands, a twist of the body, a slight inclination of the head. Then, as the juddering vibrations eased, some of the more daring folded their newspapers, rose to their feet and took cases from the overhead racks.

By the window, Clare sat motionless, her eyes still focused on the yellowing evening sky, her paperback unopened on her knee, her mind absorbed with the procession of images the last two days had left with her. Now her destination was so close, she felt reluctant to arrive; the same reluctance she'd often felt, waking in her room and wondering how the reality of the morning would fit with the images of her dreams.

The carriage was full of moving bodies now, the sunlight shut off as dark, sooty cliffs embraced the barely moving train. The brakes squealed, doors opened, her travelling companions departed as if escaping from some dreadful contagion, leaving her alone with the debris strewn around the empty carriage. Slowly, she retrieved her suitcase and travel bag from the rack, shook out the crumpled fabric of her cotton dress and stepped cautiously down on to the platform.

As she was swept into the flow of moving passengers, she picked up the acrid twang of a familiar smell. As richly evocative as the perfume of turf on the metal circle in front of the forge, it touched a memory of pleasure and excitement, of the time three years earlier when she had made her very first expedition abroad.

'Gauloise,' she said, out loud. 'Gauloise.'

'Gare du Nord, Gare du Nord,' a voice bellowed in her ear.

She laughed aloud, suddenly overjoyed. With that smell and this bustle, where else in the world could she be but the Gare du Nord?

The low light was straight in her eyes as she came out of the station and paused, deciding what to do next. It wasn't that she hadn't made a plan. She had. But at this moment she was so excited she couldn't manage anything as sensible as her plan. As if to convince herself she was really back in Paris, she needed to drink a coffee, or buy a newspaper. Just speaking a few words of French to someone might do.

'Taxi, mademoiselle. I make a special rate for you, however far you want to go.'

She smiled at the blue-clad figure, amused at the thought of taking a taxi all the way to the Bois de Boulogne.

'Non, merci, monsieur. I have to phone my friend. Sorry.'

The taxi driver shrugged his shoulders with a gesture she had never seen anywhere except in France. It reminded her immediately of Andrew, who imitated it so perfectly. She found a phone box and concentrated on dialling Marie-Claude's number.

'Clare, chérie, how wonderful. You've arrived. I'll come and collect you right away. Go and have a coffee while you wait. I'll pick you up at the taxi rank. The drivers know me now. They think I am mad, but harmless.'

Clare heard the warm, familiar voice and felt the same delight as when the guard had bellowed 'Gare du Nord' in her ear.

'No, Marie-Claude, you mustn't,' she said firmly. 'The traffic looks as bad as ever. I'll come on the Metro. It's a lovely evening and my case isn't heavy. Besides, I need to smell Paris and see some trees. Are you really sure I can stay for a night or two?'

'But, of course, you can stay as long as you like. Gerard is away at a conference. The children are visiting his mother in Provence. Your coming will save me from taking a lover out of sheer boredom. I'll go and find a bottle of wine and make us a little supper. Come quickly, Clare. I can't wait to see you.'

Clare laughed. How strange that after all the time they had spent together in Deauville and Paris, she could forget that this beautiful, sophisticated Frenchwoman could say things with just the same uninhibited directness as Jessie.

'I'm on my way,' she said. 'Fast as Superman.'

'Fast as Superman, it is. I'll be watching for you,' Marie-Claude said, laughing, as she rang off.

The first summer Clare had gone to Deauville with the St Clairs, Philippe had been going through a Superman phase. In the end, the whole family, even Marie-Claude's very elderly grandmother, had ended up saying 'Fast as Superman'. Philippe was now in his second year at lycée. According to Marie-Claude, whenever Super-man was mentioned now, he merely smiled in a rather superior and distant manner.

Still smiling, Clare picked up her case and walked across to one of the flower seller's stands. She ran her eyes over the huge buckets full of blooms. Beside her, a young man was handing over a whole fistful of notes for a sheaf of red roses. She eyed them and cautiously located the bucket from which they'd come. She drew a sharp breath, shocked by the price, amazed that an ordinary-looking young man could afford such luxury.

'Mademoiselle, I cannot understand why you come to buy flowers,' said the flower seller, a small, brown-skinned man in a flat cap that made him seem even smaller than he was. 'Surely your apartment is filled with flowers from your admirers.' He waved his hands in flowing motions to create the mounds of flowers, large and small, which must surround her.

She beamed at him. 'Naturally, monsieur. Though none of them as beautiful as yours,' she replied. 'But I have a friend I'm going to visit.'

'Ah,' he said. 'Then we must find something suitable for your friend. The roses you liked, didn't you?'

'Yes, they're quite lovely, but too expensive, I'm afraid,' she said, glancing over the summer bouquets, thinking of Marie-Claude's elegant sitting room with its Louis Quinze furniture and her collection of porcelain and china.

'But, of course, the red roses are expensive,' he said, cheerfully. 'So, young men must pay for their passion. But see, mademoiselle, the yellow roses, they too are lovely.' He drew out a long-stemmed bouquet to hold before her. 'These do not carry the premium of passion,' he confided in a whisper.

Clare admitted that they were indeed lovely. As she studied the golden blooms, only just beginning to unfurl, she remembered the pair of slim Sevres jars that stood at either end of the marble mantelpiece.

'I'm afraid I can only afford two of these,' she

said hesitantly. 'Perhaps you won't want to sell them singly.'

'Perhaps not, to most,' he agreed. 'But for you, mam'selle, it is a different matter,' he said, selecting carefully from the bouquet he had displayed. He wrapped the blooms in cellophane and tied a piece of ribbon round the stems before handing them to her.

'Thank you so much. I'm so grateful for your help,' she said, as she handed over the first of her franc notes.

'A pleasure, mam'selle. A great pleasure,' he said with a bow, as she put her travel bag on her shoulder, settled the roses carefully in her free hand and gave him a parting smile.

Even the Metro seemed full of delights as she hurried along the familiar corridors. She listened for the clatter of doors that told her there was no point hurrying, or the rush of air that suggested she might just catch the train about to emerge from the darkness. She ran her eyes over the posters, reading off their messages, restoring them to memory, as delighted to be reminded of her favourite brand of coffee as to see what ballet was being performed at Châtelet.

She had forgotten how the corridors sparkled with minute specks of some light-refracting mineral in the matrix of their dark surfaces. The first time she'd negotiated them, she'd thought of the forge and the tiny bright scraps of metal filings that lay in the soft piles of dark dust. Now these tiny points of light were themselves the jewels of the Paris underground, part of her own experience, part of present and future, no longer tied to the past.

The journey out of Paris was slow, but pleasant, the trains uncrowded as the evening moved on. Much of it was not underground at all. She looked out over parks and gardens, breathed the warm, summer air, rich with the scent of cooking. The smell of roast lamb made her mouth water and she realised she was hungry. But the emptiness of her stomach seemed nothing compared to the hunger of her eyes. It seemed to her she'd been living in a world of black and white for a very long time now. Avidly, she sought out light and movement and colour, shops with trays of fruit and vegetables arranged in contrasting patterns, striped awnings, a woman in a red dress, children kicking a yellow striped beach ball beneath the trees, umbrellas outside a terrace cafe, a gendarme, perspiring in the warm evening air, wiping his face with a spotted handkerchief.

'Oh, ma petite, how tired you must be,' cried Marie-Claude as she opened the door and stretched out her arms.

She had watched the small figure walk up the driveway and stand looking around at the well-kept gardens which lay beyond the entrance to the apartments. Such a solitary little figure, with a suitcase and a bag, carrying two yellow roses tied with ribbon. How like her, how very like her. Even when she came the very first time, an unknown student, she had brought them each a little gift.

'Come, chérie, tell me how we can best restore you. Shower or aperitif? Rest or food?'

Clare followed her up the wide marble stairs to the thickly carpeted landing, from which the main rooms of the apartment opened.

'What I should like most of all is to sit by the window looking over the gardens while you tell me about Michelle and Philippe and Gerard,' she began, aware that a picture had been forming in her mind as her arrival drew nearer. 'But perhaps I do need a shower,' she added, laughing. 'It seems a long time since London this morning, and even then, there was no hot water!'

She could see the concern in Marie-Claude's eyes and knew that the weariness of the journey was showing clearly in her face. She would have to tell Marie-Claude what had happened. But not tonight. There would be time enough. Tonight was a gift, a home coming she had not expected.

CHAPTER ELEVEN

Despite Clare's protests, Marie-Claude devoted the next three days to making sure her guest went to bed early, slept late, and ate much more than usual.

'You are too good to me. I don't deserve all this kindness and attention,' said Clare, when she woke up to find Marie-Claude putting a tray on her bedside table and drawing back the curtains.

'Eat your breakfast and we will continue our argument of last night,' she replied, smiling. 'I've been awake for ages so I have the advantage of you.'

'Mm.' Clare sniffed her coffee before sipping it appreciatively. 'I keep thinking this is all a wonderful dream. I shall wake up and find I'm in Belfast in the rain and I have a long essay due for tomorrow,' she said, laughing.

To her surprise, she saw a shadow pass across Marie-Claude's face as she turned away from the window.

'What are you thinking, Marie-Claude? Please

tell me,' she asked, as she tore a croissant into pieces and began to butter them.

'I was thinking, my dear, that your life has not been very easy for you. When you told me about Andrew and all the terrible unhappiness of poor Edward's death, I wondered if perhaps you had suffered a little *too much* misfortune. I think even the Fairy Blackstick would agree with me.'

She smiled with pleasure as Clare licked her fingers after spreading strawberry conserve liberally on a piece of croissant.

'*The Rose and the Ring*,' said Clare, grinning. 'You still remember?'

'Of course I do. It was not just the children who benefited from your efforts, my dear. Gerard and I, we loved your stories too, whether they were your English classics or your own inventions, or your tales about the forge and the people who came there. If I might make a small, loving criticism, sometimes I think you do not know the pleasure you bring. More important still, you sometimes do not expect to receive, but only to give.'

'But it is more blessed to give than to receive,' Clare retorted swiftly, a twinkle in her eyes.

More than once these last long evenings, lingering at the table by the window, they'd returned to the Jansenism that Marie-Claude had known as a child, similar in its effects to the

Presbyterianism that Clare had been exposed to in her church-going days.

'Yes, true,' Marie-Claude agreed promptly. 'But you have to let other people be blessed as well. It is selfish to keep all the being blessed for oneself.'

Clare giggled.

'Touché,' she agreed. 'One up to you, but I can't argue properly when I'm all sticky with beautiful strawberry conserve and blissful croissants. I'll retaliate when I've got my clothes on. A nightie puts me at a disadvantage.'

'If I might suggest your pretty green dress, I have a proposal to make to you, over lunch at Le Chat Vert,' said the older woman, her eyes twinkling, as she picked up the tray. The plate on which she had placed two large croissants bore not the slightest trace of a crumb.

A week later, Marie-Claude was well pleased with the progress of her protégée. With several days in hand before her husband's return from Geneva and the predictable reassertion of Clare's anxiety about intruding, she'd seen the strain and weariness fade away, the droop in her narrow shoulders disappear, the sparkle return to those lovely Irish eyes. They'd talked hour upon hour, walking in the park, over lunch in little restaurants an easy drive away, or by the window overlooking the garden, Clare's favourite place in the apartment she so loved.

As the older woman sat drinking her own breakfast coffee in the empty kitchen, she recalled just how downcast she had been a week before. She had so looked forward to having space in the day, once Michelle too had gone off to boarding school. Instead, an awful inertia had set in, the longed-for space transforming itself into an emptiness she seemed quite unable to fill.

Then the call had come from Calais, so unexpectedly, a breath of fresh air in a life grown stale, despite its pleasures and privileges. She sighed. Truly, miracles did sometimes happen and Clare had been hers.

On their very first day together Clare asked her what she was planning to do, now she had the long months of term in which to take up her own work. Ashamed of her inertia, she'd confessed only to indecision. Immediately, Clare gave her whole mind to the problem. Under her lively questioning, she felt her own mind begin to work again. Ideas began to shape. She smiled to herself. Indeed, so active had it become she wakened early each morning, found herself able to enjoy the solitary hours while Clare went on sleeping.

She poured herself another cup of coffee and gazed through the glass door to the balcony. Although it was not yet eight o'clock, an old man was at work in the gardens below, hoeing steadily between the shrubs, the sunlight filtering down through the trees and splashing his green dungarees with patches of light. She thought back to their lunch at Le Chat Vert, the pretty green floral dress Clare had worn, one they'd bought together at the end of her second summer with them.

'Now, my dear, about being blessed,' she had said lightly, hoping the wine and the liveliness of the riverside restaurant would come to her aid. 'There is something I should like to do, something which would give me great pleasure, but I cannot do it without your co-operation. In fact, I am totally dependent on you for my satisfaction. Will you help me?'

'But of course. You've been so kind to me, you know I'd do anything I could to help you. Just say the word,' replied Clare, immediately looking serious.

'I have your word?' Marie-Claude insisted, as she dropped her eyes and hoped she could maintain her sober expression.

'Yes, of course. Anything whatever I can possibly do that would please you.'

'So . . .'

Marie-Claude had permitted herself only the gentlest smile as she outlined her plan. Clare needed a job. Bien. They had studied the newspapers and talked at length. There were excellent opportunities for someone who spoke French as well as she did, but Marie-Claude thought her chances would be even better if she not only spoke like a Frenchwoman, but dressed like one as well.

Marie-Claude would take her to her own couturier for a suit, to her own dressmaker for dresses and skirts, and to Galeries Lafayette, so that she could show her how to buy scarves and accessories to add that unmistakable touch English women always envied. It would be her gift. It would chalk up so much blessedness she would have something to keep her going when Clare found her job and she had to part with her.

Marie-Claude almost repented the trick she had played when she saw the look of horror on Clare's face. She knew perfectly well the poor girl was thinking how much her shopping list would cost.

'You may pay your own bill at Galeries Lafayette if you wish,' she said, easily, gazing out of the window, to give Clare time to recover herself.

When she turned back, she was surprised to see that Clare was smiling broadly.

'Touché again, Marie-Claude. Have I been horribly arrogant and independent because I'm poor?'

'No, ma petite, never arrogant, but prickly, like a hedgehog. Defensive. You have had to struggle to survive, so you may not have noticed that often things are given for our joy, for our pleasure, as you were given to me and to my family. As I've told you, you must teach yourself to receive as well as to give. Let me help you.'

Clare had been as good as her word. She had not protested when Marie-Claude had taken her to places where she herself was well known and could command the very best of attention. She had patiently tried on item after item, walked up and down on thick carpets, adopted strange poses so that Marie-Claude could run her practised eye over the cut and line of whatever garment was under review, stood patiently while she was pinned and tucked, and listened, fascinated, to the language of the dress floor and those who earned their living creating clothes for the rich.

'Chérie,' she said, startled by the sudden appearance of a pale face at the kitchen door. 'You are awake so early?'

'I'm sorry. You were enjoying the quiet,' Clare said, apologetically. 'I had a horrible dream and I couldn't bear being alone. Today is the day.'

'Oh, I *am* sorry, Clare. How could I have forgotten? Let me make us some fresh coffee. How soon can you ring your friend in Belfast?'

'I don't know,' she said wearily, 'I haven't even checked for British Summer Time. We might be an hour ahead in Paris. I can't remember. Besides, it's often ten o'clock before anything happens. And then I have to give Keith time to cycle back home.'

'At nine-thirty I shall ring Gerard's secretary.

She is formidable. She has in her mind everything about the time, anywhere in the world. Now tell me about the dream,' Marie-Claude said firmly, as she poured coffee for them both and concentrated her full attention on Clare's pale and anxious face. 'I'm not an expert on interpretation, but horrible dreams are always better when exposed to the light.'

The hours dragged by. Neither of them could think of anything but the need to make the phone call. They tried a walk in the garden, but found themselves hastening back to be near the phone.

'Do try, Clare. I can't bear to wait any longer,' her friend declared as they came back upstairs to the apartment. 'You should have asked your friend Keith to ring you.'

'I didn't know where I'd be,' she replied honestly. 'It's awfully expensive to ring abroad. I couldn't ask him to do that.'

Marie-Claude hadn't thought of a young man not being able to afford a telephone call to Paris. She herself had never had to consider the limitations of being poor. It made her sad now and rather ashamed to think how unaware she'd been of her own good fortune. The beloved daughter of a successful businessman and now the wife of an equally successful stockbroker, she'd always been able to have whatever she'd wished for.

She watched Clare dial the operator, stood

restlessly by as she attempted to connect her. Clare put the receiver down and mimicked the prissy voice at the other end of the phone. 'All the lines to London are occupied. Please try later.'

She tried three times more with no success.

'Here, let me,' said Marie-Claude furiously, as she took the phone from Clare's hand.

Clare listened in amazement to a tone she'd never heard Marie-Claude use before. Her secretary had tried three times and been told there was no line available. It was outrageous. At the Banque Nationale one could not tolerate such poor service. Would she please ask her director to connect this call immediately. Yes, it was to Belfast. No, that was not in the Republique Irlandais, it was a part of Grande Bretagne and could be routed direct from London. Any further delay in this important call would not go unnoticed or unreported.

Marie-Claude handed back the receiver and Clare heard a sequence of clicks and buzzes.

'Six four ate, seven five nine. Hallo?'

Clare's heart sank. With that pronunciation of 'eight', it had to be Belfast, but if it was Keith's mother, then he certainly wasn't back yet, though it was now mid-morning.

'Is that Mrs Harvey?' she enquired politely.

'Aye, 'tis. Wou'd that be Clare Hamilton?'

'Yes, indeed it is. I wonder if I could speak to Keith.'

'Ach, I'm sorry. He had to go to an interview for a job. He said ye'd be ringin'. He was real sorry he couden stop. He left ye a message.'

There was a pause, and even on the thin, crackling line Clare could hear the mutters and scufflings as papers were sifted through. 'Aye, I have it in ma han'.'

Clare braced herself. The silence continued. For one awful moment she thought the line had gone dead. Then the voice came through again more clearly than before.

'Wou'd you just hold on a minit till I get ma glasses?'

Marie-Claude was signalling frantically to know what was happening. Clare shook her head in desperation, too anxious to speak.

'Here yar,' the voice echoed suddenly. 'He says "Congratulations". There was three firsts, Mary McCausland, Ernest Chambers an' . . . I can't read me own writin'.' There was another pause. It seemed to go on for ever. 'Ach, sure it says "Herself". That's why I couden read it. I was wonderin' what sort of a Christian name that was and no surname. Amn't I stupid?'

Clare stammered and asked her to repeat the message, then she remembered to ask about Keith.

'He got a two one and he's well pleased. Why don't I get him to give you a ring whin he comes in?'

'Oh no, I couldn't possibly trouble him. I'm in Paris.'

'Paris? The dear save us. Sure I thought you'd just gone back up to your people in Armagh,' she said, horrified at the thought of the distance between them.

A few moments later, Clare put the phone down, not knowing whether to laugh or cry. In the end, she flung her arms round Marie-Claude's neck and did both.

'I got a first, Marie-Claude. I got a first. Can you *believe* it?'

'Of course I can, chérie. Easily. However are we going to celebrate when I have no champagne in the fridge? We will simply have to go out to lunch when you've stopped crying,' she said, quite unaware that her own cheeks were wet with tears.

CHAPTER TWELVE

'Clare, ma petite, tu vas bien?'

As his wife released him from a warm embrace, Gerard St Clair turned towards Clare. He stretched out his arms, hugged her and kissed her cheeks.

'You look great,' he went on, holding her at arm's length and eyeing the well-cut skirt and pretty blouse she was wearing.

'Entirely Marie-Claude's doing,' Clare replied, as he threw himself down gratefully on one of the elegant settees that faced each other across the handsome fireplace. 'You'll have to scold her, Gerard. While you've been away, she's spent a fortune on what I'm wearing. She's spoiled me outrageously.'

'Good, I am delighted to hear it.'

He watched Marie-Claude carefully as she brought out three tall, fluted glasses and stood them on a silver tray. He could hardly believe his eyes. This lively, smiling woman, her blonde hair freshly dressed into an elegant chignon, looked far more like the woman he'd married. She was certainly not the woman he'd left behind less than two weeks ago.

'I smell something nice. Something beginning with "m",' he said, sniffing appreciatively as Marie-Claude went back to the kitchen and returned with a tray of canapés.

Clare giggled. Gerard always joined in whatever games the children wanted to play. One wet day in Deauville he got bored with 'I spy with my little eye' and insisted on 'I smell with my little nose'. They'd all laughed at him, for Gerard's nose, though distinctly aristocratic, was certainly not small.

'Do I detect a certain aura of celebration in the air?'

'You do indeed, my love,' said Marie-Claude, as she handed him a bottle of champagne and a white linen napkin. '*I* am celebrating your return and Clare's arrival, and *we* are celebrating Clare's success. Go on, Clare, tell Gerard your news.'

'I got my degree, Gerard.'

'Oh chérie, you are impossible,' expostulated Marie-Claude, laughing and turning to her husband. 'She got a first, Gerard. Only three in her year. And you should see the reference her professor has written for her.'

The champagne cork gave way to the pressure of Gerard's thumbs. It made the discreetest of sounds under the white napkin.

'Congratulations, Clare. That is magnificent. But just what I would have expected.'

He poured the champagne carefully into the three tall glasses, carried the tray to where she sat, and held it towards her.

'The first of many, Clare,' he said, as she carefully picked up her glass. 'There will be many more successes for us to celebrate together,' he went on, smiling at her, and then at Marie-Claude, who was watching him.

Clare had never drunk champagne before. But she had seen it drunk often enough at the Ritz cinema. Always in films, the champagne corks flew off with a bang, the glasses were wide and it fizzed all over the hero and heroine as they toasted each other. But these bubbles were so small. And there were so many of them. A torrent of minute bubbles rose continuously in the tall glass. She watched them, fascinated, while Gerard went and sat down by Marie-Claude, taking her hand, saying something Clare did not choose to hear. Even after she'd taken the first few sips and decided that champagne was indeed wonderful, the bubbles still went on rising.

Suddenly, she thought of the day she'd got her scholarship to Queen's. Young Charlie Robinson had come to meet her, raced back up the lane, poked his head into the darkness of the forge and shouted, 'She got it,' as he ran on home to tell his mother.

'Sure we've no champagne, we'll have to make do with a cup o' tea,' Granda Scott had said to Charlie Running, who'd been sitting on the bench inside the door waiting. They'd all laughed when young Charlie arrived in the big kitchen panting, one of his mother's cakes on a plate clutched firmly in both hands.

How lovely if Granda Scott could have lived to know about her first. She went on sipping her champagne, her eyes moving to the huge arrangement of summer flowers Marie-Claude had made in the fireplace. Wonderful sprays of foliage, dark blue delphiniums, a soft haze of white gypsophilia, and small pink and mauve dahlias. She thought of Charlie again and the dahlias he still tended so carefully: the same tubers that provided flowers every few days when poor Kate lay bedridden; flowers to take to Jessie's home the evening her father killed himself.

Each time she went up for a weekend to Liskeyborough to see William and her grandparents, she'd cycle over to see Charlie. He'd talk history and politics, show her the books he was reading, the notes he'd made, the figures he was putting together. He'd fry them bacon and egg for their tea, a better cook than Granda Scott had ever been. Always when they sat after their meal he would say. 'Ach, sure I miss him something desperate. Even all the years I couldn't leave Kate to go and see him, sure I knew he was there. I could hear him every morning, unless the wind was up, or in the opposite direction.'

She missed Charlie, as much as she missed Granda Scott and the forge, but at least she could write and tell him about her first. He'd be every bit as pleased as that morning when they'd celebrated with tea and Margaret's cake.

'I hope you like your champagne, Clare.'

'Yes, yes, I do,' she said quickly, 'I'm just fascinated by the bubbles. But it tastes wonderful as well.'

'Good, then you must drink some more to put us in the mood for Marie-Claude's specialité de maison.'

He exchanged glances with Marie-Claude as she put her empty glass down and went to see that all was ready in the dining room.

'Marie-Claude has told me what an unhappy time you've had, Clare,' he said, sitting down beside her. 'I hope you'll let us *both* help you. Tell me what sort of job you want and I'll see what I can find. I know a lot of people.'

'Oh, that is kind of you,' was all she could manage to say without risking her eyes misting over again.

She sipped her champagne to steady herself and talked about the possibilities of interpreting and translating. Gerard listened intently and took in all she was saying. What Clare did not know was why Gerard had such a particular wish to help her.

Since little Michelle had followed her brother to a boarding school, Marie-Claude had been suffering bouts of depression. Nothing he could do had had the slightest effect. She'd refused to see a doctor, grown silent and withdrawn, didn't even want to make love to him, though she never said as much. He'd gone away depressed and downcast himself, only to return and find Marie-Claude transformed. She looked as if she had been away on a long, relaxing holiday. He had no doubt at all in his mind what had brought about the transformation.

The meal was excellent, long and leisurely, their talk full of shared memories of the times they'd spent together. Gerard recalled Clare's first encounter with Philippe, when he was going through a difficult phase after being bullied at school. How she'd invented extraordinary games of skill which kept him absorbed for hours and gave him great satisfaction. What a relief it had brought to everyone, particularly Michelle, who'd found her brother very hard to cope with when his tantrums disrupted her quiet world, full of books and dreams and strange absorbing fantasies.

They spoke of some of the happiest times at Deauville. The early morning walks when the racehorses were being exercised, the boat trips, the expeditions along the coast, the games on the beach, the magnificent sunsets over the sea. They'd made friends with other families, some of whom still sent Christmas cards and little notes telling Marie-Claude of their children's progress and enquiring for 'the little Irish girl who told stories'.

By the time Gerard rose to make their coffee, the light was fading fast, deep shadows lengthening in the gardens below. On this edge of the city, a stillness spread like a gentle tide as evening turned towards night.

Gerard put the tray down, looked round the shadowy space by the window where they always dined when they were not entertaining and began pouring coffee.

'My goodness, Mosey Jackson would be pleased. Look how quickly the light is going and it's not nearly The Quatorze yet.'

'Oh Gerard, you've got it wrong,' Marie-Claude laughed. 'It's not The Quatorze, it's The Twelfth. Isn't it, Clare?'

Clare shook her head in disbelief.

'I can't believe you've remembered Mosey Jackson. When did I tell you about him? I don't remember.'

'It was our first year in Deauville and a lovely dusk like tonight,' said Marie-Claude quickly. 'You said that every year, as soon as Midsummer was passed, Mosey would meet your grandfather

172

and say cheerfully that once The Twelfth was over the nights would soon be dropping down. Winter would be just round the corner.'

Clare smiled wryly and nodded.

'And your poor grandfather got very depressed by this, year after year,' broke in Gerard, 'until he suddenly realised that what Mosey was thinking of was all the oil he was going to sell for the lamps once the dark evenings came.'

Clare laughed, amused that he should remember her words so exactly.

'And he sold candles too,' Marie-Claude added.

She nodded to Gerard, who bent forward and lit the small floating candles she'd placed in the centre of the table in a bowl of water sprinkled with rose petals.

'The children still talk about him,' she went on, as the tiny lights flickered and grew stronger, lighting up their faces with a soft glow. 'Do you remember, Gerard, Michelle made him a character in the last play she wrote for the Nativity at her school here.'

'She did?' asked Clare in bewilderment.

'Oh yes. In Michelle's Nativity it was Mosey Jackson who provided light for the stable.'

Gerard's efforts on Clare's behalf bore fruit very quickly. Less than a week later, she found herself walking up the steps of a major French bank and into a marble banking hall, whose chandeliers and pillars reminded her more of the Palace of Versailles than of the Botanic Avenue branch of the Ulster Bank where she'd had her account.

'I have an appointment with Madame Japolsky at ten o'clock,' she said to the elegant young woman at the reception desk.

'Mademoiselle Clare 'Amilton, n'est-ce-pas?'

Clare noticed the young woman sweep her dark eyes casually across her new costume. The glance was so brief and yet Clare was certain she missed no detail of its cut, nor the match of the gloves, bag and scarf on which Marie-Claude had lavished so much time.

Clare followed her up an impressive staircase, along a heavily carpeted landing with enormous palm trees in oriental pots, and into a waiting room with an antique desk, a selection of fragile-looking gilt chairs and a wide view over the Place de l'Opéra.

'I shall tell Madame that you have arrived,' said the young woman, speaking English for the first time.

Clare perched on the edge of one of the chairs, then remembered what Marie-Claude had told her about sitting properly. To be at all times aware of her body position, ensuring that her head, neck and bottom were all in the same straight line. She thought of well brought-up young ladies practising with their back boards and smiled to herself. But she had to admit that Marie-Claude had a point. Sitting properly wasn't an effort when you got used to it, and breathing properly certainly helped you to stay calm.

Time passed. Clare got up and walked round the room. Looked down at the traffic moving in the Place de l'Opéra. Studied the engravings of seventeenth-century Paris and the cartoons of Napoleon Bonaparte. Wondered if she'd been forgotten. She had been warned that Madame Japolsky, a native of Paris, but married to a Polish émigré, was the sort of formidable woman who might well keep you waiting, simply to test your patience. Well, if patience was required, then patience she would practise. She sat down again, crossed her ankles neatly, admired her soft leather shoes and wondered if she looked remotely like a genuine Frenchwoman.

'Mademoiselle, je suis desolée . . .'

She looked up, amused to find the most extraordinarily handsome young man addressing her with abject apologies. He was not tall, but what he lacked in height he made up for in manner. His dark eyes were liquid with charm, his gestures controlled and flowing. Madame was indisposed, it was very regrettable, but his own superior, Monsieur Robert Lafarge, hearing of the situation, had offered to see her himself. If she would do him the honour of accompanying him.

Although the next marble staircase was less wide as they approached the second floor, the elegance of their surroundings was in no way diminished. The gold frames on the huge mirrors which lined the red-carpeted landings would send Harry into ecstasies. She was heartily glad she didn't have to dust them every morning.

'Mademoiselle 'Amilton!'

The handsome young man threw open double doors, ushered her through and retreated backwards like a courtier in an Elizabethan tragedy.

For a moment, Clare thought the enormous room was empty. Then she saw there was a figure seated behind the vast rosewood desk set across the tall windows at the far end of the room. He was a very small man and he had been studying some papers with the aid of a glass. Only when the doors clicked quietly behind her and he straightened up did she see a shiny, bald head and a rather heavy face set off by a stiff white collar above a very dark suit.

He rose to greet her as she walked slowly across the thick carpet and took his outstretched hand.

'Mademoiselle 'Amilton, please sit down. I must apologise for the delay. I had not been told Madame had to return home with a migraine. The delay is unforgivable.'

'Not at all, monsieur,' she said easily. 'I had plenty to occupy me. I enjoyed the engravings of Paris and the cartoons of Napoleon. And there is a very good view of the Place de l'Opéra itself. It was an interesting room,' she said reassuringly, for he seemed genuinely distressed.

As he sat down again she glanced around her, amazed to find the long walls of the room hung with paintings of horses. Hunting scenes, battle scenes, country scenes, horses in every possible pose and position. Just to the right of the desk was a splendid study of a chestnut mare. It looked just like Conker.

'You like horses. Do you ride?' he said abruptly, as if it were a matter of great importance.

'Yes, I can ride, but my knowledge of horses comes more from observation. I lived with my grandfather, who was a blacksmith. Horses were his joy as well as his livelihood. And I also had a friend with a gift for drawing. She taught me to observe how painters tackle the difficulties, like a horse rearing up.'

To her surprise he came round to the front of his desk, leaned against it, and followed her gaze.

'As in this picture?'

'Yes. That one is very accurate. The painter must have spent a long time looking at the way this particular animal moves. Like Degas, when he watched the ballet dancers. He saw them as dancers, rather than as women. He watched how the muscles flex, the effect that has upon the skin . . .'

She stopped, aware she was getting enthusiastic. There was a sudden flicker of his eyes she could not place, but his next words made no reference at all to her comments.

'So you lived in the countryside, mam'selle?'

'In the countryside, yes. A small place, not even a village, near Armagh, in the North of Ireland.'

'Such places are often very backward,' he began thoughtfully. 'Even those who are well educated can sometimes retain their conservative views. I think perhaps your country is not very forward looking,' he said tactfully.

She smiled, thinking he was better informed and much sharper than he chose to appear. She could guess how Ronnie would reply.

'I have a friend who once taught me a French expression he thought described our country very accurately. He used to say, "Whatever the weather, they always pee behind the same tree."'

The effect on the little bald man was extraordinary. He beamed and shook his head, said he knew the expression well, asked if her friend had been in Brittany.

She nodded, said a little about Andrew's time in France, told him how upset his grandmother had been when his accent did not please her Parisian-tuned ears. As she spoke, she thought how totally extraordinary it was that she should be sitting here, in Paris, talking to some very senior official of a national bank about

Andrew and the Missus. Since she'd made her vow not to think about him, she'd broken her rule time after time. Now she'd even referred to a piece of their private language, described him as a 'friend' to a complete stranger.

'Tell me, Mam'selle 'Amilton, what do you know about money?'

For the first time since she'd come into the room, she was suddenly aware that this was supposed to be an interview for a job. She'd been so interested in the questions this little man had put to her, she'd not considered at all what her answers might be revealing or whether they were appropriate.

'I know how to live on very little money,' she began tentatively. 'I know that money is power. That it is opportunity.'

She looked at him directly and saw he was watching her closely, listening carefully, as he had listened to all she'd said. She decided that he was rather a shy man, but a very shrewd one. There was no point whatever in being anything other than herself with him. She smiled suddenly and said what she'd been thinking all the time.

'And I know, of course, that money is the root of all evil.'

He laughed. A small uneasy laugh, as if it was something he didn't do very often. Then he composed himself again.

'But, mam'selle, if you have to work in the

world of money, how will you understand the language of bankers and of banking?'

'New words and new ideas aren't a problem if you have the structure of a language,' she began. 'It would be no different for me to learn the language of banking than to learn the language of any other activity. For example, when I worked in a picture gallery that also sold antiques, I learnt about faience, and ormolu, and repoussé work. They were all new to me, but there was a context which made it easy for me to understand.' She glanced up at the chestnut mare and thought of Ginny. 'Like when a friend taught me to ride. If I didn't understand what she was telling me to do, I only had to ask her to explain.'

'Eh bien,' he said suddenly, as if he had made up his mind.

He went back behind his desk, pulled out a heavy drawer and took out a newspaper, which he handed to her. It was the previous day's copy of *The Times*.

'I am quite certain your French will prove entirely adequate for the tasks we will ask of you, but I regret that I speak very little English. Would you be so kind as to read to me from this newspaper.'

Clare took the newspaper, refolded it to avoid the columns of deaths, and scanned the inside pages. Suddenly, a thought struck her and she smiled.

'Mam'selle?' he said, leaning forward to look at her.

'I'm sorry,' she said, grinning broadly. 'I was thinking of my professor. He used to say to me: "Clare, you must read. Read every day. Always read *Le Monde*. If ever you want a situation in France, it will stand to you. Read *Le Monde*!"'

She laughed easily. 'When I write to Professor Lavalle I shall tell him he misled me. He is such a nice man, it will amuse him.'

'Lavalle? I know that name. Henri? Yes, that's it. Henri Lavalle?'

He looked across at her as if the Christian name was a matter of great significance.

She nodded. 'Yes. He was kind enough to write the recommendation which I think you probably have on your desk.'

He rifled hastily through the papers which lay in front of him, found the letter, looked at the signature and smiled as he set it aside. He turned back to her, a trace of a smile still on his face.

'I never read letters of recommendation. I prefer to make up my own mind, which I have already done, but it may amuse you to know that I went to school with Henri Lavalle, rather a long time ago in Coutances. He was a nice man even then. In fact, he was such a nice man I wondered

181

if he would ever survive in the world beyond our village. A professor, you say? In Belfast?'

She nodded, amazed by the coincidence. She felt a surge of delight that the man who had been so kind to her, who had taken such trouble to find her a French family when she needed a summer job, had somehow managed to retain his character, despite what other people regarded as his weaknesses.

'You may tell him when you write that I asked you to read *The Times* purely for the pleasure of hearing you speak English,' he said, leaning comfortably back in his leather armchair.

'Now, proceed, if you please,' he said politely. 'In ten minutes' time, I shall send for my secretary and make you an offer which I hope you will find quite impossible to refuse.'

CHAPTER THIRTEEN

After the cool spaciousness of Robert Lafarge's room, the heat and brightness of midday came as a surprise to Clare as she made her way down the steps of the bank into the crowded square. All around her men in shirt sleeves and women in light blouses headed for the shade of the umbrellas or the heavy canopies that sheltered pavement cafes and restaurants.

Suddenly ravenous, she was tempted to cross the square and patronise the establishment immediately opposite the bank. But as she tucked her folder of papers more securely under her arm, she changed her mind. The obviously popular meeting place was already crowded. Besides, she knew she was far too excited to sit down.

She turned right and kept going, walking quickly till she felt the tension ease. Half a mile from the bank, she turned left suddenly, in search of the first possible place to eat. She was delighted by her luck. Shaded by its chestnut tree, Le Cafe

Marronier was pleasant and much less crowded. She dropped down exhausted at the nearest empty table.

'Mam'selle. What can I bring for you?'

'Coffee, please,' she said, breathlessly. 'And a glass of water,' she added hastily. 'I'd like something to eat. Do you have a menu?'

'I am the menu today, mam'selle,' he replied nonchalantly.

He rattled off a list of salads and filled baguettes that left her head reeling. She could understand him perfectly, but the effort of deciding what to have almost defeated her. When he disappeared and returned immediately with her coffee and a glass of iced water, she knew she'd agreed to a filled baguette, but what the filling was now completely escaped her.

'Never mind. At least I don't have to worry if I can afford it,' she said to herself, as she searched in her handbag for a couple of Anadin. She swallowed them, drank most of the water and leaned back in her chair, remembering what Marie-Claude had said about breathing. The last hour had been so extraordinary, she'd probably been holding her breath for most of it.

Reading to Robert Lafarge had been easy enough, though he'd sat listening with his eyes shut for more like half an hour than the ten minutes he'd proposed. He'd then sent for his secretary and asked her to draft a memo of the offer he was about to make, so that both he and Mam'selle 'Amilton would have the details to be inserted into the printed contract he hoped she would sign tomorrow. He began by offering her a salary that took her totally by surprise.

It sounded extraordinarily large. The problem was she couldn't think in francs so she'd no real idea what it actually amounted to. Whenever he paused to allow his secretary to catch up with the details he was dictating, she'd made hasty attempts to convert francs into pounds, but each time she got an answer that seemed quite ridiculous.

The second time the figure was mentioned, she'd glanced surreptitiously at his secretary. But she sat scribbling away as if it were nothing out of the ordinary. Could the exchange rate have altered dramatically since she'd been in Paris two years earlier? But she'd have noticed at the Ulster Bank when she'd collected her francs for the journey.

She sipped her coffee gratefully and took out her fountain pen. The paper napkins provided by Le Cafe Marronier were quite unsuited to the nib of her favourite or any other pen, but slowly she inscribed the figures in the absorbent paper and divided the French francs by what she thought the present exchange rate must be. She stared at the result unbelievingly and checked it once more. There was no getting round it, that was what it came to. For the moment, she really couldn't believe it. Until Gerard checked it out this evening she would simply try to forget all about it.

She picked up her coffee cup and leaned back in her chair. Beyond the shade of the chestnut, the sun poured down on the cobbles, glancing off the worn facades of houses and shops. A woman in a blue dress strode vigorously along the pavement opposite. Long loaves of bread stuck out of a straw basket she carried in one hand, in the other, a bunch of flowers – white daisies and something blue – wrapped in paper from a flower seller's stand. She'd tied her mass of dark hair back with a spotted scarf, the soft fabric of her dress billowed as she walked, her bare legs brown, her leather sandals revealing carefully painted toenails. Clare watched her till she was out of sight, absorbed by her easy movement, her freedom to move through the warm air.

Among the exposed roots of the chestnut, the noise of the sparrows reached a sudden crescendo as they bathed in pools of dust, scuffling luxuriously, indifferent to the passage of mere humans. She moved her chair slightly to get a better view of the dusty bodies, cheeping and fluttering in outrage at some disruption among themselves. Quite suddenly, the crisis was resolved. A waiter shook a cloth nearby and they rose like a cloud, flew off at great speed, returning only seconds later to peck devotedly at the crumbs he'd provided.

She crumpled up the napkin that bore her calculations. Whatever her salary turned out to be, it was a salary. Slowly it began to dawn on her. She was in Paris. She had a job. Now she too could walk down a street, buy food, or flowers. She'd have a place of her own somewhere in this city she so loved. For a moment, she felt as if some great insight was about to be revealed to her. But nothing happened.

Her baguette arrived and she bit gratefully into its well-filled length. Whether it was what she'd ordered or not, it tasted wonderful. Slices of ham and Brie, garnished with fresh watercress and sliced tomato were layered generously between crusty morning-baked bread. She munched devotedly. She thought of making midday meals for herself and Robert, champ and stew, and herrings cooked in the oven, in a world where Brie and watercress were unknown, ham was a Christmas treat, tomatoes only affordable in a hot summer if all the locally grown ones ripened at the same time and produced a glut.

The sunlight filtering through the leaves of the chestnut cast dappled patterns on her plate, where only crumbs remained. She looked up into the spreading branches as she gathered them together with a damp finger and finished them off.

Under the spreading chestnut tree the village smithy stands.

Charlie was always keen on reciting Goldsmith. She could hear him now, the measured couplets resounding in his rich Ulster accent. He could quote huge tracts of poetry by heart, pouring out the lines and filling the shadowy room with the same passionate ring as his regular evening greeting, *Erin go Brach*.

Well, the smithy was gone now. It didn't even exist as a tumbled heap of stones, its door permanently open to the birds, the wind, the rain and the occasional curious passerby. The world of her childhood had gone with it, not only because Robert had grown old and died, but because the life Robert had known had disappeared with him. Charlie was right. The days of the blacksmith were over. The car would soon entirely replace the pony and trap. The electric would come to the remotest hamlets and bring with it television and telephones.

'Sure yer man ought to be in Parliament.'

She smiled to herself. Robert couldn't stand it when Charlie got launched on the subject of social change and particularly when he rode his great hobby-horse, the backwardness of the Province. He'd listen all right, intrigued by how much Charlie seemed to know about such matters, impressed in spite of himself by the passionate rhetoric of

188

his convictions. But, once Charlie had gone and Robert was taking his boots off, he'd make some dismissive remark. Not unkindly. Rather, it was more a deflection, an invitation for her to agree that Charlie was living in a world of his own, not really of much importance to ordinary folk like themselves.

But by her last years at school, she'd known Charlie was right. Later, she'd found herself grateful that Robert had gone before change had disrupted the world in which he had managed to live, relatively undisturbed, for all of his eighty years.

'What now, Clare?' she asked herself quietly, as she finished her coffee.

She had no doubt which world she belonged to. Whatever happiness she'd had in the world of her childhood was safe in the files of memory. The hardship, the effort and the loneliness of that now distant time were not forgotten. But she would not do what so many Irish emigrants had done in the past. Make a new life and never cease to long for what they'd left behind, because they chose to remember only rose-coloured pictures of the life they'd once had.

She thought of Ronnie, his dark eyes upon her, as he sang 'The Leaving of Liverpool'. He had been sad, disappointed, regretful, when he left, but once he'd gone, he had looked back with clear eyes and taken all that his new life offered him, a new life and new loves.

New loves? Well, no doubt in time there would be new loves. She felt sadness cloud the brightness of the day. Sometimes in the last weeks she simply could not stop herself thinking about Andrew. Often she dreamt about him. Once she dreamed they were making love and all was well between them. She'd woken up and felt desperately bleak and miserable as memory flowed back and told her they had parted. Parted in bitterness.

She'd confessed to Marie-Claude.

'But, chérie, Andrew was such a big part of your life. You were friends as well as lovers. Five years is such a long time when you are young. You may always love him. Women often go on loving their first love all their lives. But that does not mean they should marry him.'

The more she heard, Marie-Claude declared, the more she was convinced Clare had done the only thing possible for her at that moment.

'You must trust your judgement, chérie. It's hard, but you must. Besides it's only a few weeks since it all happened. Don't struggle to chase away the memories. Let them come to you. The more you try to put him out of mind, the harder you will make it. When you have other thoughts to occupy you, it will be easier.'

Well, there were plenty of other thoughts to occupy her now. She touched the folder, which contained copies of the printed contract and of the memo which Monsieur Lafarge's secretary had typed up for her.

Sometimes in the weeks since she'd arrived in Paris, she'd felt like a little creature that comes out from under a stone and sits in the sun for the first time. She knew she could never live in that tight, airless world she saw every time she stepped over the Richardson threshold, not even for Andrew's sake. She had to go, and now she had a job, she'd made good her escape. She was free to make a life of her own. She had dear friends to help her and the city she'd loved from the first minute she set foot in the Gare du Nord, three long years ago, an au pair on her way to an unknown family.

No, she would not look back. She would not confuse herself with regrets, with might-have-beens. Fortune had been kind. She would take all it offered with both hands and make of it the best she could.

Clare and Marie-Claude pored over her draft contract all afternoon. There were pages and pages of it. It went into minute detail about hours of work, additional payments for hours worked beyond regular office hours, hours worked during evenings, hours worked at weekends. There was even a clause about hours worked on national holidays.

'Are you sure, chérie, you won't mind being available so much of the time. It will make it difficult for you to have a social life.'

Marie-Claude was quite meticulous. She read every word of the huge document. When Clare admitted she couldn't quite grasp the details of an elaborate scheme of additional holiday, in addition to payments for extra hours beyond a certain level on a weekly, monthly and bi-monthly basis, Marie-Claude read the relevant paragraphs over and over again till she was satisfied.

'So, chérie, when you travel more than one hundred kilometres from Paris, or when travel to another country is involved, additional days' holiday will be given in addition to the additional payments,' she pronounced firmly.

Clare laughed. 'That sounds like an awful lot of addition. I haven't got over the basic salary yet, never mind all these extras.'

'You must not be too excited, chérie, till Gerard has looked at these conditions,' Marie-Claude said cautiously.

She looked so serious, Clare simply couldn't manage to be sober and sensible over the contract any longer. She began to giggle and before long Marie-Claude was laughing too.

* * *

'And what's the news from the financial sector?' asked Gerard, smiling, as he came into the sitting room and caught sight of the document awaiting his attention. He looked from one pair of bright eyes to the other and threw up his hands in despair.

'Perhaps, if I were to be given a little aperitif, I might be able to make some small contribution,' he said, lying back luxuriously in his favourite chair, while Marie-Claude poured him a drink and Clare brought him the contract.

Clare watched, amused by his performance. Gerard was adept at creating an appearance of nonchalance, almost of indifference. He flicked through the sheaf of pages as if he were scanning the morning paper just to make sure it contained nothing of interest. The only thing that betrayed him were his eyes. When they were in contact with printed matter of any kind, there was a focus so intense Clare could imagine it creating a very high-pitched buzz.

'Well then, Gerard. What do you think?' Marie-Claude enquired earnestly.

'I think "Bravo, Clare!"' he said, raising his glass towards her and grinning at Marie-Claude. 'They pay well, always have done, that's how they get the best people, but this is just a little bit special. They do not always insist upon the immediate opening of an account and the provision of funds to do so by means of an advance on salary. I've heard of it, but it is not common. It would seem, too, that there is to be a lot of travel. They will expect you to be available, but they do compensate you rather well for the inconvenience. Your lovers will have to be patient, Clare, the bank comes first.'

'Do you really think there will be much travel, Gerard?' she asked quickly, unable to conceal the excitement bubbling up inside her.

'I'm sure there will,' he said firmly. 'The inflow of American money has had a very powerful stimulating effect on the banking world. Some observers are saying that the present industrial expansion is the largest France has ever experienced.'

He sipped his drink and threw out a hand.

'As you well know, the Treaty of Rome was signed last year. It's been in force since January. Already we begin to see signs that France will become a kind of clearing house for certain European projects. Strangely, even the English are coming to us for finance. And often, when London does business with Rome, it is done via Paris. It is a surprise to us as well,' he said, shrugging his shoulders. 'But it is exceedingly good news for those banking houses who can cope with the new situation quickly. Those who have staff able to operate in a European rather than in a French context will be enormously successful.'

'So you think I should sign on,' said Clare, lightly.

'Chérie, I should be concerned for your sanity if you did not,' he said, so solemnly that both Clare and Marie-Claude burst out laughing.

Clare signed next morning, shook hands with Robert Lafarge, who was looking remarkably pleased with himself, and was immediately claimed by Madame Japolsky, who seemed somewhat put out that the chairman of the bank had managed to make an appointment so promptly in her unfortunate absence.

'If you will come with me, Miss 'Amilton, my office is on the ground floor, so that I am in close contact with the staff in my charge,' she said as they left Robert Lafarge's room.

Immaculately dressed in the height of discreet fashion, Madame had one of those angular bodies which undermine any possibility of elegance. What she lacked in poise and charm, she made up for by enhanced self-esteem. Despite her married status, Madame Japolsky reminded Clare of an elderly spinster who had once taught her in Sunday School. She wore exactly the same look of unshakeable distrust of her fellow men that had marked out Phoebe Hanson. She also gave a similar impression that she was about to pounce on you and demand a repetition of the first nineteen items in the Shorter Catechism.

'It is a little uncommon, Mam'selle 'Amilton, that such an advance has been made upon your salary. Nevertheless, I shall explain to you what exactly is involved,' she began, peering at Clare severely over gold-rimmed half-glasses which tended to slip down on her very narrow, pointed nose.

'The bank insists that all members of staff have their personal accounts here. They must never *under any circumstances* be allowed to go into debit. That I must stress. However, if there are personal circumstances which would lead to this very serious state of affairs, you must come to me right away. If we consider the circumstances reasonable, we have provision for meeting such difficulties.'

Clare nodded soberly and restrained a smile at the use of the royal 'we'. She read the document Madame placed in front of her and obediently signed the forms needed for the opening of her account.

'I will be very direct, Mam'selle 'Amilton. Your costume is very chic, well chosen, but in this position you will need many such costumes. Sometimes you will require evening dress,' she said severely. 'That is why this allowance has been made, no doubt. Not all young women have an adequate wardrobe. You will pay for your own costumes, but it is obligatory you use this designer with whom we have an arrangement.'

She handed over a business card. One glance at the name of a world-famous couturier and Clare could hardly wait to show it to Marie-Claude.

'You can be sure of excellent service. Do you understand?'

Clare nodded soberly, despite the fact that she was having the greatest difficulty in keeping her face straight.

'If you have a suitable, mature woman who can supervise your fittings it would be very convenient. But if not, I shall see to it myself. I will make an appointment as soon as you take up your post. I suggest three costumes and two evening gowns, unless you already have several of each.'

Clare reassured her that Madame St Clair, who had assisted with her present costume, would be pleased to help.

'Eh bien,' she replied, her lips snapping together to make a tight line.

Clare watched as she made a note on her file. No doubt she would take a great deal of trouble to find out exactly which of the well-known St Clair family she was referring to. The idea delighted her.

Madame clearly had something more to say. Clare adjusted her face muscles to look yet more attentive. It also helped her not to laugh, for the ironies of the situation were mounting all the time. Could she ever have imagined a job that provided a dress designer, subsidised her purchases and then produced an advance on salary with which to proceed?

'We also provide accommodation for our young staff. A deduction will be made direct from your salary, but you will certainly not find a small apartment in Paris at such a modest rent. There are, of course, certain necessary rules. Some young women find them irksome,' she said, as if a slightly unpleasant odour had crept into the room. 'The apartment provided is designed *solely* for your own use.'

Clare lowered her eyes modestly and saved up the remark for Gerard, who seemed much preoccupied with the question of her lovers and how she was to accommodate them in the busy life he expected her to have.

'Finally, Mam'selle 'Amilton, I must tell you that Monsieur Lafarge has requested that you take up your position immediately. We have important American visitors coming to Paris at the beginning of next week. One of our most experienced interpreters will be responsible for the visit, but Monsieur Lafarge wishes you to be present to assist him. I have made arrangements for you to see your apartment today. It will be made ready by Saturday afternoon. I am sure you will be available on Monday.'

* * *

'A week on Monday would have been perfect, Marie-Claude. But I suppose one can't have everything,' Clare said sadly, as she sat at the kitchen table telling her about her apartment and having to move in at the weekend. 'I was so looking forward to seeing Michelle and Philippe.'

'Yes, they will be disappointed, but there will be other times,' she said, as she began to make preparations for their evening meal. 'The children must learn that Clare is now a special person. Even you and I will have to accept that we meet when we can. You will often be away. Is there a telephone in your apartment?'

'Yes. It seems to have everything. I looked in the kitchen cupboards and there was a dinner service *and* champagne glasses. There were even fresh flowers on the coffee table when the beautiful young man took me to see it.'

Marie-Claude raised an eyebrow as she patted fillets of veal with seasoned flour and took a heavy iron pan from the cupboard.

'No, Marie-Claude,' she said, laughing and shaking her head. 'I think Monsieur Paul saves his beauty for other young men.'

The older woman raised a floury hand in one of those expressive gestures Clare found truly fascinating, a gesture which combined deep understanding and wry amusement all in one flowing movement.

'Now, tell me what else happened. Did you spend long with the famous Madame Japolsky? I wish to hear everything.'

Clare finished her tea, reached for her handbag and was about to produce the couturier's card when she stopped herself.

'Marie-Claude, is there something *you* should be telling me?'

The older woman laughed and raised her hands in a gesture of despair.

'You have such sharp eyes, ma petite. I'm sure I could take a lover and deceive Gerard. But with you here, alas I have no hope at all.'

Clare grinned happily. It was one of the joys of these last weeks to see the warmth and affection between Marie-Claude and Gerard. They seemed closer now and happier than she'd ever known them.

'No, it's not a lover. I can see that,' retorted Clare. 'Come on, stop teasing me. You've had some news. Letter or telephone?'

By way of answer, Marie-Claude washed her hands, dried them and fetched a letter from the table on the landing.

'Read it yourself,' she said, as she handed it to Clare.

Still in its hastily opened envelope, it was a single sheet with an impressive seal above the address. Clare scanned it quickly, then read it again to make sure she'd understood it correctly.

'Oh, Marie-Claude, how marvellous. What a lovely letter. No wonder you look so pleased. Fifteen years since you were his student and he says he remembers you well and would be delighted to have you.'

Clare put down the letter, got up and hugged her friend.

'Now you'll have to make up your mind exactly which topic interests you most,' she said, teasingly, 'out of the dozens we've discussed! You've only got till October, because then you'll have lectures to go to and perhaps even have essays to write,' she went on, excitedly. 'How is post-graduate work organised in France? I haven't a clue about that.'

'I shall explain, in every detail, but I refuse absolutely till you've told me *everything* that happened at the bank.'

She covered the portions of veal with a cloth and came and sat down opposite Clare at the kitchen table.

Clare smiled to herself, retrieved her handbag from the floor and took out the elegant card from the bank's couturier.

'I've got another new job for you as well,' she said casually, as she handed it over. 'Suitable, mature woman, to supervise the transformation of one Clare Hamilton. Three costumes and two evening dresses, as soon as possible. Unless, of course, I happen to have the said items in my wardrobe already!'

Marie-Claude stared at the card and shook her head slowly.

'Chérie! I am speechless. I cannot believe all that has happened in three short weeks. You have helped me so much.'

'Me, help you? Oh goodness, I think it's the other way round. Would I ever have got the job if you hadn't dressed me like a Frenchwoman?'

'Would I ever have been taken on by Professor Ladurie if you hadn't wakened up my mind again?'

'Perhaps we'd better call it a draw on the Blessedness Account or poor Gerard won't get any supper!' Clare laughed. 'Let me go and change and then tell me what I can do to help.'

They worked together as they had done each evening since Gerard's return. While Marie-Claude prepared meat for frying or grilling and made a sauce to complement what she had chosen, Clare rinsed vegetables, peeled potatoes, cut crudités, prepared a tray for aperitifs.

Clare thought of the tiny kitchen in her new apartment, the clean bright surfaces, the sink overlooking a small courtyard with terracotta pots full of summer flowers. Her first real kitchen.

'You'll come, won't you, both of you, and see my ménage?' she asked, suddenly so aware she must pack her case and leave for her own place in just a few days time.

'But, of course, chérie. We shall take you to your apartment on Saturday or Sunday, whichever day Gerard can be free. I shall unpack your clothes myself and poke my nose in all your cupboards. If we couldn't imagine you in your own apartment, how could we bear to part with you?'

CHAPTER FOURTEEN

Staring out of her kitchen window into the cobbled courtyard where summer flowers still bloomed in profusion, Clare yawned and rubbed her eyes, as she waited for the kettle to boil. Not entirely awake, she was just reaching for the coffee jar when a sudden sharp knock startled her.

Hastily, she turned off the kettle, wrapped her dressing gown more decently around her naked body and went to the door.

'Ah, mam'selle, you are safely returned. These flowers came early this morning. Your curtains were still drawn, so I did not allow the delivery boy to knock at your door.'

The dark figure waiting on the doorstep was holding a costume from the dry-cleaners, a carrier bag and a cluster of envelopes and cards, as well as the florist's box in the crook of her arm.

'Do come in, Madame Dubois,' Clare said politely, as she tried to smother another huge yawn.

The old woman smiled approvingly as Clare

began to relieve her of her burdens. Some of the young mam'selles and messieurs kept her standing at the door with their dry-cleaning and their parcels, because their rooms were so untidy, she suspected, but not this little English girl from Ireland. Even when a suitcase stood open, being packed or unpacked, her room was always so neat.

'These are beautiful, mam'selle,' said Madame encouragingly, as she lowered the box of flowers gently on to the dining table.

The other inhabitants of the bank's apartments had warned Clare that Madame la concierge, was garrulous and nosey, but she had long since decided Madame was just lonely. She'd been widowed in the war and appeared to have no friends or relatives. Her mam'selles and messieurs had become her family, and her greatest pleasure was helping them. In return, she merely wanted a little share in their comings and goings.

'Yes, they *are* lovely. I can't think who they're from. Shall we look?' Clare replied. She opened the box, took out a sheaf of roses and freesias and found the card attached to the lid.

'From London,' she said, as she translated the rather formal message of thanks 'for all her hard work'. 'Unusual for English men to send flowers, isn't it, Madame?'

Madame glowed.

'I think perhaps you prefer French men, mam'selle,' she said, looking pleased.

'I think perhaps I might, if I ever met any,' Clare laughed. 'Apart from my neighbours here and one or two colleagues at the bank, I meet far more Americans than French men.'

Madame nodded agreeably and turned towards the door.

'You must be very tired, mam'selle. It was so late last night. And you have had no breakfast yet.'

Clare thanked her and shut the door gratefully. The last thing she wanted this morning was to have to talk to anyone, but Madame was always so kind. Whatever the problem, she'd find a solution, and she'd never once forgotten anything she'd asked her to do.

Clare took the flowers through to the kitchen, filled her washing-up basin with water and put the flowers to soak, as Madame Givrey had instructed her. The tiny, bent old woman with a flower stall just outside the Metro was one of the first friends she'd made.

'You love flowers, mam'selle?' Madame Givrey said one day, when Clare chose a bouquet of white daisies mixed with bright blue statice. 'Have you always lived in the city?'

'No, Madame, you've guessed my secret,' she replied, smiling broadly. 'I'm a country girl. I used to grow my own flowers in window boxes my uncle made for me. Fuchsias and geraniums and lobelia. And I picked wildflowers too, for our table. Your flowers are lovely, but sometimes I miss the ordinary garden flowers, old-fashioned things like aquilegia and sweet william.'

'And the wild roses in the hedgerows?' she asked, her small dark eyes suddenly bright.

'Oh yes,' Clare replied, thinking of her favourite bush in the lane below the forge. 'They only last a day or two, but they're such a delicate colour, aren't they?'

After that, she often stopped to talk. She told Madame Givrey she never bought flowers when she was going away because there'd be no one to appreciate them. The old woman had nodded approvingly. Flowers were to be treated with proper respect.

'It is not just fresh water, mam'selle, that keeps flowers alive. Like ourselves, they need to be loved and cherished.'

The next time she chose a bouquet, Madame Givrey showed her how to cut the stems with a sharp knife.

'Always let them drink properly before you put them in a vase, mam'selle. That way they will last longer.'

Clare switched the kettle on again, fetched the carrier bag with her bread and croissants from the sitting room and made breakfast.

'No wonder Madame left so promptly,' she

said, as she glanced at the kitchen clock. It was a quarter to twelve and Madame, who rose at some incredibly early hour, before the earliest of deliveries, always had lunch at noon.

She carried her tray through to her chair by the window, carefully pushed aside the pile of books and maps on her low table and made room for it.

'Ouff!' she exclaimed, as she flopped down. Simply talking to Madame and making breakfast felt like a day's work.

'A whole week,' she said to herself, as she finished off her croissant, licked her fingers and sat back in her chair with her coffee. 'I don't have to do *anything*.'

This was the first piece of time she'd had to herself since the senior interpreter fell ill, right in the middle of the important five-day visit Robert Lafarge wished her to observe.

'This is most unfortunate Mam'selle 'Amilton. Most unfortunate,' he began, striding up and down his room. 'We cannot ask these Americans to come again another time, so I fear you will have to take Monsieur Crespigny's place. It is quite unreasonable to ask you, but I have no option. I have postponed this morning's meeting for one hour to see what help I can give you. Will you do what you can?'

'Yes, of course,' she said quickly. 'I'm afraid I haven't picked up all the technical terms yet, but the actual negotiations themselves don't trouble me. The problem is the financial side, particularly the interest rates. Monsieur Crespigny uses a calculator to produce a very fast translation. I'm afraid I've never used a calculator, so I'd be much slower.'

The look of relief on his face almost made her smile.

'That can be remedied very easily,' he said, pressing a button on his desk. 'My administrative assistant speaks little English, but he is exceedingly fast with figures of any kind, with or without a calculator.'

The door opened and the beautiful young man appeared.

'Monsieur Paul, you have met Miss 'Amilton, haven't you? Bien. Today you will assist her with our American guests. When a statement of a financial nature is made, you will make any conversion necessary to dollars or sterling, and pass the result to her. Also, you will carry up the technical dictionary and the large Larousse and find for her any French word with which she is not familiar, so that she can read the English translation for herself. Do you understand?'

'Perfectly, monsieur,' he said, with a bow to each of them. 'It will be a *great* pleasure.'

Clare thought she detected a slight raising of Robert Lafarge's eyebrows as he departed, but he said nothing.

She'd been terribly nervous before the meeting, held in the largest and most elegant of the first-floor reception rooms. She'd been introduced to all the visitors on Monday morning, but she'd not actually spoken to any of them. For two days, she'd just sat beside Jean-Pierre Crespigny, watching how he handled the negotiations, back and forth across the huge polished table.

Once she got started, it went far better than she could ever have imagined. At the end of the day Robert Lafarge had congratulated her, and the other members of the bank's team gathered round to encourage her for next day.

Only moments after she arrived back in her room, a stack of papers to prepare for the morning, Madame Japolsky appeared.

'Are you very tired, Mam'selle 'Amilton? It has been a very exhausting day for you.'

'Yes, I am tired now. I didn't notice until I stopped.'

'Tomorrow will be just as long, you must go to bed early tonight,' she said firmly. 'On Friday, you will have a much longer day. There will be a reception here, seats at the Opera and supper afterwards. This is the usual form when the bank entertains important visitors.'

The moment she mentioned the Opéra, Clare panicked. She'd absolutely nothing to wear, but Madame Japolsky had already thought of that.

'I have spoken to Mam'selle Pirelli today about the question of an evening dress. We think you are the same dress size. I have arranged for her to bring in one of her own dresses tomorrow morning. You must be here in good time to try it on before you go upstairs. If it doesn't fit, or if you do not feel at ease with it, I have made arrangements for her to go to our couturier and borrow a dress for you. At the bank's expense, naturally. I'm sure she will choose something attractive and appropriate.'

'It was too,' she murmured to herself, as she looked out across the cobbled river quay and watched a solitary fisherman set up camp.

She'd never forget the visit to the Opéra. The performance itself was memorable, but what would always stay in her mind was the opera house itself, the rich red and gold decoration of the auditorium, the foyer with its vivid, allegorical paintings and the grand staircase, L'Escalier d'Honneur, she'd seen so often in postcards and illustrations.

Stepping carefully down its broad, shallow steps of multi-coloured marble, wearing Louise Pirelli's blue silk dress, which was just a fraction too long for her, with Robert Lafarge on one side and the senior American official on the other, she felt thick carpet under her feet, was aware of the brilliant points of light overhead, the throng of well-dressed men and elegant women all about her, moving towards the open doors and the warm, velvety night beyond. She wondered if this was what it felt like to be Cinderella.

'Say, Miss Hamilton, what's that li'l red badge some of these guys are wearin' in their lapels?' the tall, slow-speaking Texan asked, as they descended.

As they crossed the foyer to the car, drawn up before the main entrance, with Robert Lafarge's chauffeur standing beside it holding open the door for her, she explained how the Legion of Honour was awarded and why one saw such a large number of legionnaires at the opera. The door closed behind her, she sank gratefully into the deep leather seat, smiled to herself and wondered exactly where she'd be when midnight struck.

By now the fisherman had got as far as baiting his line. As she watched, a slight breeze caught a handful of fallen leaves. Curled and dry, they moved crabwise along the edge of the quay, until a fresher gust whirled them into the water. They floated away, another golden cargo on the brown waters of the Seine.

She stretched back comfortably in a large, upholstered chair. On the evening of the hot July day when Marie-Claude and Gerard drove her over from the Bois de Boulogne, the first thing she'd done was move the chair over to the window. She'd imagined herself sitting with a cup of coffee in her hand, looking out on the passing scene, watching the barges pass up river and down.

'Not quite like that, was it?' she said aloud, laughing at herself.

She just hadn't appreciated how much work there would be. The few evening hours she spent in the apartment were almost always taken up with preparations for the next day. Papers to scan, maps to study. And whenever she did have a whole day at home, she had to catch up on her washing and ironing. There was shopping and letters to write.

Doing her housework, she often thought of scrubbing the kitchen floor at the forge house, or mopping up Mrs McGregor's red tiles after Alan Brady's shirts had dripped all over them. By comparison it was no effort at all to keep the apartment clean, but it still took time to arrange flowers, polish the windows, and keep it looking tidy. There hadn't been much left for gazing idly out of the window.

After those exceptional first weeks life had been easier, but it was no less busy. Her colleagues on the financial side were amazed by the continual flow of requests for finance, but Clare was not surprised at all.

She often recalled that happy evening when Gerard declared he'd question her sanity if she didn't take the job she'd been offered. After their meal he'd stretched out on one of the settees and begun to reflect on the whole economic and political situation in France.

'You've come at the right time, Clare. I think we're at the beginning of a period of enormous growth. It's been brewing for some time,' he began, 'but now the Treaty of Rome has been ratified, France is really beginning to think in terms of the new European market. Unlike London. The problems with Algeria might have put the brake on, but since De Gaulle was granted full powers last month, business confidence has returned.'

He put his coffee cup down and waved his hand in the air.

'Confidence is a term no one can define objectively, but we all know what happens when it goes up. And up.'

He laughed and threw his arms skywards in a great, expansive gesture.

As each new pile of submissions arrived on Robert Lafarge's desk, she began to see exactly what Gerard meant. Food producers, wine growers, hoteliers, manufacturers of agricultural implements, children's clothes, bathroom tiles. The list of companies requesting finance went on and on. It included items Clare had never even heard of, like extruded plastics and warp-knitted fabrics. She could understand the words, but could only guess what the processes were. They hadn't even got into the technical dictionaries yet.

She looked around her room. Her suitcase still sat unopened on the settee. She'd been so tired last night she'd looked in the drawer for a clean nightie to save unpacking. There wasn't one. Just like a couple of weeks back when she was packing for a three-day visit to Marseilles and discovered all her knickers were in the laundry basket. With no time to wash and dry them before the night train, she'd had to go straight out and buy some.

'Perhaps I'd better buy some more nighties as well,' she said, casting her eyes around the patches of sunlight that poured through the large window of her sitting room.

It was smaller than her room in Belfast, but much lighter, the pale primrose walls catching the light even on cloudy days. The furniture had been carefully chosen to match its proportions, so the room actually appeared more spacious than her old one, encumbered with a tall wardrobe, heavy sideboard and bulky settee. At night, the lights reflected in the river were so colourful, she sometimes sat for a little in her dressing gown, curtains undrawn, lamps unlit, watching the barges moving by with quiet urgency on the gleaming water.

She sighed and adjusted her chair so that her bare legs caught the warmth of the sun.

'What I miss most is being able to have a quiet think,' she said to the empty room. 'Feast or famine, that's the problem.'

Back in Belfast, she'd had all the time in the

world to sit and think. Too much, in fact. Often, she'd been bored, just as often lonely. Now she scarcely had time to be bored and was hardly ever alone. Even when she travelled and would have liked simply to watch the passing countryside, or let her mind float through the piled-up clouds, she was sure to have documents to be read before she arrived.

What she found most difficult of all was arriving back with her mind full of Bordeaux, or Lyons, or Marseilles, the sights and sounds of the city, the experience of working with new people, the words and expressions she'd learnt. She always had the greatest desire to sit still, even in the cramped office, with the banging and hammering of the builders moving closer all the time, but the next piece of work was waiting for her, or one more set of visitors arrived at reception. When the telephone rang on her desk, it was a real effort to get up and go out to greet them.

'I've landed, Marie-Claude, but I'm not sure when I take off again. I'm going to have a bath to try to get my head shirred,' she'd confessed to Marie-Claude on the phone, one evening.

So long ago now, on the beach at Deauville, speaking English because Marie-Claude had asked her to, she'd let slip the old expression.

'Shirred? Please, what is "shirred"?'

'Possibly it relates to the textile industry,'

she'd begun. 'Fabric is drawn together so that it lies in parallel ridges. Or perhaps it relates to the sediment settling to leave a liquid clear,' she continued, quite sure that Marie-Claude would want a proper explanation. Then she caught the look on Marie-Claude's face.

'Oh, Clare, you are so *sérieuse*,' she said, bursting out laughing.

'Yes, I am,' she'd admitted, ruefully. 'Sorry. Maybe it's my Scots ancestors and their respect for the "word" and for book learning.'

Ever after, it became a part of their shared language, just as it had been a part of what she shared with her grandfather.

She thought of him limping in of an evening, after a day of continuous comings and goings at the forge, longing for the comfort of silence and his pipe by the fire.

'Ach, sure I need to get my head shirred,' he'd say, as he pressed the tobacco into the bowl of his pipe with a well-practised thumb.

'Four years ago this month,' she said softly.

As vividly as if she were standing at the door of the house, she saw him walking down the lane to the forge on that lovely, frosty October morning, a bent figure in a flat cap and work-worn clothes. As the sun passed its zenith, she went on sitting, letting herself move round the dark kitchen, her own small bedroom, the 'boys' room' with her

217

table and books. She stepped out into the orchard, cycled down well-known lanes and visited places she'd not had the chance to think of for what seemed a very long time now.

Suddenly, she jumped up from her chair and shivered, the sun now long past its zenith. 'Time to shower and dress,' she said, and laughed at herself, aware how often still she spoke her thoughts out loud when there was no one around to hear.

As she pulled on her trousers, tucked in her shirt, she realised she was absolutely starving. She'd have to go shopping, but not until she'd looked at her post. She went to the cupboard, found a solitary tin of pâté and dipped gratefully into Madame's carrier bag for more fresh bread.

Back in her chair, she sorted her post into little piles. Two cards and three letters in one and a bank statement, an electric bill and a charity appeal in the other.

'Oh, Louise,' she laughed, as she picked up one of the postcards and tried to translate the Italian below the picture. A very large man was ogling two slim, but well-endowed young women in bikinis. It reminded her of seaside postcards from her childhood. She couldn't quite manage the Italian on the front, but scrawled on the back Louise had written, 'Wish you were here,' in English, and then, in French, the suggestion that they have a holiday together *without* 'le grand Monsieur', Robert Lafarge's nickname among the younger staff.

Clare laughed, so pleased at the thought of someone as lively and vivacious as Louise Pirelli wanting to holiday with her. Louise was the most striking woman she'd ever met. With wonderful blue-black hair, devastating dark eyes and a beautifully shaped figure, she turned heads wherever she went. At the bank, she was a constant trial to Madame Japolsky.

Madame had taken Clare to the office the two girls would share. A surprisingly small room, straight out of Dickens, a complete contrast to the Second Empire elegance of the rooms she'd seen so far. Louise was perched on a stool, swinging her shapely legs, her very high heels lying on the floor, her jacket draped over the back of a chair.

The tight-lipped expression on Madame Japolsky's face made it perfectly clear that such a relaxation in dress was not acceptable. Even out of sight in these back rooms, jackets and shoes were to be worn.

'You were feeling unwell, Miss Pirelli?' asked Madame Japolsky acidly, as she stared at the discarded jacket.

Clare tried not to smile, for Louise looked the very picture of health.

'Oh yes, Madame. Suddenly, I felt so unwell,'

she replied, rolling her eyes and putting her hand to her stomach.

It was exactly the gesture poor Jessie made once the morning sickness got going. A look of horror crossed Madame's face, till she realised she was being teased. She drew herself up to her full height and turned to Clare.

'I will leave you with Miss Pirelli for the moment,' she said, an icy edge to her voice. 'She will show you the staff rest room and bathroom.' She paused significantly. 'I hope she will also explain the standards of personal presentation we expect from *all* our staff,' she added, as she swept out of the room.

The moment she was gone, Louise burst out laughing, then held out both her hands to her.

'She is impossible, n'est-ce-pas? But I will tell you how to keep on the right side of her and what to watch out for.'

In that first exhausting week, however, they hardly laid eyes on each other. Instead, Louise would leave little notes on Clare's desk. '*Headache tablets and cologne in my drawer. Please use,*' was decorated with a very sad pussycat. '*If you need something to take home for your supper, try Ricardo in Rue Scribe,*' showed a very contented one.

Louise had been so delighted, too, when her own newest evening dress fitted Clare.

'Don't worry about dropping your champagne and canapé, chérie, Madame Japolsky will foot the cleaner's bill,' she said, as she helped her out of the dress and back into her costume. 'Good luck with your Americans.'

Even when they were going off in different directions and had only five minutes in the staff cloakroom, Louise would tell her the best place for a quick lunch or the nearest place to buy stockings. When eventually they found themselves working together in their cramped office, they shared the funniest of the misprints, new words they'd never met before and their observations on the state of Madame Japolsky's temper.

The other postcard told her that a costume and an evening dress were ready for fitting at her earliest convenience and that the autumn collection was now available should she wish to view it.

She turned to the letters. They were from home. She recognised the handwriting on all of them. She turned them over in her hand, remembering her very first Sunday evening alone in the apartment. After moving her chair to the window, she'd set up the dining table and written to her grandparents, Jessie and Harry and the Wileys. She'd also sent wee notes to all the people in her address book. Three months later, hardly any of them had replied.

It made her so sad that the people she'd shared lectures and seminars with for four years simply couldn't be bothered to write even a postcard. Only one girl out of the Honours year had responded. Mary McCausland thanked her for her congratulations, wished her luck and told her to make sure she got in touch when she came home to visit.

But there was one nice surprise. She'd never imagined Keith Harvey would make much of a letter writer, but he'd sat himself down regularly to tell her about his teaching job in Belfast and pass on news of mutual friends. She read quickly through his latest effort, as lively and amusing as the rest.

'What do you do, Clare, when someone is being rude or unpleasant? Do you try to give an English equivalent? Or do you clean it up? I've just read *Zazie dans le Metro* and greatly extended my vocabulary!'

There'd been nothing from Liskeyborough. Not a word from Uncle Jack or any of her cousins. Granny Hamilton could be excused, because of the state of her hands, but her dear brother might just have scribbled a word or two to tell her they were all well.

The next letter was Charlie Running's. She smiled when she saw how thick it was. He'd done a lot to make up for her family's silence. Although he seldom mentioned Robert, she knew he still missed him. What really surprised her was the enthusiasm with which he reported his historical researches.

His first letter had contained a vivid pictorial

account of the deployment of troops at the Battle of the Yellow Ford, together with sketch maps. In the next, he told her he'd discovered a row of trees had disappeared between a late eighteenth-century map and the 1835 Ordnance Survey. He was sure they'd been cut down in 1798, to make pikes for the United Irishmen. All he had to do was prove it.

'*Never forget, Clare, the active role that France played in Ireland's struggle for freedom,*' she read, laughing wryly at his next comment.

'*I wonder if you've had time yet to explore the history of those, like Matilda Wolfe Tone, who had to remain in France after the 1798 rebellion "for the good of their health".*'

The last was a note from Harry, a single sheet, the back of an invoice, as always.

Dear Clare,

I'm sorry I haven't managed to write since the baby was born but she's kept us busy. She and Jessie are grand even though they say she was at least two weeks early. We're going to call her Fiona Caroline after nobody in the family. Then there'll be no arguments. Any chance of you getting a holiday at Christmas to come over and see us? Jessie sends her love. I know she misses you. And so do I.

Much love,
Harry

She sighed as she looked at the familiar invoice form and the Ulster stamps on the discarded envelopes. Was she homesick? Only a few days earlier, she'd been asked the same question and it had taken her completely by surprise.

'Mam'selle 'Amilton, Monsieur Lafarge wishes to see you immediately in his room.'

Totally absorbed in translating a document, she looked up, startled, into the coal-black eyes of Madame Japolsky. Her stomach lurched with apprehension, till she remembered Madame had been in a bad mood for days and everything she said had an ominous edge to it. There was nothing at all unusual in Robert Lafarge sending for her. He did it quite regularly and he was never anything other than courteous.

She hurried up the long staircases and tapped at his door.

'Viens.'

To her surprise, he addressed her as Mam'selle Clare for the first time, a departure from his usual formality. He waved her to a corner by the window where two comfortable armchairs turned their high backs on the room and looked out over the Place de l'Opéra below.

'You are preparing for our London visit, no doubt,' he said easily. 'I have a question to ask you. When the directors of this consortium came to us here some weeks ago, I observed that you watched one of them, Monsieur Langley, a great deal . . .'

He paused, as Clare looked slightly embarrassed.

'I would appreciate it if you would give me your opinion of this gentleman.'

Clare took a deep breath, suddenly aware his question was not just a compliment but a responsibility.

'He reminded me of . . . someone I once knew well, a young man with a similar background, what the English themselves call "the public school type". I felt he was doing his best to be enthusiastic about a project in which he has no heart. He was making a considerable effort. He had done his work thoroughly in preparing his arguments and his figures. I'm sure he is very competent and perfectly trustworthy, but he has no feeling for the importation of fruit.'

Robert Lafarge nodded briefly and looked pleased. He then asked her for her opinion on the other members of the group of businessmen proposing to link a whole network of French and Italian co-operative producers directly with the English market.

'Thank you, Mam'selle Clare, you have been most helpful. We may speak again of this matter in London after our next meetings.'

He seemed to be about to stand up, but changed his mind and settled back more comfortably in his chair.

'Your friend, the one who has a gift for drawing animals, how is she?'

Clare beamed with pleasure.

'Jessie. She is very happy. Her first child was born two weeks ago, a little girl who already has blonde hair. She's too busy to write to me, but her husband, Harry, who runs the gallery where I worked as a student, writes me notes on the back of invoice forms. I'm afraid he's quite besotted with his daughter. I'm sure she'll be horribly spoilt,' she said, smiling.

'You will go and see them soon, perhaps? You must certainly be entitled to some holiday.'

'I . . . hadn't thought of it . . .'

'Remember that your airline tickets can be purchased through our reception. There are significant discounts,' he said practically. 'You are not homesick.' He paused and regarded her steadily.

She was not sure at the time whether his words were a statement or a question. Certainly she hadn't known how to reply. She turned over the envelopes in her hand. What did homesickness feel like? That was the problem. Was it there in the disappointment she felt when friends didn't write to her? Or was it an absence? A vague, unnameable sadness?

She shivered, feeling a sudden chill, though she'd switched on the heating while she was making lunch, and the light autumn sunshine was still warm on her face and legs. Perhaps she'd better go shopping. The letter from London was probably no more than an acknowledgement from the bookshop with which she'd just opened an account. It could certainly wait.

CHAPTER FIFTEEN

Winter in Paris was neither wet, nor bleak. There were rainy days when the last of the fallen leaves stuck to the wet pavements and vehicles splashed in the gutters, exactly as they'd done in Belfast, but however much it rained, Clare never felt the grey clouds press down upon her as if they would never lift again.

She was fascinated by the mist on the Seine, and the way the river traffic would then appear and disappear – silent, ghostly shapes, their coloured lights gleaming weakly, barely visible from her window. She loved the crisp mornings when frost iced the cobbles, picked out the swirling decoration on the lamp posts, outlined each individual twig on every bare tree, but what she loved most of all was the colour and life of the city.

As Christmas approached, a sense of excitement bubbled up as all the shops, both large and small, vied with each other for the most striking or most beautiful decorations. Sometimes, buying her own gifts, she was so totally delighted with the swags of tinsel, the loops of fairy lights, the exotic patterns of bells and ribbons and the pure white feathers, she'd completely forget what she'd come for and stand entranced by the glittering display.

Despite the coming holiday, the volume of work on her desk did not diminish. Then there were invitations from colleagues and from special customers of the bank to be fitted in as well. So when it arrived at last, she was grateful for the holiday itself, spent with the whole St Clair family in the apartment in the Bois de Boulogne. Not quiet days, by any means, with Michelle and Philippe so pleased to see her, so anxious to pursue some of their former pleasures, but very happy days. It was a real delight to be accepted so completely as one of the family.

It was as January and February passed, as full of activity as the months of the old year, that Clare found herself thinking more and more about the coming of spring. With the lengthening of the days, she looked hopefully for the first daffodils or any sign of the trees beginning to leaf, wondered if what she felt was some old, deep longing, born out of her life as a country girl, when the coming of spring would bring such relief, a respite from the cold and dark, the confinement of long evenings, and the anxiety over Robert's weak chest.

'Maybe it's all the fault of the Ritz cinema,' she

said to herself, one bright March day, as she moved around her apartment, unpacking her suitcase after one more visit to London.

'*Springtime in Paris*,' she muttered, as she put the street plan back on her shelf. Audrey Hepburn. Or was that *Three Coins in a Fountain?* 'Which was the one where she models the wedding dress?' she asked herself, as she dropped her underwear in the laundry basket.

It seemed as if all the films she'd ever seen, shot in Paris, or produced with painted sets in some Hollywood studio, blended together into one sunny, romantic picture. Young lovers drinking coffee in pavement cafes. Sunlight spilling down as they strolled hand in hand in the Tuileries Gardens. Kisses in the moonlight.

As her mind filled with images she'd viewed from the worn, red plush seats, she laughed aloud. The Ritz had a lot to answer for. All those Saturday matinees she and Jessie had so enjoyed. Ninepence worth of colour and light and never a sad ending among them. Lovers always reunited, families reconciled, implacable enemies converted, or despatched. For a few hours, they'd escaped into a wonderful world where hard work and boredom simply didn't exist.

But real life wasn't like a Saturday matinee, was it? People you loved died. Like Edward. People you thought loved you disappeared from your life. Like Andrew. Friends you enjoyed and valued moved into their own lives and forgot all about you. Like Ginny. Like the friends she'd made at Queen's. Waves of sadness swept over her as she stood staring at a grubby pair of shoes she'd just taken out of their wrapping paper.

'Come on, Clare. This won't do,' she said firmly to herself. 'You'll get nowhere if you only look at the losses. Consider the gains.'

She laughed to herself. That was Emile Moreau's job. And very good at it he was too. She could almost hear his quiet, slightly hesitant voice as she went into the kitchen and got out her shoe cleaning kit.

A quiet man, near to retirement, his hair almost white, he would come in calmly after the rigorous financial questioning of one of his younger colleagues.

'I think it is important that we now look, not at your losses, but at the experience your company has gained in the last period of time. If problems have been identified and addressed, then there may well be more potential than your current balance sheet suggests.'

His gentle manner and soft voice did so much to smooth ruffled feelings and rising anxiety. As she translated what he said, she would think what good sense his words made, if you took them out of the world of business and of money and into your own life. Listening hour after hour to people negotiating delicate issues across the table had taught her more than a new technical vocabulary. It had opened up possibilities she'd never thought of before.

'Don't ask why you got it wrong, ask what you've learnt,' she said, as she took her well-polished shoes to the wardrobe and closed the lid of the empty suitcase. She pushed it under her bed and sat down with a bump on the padded stool by her dressing table. Surely she'd been thinking about springtime when she'd started unpacking her suitcase. How had she managed to end up thinking of gains and losses?

Spring came for Clare, not in Paris, where she'd planned to walk under the trees in the Champs-Elysées, but in Provence. Suddenly, one morning, after a meeting in Nimes, Robert Lafarge asked to be taken to see the wine-making château whose future they'd been discussing.

It was the loveliest of mornings. The sky was a tender, fresh blue, the air mild but not yet warm. The chauffeur-driven car purred along the narrow roads so soothingly that neither Robert nor the prospective new director said a word to each other. She was free to watch the countryside slip past, the fields of newly turned earth, the red-brown soil combed into ridges and hollows as neatly aligned as a ribbed sweater. The hedges and windbreaks were vivid green with new growth. At the gable end of a solitary barn, a pear tree was already in bloom, its blossom a gleaming white against the worn and mellow red bricks of the dilapidated structure.

They stopped on the edge of an enormous vineyard. The first new growth had already broken into soft green leaves. The ancient-looking stumps marched up the hill slopes and into the far distance, like one of those drawings that demonstrate perspective.

Standing on the grassy verges that fringed the dry, stony, reddish earth, waiting for the second car to arrive with members of the château's staff, she felt the sun warm on her shoulders. She looked down and saw daisies winking up at her in the sunlight. On the air, a hint of smoke, a bonfire of hedge-trimmings. Its acrid note touched her heart. She looked at the daisies with longing, imagining herself bending down, regardless of her close-fitting costume and high heels, picking them, putting them in a glass in her hotel room in Avignon, taking them back to Paris, treasuring them more than any of the bouquets she'd ever bought from Madame Givrey's stall.

'Say, honey, what did the man say?'

The slow, mid-Western drawl betrayed not the slightest sign of irritation, but Clare was horrified when she realised she hadn't been paying attention. She'd no idea how this large American came to be a director of a French vineyard, but it was for his benefit she'd been required to accompany Robert Lafarge to the meetings in Nîmes.

'I'm so sorry,' she apologised. 'Mr Dubois is explaining that, though the soil would appear rather poor and infertile, it is the particular mixture of minerals in the soil and the aspect of the vineyard itself that give the wine its subtle quality. The high proportion of stones under the rootstocks themselves is not purely chance. It has been observed that the incidence of the sun's rays, striking these reflective surfaces, has a most beneficial effect on the early ripening of the grapes. This allows for more flexibility in the picking and a greater range of possibilities in using grapes of different degrees of maturation,' she said quickly, managing to catch up rapidly with the ponderous delivery of the earnest, thorough Monsieur Dubois.

'Say, now, isn't that surprising?'

Clare glanced up to find Robert Lafarge watching her, a slight brightness in his eye. She returned his gaze quite steadily and wondered – as she often did these days – just how bad his English really was.

A week later, Robert Lafarge phoned her at her apartment and asked her to dine with him the next evening, if she had no more interesting engagement. He named a restaurant for which she knew evening dress was obligatory, told her he would send a taxi to collect her and assured her they would not mention the establishment in the Place de l'Opéra.

The day that followed Robert's phone call left Clare little time to reflect upon his invitation. Louise had been feeling off-colour for a couple of days and finally admitted she wasn't fit to get out of bed.

'Mam'selle 'Amilton, we have a serious problem with Mam'selle Pirelli's absence,' announced Madame Japolsky, as she threw open Clare's door and strode across to Louise's desk. 'There is a piece of work here which is most urgent,' she went on, swinging round towards Clare, a sheaf of paper in her hand, a look of great severity on her face. 'I must ask you to set aside what you are doing and complete it immediately.'

'But, Madame, what I'm working on has to go to the printer's tonight,' Clare replied, picking up an equally thick sheaf of paper from her own desk. 'Monsieur Lafarge expects to sign it out by five o'clock.'

'Nevertheless, mam'selle, this German document is essential to Monsieur Moreau. He must have it before his meeting tomorrow.'

Madame's voice tone had risen several levels. Always a bad sign. Her left eye was beginning to twitch. When it looked as if she was winking at you, Louise had warned her, you really had to watch out. Paul had once told them when they were lunching together, that he'd nearly turned down the job after Madame took him off to her office and started winking at him.

'I will do what I can, Madame,' Clare said quietly. 'But if I'm called on for visitors, or incoming items, it will simply not be possible,' she added firmly.

She could hardly tell Madame she had an evening engagement. Madame would assume it was a boyfriend and simply expect her to cancel it. What on earth would she say if she knew she was dining with Robert Lafarge?

'I shall ensure you are not interrupted,' replied Madame, equally firmly. 'Ring through to my office at noon and I shall see that coffee and sandwiches are brought to you here.'

Madame was as good as her word, but even working flat out it was a near squeak. Robert Lafarge's draft contract went upstairs just before five, but by the time Clare finished the German document the building was empty, except for the caretakers and a courier, who sat patiently outside her door, reading his newspaper, waiting to deliver her translation to Emile Moreau at his home.

As she walked across the echoing entrance hall, under the dimmed night lights, she wondered if she would even have time to have a shower when she got home. But luck was with her. The Metro was very quiet after the rush hour. She was able to walk quickly in the uncrowded corridors and a train came along the very moment she reached the platform. She arrived home twenty minutes before the taxi was due to pick her up.

'Amazing what you can do with practice,' she said, as she peeled off her clothes, dropped her shoes on the rack and took off her make-up with a few vigorous sweeps.

The shower was heaven. A few minutes later, she splashed her face with cold water and sat down at her dressing table. Louise had taught her how to make-up in six minutes.

'It is easy, Clare, but you must give it your complete attention. It helps too if you are naked. Then if you drop something it doesn't matter.'

As she did what she'd been told, she suddenly remembered the story of the night Louise dropped eye oil on her only available dress.

'There was nothing else for it,' she said, rolling her dark eyes and throwing her hands in the air in a wonderful gesture somewhere between supplication and despair. 'It was my only dress – I had to wear it. I spent the whole opera visit clutching my evening bag to my stomach to cover the mark. And it *never* came out.'

Clare had no such dramas. With one evening

dress at the cleaners and another still being pinned on the model at the bank's couturier, she didn't even have to decide what she should wear. Tonight, it would be her very first evening dress, a blue silk, not unlike the one Louise had lent her for her first visit to the opera.

Dressed and ready, with minutes to spare, she hung up her costume in the damp shower cabinet to let it recover from the day's sitting and took out tomorrow's costume from the wardrobe, ready for the morning. As she heard a taxi draw up outside, she blessed Louise for teaching her all the tricks she herself had learnt in her first year at the bank. Tonight, she'd never have managed without them.

'So, you see, I too have an intimate knowledge of horses, though I never learnt to ride.'

Robert Lafarge paused, took the menu the head waiter presented to him and studied it with the same intense concentration Clare had seen him apply to balance sheets and company reports.

'If I might suggest . . .' he began tentatively, looking up and watching her, as she ran her eye over the impressive document in its red and gold leather cover.

She closed the menu and smiled at him. Not only was she sure that his judgement would be reliable, in a restaurant he clearly knew well, but she was so hungry she had no doubt she could manage whatever was put in front of her.

'When the Marquis went off to war in 1914, naturally he took his groom with him,' he continued, as the head waiter disappeared. 'Sadly, neither he, nor my father, ever came back. My mother had never been strong, though she had borne ten children. She died a year after the war ended,' he said matter-of-factly.

'So who looked after all of you?' she said quickly. 'Did you stay together or were you shared out round relatives?'

'Well, there were only four of us by then. My mother had ten children, yes, but some were born dead, some died as babies. My favourite sister died when I was fourteen. She was a year younger. She had tuberculosis, like my mother. It was very common in the countryside in those days.'

'Yes, it was the same at home,' she said, nodding sadly. 'While I was at secondary school, there was a big tuberculosis campaign in Ulster. They checked out school children with reaction testing and we all had chest X-rays. About ninety per cent of children in our area had actually been in contact with tuberculosis. Some of them had developed a high immunity. I was lucky, I was one of those. But I must certainly have been with people who'd had it.'

He listened attentively, pausing only for a moment to acknowledge a tall, silver-haired man, a member of a small party settling at a table nearby.

'It seems to have been a weakness in my family, but it may have saved my life!'

'However did it do that?'

She had to wait for the answer while Robert immersed himself in the wine list that had just been handed to him.

'You know a great deal indeed about the making of wine, my dear Clare, but will you allow me to instruct you in the drinking of it?'

She laughed and listened carefully to his discussion with the wine waiter. The name of the claret he chose to accompany the saddle of beef was not one she'd encountered, but she'd read that its year had not been a good one. She smiled to herself as she listened. Typical Robert Lafarge. This particular vineyard had escaped both the late frost and the early autumn rains and consequently had had an exceptional year.

'In 1939 when France mobilised, I failed the medical examination,' he went on. 'As a poor physical specimen with scars on my lungs, which I had not known about, I had to be given a task within my limits. I was made a Paymaster. Even armies require financial management,' he said wryly. 'So I was in Paris when the Germans made their advance. As you know, there was no fighting in Paris and it was not bombed as London was. I was quite safe. Unlike my wife and family.'

His tone was completely controlled, but she watched him carefully, nevertheless. For a moment, he paused, glanced briefly around the dining room with its panelled alcoves and brilliant chandeliers and seemed about to move on from what he'd hinted at.

'What happened to them, Robert?' she asked, gently, surprised to hear herself use his Christian name for the first time.

He smiled awkwardly.

'I am not entirely sure, Clare, though I have tried for years to find out,' he began, fidgeting slightly in his high-backed red and gold chair.

'Because my wife was pregnant with our second child, she went to stay with her sister in one of the villages on the edge of the Ardennes when I was called up. No one had thought an attack would come in that area. Some of those villages were destroyed by the Germans. There were, however, many refugees who took to the roads ahead of the advance. There is evidence that my wife and her sister escaped with their children. But, as you may know, the columns of refugees were strafed with machine-gun fire as they fled. My brother-in-law managed to trace some of the survivors from his village after the surrender. From all he could gather he was convinced his wife and mine died together with our children, and they were all buried together. The baby would have been only a few weeks old. Of it, there is no trace whatever, though one survivor insists my wife was carrying a baby in a sling before the Stukers came.'

'So the child could have survived?'

'Yes, he could. I had a letter months later that my wife had written, telling me we had a son. Someone must have found it tramped in the dust and put it in a post box after the surrender, but I was unable to trace them. I gave up hope of finding my son, if he survived, some time ago. Sometimes it is best to give up hope and get on with living. If hope is returned, well and good, but if not, one will not have spent time in vain longings. I think you may have already discovered that for yourself.'

Clare was completely taken aback. She'd been so absorbed in Robert's story she'd not noticed until the end of it that he had addressed her as 'tu', a sign that their relationship had crossed the invisible line between acquaintance and intimacy. She'd felt just the same surprise that second summer in Deauville, when, just as suddenly, dear Marie-Claude had said, 'Do let's call each other "tu".'

'Yes, I think you're right,' she said quietly. 'But my loss seems small compared with yours.'

He shook his head.

'That is a mistake so many good people make. They compare their loss with the loss of others and judge their own the less. It's not a good idea. Loss cannot be measured by some objective scale. One must look at the person, the loss, and the resources they have to cope with it. Even then, it seems to me one cannot be objective. A loss that would cripple one individual serves only to challenge and enrich another.'

At that moment the soup arrived, forcibly reminding Clare just how hungry she was. She thought about what he'd said as he sampled it carefully, broke the crisp crust of a roll and settled back to enjoy it.

'How did you lose your parents?' he asked, without looking at her.

'Typhoid fever in 1946,' she said, trying to be as matter-of-fact as he had been about his family. 'It was the last epidemic of typhoid in the UK. They died within two days of each other.'

'And you were not ill?'

'No. Like you, I was lucky. Pure chance. I didn't like milk and milk was the carrier.'

'And your brothers and sisters?'

'I have only one brother. Younger. William. He has always been difficult. He still is. Because I didn't drink milk, he wouldn't either. So we both survived. He lives with my father's parents.'

'And you went to your mother's parents?'

Clare smiled as the waiter took away their soup plates.

'No, it wasn't quite like that. I went to live in

Belfast with my Aunt Polly, who is lovely, but I was very unhappy there. When my grandmother died, I decided to go and look after my grandfather.'

She paused and shook her head.

'Given that I was only nine, it seems an amazing decision to have made, but I was perfectly clear that that's what I wanted to do.' To her great surprise, Robert laughed. 'What's so funny?'

'I am amused that the characteristics I so value professionally were already well developed at such a tender age.'

'What characteristics?'

'The ability to make up your own mind, which is a gift you have developed for yourself. And the gift of knowing who you can trust.' He paused and considered.

'Were I a religious man, which, alas, I am not, I would have to say that this particular gift is probably a gift of grace. One can develop shrewdness through experience, but what you have is an intuitive sense of what is right. In particular, as I say, you always seem to know who you can trust. I have never known you make a mistake yet.'

For a moment she was quite baffled, but before she could speak the waiter reappeared with the fish course. She was grateful for the time it took to serve, for her mind had filled suddenly with the memory of a summer day.

She and Jessie had gone down the steep slope

opposite Richardsons' gates to their secret talking place by the stream. When they came back up to retrieve their bicycles, Andrew was there, bending over hers, fiddling with the valve caps. Jessie had been hostile and suspicious, thinking he'd let down their tyres, but she had simply looked at Andrew and knew he would be incapable of an unkind act.

It was very strange that a man like Robert should speak about a gift of grace. But it was stranger still that his words should call up a memory of Andrew on their very first meeting.

It was almost midnight when Clare arrived back at her apartment. Sitting over coffee, Robert had looked at his watch, spoken of the busy day she'd have tomorrow, asked if she were tired. It was perfectly obvious he'd no more wish to end the evening than she had, so she shook her head and scolded him gently for even mentioning work.

Only when the other diners disappeared and the waiters began to walk past their table, discreetly but a little more frequently, did they rise reluctantly and move out into the palm-filled foyer.

'I should like us to dine regularly, Clare, if you are happy with the idea, but on one condition,' he said, as her taxi drew up at the kerb.

'And what is that?'

'That we dine only when none of your admirers

are available. You have very few evenings at leisure in Paris.'

'And what if I prefer to dine with you?'

He opened the car door, made sure the hem of her dress was well clear of the sill and stood looking down at her.

'I should be honoured,' he said, with a slight bow. 'I fully intend to enjoy your company until I am forced to part with you. Sleep well, my dear.'

The lights on the river gleamed in the velvety darkness as Clare settled herself in her chair by the window. She knew she should be in bed, but it had been such a remarkable evening she knew she couldn't possibly sleep. She would need to settle some of the thoughts whirling around in her head like the tiny moths circling the street lamp a little way along the quay.

How extraordinary it was that two people could get to know each other so well in one evening. Not only had they shared life histories, but they had spoken openly about even the most painful parts. They had moved on from the sadness of loss to her long relationship with Andrew and how the heartbreak of Edward's death had changed everything between them. He listened with a kind of attention she had not encountered before, even with dear Marie-Claude. She felt almost as if she was talking about Andrew for the first time, seeing her experience through the eyes of someone much older, yet able to understand her feelings.

She'd been shy of asking him how he'd managed to cope after he lost his wife and daughter, but he had been remarkably open and easy about it. Work, he said, was what had helped him through. Asserting his own right to life, despite his heartache.

'I had one wise friend who had faced great loss many years earlier,' he began. 'It was he who told me I must act. He said I'd often feel that what I was doing was a waste of time, that it brought no pleasure, or joy, but nevertheless I must act, believing that it would make a difference. And it did. I was successful in the work I chose and he was right. From time to time, I have felt both pleasure and joy. But using action to shape one's life does have its limitations. I've few friends, but those I have are mature enough to tell me the truth. They say I have become remote and unapproachable,' he ended sadly.

'I don't find you at all unapproachable.'

'I'm glad of that. Perhaps there is hope for me yet.'

'Don't you think perhaps your job requires you to be unapproachable?'

'Yes, that is so. But perhaps I have allowed the demands of the job to shelter me from a proper engagement with my fellow creatures. What do you think?'

She'd been amazed he should ask her such

a personal question. But then, why not? She'd already shared more with him than with most of her oldest friends.

'I think it's very easy to develop habits. When I was a student, I was often lonely. Yet there were people who would have been glad to see me, places I could have gone. I sometimes wonder if loss breeds loss. That those who've lost loved ones expect to lose what they value. And because you fear loss, you defend yourself by trying not to be too involved.'

She'd been amazed to hear her own answer, but Robert had smiled gravely and said something complimentary about her seeing more already than many he had known who were twice or three times her age.

Beyond her window a couple strolled into view, arms entwined. They stopped, embraced and moved on. She wondered if they were lovers with a place to go to, or whether, like she and Andrew walking by the Thames two years ago, the choice was to walk all night or return to their respective hostels.

'You ought to go to bed, Clare Hamilton,' she said severely. 'You'll need more than a good layer of foundation and rouge if you don't get some sleep.'

But she didn't move an inch.

So much of their conversation had been

thoughtful and serious and yet they had laughed often.

'Say, honey, what did the man say?'

She'd looked around, startled, sure one of the nearby diners had spoken. But when she turned back, Robert was grinning broadly and looking pleased with himself.

'Robert, I thought so,' she said, moving to English. 'I was sure you understood English far better than you pretended. So you speak it as well.'

'Most, certainly not,' he replied, returning to French. 'There is a very good reason. I worked with an American organisation at the end of the war. That's when I learnt my English. I can follow a good deal of what is said, but I have an appalling accent, probably a worse English accent than the French one your friend Andrew acquired in Brittany. It would be quite unsuitable in my position,' he said, deliberately sounding pompous.

She laughed and shook her head.

'Don't you get bored, hearing everything twice?'

'I even get bored sometimes hearing it once,' he said abruptly. 'But not when you are there. I see things differently when I look through your eyes. It is most illuminating. And very good for business. But that is a subject of which we may not speak. Have you forgotten our promise? Perhaps when we dine together in London next week, we may speak of business, but not tonight.'

Clare yawned. Suddenly, her tiredness had caught up with her. As she drew back the covers and slid gratefully into bed, she thought of that July day last year when he had asked her to read *The Times*, and then offered her a job and a salary she couldn't possibly refuse.

CHAPTER SIXTEEN

'There is a telephone call for Mr Lafarge,' said the waiter, as he stopped beside their table and caught Clare's eye.

Robert lowered his newspaper and looked at her.

'From Paris?' she asked, as she put down her toast and wiped crumbs from her fingers on a large damask napkin.

'I'm sorry, I don't know. The young lady on reception asked me to come and tell you because she's new and doesn't know Mr Lafarge,' he explained before he moved away.

'I'll go and see who it is,' Clare said, getting to her feet. 'If it's Paris, I'll ask them to call again in half an hour. If it's about today's meeting, I can take a message. All right?'

Robert nodded and retired gratefully behind *The Times*.

Clare moved quickly through the large dining room full of the smell of bacon and egg, the rustle of newspapers and the sound of well-bred English voices. Robert was not a morning person. Even in Italy, where he spoke not a word of the language and could only read the exchange rates, he still insisted on having his newspaper.

'Good morning,' she said, picking up the phone and trying English first. 'This is Clare Hamilton, Mr Lafarge's assistant.'

'Clare! What a relief. I thought I was going to have to use my schoolboy French.'

'Charles,' she replied, laughing.

One of the things she liked most about Charles Langley was his disarming honesty.

'Has something gone wrong?' she asked quickly. 'We were expecting you and John Coleman at nine-thirty.'

'Well, it's good news in one way, but there *is* a real problem. I don't know how Robert Lafarge will take it. John's wife went into labour last night. It's her third pregnancy, but they lost the first two. Naturally, she's in a bit of a state. John's even worse, but he's trying to do the stiff upper lip bit. He's with her at the hospital and he really can't leave her at this stage.'

'And he's the one that's worked out the growth projections?'

'Absolutely. I'd have swotted them up if I'd been coming to Paris, but there was no point when you were coming here and I could bring him with me. Will your boss be furious, or can you charm him? I'll turn up and grovel, but I can't waste his time trying to have a meeting. Is there any hope we could have the meeting tomorrow, or were you flying back tonight?'

'No, he's booked on the evening plane tomorrow,' she replied. 'There's nothing in the diary, but I think he wants to do some shopping.'

'Sounds hopeful, if you can persuade him. I could take you both shopping today and then out to lunch. Do you think he'd like a Langley Town and Country Tour? I think it's going to be a nice day. I really do feel bad about this, Clare, but poor old John is up to thirty thousand. Lafarge is a bachelor, isn't he?'

'No, Charles, he isn't. He lost his wife and daughter during the German advance. There was a baby son that might or might not have survived.'

'Oh lord, Clare, that's tough,' he said, with an audible intake of breath. 'Makes one's own problems seem pretty trivial,' he added resignedly. 'What shall I do? Give me good advice.'

'Well, I think you should appear, but leave it till ten. I'll tell him you've offered to take us shopping or whatever he wants to do. With any luck, he'll suggest tomorrow. Can John get in touch with you?'

'Yes, he'll ring my secretary from the hospital as soon as there's any news and I'll keep in touch with her whenever I can get to a phone.'

'Right, I'll do what I can. See you at ten.'

The moment Clare sat down, Robert folded his paper and signalled to the waiter.

'London or Paris?' he asked, as the waiter set down a pot of coffee, a rack of toast and a well-polished cup and saucer bearing the hotel's crest in gold.

'Yours was getting cold,' he said abruptly, as he poured her a fresh cup. 'Now finish your breakfast,' he added firmly.

'It was Charles Langley,' she began, as she buttered the hot toast. 'John Coleman's wife went into labour last night. They've lost two babies already.'

'So, no meeting today. Is tomorrow a possibility?'

'Yes, distinctly so, if baby arrives today. Charles has offered to take us shopping and then to lunch. He thought you might like a tour of London or a drive out into the countryside. It looks as if it's going to be a nice day.'

'What time's he due?'

'I said ten.'

'Good. I hate nine-thirty meetings.'

He stood up unexpectedly, paused for a moment.

'I'll meet you in the foyer at ten. I have some things to see to.'

He tramped across the dining room and

disappeared in the direction of the lifts, a small, almost square figure with dark, thinning hair and a very determined set to both his face and figure.

Clare watched him as she ate her toast. In the two weeks since they'd first dined together, she'd discovered the second Robert in her life was often as silent and awkward as the first. The better he got to know her, the more he let it show. He was never bad-tempered, never discourteous, but he no longer concealed either his irritation at changed arrangements or his discomforts. This morning, his inside was playing up. She'd noticed the discarded foil of his indigestion tablets by his plate when she came down to join him. Eating breakfast usually helped, but until he'd been to the bathroom he wouldn't feel much better.

She looked at her watch. It was only ten to nine. She sat drinking her coffee and watching people standing up, collecting themselves and moving towards the foyer and their day's work. Men in dark suits with loud voices and identifiable accents. Women, smartly dressed, up in town to go shopping. A handful of tourists in casual clothes being shepherded by their courier. A group of twenty men and women, who got up together and turned out of the dining room towards one of the smaller conference suites.

Clare thought of John's wife lying in some labour ward. Poor woman. To lose two babies.

She wondered if they had both been born dead or if they had simply not survived for very long, like Robert's brothers and sisters. Robert's wife had lost a child too before their daughter was born. Then Robert had lost them both and his son, whom he had never even seen.

Sometimes the world seemed such a cruel place. She couldn't really accept that everything was the will of God, the way it had been put to her from the pulpit all through her schooldays. It just wasn't logical. If God was all powerful, then why did he let it happen? And if he wasn't all powerful, why did the Church try to insist that he was?

The image of Robert's wife with her tiny baby and her five-year-old daughter haunted her. At Film Society, with Keith Harvey she'd once seen a newsreel about the fall of France. The sad columns of people trudging away from burnt-out villages or fleeing before the German advance. Women and children and old men, carrying bundles, pushing prams stacked high with possessions, pulling carts because all the horses and donkeys had been requisitioned for the army. Moving as quickly as they could, hampered by children who could walk no faster and cried in fright when the planes passed overhead. Diving for the ditch when they heard the rattle of their machine guns.

Suddenly, she realised she was the same age as Robert's daughter would have been, had she survived. The baby boy would be William's age. In her own mind, she'd always think of him as little Robert, calling him after his father, just as generations of women in her own family had named a son either Robert or Thomas.

Beyond the tall windows with their heavily draped velvet curtains, the traffic flowed down Park Lane under a bright blue sky dappled with small white clouds. If the weather were like this tomorrow evening when she flew to Belfast she'd be able to see more of the green hills and little fields than she'd ever seen before.

'Can I bring you some more coffee, Miss Hamilton?'

The voice drew her back to the present. She smiled up at the waiter who'd served breakfast and brought them the message about the telephone call.

'No thank you. That was splendid. It's time I did some work!'

She went to reception, checked there were no letters or telegrams for Robert, collected her key and went up to her room. She couldn't decide what was making her so sad, Robert's loss, or the Colemans' loss, or some loss of her own she could put no name to.

'How do you do, Mr Langley?' said Robert Lafarge, pronouncing each word slowly and carefully.

Clare smiled to herself. The words were fine, but the intonation was all wrong. It sounded more like, 'How do you do a reverse turn, or a back flip, or a victory roll?' She had a feeling he was teasing her, but couldn't be sure.

'Je suis très bien, merci, Monsieur Lafarge,' replied Charles Langley, speaking French for some reason best known to himself.

'Bon. Bon.'

Having shaken hands most cordially, Robert turned to Clare and addressed her at a speed she knew Charles couldn't possibly follow.

'You will explain to Monsieur Langley that I appreciate his difficulties. We will meet tomorrow at ten, all being well with the Coleman family. As for today, I would be grateful if he would entertain you. I have made my own arrangements, but will expect to see you at breakfast at eight-thirty tomorrow.'

He turned away before she could protest and beamed at Charles Langley, while he waited for her to translate.

From the look on his face, it was perfectly obvious Charles hadn't managed to catch so much as a word. She could do nothing other than give an exact translation.

It was now Charles's turn to smile broadly. He assured Robert Lafarge, in English, that he would be most happy to entertain Miss Hamilton. He could rest assured that she would be well looked after.

Clare translated, they shook hands again, exchanged good wishes in each other's language. Robert wished 'Miss 'Amilton' a pleasant day, and went off looking pleased with himself.

'Well then, what shall we do? Where would you like to go? Would you mind if we call in at my office on the way?'

'No, of course not. I'll go and get my coat. Is it as nice as it looks outside?'

'Yes, it's lovely, but there's a chilly edge to the breeze. You'll certainly need a coat over that suit. Unless you want to go shopping?'

'No, definitely not. I was wondering if we could walk in a park. I have some flat shoes upstairs.'

He looked at the high heels that complemented her spring costume and nodded wisely.

'Bring them with you and I'll call a taxi.'

'Haven't you got your car?'

'Oh yes, but it's up in Covent Garden. You don't think I'd turn up here in less than a Rolls, do you?'

Ten minutes later, as Clare settled back in the taxi, she felt her spirits rise. She was even prepared to be grateful to Robert for organising her day without consulting her. Charles was a nice man, too nice, perhaps, but she'd always liked him. They'd met several times now in the course of business and got on well. Once, when Charles had stayed an extra night in Paris, they'd had dinner together.

'So which of the character-forming establishments *did* you go to?' she asked gaily, when she stopped laughing at one of his stories about his school days.

The answer took her so totally by surprise, she felt the colour drain from her face.

'You must have known Andrew Richardson,' she said slowly, as she collected herself.

'Goodness, yes. Richardson was my fag. Nice chap. Had relatives in your part of the world. Went to Cambridge. Law, I think. Or was it history?'

'It was law.'

'Do you know him?'

'Yes, rather well. We were engaged. But it didn't work out.'

'Oh, I *am* sorry. That makes two of us. My wife left me last year. We'd only been married two years. I came home one day and she was gone. Two lines on the back of a shopping list to say don't try to find her, there was no point. She went off with a cousin of mine she'd known for years,' he explained bitterly. 'What happened with you and Richardson?' he went on when he'd recovered himself.

She told him as honestly as she could.

'Sounds just like him. Bloody fool. Pardon the expression. He always did what people wanted him to do, never mind what he wanted. *I'd* have taken you to Canada.'

She glanced away from the look he gave her.

'If I'd been in his position,' he added quickly.

The streets were full of people, the shop windows dressed with giant sprays of blossom, flourishing daisies and sprouting branches, a background for costumes in delicate pastels, soft leather shoes with very high heels, and summer dresses in linen and flowered cotton.

She registered the passing scene with a corner of her mind, but had not the slightest wish to be any part of it. She was glad when the taxi turned away from the main streets she recognised and nosed its way down through a maze of side streets only just wide enough to drive through. It pulled up beside a pavement stacked high with boxes and the debris of the early morning market. Beyond, a tall narrow building still carried its rather old-fashioned sign, 'Langley and Son, Fruit Importers'.

'Sorry about this. You get used to it, but it's hard on visitors,' he said, drawing her gently away from a squashed tomato on the pavement. 'It's better upstairs.'

The stairs were steep, but at the end of a surprisingly broad landing he threw open a door into a large room, beautifully restored to its former elegant style, with moulded cornices and a plaster-work ceiling, full of light, and carpeted from wall to wall. The furniture was Scandinavian – a polished teak desk, leather swivel chairs, stainless steel lamps, polished metal filing cabinets. On the walls were photographs and etchings of early aeroplanes, biplanes and gliders.

'What a lovely room, Charles,' she said, as she slipped off her coat and gave it to him. 'Do you fly?'

'When I can. There's a light-aircraft club down at Biggin Hill. I wanted to go into the air force when I left Oxford, but they wouldn't have me. Low level of colour blindness. Besides, father wanted me in the business.'

One more of them, Clare thought to herself. Andrew does what his uncle wants, Charles does what his father wants. Men with offices keep their secrets on the walls of their room. Robert's horses, Charles's planes. She wondered if Andrew would put pictures of prize cattle on his wall if ever he had a room of his own.

'Can I leave you to look round while I check with Julie? There may have been a call from John.'

'Yes, surely. Can I look at your books?'

'At anything you like,' he said easily, as he strode across the room and out on to the landing.

She was still looking out of the window at the pavements below when he came back only minutes later.

'Good news?' she asked as she swung round and saw the huge grin on his face.

'Absolutely great. Little boy arrived half an hour ago. Bad moment with cord round the neck, but they were more than half expecting it. He's absolutely fine. They haven't even weighed him yet, but he's at least seven pounds. Poor Jane can't stop crying, but John says she's all right, no stitches or anything nasty, just pure relief.'

'How wonderful. Isn't it lovely when things work out right?'

'Yes, wish it happened more often. How shall we celebrate? Town or country? I can do better than a park: I can take you to Ashdown Forest, on to the Downs, perhaps, show you my home at Penshurst. There's a good pub near there called The Spotted Dog, if you like traditional English pubs.'

'Charles, I've never been in *any* kind of English pub. I would love that, if it's not too long a drive. My geography of Kent and Sussex is a bit hazy now, though I think I could still draw the sketch map of the Wealden Dome with the centre eroded out.'

'More than I could. I was lousy at geography. You can look at the road atlas if you want, but the nicest little roads aren't on it. They're in my head. Right, let's go.'

'Can I leave a message for Robert Lafarge? I don't know what he's planning to do, but he'll be pleased when he hears about the baby.'

'Yes, of course. Dial nine for an outside line. I'll go and bring the car down. Probably take me about five minutes. Sometimes the phone plays up. If it does, go and use Julie's.'

Once free of the traffic in central London they moved speedily through the suburbs, and within half an hour were driving in rich, green countryside with half-timbered houses and villages already bright with summer flowers. Newly leafed trees, almost touching across the narrow roads, filtered the bright sunlight into dappled shadows as stretches of woodland alternated with small hamlets, clustered groups of older houses and a few recent developments of bungalows.

'I used to wonder if stagecoaches outside hostelries really existed,' Clare said, as they passed yet one more Old Coach Inn. 'They used to appear every Christmas in the box of cards, but we haven't got anything like that in Ulster. I thought perhaps stagecoaches and oak beams were like Santa Claus, purely for the festive season.'

Charles laughed and nodded towards the view as they crested one of the higher hills.

'Is Ireland really so different from this?' he asked.

'Can't speak for Ireland,' she said cheerfully. 'I only know Armagh and bits of County Down and the north coast of Antrim, but they're very different from this. Not so many trees. Little green hills, but lots of them. Tiny fields compared to these,' she began, scanning the well-cultivated lowland spread out below the steep hill they'd just climbed.

'Go on,' he said, not taking his eyes from the narrow road. 'Tell me more. I've never been to Ireland. Is it really greener than this?'

She laughed.

'Yes, it is actually. But the main difference is that Ireland is shaggy. This is all so tidy. Those fields look as if they'd been vacuum-cleaned after they were harrowed. The bits of Ireland I know are more unkempt, more unruly, I suppose. But then, this land has been cultivated for such a long time in comparison.'

'Domesday Book and all that?'

'I wish we had a Domesday Book for Armagh. I'd love to know exactly what was going on in my small corner. I doubt if much of the land was cultivated before the seventeenth century. Mostly, it was pasture for cattle. According to my grandfather's great friend Charlie Running, Armagh was settled by planters from Warwickshire. That's why there are so many apple orchards and why we have a Shakespearean turn of phrase.'

'I haven't noticed that,' he said, glancing at her as the road straightened out.

'But I haven't lapsed into dialect yet. I'm still speaking standard boardroom English.'

'I'll keep listening. I could listen to you all day.'

Clare was delighted by The Spotted Dog, and amused by Charles's practised stoop as they came into the bar with its huge oak beams close enough to touch, sporting prints and well-polished brassware. 'It appears that true-born English men were smaller in days of yore,' he said, sitting down beside her on a bench, well polished by generations of bottoms. 'We can eat here or go through to the dining room,' he said, nodding towards an almost empty room, laid out with pink table linen and white napkins folded in stemmed glasses.

'I like it here,' she said promptly.

'Good. So do I,' he said, picking up the handwritten menu and glancing at it. 'Daisy does a good cottage pie. Steak and kidney pudding is splendid if you're really hungry and the fish and chips is the best in Sussex, so my father says. Though that's probably because he knows Fred goes up to Billingsgate in the middle of the night to choose his own fish.'

'I'd love fish and chips. I can't think when I last had any.'

'No, the French don't seem to have the knack of it. I can't imagine a pomme frite ever tasting like a good old English chip.'

The landlady herself came to take their order and welcomed Charles like a long-lost friend.

'Daisy, this is Clare,' he said, when she paused for breath. 'She works in Paris and hasn't had fish and chips since she went.'

'Well, we'll soon put that right, won't we?' said Daisy, shaking Clare's hand and smiling at her. 'You must be dying for a bit of good English nosh,' she said, winking at them.

The food was as good as Charles had promised and Clare hungrier than she'd imagined, given the full English breakfast served in Park Lane. Although it was now the middle of May, a pleasant wood fire burned in the huge fireplace, filling the whole room with the scent of its fine bluish smoke. She looked around as they ate, taking in the details of the comfortable and welcoming room, the small tables, the cosy alcoves. How strange it was to step into someone else's world, full of the people they knew, the places dear to them.

It was as if you made a picture of the world through what you did, what you saw, the people you knew well. And yet, living in the very same place, whether it was Armagh, or Penshurst, or Paris, another person could make a totally different picture. She glanced towards the two women at the nearest table, clearly old friends. They were talking about their girlhood in Simla and mutual friends who had just gone back for the first time since 'the old days'. They knew Daisy, so presumably they lived here, somewhere among the leafy lanes, the sudden steep hills and the wide views over almost flat lowland. She wondered how those early years fitted into the picture they'd made.

'Have your parents always lived in Penshurst?'

'Mm,' he nodded, as he demolished the last of his chips. 'I was actually born there, though that wasn't planned. I had the bad taste to arrive early. Fortunately, the midwife lived just round the corner and had a phone. My poor father hadn't the remotest idea what to do, so he made a cup of tea.'

'At least he could manage that,' she said, laughing. 'Where I come from, some men would think that was letting the side down. Teamaking is woman's work.'

'You get over that in the army,' he said, leaning back comfortably. 'Two years away from home and no one to do things but yourself. Unless you get a commission, of course. Even then you learn all the practical things in basic training, bed making, sewing on buttons. If your kit's not up to scratch you're up on a charge. CB and all that.'

'What's CB?'

'Confined to barracks. Fate worse than death. You die of boredom.'

'And a commission?'

'That's when they think you're officer material. They put a pip on your shoulder and call you a soldier of the Queen, or King, as it was in my case. Poor man died while I was in Egypt and we had to put on a grand parade for the Accession.'

'So you went into the army?' she asked, surprised.

He laughed wryly.

'No, my dear Clare. I didn't *go* in. I was called up. National Service.'

'Yes, of course. I'd forgotten. We don't have National Service in Ulster. It sounds like a good idea.'

'It doesn't feel like a good idea while you're doing it, but I think I agree with you. Very character-forming and all that. Caroline used to appreciate my domestic skills.'

The bitterness broke through every time he mentioned her. She wondered if she sounded as bitter when she spoke of Andrew.

'Why do you think she married you?'

'I've asked myself that one too. Sometimes I can't think why anyone would want to marry me.'

'Oh Charles, don't be silly,' she said, laughing. 'You're terribly marriageable. Surely the problem was that a lot of women wanted to marry you, but not always for the right reasons.'

'What are the right reasons?' he said promptly.

'Well it's not about domestic skills, or good looks, or entry to a particular social milieu, or money, or position. I think it's about being able to make a life together. Supporting each other. Accepting the weaknesses as well as the strengths.'

'But aren't men supposed to be unfailingly strong?'

'Only in certain women's magazines,' she said crisply, as Daisy reappeared to take away their empty plates.

'Not much for Fido,' said Charles, as she picked them up.

'Good. That's just what I like to see. Apple crumble, blackcurrant tart or jam roly-poly with cream or ice cream?'

After their meal, they walked through to the minute garden at the back of the pub. Perched on a narrow ledge, above the steep drop of the hillside, a few tables with furled umbrellas were surrounded by a mass of green foliage and terracotta pots filled with geraniums.

'The hollyhocks are marvellous in July,' Charles said, as he saw her eye the tall stems already stretching higher than her head.

'I used to embroider hollyhocks and crinoline ladies with watering cans under trellised arches. But I've never seen a real hollyhock before. Bit like stagecoaches and hostelries. You really are completing my education,' she said, laughing, as they moved to the edge of the terrace and gazed out over the sunlit countryside beyond.

'I haven't finished yet,' he said, smiling with pleasure. 'Next comes the cultural bit of the tour. Have you read *Winnie the Pooh*?'

'Yes, I have indeed,' she replied, surprised he should even have heard of one of Aunt Sarah's children's books.

'Good. Well I shall now take you to the Top of the Forest. It's actually called Caesar's Camp, but Milne lived close by so everyone knows that's what he used. We can walk off lunch there. And the view is good. On a clear day, you can see for miles.'

'Sorry about the smell,' he said, as he pushed open the front door of his house in the Cromwell Road and waited for Clare to go ahead of him towards the open door of the sitting room. 'It's Mrs M. Her passion for lavender polish is exceeded only by her passion for Dettol and Vim. I drew the line at Jeyes Fluid. Here, let me take your coat.'

'What a lovely house, Charles,' she said, as she handed the coat to him. 'And a garden as well?' she added, as she moved toward the French windows.

'More a large back yard really, but I've a friend who specialises in town gardens. Amazing what you can do when you know how,' he said, as he dropped his briefcase and turned towards the kitchen.

'I can make tea, but there may not be any cake,' he said seriously. 'Make yourself at home.'

He waved a hand at the sitting room, a light airy room with the same spare furnishing as his office, but a more lived-in look.

She took him at his word, slipped off her high heels and went straight to the French windows. Immediately outside, a small cobbled area had a pool at its centre. The old walls were draped in climbers. One of them, a pink clematis, was covered in bloom. Raised flowerbeds had been shaped to make the whole space look larger and longer than it really was.

She stared at the rich greenery, the varied texture of shrubs and the patches of colour and thought about the long day they'd spent together, the continuous play of sunlight on the rippling countryside that ran, ridge upon ridge, till the chalk finally met the sea.

Suddenly and unexpectedly, across all the years, the back yard in Edward Street came into her mind: the single flower bed made of old bricks, carefully draped with trailing lobelia; the honeysuckle growing up the wall of the outside lavatory; her mother picking a posy to put on the table.

'You're in luck, Clare. Mrs M. left me a lemon drizzle. She sometimes does if

He broke off and put the tray down hastily, as she turned towards him, her eyes bright with tears.

'Clare, what is it? What's wrong? Have I said something? Done something?'

She shook her head helplessly, quite overwhelmed by his concern. He came and put his arms round her, held her close, fished out his handkerchief and gave it to her.

'I thought of the garden at home. before my parents died. I suddenly felt so lonely. Does that ever happen to you?'

'Yes, yes it does,' he said, holding her close and stroking her hair distractedly. 'What can I do to help?'

'It's been such a lovely day. I can't think why I should feel so sad.'

'Has it really been a lovely day?' he asked, looking down at her.

'Yes, I've enjoyed every bit of it,' she said, sniffing, and trying to mop up her tears.

'You've shrunk,' he said. 'I could have sworn you came up to my shoulder just a little while ago.'

She giggled and looked down at her stockinged feet.

'All part of trying to be sensible and grown-up when sometimes I don't feel it,' she said, looking up at him.

He kissed her gently. When she didn't move away, he took her more firmly in his arms and kissed her passionately.

'I should so like to make love to you. Would that be grown-up and sensible?'

'I don't know, but it would be nice.'

* * *

Clare opened her eyes and saw a Spitfire dipping its wing in a brilliant summer sky. She knew it was a Spitfire, because Uncle Jack's friend who worked in the aircraft factory during the war made models of Spitfires on polished metal stands. The one he'd given Uncle Jack had sat on the mantelpiece at Liskeyborough for years.

Clare moved her head to look at the other pictures in Charles's bedroom, but she didn't recognise any of the other aircraft, nor the pictures of mountain peaks, some of them iced with snow.

'Tea, my lady?' said Charles, coming in with a tray and two china mugs. 'No cake, it might spoil your dinner.'

'Goodness, what's the time?'

'Time to get some clothes on, though I must say you look delightful without. Not quite the thing for Andoni's.'

'What's Andoni's?'

'I hope you'll like it. I took a chance while you were asleep and booked a table. It's a Greek restaurant. Not posh at all, but the food's good and the waiters are fun. You said you and Louise were going on holiday to Greece in the summer, so I thought you might enjoy it.'

'What a kind thought. I've never had Greek food.'

'And never made love to an Englishman?'

Clare was quite taken aback. To begin with, she wasn't sure whether it was a statement or a question. She'd only ever made love to Andrew. Did he classify as an Englishman, when he was born in Ireland and was passionate about Ulster?

'What makes you say that?' she asked, hoping he wouldn't notice she was blushing.

'I've been told the only way to make love to an Englishman is to lie back and think of England.'

She laughed and put her free hand out to touch his cheek.

'You're teasing me again,' she said easily.

'I wish I was,' he said, his eyes flickering away from her gaze. 'I know I'm no great shakes in bed.'

'Charles, what *are* you talking about? You were lovely. I was so sad and you were tender and passionate . . . what *do* you mean?'

She sat up in bed, put her mug on the bedside table.

'Now tell me what makes you think that, or can I guess it in one?'

'After today, I'd say you'd guess it in one.'

'Well, she's wrong, completely wrong.'

He smiled, put down his mug of tea and kissed her gently.

'Bless you for saying so. Time we were going,' he reminded her.

'No it isn't,' she said, shaking her head

vigorously. She put her arms around him and kissed him. Moments later, he dropped his dressing gown on the floor and came back into bed.

'How do you like your coffee?' Charles asked. 'Sceto, metrius or glika?'

Clare caught the hint of laughter in his eyes and laughed too.

'Sugar. No spoonful, one spoonful, two spoonful,' the waiter said helpfully, as he brushed crumbs from the tablecloth and wiped perspiration from his forehead. 'Real Greek coffee. Ess strong.'

'He's right,' agreed Charles. 'Take the skin off your mouth if you're not careful. I go for the two spoonful.'

'Right then, I'll try that too. Glika,' she said, smiling at the waiter. 'And the others? Sceto?' she asked, counting on her fingers.

'Sceto, metrius, glika,' he repeated, with a broad grin. 'I teach you speak Greek.'

'I bet he would,' said Charles, as soon as he was out of earshot. 'He'd teach you more than Greek. And I wouldn't blame him.'

He reached for her hand across the small candlelit table.

'I don't know how I'm going to part with you.'

'It's been such a lovely day, Charles. I don't think I'll ever forget it,' she said, looking at him steadily.

He smiled wryly and shook his head.

'What you mean is that you don't really fancy me.'

'No, that's not what I mean,' she said vigorously. 'It's not a question of fancying you. I think you're the nicest man I've met for a long time. I really enjoy being with you. It would be very easy to fall in love with you.'

'Then why not?' he asked, looking distinctly brighter.

'Because I know it wouldn't work out and I just couldn't bear to hurt you. Not after what happened with Caroline.'

'But why shouldn't it work? We get on well, don't we?'

A sudden pulse of anxiety touched his mouth and eyes.

'We do, don't we?' he said, urgently.

'Yes, we do. But getting on well isn't enough. I've learnt that the hard way,' she said softly. 'Don't be cross with me,' she went on, putting her free hand on top of his. 'I don't think I can explain, Charles, but I can imagine the sort of girl who really could make you happy. I'd be so delighted if it was me, but it's not.'

'You really don't think it ever could be?'

'No, I don't. But we can be a lot closer than "just good friends",' she said honestly. 'If you wanted to, that is.'

'You mean we'd see each other sometimes?'

Clare looked at the clear grey eyes watching her. For one moment, she felt such a tenderness for this dear, uncomplicated man and such a weariness with the effort of her own singular life she longed to say words that would make him happy, words that would move her into the protective warmth he was offering her.

'I'd love to see you. Of course I would. As often as I'm over here or you're in Paris, we'll meet. We'll share our secrets and encourage each other.'

'But you won't let me carry you off here and now and live happily ever after,' he said, managing a wry smile.

She beamed at him, shaking her head, relief mixed with pleasure as she saw his spirits lift.

'I think happy ever after is going to take us both a bit longer. But it's worth a try, isn't it?'

CHAPTER SEVENTEEN

'You have your wish, my dear,' said Robert Lafarge, as they walked out of the hotel to the waiting car. 'It will be beautiful for your homecoming.' He looked up at the almost cloudless sky, while they waited for their cases to be loaded into the boot.

'Yes, it will be a lovely evening here, but the clouds may come to meet me,' she said, laughing. 'On any sunny day in Ulster you suddenly see great clouds in the west. The next thing you know, it's pouring with rain. And all the time London basks in the sun. Sometimes it might as well be two different worlds,' she said cheerfully.

'You are excited about your journey? Or is it the attentions of the handsome Monsieur Langley? Something is making your eyes sparkle even more than usual,' he observed dryly, as they settled themselves comfortably in the chauffeur-driven limousine.

'I don't know,' she admitted honestly. 'It seems such a long time since I left Belfast, though it's not even a year ago till July. So much has changed. I don't know how I feel. Perhaps I'm more agitated than excited,' she said easily.

'You will come back, won't you?'

'Robert!' she exclaimed, amazed by the edge of anxiety in his tone. 'What on earth are you thinking of? Why would I not come back?'

He looked sheepish, gazed out of the window at the boarded-up houses below a newly built flyover.

'Perhaps an old love will claim you,' he said flatly, without looking at her.

'If something like that happened, you'd be the first person I'd come and tell.'

'Eh bien.'

She smiled to herself. When Robert said 'Eh bien', it meant that he was satisfied, content, at ease, a meaning not to be found in the dictionary. It reminded her of the first Robert. The way he used to say, 'Well.' It had taken her quite a while to work out this was his own way of saying, 'Yes, so be it.'

Outside the Domestic Terminal, Robert insisted on getting out to see she had a trolley for her cases.

'Bon voyage, chérie', he said, kissing her on both cheeks. 'Come back safely.'

She hugged him and said nothing, because she thought she might cry if she did, and stood watching him drive off to the International Terminal for his flight to Paris, waving to the car even though he probably couldn't see her through the crowds of passengers. Partings were so painful, even when they were only for a short time.

She stood on the escalator and looked down at the pattern of moving people below. All rather different from Auntie Polly going off to Canada with Uncle Jimmy when they were newly-weds. Grange band had turned out in force for them on the morning of their departure. Marched them into Armagh Station with all their family and friends, then lined up on the platform to play 'Auld Lang Syne' as the train steamed out.

'The captain and crew of Vanguard flight VA five, two, three, eight, welcome you aboard . . .'

Clare smiled. The voice was using a prepared script, but the careful pronunciation had done little to modify the stewardess's accent. It had more than a hint of Scots, but that 'eight' was a particular old friend. As her fellow passengers settled themselves, she heard the short vowels and rapid delivery of Ulster voices all around her. Her homecoming had already begun.

The sky stayed clear as they corrected course over the Chilterns and flew north towards Liverpool. The only cloud was over the Lancashire coast. It looked like puffs of smoke from a bonfire. The sea beyond lay still, its clear blue darkening to navy as the sun went west, the slanting light still strong on the long May evening.

She sat looking out of the window, her book unopened on her knee.

'An old love may claim you.'

Robert's words came back to her as the wing dipped and they crossed the County Down coast, flying north-west towards Belfast, where the lough gleamed in the sunlight, the air so clear she could see both the hills of North Down and the Mournes, sharply outlined against the southern sky, now turning to pale gold as the light faded.

With the city below them, she picked out the curves of the Lagan. On the edge of the city, it flowed between patches of woodland. The whole broad, green lowland that led into the heart of Ulster appeared briefly as they flew inland, following an arcing curve that swung them north over the darker, hard-edged hills that bounded the city. Suddenly, the vast mass of Lough Neagh appeared, as they began to lose height, glistening and sparkling in the evening light. All around it, as far as the eye could see, in every direction, rich with the green of summer, edged with hawthorn hedges, white with blossom, the small, irregular fields lay side by side, as well fitted together and as comfortable as the patches in a quilt.

Looking down, anxious not to waste one moment of this extraordinary experience, able to make a map of her world unlike any map she'd ever had before, she saw how ambiguous Robert's words had been. There were more loves that could claim you than the love of a man.

The landing at Nutt's Corner was smooth, but it took her slightly by surprise. One moment there was nothing below the wing but the lough with a fringe of water-loving trees. Next, the hares that had been feeding quietly on the rich grass fringing the runways twitched their ears and scattered in all directions, as the plane touched down and the engines roared into reverse. They taxied slowly towards a long, low building. She had arrived.

'Clare, you're looking powerful well, as they say. Did you have a good flight?'

Harry hugged her, completely disregarding the flow of passengers trying to move through the small, dilapidated building that constituted the reception area.

'It was great. I just wished I'd had longer. I could see for miles. I think I saw the hills of Donegal as we turned over Lough Neagh.'

'Oh you would have. On an evening like this, you'd see most of the north. Come on and we'll see what they've done with your case.'

'New car, Harry?' she asked as they turned out of the airport, between the same hawthorn hedges she had looked down upon.

'D'you like it?'

'Very posh. Is business good?'

He nodded vigorously as they cleared the handful of cars leaving the airport and headed for the city.

'How are Jessie and Fiona?'

'They're grand,' he said, less convincingly.

She looked at him sharply, saw lines around the eyes that she was sure had not been there a year ago. But then, they were both a year older. Harry must be nearing thirty and Jessie was twenty-four in June.

'It was awfully good of you to come for me. I could have got the bus and had a taxi from Victoria Street.'

'Sure, it's a chance to show off,' he said lightly. 'Jessie and I don't go out much, though my mother's happy to babysit,' he went on uneasily. 'You'll see Jessie changed,' he said honestly, 'but then I suppose we all change, whether we like it or not.'

Harry fell silent and Clare studied the pattern of fields and hedgerows till the road bent in a steep horseshoe and began to run rapidly downhill towards the city. The sun was going down into grey-purple cloud. Across the lough, the hills of Down looked more remote now, as the light dimmed towards dusk. They drove through shabby suburbs, where children played on pavements and men stood on street corners.

The rows of back-to-back houses that turned

their gable ends to the main road had not changed, the open spaces where weeds grew high were still there – a legacy of bombs that had missed the docks, or had been dropped on the roofs of weaving sheds that shone in the moonlight in mistake for the regular targets, the aircraft factory and the machine sheds of the shipyard.

Here and there, with windows boarded up, an empty house peered blindly across a street, once quiet, now full of traffic. Dwarfing these tiny houses, a red brick chimney towered above a solid four-storey mill, its windows alight with sudden gleams of gold as the sun slipped from under the cloud and dropped further towards the horizon.

Sadness crept over her as they moved on, down into the heart of the city, past the end of Linenhall Street where two summers ago she'd lived and worked. Up into Shaftesbury Square, on past the front of Queen's. She barely glimpsed tree-lined Elmwood Avenue where she'd worked so hard for four long years. To her surprise she found herself thinking of the roads to Salter's Grange and Liskeyborough, equally familiar when she was a little girl, when she called out the names of farms and houses, places her father had taught her. What she'd expected to feel driving these last two miles through streets and roads she knew so well, she didn't know. What she did feel was a sense of loss, of disappointment. There was no welcome for her from the city she knew best.

'Ach sure there ye are. I thought ye'd a' been another half hour. I say, the style's crushing.'

Jessie turned at the bottom of the stairs, Fiona in her arms, as Harry opened the front door and stepped back to let Clare go ahead of him.

'Hallo, Jessie. It's great to see you.'

She'd have liked to give her old friend a hug, but she couldn't hug her with Fiona in her arms.

'Hallo, Fiona,' she said quietly, touching the baby's arm with her finger.

'Say hallo, Fiona,' said Jessie softly, as the child wriggled shyly in her arms. 'Mind you, we'd get an awful shock if she did, an' her not eight months yet. Say Da-Da.'

Harry held out his arms for the baby, but Jessie seemed not to notice. She went on talking to her while Clare and Harry waited.

'I'll just bring your cases in, Clare,' said Harry, who was beginning to fidget.

'Cases? How long did ye say ye were stayin'?'

Clare laughed for the first time since she'd arrived. This sounded more like the old Jessie.

'I've been working in London for three days, so I have all my stuff from that. Two suits and an evening dress. And all the bits.'

'Listen to it,' Jessie said, addressing the baby, 'an' I'm like a tramp.'

'No you're not,' Clare protested.

'Yer just sayin' that,' she said sharply. 'Come on up an' I'll show you yer room. It was where we used to keep the paint.'

Clare climbed up the wide carpeted stairs behind her, remembering the noise their feet had once made when the whole house was bare boards. The room where they had kept paint, brushes and dustsheets, was now equally transformed. A pretty rose-patterned wallpaper matched curtains and bedspread, the carpet was a paler shade of rose, and white paintwork picked out the deep-set window and the built-in wardrobe below the slightly sloping ceiling.

'What a lovely room, Jessie. Did you choose this paper?'

Jessie shook her head and bent towards the baby.

'No, Harry got it. By the time Fiona came, I'd had enough of decoratin'.'

'Well, it looks lovely, really lovely.'

'You like it then?' said Harry, coming up behind them.

He put down her suitcases under the window and looked pleased as he ran his eye round the room.

'I'll away and put Fiona to bed.'

Jessie disappeared along the landing without a backward glance.

Clare watched her go. When she turned towards Harry she saw him gazing after her. She caught a look that made her heart sink. For a moment, she could think of nothing to say. Then it came to her. Standing in the hall, waiting for Jessie to move, she'd smelt food cooking.

'Can I give you a hand with the meal, Harry,' she said gently.

He nodded sharply as if he didn't trust himself to reply. As they moved back out on to the landing and headed down the stairs, he turned on his heel and smiled at her.

'That would be great,' he managed. 'It sometimes takes Jessie a while to settle her.'

Next morning, Harry brought Clare her breakfast in bed. He'd made her a pot of tea and toasted some soda farl. She loved soda farl, but these pieces had curled up in the toaster and come out burnt at the edges and pale in the middle. Just like old times, she thought, as she removed some of the burnt bits. A pity he'd forgotten the marmalade.

She sat up in bed and munched unhappily. Although it was Saturday, Harry was wearing a suit and hurrying to get away. In another life, he'd once done a Saturday to give her a day out with Andrew, but she'd a feeling that Saturdays were now a regular event. She wondered how much time Harry spent at home. She wondered more if Jessie noticed his presence even when he was there.

'Sure, tell us all about Paris,' Jessie had said, last evening, as she served the roast chicken.

'Well, I have a lovely wee apartment,' began Clare. 'It looks out over the Seine. I can sit and watch the barges at night, all lit up.'

'Are ye not out enjoyin' yerself? Shure I thought Paris was supposed to be romantic.'

'Don't forget Clare's a working lady,' said Harry, as he helped himself to the vegetables they'd prepared and cooked together.

'Have ye found yerself a Frenchman yet?' Jessie went on.

'Oh, the place is full of them. They're not hard to find.'

Clare was pleased that Harry laughed, but Jessie was not amused. She picked irritably at the very good roast chicken and ignored the wine Harry had brought out with such enthusiasm.

'There's not much point bein' in Paris if yer sittin' in every evenin'.'

'Oh I'm very seldom in. I'm often away. And sometimes we have visitors at the bank and they have to be entertained.'

'In evening frocks?'

'Yes, has to be. The bank takes its visitors to the Opéra. It's very posh. All red and gold. Big marble staircase and chandeliers. Paintings and statues everywhere. Harry would love the decor. You'd enjoy the style, Jessie. Some of the women are very elegant.'

'Ach, sure there's no being elegant once there's a baby.'

Clare abandoned the soda bread, poured another cup of tea, looked around the pretty bedroom and wished she hadn't come.

The morning that followed did nothing to improve her spirits. A fine mizzling rain was falling steadily. It brought out the rich greens in the garden, where rolling lawns and new shrubs had replaced the weed-infested space and dank rhododendron shrubbery she remembered so well, but it filled the house with a grey light that the new carpets and beautiful polished furniture did nothing to offset.

When she'd finished breakfast, she had to go to the downstairs cloakroom to have a pee. She waited half an hour for the bathroom while Jessie changed Fiona. Washed and dressed, she went downstairs to find them, but the kitchen was fully occupied by a large woman taking the gas cooker to pieces so she could scrub all the bits. The sitting room was immaculately tidy and stone cold, full of the chill of unused rooms. As she went back upstairs for a sweater, she heard a sound from one of the bedrooms. Through the open door, she saw

Jessie sitting by Fiona's bed reading a story to the sleeping child.

That set the pattern for the day. Everything revolved around Fiona. She herself was a good-natured child, given to sudden smiles and waving of small, podgy arms. Clare had no difficulty in entertaining her in the rare moments when Jessie left them together.

'How is Aunt Sarah?' Clare asked, as they settled in the window seat of the dining room with their coffee after a picnic lunch at the kitchen table.

'She's fine. Can't walk much, but has all her marbles.'

'Can she manage her shopping?'

'Don't know at all. Ye may ask me mother when you go up.'

'I'll be going to see her. What'll I say when she asks for you?'

'I'm grand.'

Clare tried the odd 'Do you remember?' but Jessie was dismissive, if not actually disparaging. Eventually, as one attempt after another came to nothing, she asked Jessie if she did any painting these days.

'Sure there's no more to do,' she said with a short laugh. 'Have ye not looked round yet? Harry has it all done. He got a man in to do the papering and he did the rest.'

'I meant your own painting, watercolour and oils.'

'Ach, for goodness' sake, Clare, how would I have time for that now? Ye don't know what it's like at all.'

'No, I don't, Jessie, but I know most women try to keep up something they're good at.'

'Ach, I wasn't much good. It was just a pastime.' She broke off. 'I think maybe I hear Fiona.'

Clare finished her coffee and listened. She couldn't hear anything.

'Well, what d'you think, Clare?'

'I think it looks wonderful. Far more spacious. And I love the new lighting.'

Harry looked pleased, as Clare stood taking in every detail of the extended gallery. The storeroom had gone, the extra space integrated into the main room.

'But what about storage?'

'Come and see,' he said, a grin on his face that told her how excited he was. 'I'll go first in case there's a paint pot in the wrong place,' he said, looking at her navy trousers and the light, reversible raincoat she was wearing.

She followed him up the steep stairs to the flat. The doors stood open. The kitchen now displayed newly fitted pine units, new cooker, fridge and breakfast bar. The sitting room was ringed with metal shelving, stacked with boxes and cartons; the bedroom was now Harry's office.

'How about this?'

'What a lovely desk, Harry. Where on earth did you find it?'

'In an outhouse once used as an estate office.'

He told her how he'd searched for someone skilled enough to restore the damaged veneer work and someone to match the worn leather. It had taken months to restore the polish where the back had been mouldy with damp, but he'd persevered.

She glanced at the walls of his room. She was not surprised to find a group of prints of well-known houses, mostly Georgian, some very old sepia-coloured prints of his grandparents, two studio portraits of Jessie and a large photograph of Jessie and himself with Fiona held between them.

'Are you sure you won't let me drive you up to Armagh? It's no distance at all.'

'Oh yes it is, Harry. I know the way the work piles up if you're not in the gallery first thing on a Monday morning. But I've some business to do before anyone comes along. I owe you a hundred pounds and an awful lot of favours. I suppose you wouldn't accept interest?'

'You suppose correctly. I would be offended,' he said, trying to look severe.

He walked across to the safe and opened it while she wrote her cheque.

'Are you sure you can afford it, Clare? There's no hurry at all, you know. Things are going well, as you can see.'

'Yes, I can, Harry. And I'm so delighted. You've worked so hard. But I might be broke again some day,' she said laughing, as she handed him the cheque and he put a small red box in her hand.

She stood looking at the box quite unable to speak.

'Oh Clare, I'm sorry. I'm an absolute fool.'

Harry snatched the box from her hand and replaced it with a larger box that now held the two gold rings she'd found under the settle in the house by the forge.

She took them out and touched them, quite overcome by the memories that had flowed back when Harry put the box containing her engagement ring into her hand. She hadn't needed to open it to see the wink of the garnets surrounding the tiny fragment of diamond, nor put it on to feel its snug fit round her finger.

She took a deep breath and looked Harry straight in the eye.

'How is Andrew?'

'He's all right now. But the estate's in a bad way. I've been able to help him a bit, selling stuff,' he said carefully.

Harry had always been honest with her, but she could see he was having doubts about whether or not he ought to say more.

'Go on, Harry, I want to know.'

'I think he has a girlfriend. She's been with him a couple of times when he's brought stuff up here. Tallish, red hair. Didn't catch her name.'

'Ginny?'

'Yes, that's right. Nice girl. D'you know her?'

'Yes, I do. She *is* nice. She taught me to ride.'

'But isn't she his cousin?'

'Only by marriage. Edward was his cousin. Ginny was Edward's half-sister,' she explained, amazed she could feel so calm, when the sight of the little red box had thrown her completely.

'Time I was going for that bus, Harry,' she said briskly. 'Will you keep these for me?'

'Don't you want to take them with you?'

'No, they belong in Ireland. You can charge me rent.'

'I shall,' he said, putting the box with the gold rings back in the safe and standing up. 'A big hug as often as you come home,' he said, putting his arms around her and holding her close.

'Come in, come in, Clarey dear. Sure I'm glad to see you. You're lookin' the best. I think the French capital is agreein' with ye.'

'It's lovely to see you too, Charlie. How's the work going?'

'Not bad, not bad. I've become very pretentious in my old age. I no longer have a sitting room in which nobody sits, I have made it into a writing room. Come in, do. These old wing chairs are far more comfortable than those damned armchairs that go with the settee. I got rid of them. Sure once I sat down in them I couldn't get back up again.'

'I have the same problem at airports,' she said cheerfully. 'They must think all passengers have long legs. If I sit back in their armchairs, my feet don't touch the floor. If I want my feet on the floor, I have to sit up straight, then my back aches,' she went on. 'These are great. Where did you get them?'

'Sale room in Armagh. There's great stuff about if you have the time to look. I go in regular, because they sometimes have books. Job lots. They buy them at auctions, a pound for a boxful and then sell them for a bob or two each. Makes a good profit and I'm happy to buy. But there's some fine old libraries being sold off like that, more's the pity.'

Clare looked round the tiny, cluttered room. Apart from Charlie's desk and the pair of wing chairs that looked down over the uncut grass to where the pump still stood on the far side of the road, there was a settee, entirely covered with books and newspapers, and three lopsided bookcases leaning drunkenly against each other.

The faded wallpaper was covered with sections cut from the one-inch and two and a half inch maps of Salter's Grange, sketches of roads, fields, the location of derelict houses and lists of books to be consulted, all stuck up with drawing pins. On a calendar of Majestic Canada, hanging on a nail, she could see her own name written in large letters in the square allocated to the third Thursday in May.

'I'm sure you see great changes since you've been away. New houses, roads and schools and suchlike.'

'No, actually, I don't think I've noticed anything like that. Perhaps I haven't been in the right places. I did see a bridge for the new motorway from the bus.'

'I'm afraid I was being sarcastic,' he said with a laugh. 'I'm sure you know that Armagh Rural District has great plans. They have one thousand, nine hundred and twenty-four houses unfit for habitation. Twenty-four per cent of all rural housing. They're planning a programme to replace them. They expect it to take thirty years.'

'Thirty years?' she repeated. 'You're joking, Charlie.'

'I wish I was. I don't know what's the matter at all, things are just not getting any better. Not round here anyway. Sure, the urban district needs five hundred and fifty houses just to clear the slums in the town, never mind start housing the young couples. Listen to this, Clarey.'

He scuffled down a pile of copies of the *Armagh*

Guardian, found the one he wanted. '"*The building of houses is, as you know, a very slow process, especially in Armagh,*" he read. 'That's the Chairman of the City Council. I'm sure it's not like that in France.'

'No, it's not, Charlie. There's an awful lot of new business and industry. But then there's American money coming in.'

'And sure what's to hinder us getting American industry in here as well? This country is being run for the gentry and the landowners. They're doing fine. Them and a few big people in linen and textile machinery. But they may watch out. When Japan and Germany get back on their feet, they'll take the legs from under them.'

He threw back his head and laughed.

'Ach dear, Robert would have thrown me out if I'd said that in front of him, God bless him and rest his soul. I think he thought I was a communist forby being in the IRA. Did you know they were active again?'

'No, I'm afraid I only hear what gets as far as *Le Monde.*'

'An' I'm not too surprised it didn't make it. One meal lorry and one culvert down near the border in Fermanagh. Not exactly strategic targets. But de Valera condemned it anyway. Him and Brookeborough, six of one and half a dozen of the other, as far as go-ahead governments are concerned. I think ye're better off in France, Clarey.'

'That reminds me,' said Clare suddenly. 'Matilda Wolfe Tone. That's what she decided. She said she was French, not Irish. She sent her son to the cavalry school at St Germain and he went and fought with Napoleon. She even managed to get herself a French pension.'

Clare opened up the back of her handbag, took out folded sheets of handwritten text and gave it to him. He scanned the lines avidly.

'This is great. I had a feeling the same lady was no weeping widow. It was good of you to do all that work for me.'

'I wish I had, Charlie, but I can take no credit. All I did was translate it from French. My friend Marie-Claude did the work. She's gone back to do another degree in history. She says you've given her a good idea. She hasn't decided yet, but she might take up the role of Irish émigrés in French political life.'

'Well now, isn't that very interesting. Will you give her my kindest regards? I am much in her debt,' he said, as he laid the neatly written sheets on his desk.

Cycling back to Liskeyborough in the last of the evening light, the smell of hawthorn heavy on the evening air, Clare decided that her visit to Charlie was the best thing yet. Amidst all the disappointments, the hours she had just spent stood out like an island of pleasure in a sea of discomforts.

It had never occurred to her how hard it would be to be a visitor in the home of old and dear friends, seeing their life at close quarters, picking up the tension and awkwardness between them. She'd been so miserable most of the time she'd been with Jessie and Harry, she was positively looking forward to going to see her grandparents. In the event, that had turned out even worse, from the first moment she'd stepped into the house.

'Hallo, yer a stranger. Put yer case in the room outa the way. Mrs Loney is due anytime to do the turns.'

'How are you, Granny?'

'Ach, just the same. An' yer Granda gets deafer. He only hears when ye tell him to come to his tea.'

'What about William?'

'What about him?' she said bitterly. 'He's had a dozen jobs since he left school and lost them all. He won't be told anything. Not the same boyo. All he's interested in is motorbikes and cars. If it weren't for wantin' the money to buy one or other, he'd likely not go to work at all.'

Clare sighed as she turned off the main road and took the narrow road through Annacramp, past the new Grange School that had replaced

300

Aunt Sarah's schoolroom in the 1930s. The south-facing hedge beyond where Alfie Nesbitt used to live was full of honeysuckle. She'd like to stop and pick some, but Granny Hamilton seemed not to care about flowers any more. It was Granda who filled the tub by the door with marigolds and nasturtiums and Granny who didn't want them in the house because of the mess they made when they died.

Monday had been a difficult day, her attempts at conversation no better received by her grandmother than by Jessie. She'd retreated to the workshop and fared slightly better with her grandfather, despite his difficulty with his hearing aid, but in the end, she'd gone for a walk, tramping up the road to climb Cannon Hill.

She'd stayed there till tea time, hoping the presence of Auntie Dolly and William might make things easier.

'Hello, Clare, how are you?' said William, coming through the door and drawing up to the tea table in oil-stained dungarees.

Granda looked at him severely. He got up, ran his hands under the tap at the kitchen sink, wiped them roughly and sat down again.

'How's Paris?'

'Great,' she replied, smiling at him.

She was amazed at the change in his manner towards her. It was the first time she could ever remember him saying 'Hallo', without having been told to, and never before had he shown the slightest interest in her affairs.

'Would you like to see the new lamp and saddle I've put on your bicycle, Clare?' he said as they finished their meal.

Granda hadn't been able to make out what he was saying. Granny assumed he was getting out of the washing up as usual and Dolly looked at Clare blankly, as puzzled by this sudden change of attitude as she was.

As they walked towards the barn where he kept the bicycle, Clare made enquiries about his present job, but William was striding along so quickly she had difficulty keeping up with him.

'A bicycle's all very well when yer young, but I want a car,' he began, when they stepped inside the low stone building. 'Dolly says the money's great where you are, Clare. Will you lend me a hundred pounds?'

It was raining steadily when Harry drove her to Nutt's Corner the following Saturday. Jessie hadn't wanted to come. The car, she said, made Fiona sick. They'd said their goodbyes in the hall while Harry put her cases in the boot.

'Don't be long till yer back,' said Jessie.

Clare wondered if she meant it, or whether she was just saying the traditional phrase out of habit.

She waved to her as they slid slowly down the drive. Looking back, she saw Jessie slowly waving Fiona's arm.

'Thank you, Harry dear, you've been so good to me. I'll give you a ring any time I'm in London and I can talk to you at the gallery. I know Jessie's not herself, but I'll have to think about it. Take care of yourself, won't you.'

He hugged her tight and kissed her cheek.

'What would I do without you, Clare?'

She felt tears trickle down her cheeks as she picked up her cases and headed for the check-in desk. There had been good things, and Harry and the success of the gallery had been amongst them. But overall it was a week she'd never want to live through again.

She watched the terminal buildings slide by, the rain-streaked window of the Vanguard blurring their outline. The engines roared and for a few brief moments she glimpsed the small, sodden fields, the white blossom dropping, its gleaming softness gone. The lough, grey and misted, lurched uncomfortably to one side as the wing dipped and the aircraft turned upwards and eastwards. Greyness enveloped her, clinging and featureless. Like the long minutes and hours of cold and boredom she'd endured all through the last week.

She wondered if she would ever come again, or if, like Matilda Wolfe Tone, she would decide she was French, her life to be lived in another country.

The grey mist began to thin. Gleams of light caught the rain-drops running off the wing. Then suddenly, joyously, the light returned. Sunlight poured down on the mountains of pure white cloud that now lay below them. She felt herself relax; the effort of the past few days flowed away. No doubt there were lessons to be learnt. No doubt, indeed. But it could all wait. Here and now she was happy and knew she was happy. This time she really was going home.

CHAPTER EIGHTEEN

When Clare opened the door of the room she shared with Louise on the following Monday morning, she gasped in amazement. The room was completely empty. Gone were the high desks and stools, the ancient bookcases and filing cabinets, the straight-backed chairs and worn strips of carpet. The only sign of life in the deserted room was a huge sheet of wrapping paper attached to one pocked and pitted wall. She looked at it and laughed.

'Welcome home,' it said in English, the big letters written with a one-inch paintbrush. Below it, in biro, a further message in French: 'Come and find me, I've missed you, Louise.'

For a moment Clare stood looking round the empty room. It suddenly dawned on her that all was quiet. At long last, the hammering and banging had stopped. She turned on her heel, set off towards the corridor that led to the new suites and was confronted by Madame Japolsky, who shot out of her office opposite at the sound of footsteps.

'Ah, Mam'selle 'Amilton, you have had a good holiday?' she began. 'Monsieur Lafarge wishes to see you immediately,' she went on, without the slightest pause for any reply to her question.

She edged past Clare so that she could peer up at Louise's notice through her minute, gold-framed spectacles.

'When you have seen him, I shall show you to your new office,' she added severely. 'Naturally, there will be new arrangements.'

Clare crossed the banking hall and climbed the familiar flights of stairs, walked along the familiar landings. Every time she passed those elaborate gold frames, she thought of Harry, just as she had done when Paul had conducted her to Robert's room the very first time and ushered her into the royal presence like a courtier of Louis Quinze himself. Dear Harry. He'd always been so good to her. Unpacking her suitcases the previous day, she'd thought about the lovely home he'd created, about Jessie wandering round it, half in a dream, relating only to little Fiona.

'Viens.'

As she opened the door, she found Robert was halfway across the room to meet her.

'Good. You look well,' he said, kissing her cheek.

His telephone rang and he turned away, strode back to his desk and picked it up. 'Paul, I am engaged. I do not wish to be disturbed. No, not by anyone. I will tell you when I am free.'

Grinning broadly, he waved her to an armchair by the window.

'Did you have a good holiday?'

She laughed and smiled warmly at him.

'Madame Japolsky asked me that. But *she* didn't wait for a reply. I've been trying to think what I'd say if you asked me.'

'I am quite willing to wait for a reply,' he said, settling back in his armchair.

'It was a mixed experience, Robert, and not a very happy one. There were good things. I had a lovely evening with my old friend Keith Harvey, and Charlie Running was so pleased to see me, so were Aunt Sarah and Mrs McGregor. But the visit to my grandparents was rather depressing. They are ageing visibly and aren't at all happy. My brother asked me for money before we'd been together for five minutes.'

'Did you give it to him?'

'No. I told him I'd have to talk it over with Granda Hamilton. He wanted the money to buy a car and I was uneasy about that. He once broke his leg riding a motorbike he'd taken without permission. He's unreliable about most things. Granda said he thought a car wouldn't be wise.

So I didn't give him the money. I did give Granny money for any clothes he might need. But he said I was mean, and didn't speak to me again after that.'

Robert nodded thoughtfully.

'And your friend Jessie. Was she pleased to see you?'

'I really don't know. Harry was. But Jessie was quite sharp with me at times. Something's wrong, but I don't know enough about having babies to understand. I'll have to talk to Marie-Claude. Jessie seems totally preoccupied with Fiona, spends far too much time with her, and almost none with Harry. He's as loving as ever, but it can't be easy for him. She's not the girl he fell in love with.'

Robert nodded again. 'And did you meet up with Andrew or your friend Ginny?'

'Not directly. I found out from Harry that Ginny is now Andrew's girlfriend,' she said matter-of-factly. 'I suppose I should have guessed that when she didn't write to me. Ginny's always been fond of Andrew. When we were engaged, I used to be surprised she was never jealous. But I'm sad about Ginny too. We came very close to each other when Teddy died. I miss her. But they seem to be very happy together. I saw a photograph of them in a magazine at the airport. At a Hunt Ball,' she ended, laughing wryly.

'So, you are glad to be back.'

'Yes, I am. My empty apartment was far

more welcoming than either of the places where I stayed. Paul had arranged some flowers from the courtyard for me, and Louise had put something for my supper in the fridge. The minute I arrived, Madame Dubois came to see if there was anything I needed,' she went on, smiling. 'I think I might do as Charlie suggests and become a Frenchwoman like Matilda Wolfe Tone.'

He smiled unexpectedly.

'She was the wife of the revolutionary in whom Charlie had an interest?'

'Yes, that's the one,' she said, nodding. 'I don't know quite where she fits into his book, but it seems to me she made a far better life in France until she went to America. Charlie says Ulster is simply not moving with the times.'

'Do you think he's right?' he asked soberly.

'Yes, sadly, I do. Even Keith, who's a very easygoing man, says all the urgent questions are being ignored. He's planning to go to Australia when he's had two years' experience at his present school.'

'I am sad for you. I, too, went back to my part of France and found that what I'd left behind was better left behind. But I am glad you have the wisdom to accept what you see. The worst thing one can do in life is go on seeing situations as once they were, or as you wish they might continue to be. Both individuals and groups fall prey to such fantasy. It is a very dangerous thing.'

He gathered himself and straightened up in his armchair.

'It looks as if we shall have an opportunity to dine together later this week,' he said, waving a hand towards a pile of papers on the desk behind them. 'Bordeaux,' he added.

'Good,' she said, smiling. 'This time, thanks to you, I know the wine but not the region. Usually it's the other way round.'

'I shall want to hear much more about your visit then, but meantime, I have a favour to ask of you. You must refuse if you feel uneasy, but I very much hope you will say yes.'

'I shall certainly want to say yes, Robert. What is it?'

'Emile Moreau's farewell party next week. It will be a large affair. As well as Emile's own family and guests, we will be asking important customers, particularly those he's been involved with in recent years. There will be some government ministers and some colleagues from the financial world,' he said solemnly. 'Including your friends the St Clairs,' he added, more cheerfully. 'I shall have to make the inevitable speech, but I should like you to present the gift from his colleagues.'

'But why me, Robert? I like Emile very much, but there are so many people who have known him much longer. Surely one of them would be more appropriate.'

To her surprise, Robert laughed.

'I thought you'd protest. But I have good reasons for my request. Emile is a shy man. There is considerable interest in his retirement in the serious newspapers and the financial journals. We shall have to admit the press and submit Emile to being photographed. He may tolerate it better if you are by his side. He always seems easier in your company.'

'Does he?'

'Yes, he does. I have observed,' he said crisply. 'Besides, I need a young face in these photographs. Yours is the youngest I've got,' he said, decisively.

'May I ask why?'

'Yes, you may,' he said, nodding, as he stood up, collected the pile of documents on his desk and handed them to her. 'The photographs taken at this event reflect upon the bank. There is no better way of declaring our perspective on the future than by having an attractive young woman among all the old-timers.'

Clare smiled and shook her head. Robert had made up his mind. And, when he had, as always, he was able to find good reasons to support his decision.

'Yes, I'll do it,' she said, smiling. 'You've picked the right week. I have a new dress that should be ready in time.'

'Good,' he said, looking pleased. 'I'll ensure that there is an appropriate interval between the bank and the Champs-Elysées in which to prepare yourself.' he said, as he walked with her to the door. 'Unlike the last time we dined!'

'Well, Clare, what do you think?' demanded Louise, as Madame Japolsky shut the door behind her. She took off her jacket and dropped her shoes on the carpet.

'Can't quite believe it,' Clare replied, as she surveyed their new retreat. The modern furniture reminded her of Charles Langley's office: teak desks, a glass coffee table, swivel chairs upholstered in soft leather. But the colours were gentler than in Charles's room. Grey and pink on the walls to match the carpet, white on the tall windows looking out on to the cobbled courtyard. On the floor a soft, rose-pink carpet on which Louise was luxuriously curling and uncurling her toes.

'I hope you took in Madame's strictures about the use of the bathroom, Clare,' said Louise, pulling a face.

Clare giggled. 'I liked the bit about not cooling wine in the bidet,' she said, grinning. 'I'd never have thought of that if she hadn't mentioned it.'

'I'm so glad to see you back, Clare. I've moved your things as best I could,' she explained, as Clare began to open her drawers and take out what she needed for the morning's work.

'Was it awful leaving all your family and friends?' Louise asked anxiously. 'I cry every time I leave Ravenna, though I love it here,' she said, as she took down a dictionary from the bookcase and unscrewed the cap of her fountain pen.

'Not as bad as I expected. I'll tell you all about it. D'you think we'll manage a lunch hour today? I'd love to take you to Franco's. It's been my turn for ages now and we never coincide.'

'Ah, but we will, we will. I've bearded Madame in her lair. We've got the two weeks in July we wanted and I've made a provisional booking. Two weeks in Greece without le grand Monsieur. How about that?'

'Wonderful, just wonderful,' Clare replied, as she took a pad of lined paper from a deep drawer. 'Meantime,' she said, laughing, 'I shall be spending the morning in Bordeaux.'

'Good, you are home already. I've been thinking of you all day,' said Marie-Claude, the moment Clare picked up the phone. 'Has your dress arrived?'

'Yes, it came yesterday. I do hope you like it. It's the first one I've chosen without you to help me.'

'But, chérie, you are a good pupil. You have outgrown your teacher. Will you tell me the colour, or is it a surprise?'

'I never thought of surprising you. What a lovely idea. Yes, I shall keep it a dark secret. I'm dying to see you in evening dress. I'm sure you will look lovely and Gerard will look terribly distinguished.'

Clare heard Marie-Claude laugh. She muttered about Gerard's cavalier attitude to evening dress.

'I'm not sure we'll even get speaking to each other if the American ambassador turns up,' Clare said suddenly. 'If he does, Robert will pretend he doesn't understand a word of English rather than lose face with his mid-west accent and I won't be able to leave his side all evening.'

'Don't worry. I shall take my opera glasses and peer at you from afar,' she replied, teasing her. 'But the moment you spy a day off, I insist we have lunch. I'm dying to tell you about my studies. Prepare to nod indulgently while I bore you to death. Now, I must go. I intend to lie in the bath for ages. I hope you are going to do the same.'

'Yes, I am. I don't think I've ever managed a bath before an evening engagement,' she said. 'I wish I wasn't so horribly nervous,' she added, honestly.

'Cherie, I don't believe it,' Marie-Claude replied, her voice full of amazement. 'You have only to give Emile his prize for being good. He will kiss you no doubt. Do you mind that?'

'Oh no. It's not that. I think Emile is a dear man. Right from my first week he helped me with all sorts of things. No, it's the photographs I'm dreading. I look horrible in photographs.'

'And when were you last photographed, chérie? On the beach at Deauville playing cricket, perhaps?'

'I don't remember. I suppose it was a long time ago.'

'And probably on someone's old box Brownie?'

'Yes,' she said, laughing. 'How clever of you. I think you're right. Jessie's mother had one and I remember Aunt Sarah taking a picture of Jessie and me. The sun was in my eyes or I blinked. I looked most peculiar anyway.'

'You really mustn't worry, Clare. These Press people know what they're doing. Just smile *gently* if they ask you to. When you present Emile's gift, look at no one but Emile.'

'I wouldn't anyway.'

'Well, there you are. You see, you know what to do instinctively. I'm sure the evening will be a great success. You will probably captivate the American ambassador. Gerard will be triumphant and I shall glow with pride and reflected glory. Go and have your bath. I shall think of you. Once you begin I'm sure you won't be nervous at all. Good luck.'

Clare didn't enjoy her bath. She lay there thinking of all the things that could go wrong: from her knickers falling down, to spilling her wine, tripping over her few words to Emile, or mistranslating some important comment from a foreign visitor.

'Come on, Clare. What *is* wrong with you?' she demanded, as she sat naked in front of her dressing table, an array of bottles, brushes and pencils lined up in order of use in front of her.

'Maybe it's the dress,' she said to herself. 'Perhaps it's unlucky.' Auntie Polly used to think certain colours were unlucky. And pearls, of course. 'Pearls for tears, Clare,' was what she used to say. Well, that was no problem. She hadn't got any pearls. In fact, the only decoration she was wearing tonight was a tiny spray of two yellow rosebuds, a tribute to Emile, a passionate gardener, who intended to devote part of his new-found leisure to growing roses.

'There's nothing to be done but get on with it. If it's going to be awful, it'll still be over by midnight. If it's not, you'll feel a fool for having worried yourself silly.'

She did her best, but the sense of anxious tension just wouldn't go away. She left putting on her dress to the last possible moment because she kept having to go and pee, yet the moment she put it on, she felt better.

She picked up her evening bag and checked the contents. Key, hanky, powder, lipstick, slim notepad, biro, supply of Robert's cards. She counted the remaining Anadin in the paper strip. Three lots should be enough: Robert, herself, and perhaps some other poor soul. She was amazed at the way men who regularly suffered from headaches never thought of carrying tablets, especially when they had so many pockets.

The June evening was so warm she decided not to bother with a wrap of any kind. She would go as she was and probably be grateful for her bare shoulders and back when she reached the even warmer restaurant. She glanced in the mirror to make sure her roses were lying easily on the single shoulder strap, then went and stood by the window looking out at the sunlight on the river.

Robert's car drew up almost immediately. To her amazement, Robert himself sat beside his chauffeur. He was looking profoundly uncomfortable.

'I was ready early, so I came to save Gilles an extra journey,' he explained, with a certain lack of conviction.

'Oh good, I wasn't looking forward to arriving by myself.'

'Why ever not?' he asked sharply, as he opened the door for her and climbed in beside her.

'It's silly, I know, and I've scolded myself thoroughly, but I'm nervous.'

To her surprise and delight, he smiled broadly. 'Oh good, so am I.'

She felt the tension ease as Gilles drove sedately

along the quay and turned towards the Arc de Triomphe.

'We're still early, Gilles. Can you take the longer route, please?'

'Certainly, monsieur.'

'We are reprieved. How shall we spend our leisure?' he asked. She thought for a moment.

'We could discuss the international monetary situation,' she said slowly, with as serious a look as she could manage. 'Or I could tell you a joke,' she added wickedly.

He laughed and sat back more comfortably in his seat.

'You look extremely lovely this evening,' he said, as matter-of-factly as if he were commenting on a balance sheet. 'Why have you never worn green before? It suits you particularly well.'

She blushed and laughed at herself. 'Do you really want to know?'

'Most certainly, I do.'

'My school uniform was green and I vowed when I left school I would never wear green again.'

'And you actually changed your mind. How extraordinary,' he said severely. 'Just how did this unlikely event occur?'

She smiled to herself, comforted. If Robert could tease her, he must already be feeling a lot easier than when he'd arrived at her apartment.

'I tried on the model dress, just to please the

Madame, who was being so helpful. I liked the feel of it. I was going to ask if they could make it up in another colour, but as I turned round, I saw the girl who had come to pin the hem. She was looking up at me with big round eyes. So I asked her if she liked it. She just kept nodding. She's a very shy girl. But I knew then the dress was right. Perhaps she was seeing something I couldn't see.'

'She certainly was. I think Madame St Clair will be proud of you.' He settled himself more comfortably and looked at her sideways. 'Now tell me a joke, please, before we arrive.'

'What is smooth and yellow and highly dangerous?' she asked, falling back on the last series of jokes Philippe had entertained them with before he went away to school.

'I do not know,' he said solemnly. 'What is smooth and yellow and highly dangerous?'

'Shark-infested custard.'

Robert was still grinning as the car drew up outside the restaurant in the Champs-Elysées. The door of their car was opened by an elegant figure, so beautifully uniformed he looked as if he might have survived the Revolution. Robert gave her his hand and, as she stepped out, she saw below her satin evening shoes that red carpet had been laid across the pavement. Ahead of her, the entrance to the restaurant was banked with flowers, their perfume wafting towards her on the warm evening air.

'Monsieur Lafarge, ici, s'il vous plaît Mademoiselle, ici, ici.'

Clare registered the sudden flare of a flash bulb. From two clusters of young men twisting themselves into the most uncomfortable positions came a stream of requests. 'This way, monsieur. Mademoiselle, this way, please.'

To her surprise, Robert smiled obligingly, took her by the elbow and made sure all the young men had their opportunity. He bowed to them when they had finished and ushered her into the foyer, as magnificently decorated with flowers as the entrance had been.

'Now, Mademoiselle Clare, to work,' he whispered. 'You've made an excellent beginning.'

Marie-Claude was quite right. From the moment she set foot on the red carpet, she was too busy to be nervous. She remembered all Marie-Claude had taught her. How to sit when wearing a low-cut dress. Which of the phalanx of glasses to use for water. How to avoid drinking too much wine when waiters constantly refilled your glass. Paul had briefed her on how to address ambassadors and other dignitaries, while Jean-Pierre Crespigny had shown her when not to translate a greeting or phrase the context made clear.

By the time she stood up to present Emile with

his gift, a good meal and a cautious amount of wine had settled the butterflies in her stomach. Moving past the tables that surrounded the small dance floor she felt perfectly easy, prepared to say whatever words came to mind should the one's she'd prepared desert her.

'Bravo, Clare.'

She recognised the familiar voice. It was Gerard St Clair. She did not turn towards him but she smiled with delight as she stepped up on to the dais where Emile was waiting.

'Clare, you are wearing roses,' he said quietly.

'For your future, Emile. May it be full of roses, of every kind.'

She added a few extra words to those her colleagues had suggested, handed him the cut-glass rose bowl and an envelope containing a very large cheque. The flash bulbs popped all around them, but neither she nor Emile paid the slightest attention to them as he kissed her cheeks and thanked her.

It was only as she made her way back to her place beside Robert that she noticed a young man with dark hair and even darker eyes. He was looking at her as if she was the only woman in the whole glittering assembly.

'Clare you look wonderful,' said Marie-Claude, touching her shoulder gently and smiling at her in the mirror.

'Oh Marie-Claude, how lovely to see you.' Clare turned and kissed her. 'I hoped you'd appear, even if you didn't need to. Your nose never shines.'

'True, but, unlike you, I've been enjoying my wine. I must go and make myself comfortable. Don't go away, I have something to say to you.'

Turning back to the mirror, Clare watched her friend weave her way through the crowded powder room, full of the rustle of gowns, the mingling of perfumes and the laughter of women released from the formalities of a presentation dinner. As she pressed powder carefully on her warm face, she was suddenly aware of the picture the broad expanse of glass reflected back. It was one thing standing in front of her own long mirror at home, anxiously checking every detail, quite another to see herself like this, as she must appear to others. The emerald silk dress did look wonderful, she had to admit, its style and cut, the way it complemented her creamy skin and dark curls. The little seamstress had been absolutely right.

As she carefully applied lipstick, she saw herself set against a background of self-possessed women, moving to and fro behind her, for the most part what Ronnie would call 'the great and the good'. Women of all ages, some severely formal in their dress, silver-haired and wearing velvet and pearls, some bedecked in jewels, some wearing tiny orchids, others large corsages of flowers. A stunning blonde in a red dress. An awkward-looking woman, heavily sequinned. They greeted friends, adjusted skirts, or necklaces, tucked back strands of hair from chignons, ran damp fingers along eyebrows. She smiled to herself. She looked perfectly at home amongst them, as if she had been attending such occasions all her life. The face that looked back at her now, smiling with pleasure as she caught sight of her friend returning, seemed to say that she was managing to enjoy herself after all.

'Cherie, have you noticed that young man at the next table but one?' asked Marie-Claude, bending over her and whispering.

'Dark hair and eyes?'

'Yes, and distinctly handsome. Do you know him?'

'No, never seen him before.'

'His eyes have never left you. With the greatest of discretion, he has watched you all evening.'

Clare laughed and shook her head.

'What's so funny?'

'And all the time he's been watching me, you've been watching him, just as discreetly. You're as bad as Gerard,' she said, squeezing her arm. 'But can you really believe it, Marie-Claude? Can you?'

'Believe what, chérie?'

'Tonight. Here and now. Your protégée. The poor, sad little refugee from a broken love affair who came to your door last July. You have been

323

so kind and taught me so much. How can I ever thank you?'

'And what about me?' Marie-Claude protested. 'A poor mother with an empty nest, wondering what to do with the rest of her life. So depressed I couldn't even appreciate my dear Gerard.'

Marie-Claude broke off suddenly. The room was emptying around them.

'My dear we must go,' she said quickly, walking her to the door. 'Robert may need you just now. I'll ring tomorrow morning, late, or until I catch you, to hear what happens next.'

They parted as Marie-Claude reached her table. Gerard stood up to help her to her place, looked at Clare and gave her a tiny wink.

Suitably refreshed during the interval for the presentation and speeches, the band put away the light classical music they'd played during the meal and launched into a selection from Glen Miller with considerably more enthusiasm. As Clare sat down again, she could feel her feet tapping. She wondered if Robert ever danced and whether anyone else might ask her. She longed to dance.

For a few moments no one moved except the waiters bringing brandy and liqueurs and serving more coffee. She was puzzled. Here was this lovely floor, this marvellous music. Why on earth was no one dancing? The band paused between numbers. She saw Robert nod across the table to Emile.

324

They exchanged glances. Emile rose in his usual dignified manner, excusing himself to his elderly sister, and came and stood behind her chair.

'Mademoiselle Clare, may I have the honour . . .'

'That would be lovely,' she said, as he drew her chair away, took her hand and led her to the dance floor.

The band struck up immediately. To Clare's absolute amazement, Emile danced her vigorously round the empty floor to the strains of 'American Patrol'. She was so delighted to find herself dancing again after so long and to that particular tune, she hardly noticed the discreet round of applause, after which other couples joined them on the floor and Emile had to be more circumspect in his manoeuvres.

'Thank you, my dear,' said Emile, bowing slightly, as he took her back to her place. 'You make *me* feel young again. See what you can do for Robert.'

Robert grunted as Clare settled herself beside him. She hadn't realised quite what good friends the two men were till this evening. She wondered if it was because they were both widowers. Perhaps having to remake a life after great loss had created a special bond between them.

She looked at Robert encouragingly. To her surprise, he blushed. Given the heat and the amount of very good wine they'd all drunk, his change in colour was almost certainly invisible, but she knew Robert was quite aware of it.

'Have all those pressmen gone home?' he asked, leaning across the large, round table to where Paul sat entertaining an official from the Ministry of Finance and his wife.

'Yes, monsieur. They were given supper with the band and have gone away happy.'

'Humph.'

Robert straightened himself up, ran a finger round the left side of his collar and stood up.

'Mademoiselle Clare,' he said formally, as he looked down at her.

Dear Robert, she thought, a wave of tenderness sweeping over her. That gesture with his collar had gone straight to her heart. She'd known it for some time even if she'd not admitted it herself, that here was a man just as vulnerable as the first Robert. The one a country blacksmith, the other the chairman of a leading French bank. A whole world of time and distance separated them, yet each was as much prey to simple anxiety as the other. She wondered, could that be why she loved them both?

'Thank you,' she said, smiling.

They walked to the floor and began to dance. Robert was no dancer, but he knew the steps and went through them meticulously, though without much relation to the music, so they managed well enough. After a couple of circuits, he began to listen to the tune and to relax. By the third number in the sequence, he began to move with the rhythm. She could see he was almost enjoying himself.

'You love dancing, don't you?' he said, choosing a more adventurous turn, as the band increased the tempo.

'Yes, I do. I've always loved it from the very first time I danced. It was at school, with Jessie, in green knickers. I really do prefer a dress.'

Robert laughed.

'Emile is right: you make me feel young. But not young enough to dance into the small hours,' he added sadly. 'I shall be leaving shortly with Emile and his sister, but you are to stay. Enjoy yourself. You've done a good job this evening. I wish I could be there to see Henri Lavalle's face when he opens his copy of *Le Monde* and sees you smiling back at him.'

'And you too, Robert,' she reminded him.

'Yes,' he said thoughtfully. 'He may be amused to see that I now possess a shirt with a collar.'

Robert and Emile leaving was a sign for the more senior guests to follow. The man from the Ministry of Finance and his wife said their goodbyes and Paul promptly asked Clare to dance. He was a splendid dancer, his footwork so precise and yet fluid they appeared to float round the floor without the slightest effort.

'That was marvellous, Paul. I think I need another glass of water,' she said, laughing, as they stopped in the middle of the floor and made their way back to the empty table.

'Would you like some as well?' she asked, as she picked up the jug.

'No, my dear Clare. I never drink water when there is wine,' he said cheerfully, reaching across the table.

Before he could turn back towards her, a figure appeared behind her chair. It was the young man with the dark hair and the even darker eyes.

'Clare,' he said, without more ado. 'May I have the pleasure of the next dance?'

As she stepped on to the dance floor and he held out his arms to her, Clare knew she'd dance with no one else that evening. Before he had even spoken to her, she'd read a quiet determination in his manner. He would be discreet, as Marie-Claude had observed. He would be courteous, as indeed he had been, in not approaching her till all possible duty had been done. But now that he had spoken she sensed he would not let her go.

They moved together easily. Less flamboyant than Paul, yet full of a pent-up energy, she sensed he was matching their steps before he spoke.

'Let me introduce myself, Clare,' he said smiling. 'My name is Christian Moreau. I have been grateful to my dear uncle often enough, but never more than tonight. He said I would like you, an understatement worthy of the English.'

Clare laughed, could think of nothing whatever to say. But Christian needed no reply. He looked down at her, his tanned cheeks and dark hair so close she caught the hint of his after-shave, his eyes deep and intense.

'We shall dance till the band goes home and then I shall take you to a nightclub in Place Pigalle. There we can dance till dawn. I think you will enjoy that.'

CHAPTER NINETEEN

'So, I am going to lose you,' said Robert unexpectedly, as they settled themselves with coffee on the balcony of their hotel. Although the evening was warm and pleasant, the few inhabitants of the dining room had not even stirred when Clare and Robert moved towards the balcony doors. They sat on in the stuffy gloom created by the heavy furniture and the rich velvet curtains, the hot-plates on the sideboard, the candles on the tables, completely cut off from the long fingers of sunlight that picked out the sharp limestone crags and rich green foliage plunging down into the deep-cut valley below.

Swollen by unexpected late summer rain, a small tributary of the Tarn rushed noisily over its rocky bed, swirled vigorously beneath the cliff opposite their viewpoint and lapped gently on a beach of white pebbles directly below them.

'Who told you that, Robert?' she asked, puzzled, as she poured his coffee.

All through their meal, they had talked about the proposals in hand. Robert was not entirely sure the old-fashioned hotel could transform itself into a centre for climbing and water sports, but he had listened attentively to the group of businessmen who were putting up half the money.

In the afternoon, he'd insisted on being driven round the surrounding area. Clare was intrigued by the rugged limestone country, the sudden gushing streams, the rich vegetation clinging to steep slopes. An empty landscape with few patches of cultivation except where the river flowed in a wider valley and cattle grazed in the rich meadows.

They'd stood looking across at the hotel from the other side of the steep valley, driven slowly through the nearby villages, visited a local viewpoint. Robert had agreed to make a decision before they left in the morning. Now, he asked her what she thought.

'I think they have the right idea,' she said. 'So many people want to escape from the cities and be active, not just sit around. After all that's what most of them have to do, most of the time, during working hours. Other parts of France have developed water sports and rock climbing, I know, but this place has both. And there's good walking too, once they signpost the paths. That means you have a spread of activities. Safer than having just one. Even in sport and pastimes fashions change.'

He'd seemed particularly pleased by her comments, though he'd said little.

There was a comfortable pause. She decided to ask the question that had been in her mind all day. 'Why did you bring me with you, Robert, when everyone speaks French?'

'Do you want the professional reason, or the personal one,' he replied, crisply.

'Both,' she replied, equally crisply.

'Personally, I bring you because I don't get bored if you are with me. Professionally, I know you'll react to anyone who isn't telling the truth. The first time it happened was when I thought Charles Langley might not be quite sound. You reassured me, and that enterprise has been a great success.'

'But I might have been wrong,' she said, suddenly anxious.

'Of course, there is always that possibility, but your score so far is remarkably good. You must have realised by now that my job isn't about money, it's about risk, and people are the largest part of the risk. It's my task to assess them. If I make a mistake it costs the bank a lot of money. If I am too cautious, that's just as bad, the bank makes no money. The calculated risk is the heart of the matter. I told you once before that you have a gift for assessing people. You always seem to know who is to be trusted. And I have learnt to trust your judgement.'

Clare sat listening to the rush of water and the cheep of sparrows that had found the crumbs beneath a nearby table, waiting for Robert to explain why he thought he was about to lose her. As he seemed reluctant to return to the subject, she prompted him gently.

'Madame Japolsky says you have asked for a long weekend in lieu of your extra hours and that you have booked a ticket to Toulouse.'

Clare laughed.

'Honestly, Robert, you are impossible. I shall only be gone three days. Christian wants to show me his part of France. He says his parents have never met anyone from Ireland and they keep asking him to bring me to see them. I promised ages ago I'd fly down the first long weekend you could spare me,' she explained. 'I would have told you,' she added gently.

Yes, you would. But I see you do not understand why I think I am about to lose you.'

'No, I don't.'

Something was upsetting Robert, but she couldn't work out what it was. Certainly, she'd made no secret of her growing relationship with Christian. He knew they'd spent every possible minute together in the last three months and that he'd flown to Greece to share a week of the fortnight's holiday she and Louise had already booked.

'Being in love suits you,' he said abruptly. 'It makes your eyes shine. But I am impressed. However much you may think of your handsome admirer, you still manage to keep your mind on your work. A most unusual feat for young women in love, in my experience. But that's only one of the problems it produces.'

'And what are the others?' she asked, her curiosity getting the better of her.

'They tend to be extravagant. But again, you'd never be guilty of that. Your housekeeping bills wouldn't feed a mouse,' he said matter-of-factly.

'Robert!' she said laughing, 'How on earth did you guess that? I sometimes can't believe how little I spend. I don't have time to go shopping, even if I wanted to. And I so often have meals while we're working, I hardly ever have to cook at home,' she went on. 'But how *did* you guess?'

'I didn't,' he said sheepishly. 'I monitor the accounts of all our young staff. I know it seems an intrusion, unpardonable were it not done for their own protection. Many young people are overwhelmed by the salaries we offer. Jewellery, evening gowns, sports cars. Monitoring the account gives me early warning of the weaknesses I may expect.'

'And what are mine?' she demanded, grinning at him.

'Abstemiousness. You are too hard on yourself.

You should relax a little. You look as if you're saving for a rainy day when the climate is perfectly dry,' he said crisply. 'Were I not about to lose you to a wealthy young man, I'd offer you some advice on investment. But you'll hardly need that in *his* situation.'

'Robert, do you think I'm going to elope with Christian?' she asked, laughing. 'Christian has never mentioned marriage. I know he loves me and I love him too, but we've never talked about getting married. Not yet, anyway. We've only known each other three months and, apart from that week in Greece, we've only met when we're both free, which isn't often.'

It was true their free hours didn't often coincide, but when they did, their time together was very exciting. From that first evening when they had danced and talked all of the short night, had walked the empty streets and up the steps of Sacré-Coeur to watch the sun rise over the stirring city, to the weekend in the French Alps when they had first become lovers, lying naked, the doors of their room opening to a balcony that framed rugged peaks still dusted with snow, sharp outlines against a star-filled sky, there'd seemed a kind of magic in every meeting.

'Clare, my dear. Christian Moreau comes from a privileged background about which I know relatively little. But I have known Emile a long time. I can assure you that a man like Moreau will not ask you to marry him until you have met his parents. It may seem a little old-fashioned. Or you might say it is a matter of courtesy to them. They will certainly not object, of that I am quite sure. I think your weekend at Moreau's château will almost certainly involve his proposing to you, and, in the circumstances, I imagine you are rather unlikely to refuse him.'

Clare did not sleep well that night. At the time, she thought it was the sound of the river beyond her open window. Its noisy flow seemed to enter all her dreams, an insistent presence, like an unanswered question continually repeating itself.

She woke at six with a headache and couldn't go back to sleep again. Given the long drive to Avignon and how difficult Robert could be in the mornings, a headache was not to be recommended. She took two Anadin and had a long, leisurely bath. As she lay soaking, feeling the tension drain out of her, she heard Louise's voice, so clear and sharp.

'If you marry Christian your children will be French.'

She'd said it suddenly, when they were sitting under an olive tree above the stadium at Delphi sharing a melon.

'But, of course,' she laughed. 'They could hardly be anything else.'

'I don't think I could have French children,' Louise went on. 'I thought about it once, when there was this wonderful Frenchman,' she said, rolling her eyes. 'Before I met you,' she added. 'I thought about taking the children home to my parents, showing them the places I love. I just couldn't do it. I could teach them Italian, that's easy with children. But I couldn't teach them to *be* Italian. It wouldn't be right anyway. Could you do it?'

Clare was grateful for the Anadin and the bath. The headache had eased by the time they left and the drive to Avignon was pleasanter than she expected. Robert was silent and preoccupied most of the way, leaving her free to take in the detail of this unfamiliar and fascinating countryside. He told her he had an afternoon engagement and they were being entertained by some local businessmen in the evening.

'What will you do this afternoon?' Robert asked as they finished an unusually silent lunch. 'You've read all the documents, I expect.'

'Yes, I did that before we left Paris,' she said. 'There's something I've wanted to do here since I started learning French.'

'And what is that?'

'I'm going to find the "pont" in "Sur le pont d'Avignon". Only I've been told they didn't dance *on* the bridge, but under it.'

'I shall be back by six-thirty. I would enjoy your company but I wouldn't wish to inflict this duty upon you. I am going to visit my eldest sister. She moved to Provence for the good of her health and now complains about the heat,' he said tartly, as he rose from the table.

Clare went to her room, changed her costume for a blouse and skirt and her high heels for walking shoes. She put some money in the pocket of her skirt, picked up a street map at reception and headed for the river.

She walked briskly, grateful to be by herself, outdoors on such a lovely, warm September day. How long was it since she had been free to walk in comfortable shoes, without a handbag, or briefcase, or a pile of documents under her arm? A light breeze tempered the warmth of the afternoon, but in a short time she began to perspire.

'What's the hurry, Clare? You'd think you'd a train to catch,' she said to herself sharply, as she came down to the river bank. She found a summer seat and sat down gratefully. For a little while, she did nothing but watch the river flowing, fast and deep, sunbeams glancing from its slightly rippled surface.

'Marry him. Now? *This year. Next year. Sometime. Never?*'

She'd been completely taken aback when Robert had said that Christian was sure to ask her to marry him, once she'd met his parents. It had never occurred to her. It was one thing sharing thoughts about marrying a man from another country with Louise, but quite another actually to be faced with the prospect so suddenly. Besides, she'd been so bound up in their loving, the pleasure of sharing all that they did, she'd never thought beyond their next meeting.

Marrying Christian would mean leaving Paris, of that she was certain. Christian loved the city as much as she did, but his home was in the south, north-west of Toulouse, a region she'd never visited. His family had been wine growers for generations. How they'd amassed the wealth that clearly impressed Robert, she had no idea. Christian seldom spoke about his work or asked about hers.

Christian knew Paris very well. He'd been to school at Henri Quatre, on the Left Bank, then gone to the Sorbonne. He knew parts of the city as well as she'd known every hedgerow and tree, every path and lane, in the few square miles of her own world.

'Where shall we go now? Do you like sculpture? Good. Then we will go to the Rodin.'

She could hear his voice, feel his arm round her waist, his hand in hers, his lips brushing her cheek, as they visited all the places she'd not had time to see in this busiest year of her life. They'd sailed up to the top of the Eiffel Tower, had dinner on a river boat that chugged past her own apartment, driven to Versailles and carried candles in the Catacombs.

He'd insisted she saw everything she'd ever heard of, or read about, and he would be her personal guide. A very knowledgeable guide he was too. Not only could he tell her the history and significance of every building they viewed, but he had that same passion for French literature she'd first met in Henri Lavalle. He'd read everything she'd read and much more. There seemed to be no limit to his experience and enjoyment of French culture. Whatever she mentioned, he responded to it with enthusiasm, sweeping her along, cherishing her with his love, enfolding her in the richness of his world.

'Hallo, doggy,' she said, her reflections interrupted by a young spaniel who came trotting purposefully along the river bank wanting to be friendly.

'What's your name?' she asked, fondling his ears and looking for a disc on his collar. 'Conker,' she read. 'And you are too,' she said, stroking his gleaming chestnut coat.

She thought of Ginny, of those fresh August mornings, when she'd taught her to ride, walking her round the small paddock at The Lodge, Andrew and Edward perched on the gate, teasing and encouraging her.

Conker barked at her. It was not a hostile bark,

more a communicative noise. Clare looked at him closely, not sure exactly what it might mean. An invitation to play, perhaps?

'Come on, hop up here beside me,' she said, patting the summer seat encouragingly.

Conker obliged immediately, leant forward and licked her nose. She hugged him, close to tears, quite unable to resist his good-naturedness or the memories that flooded in upon her.

'There he is. There he is.'

She turned to find a young man and a much younger girl hurrying towards her. Conker spotted them too, jumped down and greeted them with ecstatic barks. Then he ran back to Clare and barked at her too.

'Thank you so much, Mademoiselle. I hope he's not been a nuisance. He gave us the slip,' said the young man apologetically, as he put Conker back on his lead.

'No, he's lovely. I like dogs.'

'Do you have one?' the girl asked.

'No, I work in Paris and travel a lot. When I was very little my grandfather had a spaniel just like Conker, but he was pure black. He used to lick my nose as well.'

The girl sat down beside Clare, introduced herself as Madeline and asked her what it was like living in Paris. To her surprise, Clare found she was grateful for the interruption. She'd looked forward to having time to think, but now she had it, it seemed only sad thoughts were coming upon her, when she ought to be so very happy.

The young man would be about eighteen or nineteen, she thought, the same age as William. Sturdy, slightly square, and very good-humoured, he was only a little taller than his sister, who'd just informed Clare that she was twelve and two months old.

Clare laughed when he said his name was Robert.

'There are so many Roberts in my life,' she responded, without thinking. 'My grandfather was Robert and my boss is Robert.'

She was about to add, 'You remind me of him,' but it seemed such a strange thing to say she stopped herself in time.

'Robert is very clever,' said Madeline proudly. 'He's always winning prizes at school. Last year he won the medal for mathematics. Father says he doesn't know where he gets it from, because Mother is hopeless at sums.'

'You don't look at all like each other,' Clare said, smiling, as she looked from one to the other.

There was something so open and easy about the two young people. Robert was the quieter of the two. He was not so much shy as thoughtful. He was clearly quite used to Madeline doing most of the talking.

'I shall soon be taller than Robert,' said Madeline, teasingly. 'But he's a nice brother. I'm so glad Mummy escaped with him. She ran away when the Germans came. His own father was killed fighting them.'

'Do you remember him at all, Robert?'

'No, I was only weeks old when my mother came south. I don't even remember not having a father.'

'Our father is a custodian at the Bishop's Palace. Have you been there?'

'No, I haven't.'

'Would you like us to take you there? Robert knows everything about it. He'll tell you all the history. I always get the dates mixed up and forget the names of the Popes,' she said cheerfully. 'Wouldn't that be a good idea, Robert?'

Robert smiled and nodded and got to his feet. He'd been kneeling down stroking Conker, who was lying luxuriously on his back with his paws up.

They set off with Robert and Conker leading the way. She watched his sturdy figure moving ahead of her while Madeline continued to chatter happily by her side. There was no doubt about it. He did look like Robert, particularly from the back, but then, she considered, so did thousands of other French boys. It was a type, possibly one she would recognise if she knew Brittany. Many women had escaped the German advance from the north and east. There was no reason to think that Robert and Madeline's mother might have known Robert Lafarge's wife. Nevertheless, she would find out exactly where she had come from, just in case it might be of some use to the second Robert in her life.

Next day, Wednesday, they finished their meetings in time to catch the afternoon express to Paris. Robert was pleased. He'd done his duty with his sister, who had been as unpleasant as he expected, and he'd completed arrangements with the Avignon group, who had been much more progressive than he'd expected. He was tired out.

While he fell asleep behind the financial pages, Clare sat staring out of the window, absorbing the sunlit countryside as it sped past, parched and dusty, after a hot summer. The sun still blazed down out of a clear blue sky, reminding her of the fields of sunflowers she'd seen earlier in the year, near Orange.

She'd always been fascinated by sunflowers. At school, they'd once planted the large seeds in two-pound jam pots, placed between the glass of the jar and wet sand insulated by blotting paper. Quite quickly they had sprouted both roots and shoots. When they'd finished their experiment, drawn sketches in their biology exercise books, labelled the parts and planted the seedlings outdoors, they'd grown to almost two feet high. Here, in the south, the sunflowers she'd seen towered above her head, their huge faces fringed with bright yellow petals, their massed seeds home to dozens of harvesting insects.

Here, the countryside was exotic. Full of colour, passionate, like a Van Gogh painting. Fields of lavender like purple lakes, fields of stubble bleached white by the sun. The brilliant flash of the Rhône, caught in glimpses. Houses and factories in brick or plaster reflected the light, pinks and blues and dazzling white, or remained quietly shabby, even their peeling paint and fading tones glowing warmly.

The rhythm of the train was soothing, the comfortable carriage empty but for themselves. She leaned back, her guide to Toulouse and its environs open on her knee. There was so much of it, this huge country, and she'd been lucky to see so much in such a short time. But she could not say she knew it. Could anyone say they 'knew a country'? You could know a piece perhaps. A village, a small town, a locality. The way she knew The Grange, Armagh, the streets and roads round Queen's.

She thought of Charlie Running, his wall covered with bits cut from maps, sketches he'd made. That was a way of knowing a piece of a country. But it was only one way. There were others. You could say Robert knew France in terms of its financial institutions. The problems he tried to solve were particularly French. No doubt his counterpart in London or Milan would face very different problems.

She paused, laughed at herself. Between the effects of lunch and the heat, she was far too sleepy to solve any problem, particularly one she wasn't sure she could identify in the first place.

By the time they arrived, late in the evening, Paris was cooler. It was even cooler in her own apartment when she stepped into the dim room, the curtains and blinds meticulously closed by Madame to keep out the sun. She dropped her suitcase, drew them back, opened the windows, propped open her kitchen door to catch the slight breeze from the courtyard. Only moments later, the expected knock came.

'Here you are, mam'selle, your lovely green dress, the blue costume and your breakfast,' said Madame, handing over the garments on hangers from the dry cleaners. 'You will see a small packet and your post with your bread and croissants,' she explained, pointing a bony finger into the plastic carrier bag. 'It made it easier to carry.'

'Thank you very much, Madame.'

'You look so tired, mam'selle. It is the heat. I will not come in. Tell me tomorrow evening what you need for your return from Toulouse.'

Clare hung up her dry-cleaning, put the bread in the bin, the small packet and the post on the low table by her chair in the window.

With a sigh of relief she stepped into her bedroom and peeled off her clothes. She felt as if she'd been wearing them for a week. She hung her costume over a chair and made for the shower.

'Oh, that *is* better,' she said aloud, pulling on a dressing gown and tramping barefoot back into her sitting room.

She picked up the packet, small but sturdily wrapped. It had been registered, and signed for by Madame. On the back, the slightly torn custom's declaration said 'Recipient's own prop.'

'I could do with a prop, this evening,' she said, smiling to herself, as she struggled with the heavy brown parcel tape.

Inside, she found a small red velvet box like the one in Harry's safe and a stiff sheet of embossed paper, badly creased by having been folded round it. She opened the letter, smoothed it out and peered at the short paragraphs in the fading light.

Dear Madam,
In accordance with the wishes of the late Clarissa Madeline Richardson, I am forwarding to you the enclosed brooch.

Following the decease of the

aforementioned person, a note found in her
personal possessions and forwarded to us by
her executor, Mr Andrew Richardson, reads
as follows:

'My emerald brooch to Miss Clare
Hamilton, formerly of Salter's Grange,
now resident in Paris, with this message,
'Congratulations on your success. I hope
you will marry your Prince.'

We have provided for your convenience a
receipt for the enclosed item. If you would
be so good as to sign it, we would appreciate
its return to our Belfast office at your earliest
convenience.

'So she's dead. Poor woman,' Clare said, tears
trickling unheeded down her face. 'That's why I
could get no reply when I phoned June. She must
have been in hospital, or already dead. I should
just have gone up to Wiley's. Someone there would
have told me.'

She picked up the box. Yet again, for one
strange, disturbing moment she'd thought it was
the box containing her engagement ring.

'How silly of me,' she said as she opened it.

The brooch inside was small, just a single stone,
set in a filigree of gold wire. Even in the dusk, it

caught light from the quay outside to glow with a green fire. Could it really be an emerald?

She tried to read the letter through again, but the light had gone. She drew the curtains, put on a lamp, scanned the paragraphs. But no amount of reading was going to answer the questions that sprang into her mind.

Was the admirer who had pursued the Missus from Paris to Deauville the man she should have married? Or had she given him up to marry the Senator? Why had she kept the brooch all these years, when they'd been so short of money?

'I'll never know now,' she said quietly, wiping her eyes. 'I just know I must get to bed. It's a full day tomorrow and Toulouse on Friday.'

Not even the thought of seeing Christian had the power to cheer her as she hid the brooch carefully among her clothes and climbed wearily into bed.

CHAPTER TWENTY

'Mesdames, Messieurs. Attention, s'il vous plaît.'
Clare obediently paid attention. The early evening
flight to Toulouse had been delayed for technical
reasons.

Sitting by a window, drinking Perrier water,
she watched other aircraft come and go, wondered
what the phrase 'technical reasons' might actually
mean. Perhaps a wheel had fallen off, or an altitude
meter had started recording while the aircraft was
still on the ground. On the other hand, it could
be something quite different. The in-flight drinks
hadn't arrived, perhaps, or the pilot was delayed in
a traffic jam, or the documentation for a box to be
placed in the hold had disappeared.

She smiled to herself, thinking of the tactful
reasons the bank used to turn down a request for
finance. Courtesy was always an objective. The
area of concern might be referred to, but only in
general terms. Unless one was going as far as to
offer an assessment of the problem, it was policy

to use a phrase like 'not in the best interests of the bank'. It was only another variation of 'technical reasons'.

The delay lasted about an hour, but the flight itself was unexceptional, only the landing rather unpleasant as they lost height through thick cloud, the tail end of one of the thunderstorms generated by the heat of the last week.

She spotted Christian before he saw her, surrounded as she was by the dark suits and striding figures of returning businessmen. He was scanning the dark stream intensely, his tanned face staring and expressionless. The moment he saw her, he smiled, that warm expansive smile that had so captivated her.

'My poor little one, you must be so tired. Was it a bumpy flight?'

He slipped an arm round her, kissed her cheek and drew her towards the baggage area. 'Which ones are yours?'

'Just that one,' she said, laughing. 'With the Athens sticker. The wretched thing wouldn't peel off,' she said easily, glad to have arrived and found him waiting for her.

She noticed a tightening in his face as he left her to retrieve the case. He hurried back to her and shepherded her towards his car.

'New car, Christian?'

'No,' he said absently, as he reversed at speed

and then headed for the exit. 'This is the one I always use here. I keep the Renault in Paris.'

He drove fast through the suburbs of Toulouse, and even faster when the city had been left behind.

'Your flight was late,' he said flatly. 'You will want time to change before dinner. Travelling on a Friday night is always more tiring,' he added, with a glance towards her.

'What do you usually wear on a Friday night?' she asked lightly.

She thought longingly of a pair of trousers and a cool over-shirt.

'Oh, just a suit. I don't bother with a dinner jacket, though my father always does. I expect you've brought a short evening dress. Easier to pack,' he said brightly, without taking his eyes off the road.

The road was twisty and wet from the thunderstorm, though the sky had cleared and there was freshness in the air. She concentrated on the countryside to distract herself from the speed of the drive. Perhaps it was the flight, but she almost felt slightly car sick.

'Not far now,' he said, reducing speed marginally on even narrower roads. 'My parents moved out of the château some years go. They found a more comfortable house about five miles away, between Pescadoire and Puy l'Eveque. It was built by an American recluse in the nineties, a strange mixture of styles, but there are no draughts. My mother says she's too old for a draughty château,' he said, flashing her a warm smile.

'And you live with them?'

'No, of course not. I have a small suite in the château. I'll take you there tomorrow.'

He swung off the road on to a broad gravelled drive lined on one side with poplars, on the other with flowering shrubs. The shrubs gave way to a broad lawn, remarkably green compared with the dried-out look of the countryside, which the rain had done nothing to modify.

'Good,' he said, looking at his watch, as he came round to open her door. 'Just eight o'clock. We have drinks on the terrace at eight-thirty and dine at nine. Come down as soon after eight-thirty as you can manage. Gabrielle will take you to your room.'

The house was large. Three storeys. Pink, with shutters, like many houses she'd seen in the south. But, unlike them, it had a porch with Grecian columns painted white and a wide fan of shallow steps leading up to the front door.

The hall was even more extraordinary. It reminded her of baronial halls in films like *The Adventures of Robin Hood*. There were beautiful oriental carpets on the polished wood floor, suits of armour, heraldic shields, and a number of flags, so faded with age they were almost transparent.

'This way, mam'selle, if you please,' said Gabrielle, taking her suitcase from Christian and heading for the stairs.

'Don't be late,' he said, smiling warmly, as he disappeared.

'If there is anything you need, mam'selle, will you please ring,' she said, throwing open a bedroom door and indicating a heavy gold rope by the fireplace. 'Your bathroom is through here,' she went on, opening a heavy panelled door into a room almost as large as the one in which they stood.

'Thank you, Gabrielle.'

Gabrielle bobbed a curtsy and Clare managed to keep a straight face until she'd closed the door gently behind her.

'Whee . . .' she said, as she dropped down on a sofa placed across the end of the four-poster bed. 'You nearly put your foot in it, Clare dear.'

She opened her case quickly, took out her make-up and dressing gown and shook out the new plum velvet cocktail dress she nearly hadn't brought. She wasn't even sure she liked it, now she saw it lying on the bed, waiting to be worn. But Louise said it looked good when it arrived from the couturier's yesterday. She'd put it in just to be on the safe side, in case Toulouse might think itself quite as smart as Paris, if Christian wanted to take her out to dine.

The room was gloomy now as the light faded,

despite its two large, high windows overlooking the garden. Another beautifully green lawn with paths and pergolas covered with roses, leading to other areas defined by box hedges. She had such a desire to run out of the house, down one of those paths and let the freshness of the evening envelop her. She sighed and smiled as she felt her shoulders give a passable imitation of a classic Gallic shrug.

'Come on, Clare. You haven't got time. Just do a Louise.'

She parked her suitcase in the bottom of a huge wardrobe, where a summer dress and her light trousers already hung in solitary splendour, and two pairs of shoes occupied a small corner of a shoe rack with enough capacity for a football team, and examined herself critically in the long mirror. She sighed. She had broken a golden rule. Never wear a new dress for the first time when about to go out. The dress was nicer than she thought: she liked the soft fall of the fabric and the fit was impeccable, but the deep V-neck needed a necklace.

She scolded herself. Marie-Claude had taught her to use costume jewellery as she used scarves and belts and she'd built up quite a collection of brooches for her costumes and earrings for her evening dresses. But no necklaces. It was not a matter of expense. She just hadn't seen the need until now.

She wondered if the brooch from her blue suit might offset the bareness of the neckline. The blue was deep enough to wear with the plum, yes, but its setting in white metal was quite wrong against the soft fabric. The richness of the dress needed gold.

'Ah.' she breathed, as an idea came to her.

She went to a drawer where she had unpacked her underwear and took out the small red jewel box. She'd only brought it because she'd promised Madame never to leave real jewellery in her apartment and she hadn't had time to do anything else with it.

'Oh, what luck,' she said aloud, as she tried it out at different points on the draped shoulders and fitted bodice. 'It looks good wherever I put it.'

She turned off the battery of spotlights around the dressing table and stood for a moment in the darkened room. Everything was silent. No friendly household noises came to her, no smells of food, no tramp of feet. The house had a dead feel about it. The hall itself looked like a museum, but her bedroom was more like a stage set for a costume drama, waiting for the cast to bring it to life. Little Gabrielle, in her black dress and starched white apron, merely added to the illusion, a Miss Muffet cap perched on her dark curls, like the one she'd worn herself at Drumsollen.

Strange that the place should so remind her of

Drumsollen, given a different country, the great difference in the style of furnishing. Perhaps it would all become clear to her, after dining with the inhabitants.

She walked slowly downstairs, half expecting the baronial hall to be lit by flickering torches, but it was not. Concealed spotlights played on key exhibits and threw long, menacing shadows up the high walls and across the timber-beamed roof. She paused at the foot of the staircase. At last, there were signs of life. The chink of glasses and the higher notes of a woman's voice. It was exactly eight-thirty. She walked towards them.

'Clare you have been quick. Well done,' said Christian approvingly, as he arced his arm around her without touching her, drawing her into the conservatory, which gave on to a lamp-lit terrace.

Christian's father rose at once. A little taller and somewhat older than Emile, he had broader shoulders and bushy eyebrows, but little of Emile's gentle hesitancy. He was wearing evening dress with the fleche of the Legion of Honour in one lapel.

He waited, patiently enough, while Christian introduced Clare to his mother, a tall, aristocratic woman with iron-grey hair and papery skin on which her rouge sat unhappily, despite its skilful application.

'How do you do, Miss Hamilton, I'm sure we may call you Clare,' she began, in English, extending her hand limply, her fingers cold.

'How do you do,' Clare replied, wondering which English habits of speech Madame Moreau would expect. 'Yes, of course, you may,' she added easily.

'I regret my English always was poor, completely non-existent now,' said Monsieur Moreau abruptly, in French.

Clare smiled at him as she shook his hand. 'But that's much better than having an unfortunate accent. So my boss says. He learnt his English from the Americans after the war and refuses to speak it at all,' Clare replied, in French.

He grunted, and sat down again looking relieved.

'Christian, Clare has nothing to drink. What are you thinking of?' Madame Moreau demanded, reverting to French, her tone sharper, less rounded than when she spoke English.

But at that very moment Christian appeared from behind Clare's chair carrying a glass of white wine.

'Thank you,' she said politely, as he handed her the glass without looking at her.

Clare had a sudden desire to giggle. She spoke to herself severely. If she felt like giggling now, how on earth would she feel if she drank wine on an empty stomach? She'd broken another of Louise's golden rules. Always eat something before you go out, in case the meal is late. While Louise drank milk, Clare usually had cream crackers or plain biscuits, but that was one more thing she'd forgotten to pack. She really wasn't scoring very well tonight, and the evening was only just beginning.

She took a very small sip of her wine and waited.

Madame Moreau turned towards her with a slight inclination of the head, speaking now in French.

'You must think us very old-fashioned, Clare, with our silly old flags and trophies. Charles is the keeper of the family history and it does go a long way back,' she said, stroking the grey silk of her full-length gown.

'But family history is so interesting,' Clare replied. 'I think I saw the device of Henry of Navarre in the entrance hall, but perhaps I was mistaken.'

'Oh no, not at all,' Madame replied, her eyes opening a little wider. 'Henri Quatre was a very important figure in our family history. Without his protection we Huguenots would not have survived. I'm sure you are familiar with his efforts on our behalf and what happened when the Edict of Nantes was finally revoked.'

'Yes, indeed. A very dark episode in French history, though one which my own country has benefited from.'

'It has?'

'Yes, very much so. While England and the Netherlands seem to have welcomed the silk workers and goldsmiths, we in the north of Ireland had the benefit of Louis Crommelin. He and other Huguenots transformed the existing textile industry and gave us our famous linen industry.'

'And your family, are they also Huguenot, as we are here?' she went on, with a slightly more than courteous interest.

'Most of the families I know well seem to have Huguenot links,' Clare replied, thinking of all the aunts and uncles who worked in the mills round about Banbridge. 'But they also have strong ties with the Calvinists in Scotland,' she added, now that the drift of Madame's questioning was quite clear to her.

'How very interesting, my dear,' she said warmly. 'You must ask my husband to take you on a tour of our treasures. But not until you have had some supper. We are neglecting our duty while we enjoy your company,' she said, standing up and sweeping out of the room, just as a distant clock struck nine and a young man appeared to announce that dinner was served.

* * *

Clare was grateful when the first course turned out to be a comforting soup. Madame, it was clear, did not permit conversation with the servants present, so it was not until they departed and Clare was feeling distinctly more like herself, that Charles Moreau addressed her.

'Christian says your plane was delayed. Were there thunderstorms further north?'

'Yes, I think there were, but the main delay was in Paris. Technical reasons, they said. Coming in to land in Toulouse was nasty. I think we flew through the edge of the thunderstorm moving away south.'

Moreau nodded.

'But there was no rain on the drive back?' he asked, turning to Christian, who had not said a word since the meal began.

'No, none at all, but the road was wet over large stretches. There was water actually lying by the roadside on the far side of Pescadoire.'

'It rained here about seven, but only for a few minutes,' said Madame Moreau. 'Did you not have that up at Chirey?' she went on, addressing her husband for the first time.

All conversation ceased as Gabrielle and the young man removed the soup and served fillets of trout, beautifully arranged on translucent china plates, rimmed with gold and decorated with the family crest.

'Clare, you must forgive this boring

conversation,' said Madame, with an indulgent smile, when they had gone. 'You have discovered that it is not only the English who talk about the weather.'

'I have certainly discovered that rainfall in early September is a serious matter with the vendage so close at hand. I wondered if it might have begun already, at least on the south-facing slopes.'

'You are quite right, Clare,' said Monsieur Moreau, looking somewhat taken aback. 'We would have begun by now had it not been so very dry.'

'So you do need the rain to swell the grapes, but you do not need thunderstorms to risk damaging them,' she said, smiling at him. 'It must be a very difficult time.'

'Yes, it is,' he said firmly. 'With our table wines, there is no difficulty. We have a range of vineyards over a wide area. We can compensate and balance by careful blending. There is some satisfaction in producing a quality wine in very large quantities. But at Chirey itself, we've always had ambition.'

'Aiming for a great year?'

'Precisely.'

'I should have told you of Clare's interest in winegrowing, father,' Christian broke in quickly.

'Indeed,' said the older man. 'But surely there is no winegrowing in Ireland,' he said, smiling for the first time.

'Sadly, no. At least not since the fifth century, when the climate was warmer than it is now,' she replied. 'No, my knowledge is all of the French industry. It began one morning near Avignon when I discovered the benefits of the large pieces of stone lying around looking untidy in a very well-ordered vineyard,' she said, laughing. 'From then on I listened as well as translated. What fascinates me is what affects the grapes, the small variations of soil, of site, even before you introduce the variables of rainfall and sunshine, and hazards like frost and thunderstorms. It surprises me great years can occur at all with so much to prevent them.'

'We have had one or two since the war,' said Charles Moreau, looking at her steadily. 'But not here at Chirey. You are right. Success can be almost within one's grasp and something goes wrong. It can even be as small a thing as a key workman being ill when the presses are being set up. You must come up to Chirey tomorrow and I will show you round.'

'I should enjoy that very much,' said Clare honestly, as Madame raised a warning hand to indicate that the servants had once again come into the room.

The meal was lengthy and the food very good. All three Moreaus now felt free to talk about the wine-making that was their consuming passion, about the history of their vineyards and the successes they had had over the years.

By the later stages of the meal, Clare felt steady enough to drink her wine. Served from unlabelled bottles, it had to be from one of their many vineyards. She hoped no one would ask her opinion on its quality for when she was as tired as she now felt, wine tasted merely pleasant or unpleasant. All subtlety was lost.

'Come, Clare, let us leave these gentlemen to their speculations. You will have heard more than enough of the family's preoccupations for one evening,' said Madame Moreau. 'Gabrielle will bring more coffee to the sitting room when you join us,' she said, with a meaningful look at her husband.

The sitting room was on the opposite side of the baronial hall. Its heavy velvet curtains were already drawn, a small fire of logs glowed on the hearth of an enormous marble fireplace. A tray of coffee sat waiting on a low table.

'Do come and sit beside me, my dear. This room echoes so when it is not full of people,' she said, waving Clare to a white and gold armchair close to the long settee where she had seated herself.

'I'm afraid you've heard a great deal about the Moreau family tonight. I'm much more interested in hearing about your family. Christian is thoughtful in so many ways, but he has told us so little about you. Terribly selfish, keeping you all to himself. Now do tell me, where did you learn to speak French so beautifully?'

Clare smiled to herself and sipped her coffee. She was about to be interviewed for the position of lady wife to the heir apparent to the Moreau estates, the extent of which had taken her by surprise even after Robert's wry comments. She'd reckoned this was going to happen sooner or later, but she'd hoped it might be later.

'I used to listen to the radio when I was a little girl,' she said, deciding on the direct approach.

'But surely you studied in Paris?'

'Only since I've been working there. Before that, I looked after two children at Deauville, au pair to the St Clair family during my long vacations in order to learn colloquial French.'

'How charming. Deauville is delightful, isn't it?'

Clare agreed that Deauville was delightful and remarkably unchanged since the turn of the century, according to one of her friends. She thought Madame seemed distinctly taken aback at the mention of looking after children, but she smiled indulgently at the mention of Deauville, and nodded at the mention of the St Clairs.

'You must forgive me making a personal comment, but I have been admiring that pretty little brooch of yours. Such a delightful choice with that dress. It looks as if it might have a story. Am I right?' she asked archly.

'Yes, you're quite right, but the story is still a mystery. It was given to me by an old lady to whom I spoke French. I'm almost sure it came from an admirer while she was in Paris or Deauville with her chaperone, around the turn of the century, but she didn't marry him.'

'What an interesting story, Clare,' she said, enthusiastically. 'France seems to have been so much a part of your life, even when you lived in Ireland,' she added, with a little laugh. 'I find it hard not to think of you as a Frenchwoman, except for your hair. Your beautiful, dark, Irish curls,' she said with a sweet smile. 'So romantic. I'm sure Christian . . . Ah, here they are,' she said, breaking off, as Charles and Christian came into the room. 'Christian, darling, do ring for more coffee. She should have brought it by now.'

Clare ran a hand through her beautiful, dark, Irish curls and shivered, though the room was warm. She was back in Greece with Christian, lying in a shaded hotel room during siesta.

'I love your hair,' he had said, running his fingers through it. 'So fine, and so dark. I wish there were more of it for me to stroke,' he said, kissing her. 'Why don't you let it grow for me? Pin it up by day and let it down at night when we make love.'

She'd laughed and told him what hard work

long hair was, how poor Louise spent hours in front of her mirror. At the time, she'd thought nothing of it. But Christian had come back to the subject of her hair, many, many times, coaxing her and teasing her with great persistence.

Now she knew why. With all the charm and skill in conversation his mother clearly prided herself upon, she had indicated unambiguously that French women of her class and standing simply did not wear their hair in dark curls.

Despite her unease about Christian and the way he'd behaved since she arrived, Saturday turned out to be a very enjoyable day. After breakfast, Charles Moreau drove her to Chirey and gave her his promised tour of the wine presses and cellars of the château. When he'd answered all her questions, he handed her over to Christian, who drove her to the Gorges d'Anglais for a picnic lunch, followed by a lengthy tour of the Lot valley and the countryside around Cahors.

The day was hot, but freshened by a slight breeze, the roads almost empty of cars. Christian himself was relaxed and easy, once again the lively companion she was familiar with, as enthusiastic about mediaeval architecture and the unspoilt villages of his home territory as he'd been about the sights of Paris itself. He spread the landscape before her, driving from one viewpoint to another, stopping wherever there was a particularly interesting feature to be pointed out to her.

'I will take you to a nightclub where we can dance till dawn. You will like that.'

The words came into her mind as they drove back through Puy l'Eveque. Today, she'd been so aware that Christian always *told* her what she would like. Until now, she'd simply not noticed, because she'd so enjoyed his company and so much of what they'd done together. Truly, she could say he'd swept her off her feet from that very first evening.

Her friends were delighted to see her so happy. Robert had told her that being in love made her eyes shine. Yes, she *had* been happy. She *did* love him. So why did the thought of marrying him fill her with such misgiving?

'Tomorrow, I will show you my favourite view. You will like it,' he said, as they drove up the gravelled drive, past the green lawn where the sprinklers were hard at work.

'I hope you aren't tired,' he said, a hint of unease in his voice. 'My mother has invited some friends to meet you. Even I shall have to dress this evening,' he said, as he opened her door, kissed her cheek, walked with her to the bottom of the stairs. 'Eight o'clock on the terrace. Don't be late,' he went on, with a winning smile.

'Of course I won't be late,' she replied, turning

away quickly and running lightly upstairs.

She shut the heavy door firmly behind her, threw her handbag on the smooth, pink silk bedspread that covered the enormous four-poster and dropped into a settee.

'It's your own fault, Clare. You weren't paying attention,' she said aloud. 'The signs were all there, you just didn't choose to see them.'

She went to the window and stood looking down the length of the back garden. For some unknown reason, she thought of Mrs McGregor's garden in Belfast, that tiny strip of green beyond the back yard and the dustbins. She could see herself standing by the window in the gloomy kitchen, waiting for the kettle to boil. Waiting for life to begin.

The Moreau garden ran a long way from the house, till it ended abruptly below a stand of tall poplars that shut out the sky. The sprinklers were hard at work here as well, hazy rainbows shimmering wherever the sunlight fell at the appropriate angle on the rain of their arcing jets.

She stared at the rainbows, entranced by their delicate colour. Suddenly, the water jets sagged, the rainbows disappeared. A gardener appeared, disconnected the green hoses, collected up the metal fountains, walked back and forth, his arms full of equipment, then reappeared with a broom made of long twigs. He brushed the grass gently where the sprinklers had stood. By the time drinks were served on the terrace, the grass would be dry and perfect, unmarked by any sign of human activity.

'You have enjoyed the evening?' Christian said, slipping into the empty seat beside her, as the first guests rose to say their goodbyes.

'Yes, I have. I particularly like Monsieur Le Maire. I've learnt so much about the surrounding villages. Quite a few things you didn't tell me,' she added steadily.

'Oh, I shall tell you much more, when we have more time,' he said, looking at her meaningfully. 'Mother has suggested you come to church with us in the morning,' he went on, looking pleased with himself. 'I'm sure you won't mind. It is rather boring, but it pleases them.'

Clare cast her eye round the sitting room and saw there were people well within hearing distance.

'I would come, of course. But you didn't tell me we would be going to church,' she said, smoothing the sharpness from her voice. 'I haven't a hat, or even a suitable scarf.'

'I'm sure we can solve that problem,' he said, getting to his feet immediately.

She watched him cross the room, wait his moment, then bend down and whisper in his mother's ear. She nodded and smiled. Aware that both mother and son were looking towards her, Clare glanced away, and studied the detail of a large, allegorical painting close to her.

It was being arranged. Suitable headgear would be provided. Hardly a felt hat with an upturned brim and bead elastic under the chin like she'd worn for Sunday School in Armagh, before her parents died, or a straw hat, like any of those Auntie Polly had sent from Toronto. Certainly not a beret like she and Jessie had worn as schoolgirls. Berets, she was sure, were only worn by work people.

The small church in the nearby village was much older than the church on The Mall in Armagh. Built when the French Protestants had been given protection by the Crown, it was remote enough to have survived the destruction that followed the change of heart of 1685. A solid stone building, a strong mediaeval influence in its pillars and lancet windows, it had a familiar bareness, wooden box pews and a musty smell.

They arrived just before the service began, walked two by two down the narrow central aisle to the family pew just below the pulpit. Every eye was turned towards them, a fact that Madame Moreau appeared to relish and Charles Moreau studiously ignored.

Clare found herself sitting rigid, oppressed by the setting, the smell of damp and the familiar torrent of words. Reading, prayers, sermon, all seemed to merge into one homogenous deluge. It didn't help that the theme for the day was Original Sin.

Surely, she thought, if you tell people how sinful they are, you only reinforce their weakness and if you *are* born sinful what can you do about it? She'd always thought it a counsel of despair. When Granda Hamilton had taken her to the Quaker meeting, at least they'd had peace and quiet. And when the people rose to speak they didn't say the same things over and over again.

'Do you take this man to be your wedded husband?'

If she were to marry Christian, they'd stand over there, only feet away from the family pew. The front rows would be filled with the great and the good, the back with the workers from the nearest vineyards, probably a large part of this present congregation. She would wear a simple but stunning creation from Paris. Gerard St Clair would give her away. Louise would be her bridesmaid.

And what then? A marquee in the courtyard of the château, grape baskets and donkey carts carefully hidden away in the cellars. Flags flying? Oh yes, let's have flags, she thought, looking round the bare walls with neither statue, nor carving, stained glass, or cross to relieve the bareness.

She gazed up at the preacher, a look of rapt attention on her face. She'd heard it all before, so there was no need to listen. Besides, there was the rest of her life to arrange.

No doubt she and Christian would live in the château. She hadn't seen his suite yet, but that would be this afternoon. The château would be reinvigorated. They might even be permitted to remove the draughts. Then there would be the children.

'We will have beautiful children. You will like that.'

She could almost hear him saying it. This man, sitting by her side, his handsome face in profile, listening attentively to the penalties of sin, both sins of omission and sins of commission. Most likely he was thinking his own thoughts just as she was.

By the time the highly articulate figure threw his arms in the air and blessed the congregation, she was stiff and cold with tension and the effects of the hard wooden seat. They were dismissed into the warmth and sunshine and the sidelong glances of the departing parishioners.

The courtyard of the château was full of activity when Christian swung his sports car up the steep slope between the huge stone pillars that had once supported the portcullis.

'What's happening?' she cried.

'We've decided to begin in the morning,' he said, getting out of the car, taking her hand and leading her through the throng of people coming and going. 'It's a pity you have to go back tonight, but there'll be other opportunities.'

They walked up stone steps into the château itself, crossed a huge empty hall, climbed a curving stone staircase. The place felt like a cave quarried out of stone. She could feel the damp chill producing goosepimples on her bare arms. At the end of a long corridor, Christian opened a door into a pleasant sitting room, lit by a large window looking south. Warmed by the sun, the heat was blissful after the dank feel of the empty lower storey and the staircase.

The whole suite was pleasant enough, the view down into the courtyard impressive. He led her through the well-furnished rooms, showed her his bedroom, the kitchen and bathroom.

'It's quite possible to be comfortable in a draughty château,' he said, laughing. 'But Mother has a point. To use the whole château, one needs to be young and have lots of good ideas. You would enjoy such a challenge, wouldn't you?'

'I always enjoy a challenge,' she said, honestly, as she turned away towards the window.

'Now I will show you the most splendid view of all,' he said, holding out his hand to her.

Another corridor, another staircase, much steeper than the last. They paused at a small door set deep into the stonework. A final steep flight and they were standing at the highest point of the château, the figures in the courtyard below them reduced to small dark shapes.

There was little space to spare in this high eyrie. They stood close together and scanned the landscape laid out all around them. The sky was clear, not a cloud to be seen, but the heat had generated a haze, which made the far horizon shimmer like a picture viewed through the fumes of a Tilley lamp.

The rugged, dissected country ran, ridge upon ridge, towards lower land far away, the sides of the low, eroded hills ribbed with the rich green of vines in full leaf and fruit. Small villages blended into their hillside sites, their building stone the very same rock upon which they stood.

Twisting roads, appearing and disappearing, today empty dusty ribbons, tomorrow filled with the laden carts now being prepared in the courtyard below. On the tops of the hills the bare rock gleamed between areas of sparse vegetation. Here, on the 'causses', farming was a matter of scraping a living in the more favoured hollows.

Clare took it all in, fitting together what she could now see with her tour of yesterday and all the local mayor had told her last night at dinner. It had its own harsh beauty, but it was a hard land, unforgiving, enclosed and remote.

'This is my favourite view,' he said, proudly.

She waited, becoming more and more anxious by the minute.

'You would be happy here,' he said, smiling as he took her hand.

For a moment she felt desolate, locked in a situation she had allowed to happen and from which she could see no easy means of escape. Then it came to her. With a fluency and ease that afterwards amazed her, she found words – the words she needed.

'It is a splendid view and quite wonderful countryside,' she said, smiling. 'I'm so grateful to have seen it. But I could never be happy here,' she went on, shaking her head. 'I would never stop longing for the little green hills of my home in Ireland.'

CHAPTER TWENTY-ONE

The week following her return from Toulouse was one of the most miserable Clare had ever spent. Although she knew she'd done the right thing and was grateful she'd been able to do it in the way she had, she just couldn't get over the aching sense of loss. Between one week and the next, a bright light had switched itself off, leaving her feeling sad and abandoned.

The facts of the matter didn't help. She struggled with the sense that some treasured hope had been taken away. The joy that had swelled up in the months gone by had burst like a bubble.

It might have been easier if Robert or Louise were there to welcome her back, but they were both away in Italy. Without Louise to fill it with her vivacity, their room seemed large and empty. She missed Robert too. Often, several days would pass without her seeing him, but she always knew he was there, upstairs, working away at his large desk, surrounded by his paintings.

In odd moments of the day when her mind was free to wander, walking to the Metro, having lunch in some little place near the bank, shopping for her supper on the way home, she thought about Christian. Not the Christian she had come to see so clearly in his own habitat, but the lively presence that had swept her up with such enthusiasm after the sad disappointment of her first visit home. There was a contradiction there. An enigma she could not resolve.

'Nothing to do but grin and bear it, Clare,' she said to herself on the Friday evening, carrying her supper tray to the low table, as the setting sun cast long fingers of light deep into the room. 'It happens all the time. People fall in love. They see someone they hope is there. Time proves them wrong and they fall out of love again.'

She sat for a long time in the fading light watching the couples who strolled past. There were always lovers walking by on the quays, hand in hand, arm in arm, stopping to kiss from time to time, just as she and Christian had done in so many parts of the city.

'Would it have been different if he'd been a Parisian?'

She thought of all the times they'd been together, free to wander through the city, from that very first evening when they walked the cobbled streets from Place Pigalle and climbed the broad, white steps to Sacré-Coeur. For three months, they'd made

Paris *their* city, possessing it, as lovers do, enjoying its colour and life, drinking coffee in cafes in unexpected places, stopping to look at a street artist at work, strolling by the river, tramping the galleries of the Louvre, or enjoying the broad avenues of the Bois de Boulogne. If Christian had been a Parisian they would still be together, somewhere in the city, watching the light fade in the Tuileries Gardens or heading for a favourite restaurant on the Left Bank.

She laughed at herself. Christian could hardly be a Moreau, of Huguenot descent, heir to one of the largest accumulations of vineyards in France, and be a Parisian. His background and upbringing had certainly contributed to the sort of person he was. Change any of the factors and he would have been different. And if he had been, they would never have met in the first place.

'Nothing for it, Clare. As the song says: "Pick yourself up, dust yourself down and start all over again."'

She took her tray to the kitchen, set the filter machine going and stared out at the fading summer flowers. A figure moved in the apartment on the other side of the courtyard. She waved and smiled. Paul was doing his washing up. Dear Paul. Could she ever have imagined such a strange young man becoming such a good friend?

She made a note on her kitchen reminder pad: 'Take brooch to work tomorrow.'

It was Paul who had solved that problem. She had asked him about insurance but he'd suggested a deposit box. He said it didn't matter how little you had to put in one, given that staff could have one without charge, she might as well. He would arrange it for her.

Her coffee machine made spluttering noises, gurgled and stopped. She filled up her cup and went back into the living room. 'Mosey Jackson would be pleased,' she said aloud, as the golden fingers on the carpet died away.

Suddenly, the evenings were noticeably shorter. September was moving on and the first yellowed leaves, exhausted by warmth and a drying wind, were drifting along the edge of the quay, spilling over into the brown water and floating off to accumulate under the nearest bridge, bright patches on dark water.

Beside her chair she'd collected up a pile of books for learning Italian and a small tape-recorder. She turned towards them.

'Come on now, Clare. Let's see how far you can get before Louise comes to help you.'

Robert sent for her as soon as he arrived back from Italy, as she knew he would. She told him the bare facts of what had happened between her and Christian.

'So you won't be losing me after all, Robert.'

To her surprise he said very little, though he listened carefully and looked most thoughtful. A few days later, she found a note from him when she got back to the apartment. Notes from Robert always meant the same thing. She smiled as she opened it.

He had the most endearing way of using exactly the same formula whenever he asked her to dine: 'if she had no more interesting engagement and if she were not already committed to Louise or the St Clairs.' On this occasion, however, he named the eighth of October, and continued: 'if she had not already made arrangements for celebrating her forthcoming birthday.'

'Good gracious, I'd almost forgotten,' she exclaimed.

She would be twenty-three on October the eighth, the day on which her parents had married twenty-four years earlier. 'Our anniversary present,' she said quietly, remembering her mother's words.

Robert must have looked up the date in his files. On the other hand, he might have consigned the date to his prodigious memory the day he offered her the job. She never ceased to be amazed at just how much information he had at his fingertips, whether it was when they worked together or when they dined.

When they talked about more personal matters he could remember every detail she'd ever shared with him, referring as easily to her grandfather or Charlie Running, Jessie or the gallery, as he did to the St Clairs.

She took the cap off her fountain pen. Of course she would dine with him. She would look forward to it especially.

A small handful of birthday cards arrived at the apartment in the days immediately before Clare's birthday, some with notes, some with letters. The most welcome one was from Jessie, a really lovely card of late summer flowers. Clare smiled when she saw that Jessie had started to write a short message inside the card, but went on to fill up the whole back of it, despite the awkwardness of writing on its shiny surface. It wasn't the first time she'd written, but it was the first time she'd said anything about herself. It had a warmth about it so sadly missing when she'd been with her back in the spring.

Wee Fiona is great, though she's into everything now she's walking. No. 2 is on the way, due early next May (we think). I hope I'm going to be able to manage the two of them. I maybe shouldn't have had another so soon, but I didn't want there to be years between them, like me and John, who never really got on. I go to this specialist

*in Cadogan Park (no hope of me spelling
the word he calls himself) and he says I may
have a little more difficulty with the second.
I don't quite get what he's on about, but he
says rest is the thing. I suppose he ought to
know, he charges enough. Any word of you
coming over for a holiday? I know I haven't
written much and Harry drops you the odd
line but I do think of you a lot. I miss you.*

    Love and hugs,
    Jessie

Clare propped the card on the mantelpiece.
She was so grateful to have a real message, but
something about it really troubled her. Yes, it was
more affectionate, more like the loving Jessie she'd
known, but it certainly wasn't the voice of her old
friend. This was a Jessie who seemed harassed and
anxious. Not anxious about anything specific, just
anxious in herself. No trace at all of the girl who
had charged into life and emerged triumphant.

She was still pondering over Jessie's words as
she opened Ronnie's card. She began laughing
the moment she pulled it out of its bright yellow
envelope. Charlie Running sent a view of Armagh
from the Newry Road. Aunt Sarah's handwriting
was terribly shaky but there was nothing shaky
about her message of good wishes. And lastly, there
was one from June and John Wiley and the girls,

signed by all of them in blue biro and decorated with kisses. Inside, June had added a note to say she was so sorry they missed her when she was over. After the Missus died, they'd had a holiday down in Newcastle for a week to have a bit of a rest. She hoped she'd be over again soon. They had the telephone now. Be sure to give her a ring and let her know when she was coming.

To her great surprise, there were more cards waiting for her when she arrived at work on her birthday itself. A brightly coloured Italian one from Louise, with champagne bottles popping and all the Italian superlatives flying around like birds. She laughed and hugged her friend before she went on to open the rest. It seemed as if all her colleagues had found out about her birthday, even Emile's replacement, the rather formal Monsieur Mauriac, and the formidable Madame Japolsky, who sent a discreet engraving of the bank premises with carriages tastefully arranged beyond the steps. As Louise said wickedly, it stood out from the others rather like Madame's nose itself.

'I'm glad you wore the green dress tonight,' said Robert, as the waiter removed their plates and rearranged the table for dessert. 'Each time you wear it, I wonder if it's because you come from the Emerald Isle that you look so good in almost any shade of green,' he said, matter-of-factly. 'But you haven't worn that dress for some time now.'

'Haven't I?'

'No, you haven't. Not since you despatched a certain exceedingly eligible young man.'

'Oh.' She blushed slightly and then laughed. He was quite right. Recently, every time she put out a hand for an evening dress, she'd chosen the blue or the gold, but she hadn't noticed it herself.

'I wondered if you've worked out why you really rejected him,' he said, looking at her steadily over his dark-rimmed spectacles.

'But I told you, Robert.'

'Yes, you gave me a very sensible account of why you didn't think marrying him would be a good idea, but you didn't actually tell me why you rejected him.'

'Well, the two do go together, don't they?'

'Yes, but there is much to be learnt by separating the man from the ménage.'

'Fair point, Robert.' She paused and went on more slowly. 'I'm not sure I can do that.'

'Have a try.'

'Well, what I now see is that Christian needed me. Not the me that I am, but the person he thought I could be. Of course, he was quite right. I could have done what he wanted, if I'd put my mind to it. What he wanted was someone presentable, who would satisfy his parents, entertain his guests and provide him with children, a son, in particular, I should imagine. He couldn't exactly check out my childbearing potential, but he certainly did check out the rest.'

She paused, sensing there was yet more to say.

'Once I got to Toulouse and saw what he was doing, everything else fell into place. In all our time together, I realised he'd never wanted to know about *me*. Oh yes, he'd ask me what I thought about this painting or that sculpture, had I seen *Les Enfants Terribles*, did I like Baudelaire? He asked lots of questions, but never once did he ask about my home or my family. I don't think he'd have taken a great interest in Charlie Running or Mosey Jackson,' she added wryly.

They both laughed.

'Sometimes I've felt angry with Christian for choosing me to fit into his life,' she went on. 'More often, I've been angry with myself for ignoring all the signs. He was very egocentric and very determined. Perhaps I was flattered. And I shouldn't have been. I certainly won't make that mistake again.'

'You are being hard on yourself, aren't you?'

'Am I?'

'Yes, you are. You are young and attractive. An equally attractive, but not quite so young man comes along, shares many of your interests, enjoys your company. What is more likely than you should fall in love?'

'But should I not have seen why he was so happy to fall in love with me?'

'But how could you? You only had part of the picture. Why do you think I insist we drive round twisty roads and tramp through vineyards? The picture a person presents at the conference table is the picture they choose to present. One needs the broader context and the history to be able to read it accurately. You've always grasped that.'

'Yes, it always made sense to me at work, but I hadn't thought of applying it to my lovers,' she said wryly, grinning at him. 'I should have paid more attention to Christian's background, shouldn't I? After all, he never told me anything about himself, and I didn't ask.'

'Indeed yes. His background and upbringing taught him to expect to shape his life as he and his family have always shaped it, with their own interests firmly at the centre. Perhaps it's inevitable if one is very rich. What do you think?'

'No, I don't think it's money in itself. The Richardson family had lost all their money, but the Missus still behaved as if the world revolved around them.'

'Yes, but that family once had money, political power as well, if I remember correctly. Habits die hard. I've known men with hardly a sou in their pockets behaving as if they were still millionaires.'

'Is it power then, Robert? Is that what makes

Christian so convinced he can always have what he wants.'

Robert grinned broadly.

'I once interviewed a young woman who told me that she knew that money was power. She got the job.'

They both laughed, as the waiter arrived and Robert turned his attention to the menu's impressive list of desserts.

'If I might persuade you to the strawberry gateau,' he said, turning towards her. 'There is a rather special Château Latour Blanche that might be worthy of the occasion. The strawberries will be North African no doubt, but they should be reliable here.'

'I love strawberries,' she said, smiling.

After all this time, she was still amused by his total absorption in any decision involving what they should eat or drink.

The waiter served the dessert, then brought two delicate, engraved wine glasses lying on a bed of ice. He picked up each glass in turn with a white napkin, placed one before each of them, and poured a small measure of the pale yellow liquid into Robert's glass.

Robert picked it up, sniffed gently, took a tiny sip. Clare waited patiently. Nothing in the world would prevent Robert from giving the wine his fullest attention.

'Yes,' he said, positively, turning to me waiter. 'You have not disappointed me. You may tell the maitre I said so.'

The young man's face remained impassive. Clare saw a flicker of anxiety as he stepped back from Robert's chair to pour the delicate wine into her glass before returning to fill Robert's.

'Monsieur says you have not disappointed him. He is pleased,' she said softly, speaking Italian. 'You may tell your boss he said so.'

'Si, signorina,' he said, a broad smile spreading across his face. He bowed to them both and retired.

'Another willing slave,' said Robert dryly. 'How did you know that?'

'I didn't. I had to guess.'

'Well, we shall certainly have exceptional service henceforth,' he said, raising his glass. 'To you, my dear. Happy Birthday.'

The Sauterne tasted as she imagined nectar ought to taste. Smooth and sweet and rich, yet not at all cloying. She wondered if that was because the wine was so well chilled that beads of moisture formed on her glass.

'What do you think?'

'Wonderful. How can it be so rich and yet not be sickly?' He smiled, delighted.

'You could ask them yourself next week when we go down to the Gironde. On the other hand, you've probably started reading it up already and will know more about it than the people sent to impress us.'

She smiled, and wondered if he would return to the subject of Christian Moreau. It no longer hurt to speak about him, but there was still something about the whole affair that evaded her, some thought that teased on the edge of consciousness, like a word you can't remember.

'I dined with Emile last week,' Robert began, as he picked up his fork and sliced into the dry, crumbly texture of the strawberry gateau. 'He sends you his best regards. I think he is sad not to be able to welcome you as a niece, but he wasn't surprised when I told him that it was not to be.'

The gateau was superb. It was some moments before Robert went on.

'It seems Charles Moreau had a heart attack some two years ago. Not a major one, but a warning. Christian has been under some pressure to settle down. Emile thinks Christian has not given any thought to his relationships with women. He has seen them mainly as a source of companionship and pleasure. It has not yet occurred to him that a woman of any spirit might have thoughts and ambitions of her own.'

Clare nodded, a slow smile lighting up her face.

'A blessing on dear Emile. He's put his finger on it. Christian has just never thought about a woman as a person. And it would never occur to him that such a creature might have "thoughts and ambitions of her own". That's what you said, wasn't it, Robert?'

'Yes, I did,' he said, looking pleased.

'That's the bit I was looking for,' she began, taking a deep breath. 'If ever I marry anyone, he'll have to be aware of my "thoughts and ambitions". It's not that I wouldn't compromise, or change my life, or do something different from what I do now. It's the being thought about that counts. Unless a man can get beyond his own wishes, I'd rather make my own life with my dear friends and a job I love doing,' she said, much more firmly than she had intended.

'Bravo, Clare. I shall drink to that,' he said, raising his glass. 'Not many young women would have turned down one of the wealthiest young men in France. I think Emile was rather pleased. And, of course, so am I,' he added, smiling broadly.

She looked at him closely. All evening, there had been a kind of suppressed excitement about him, as if he were enjoying a secret known only to him. It was something he intended to share with her, of that she was sure, but it would most certainly be in his own good time.

They finished the delectable gateau and drained their glasses. 'May I pour you another glass, or do you wish to practise abstemiousness?' he said severely.

'Good heavens no.'

She laughed as he refilled her glass. The more severe he was, the more he was enjoying teasing her. 'I really can't see how you can call me abstemious, even if my housekeeping is modest,' she said, picking up her glass. 'Have I ever said no to any of the wonderful food you've chosen for me? Or the wines you have offered me?'

'No, that's true,' he admitted reluctantly. 'You don't play with your food like some young women do. And you enjoy good wine. But I see no jewellery. You buy your jewellery like you buy scarves, or handbags, simply to complete an outfit. Madame Japolsky has no cause for complaint. You always look perfectly turned out. But I see no diamond brooches or gold necklaces. Not a thing from Cartier,' he said, with a shrug of his shoulders.

'But Robert, even if I were terribly rich I don't think I'd buy jewellery from Cartier.'

'Why not?'

'I don't know.'

'You have a silver pendant you sometimes wear with your plum dress. It is very attractive.'

'Oh, that *is* precious,' she said quickly. 'Michelle and Philippe gave me that last Christmas.'

He grinned broadly and sipped his wine.

Clare was perfectly aware that the wine had made her face glow and she probably needed to apply powder to the end of her nose, but Robert was in such very good spirits she decided not to bother. He seemed to be enjoying himself even more than usual.

'I did not send you a birthday card, Clare. I am too discreet,' he said, teasing once again. 'But I have allowed myself the indulgence of a gift. If you are abstemious, I see no reason why I should be.'

He slipped a hand in his pocket and brought out the kind of black velvet box that can only contain jewellery. He slid it across the table to her.

'Robert!' she gasped, as she opened it.

'Don't be alarmed. They're not emeralds. If they were, you'd probably keep them in the bank. But they've been designed specially for you. I once did the accounts for a goldsmith. And I learnt a thing or two, like you learnt at your friend's gallery.'

Clare sat gazing down at the silk-lined box. A necklace, a bracelet and a pair of matching clip-on earrings winked and gleamed in the light, sparkling with cut green stones set in a delicate gold tracery that reminded her of lace.

'They are so beautiful,' she said slowly. 'I don't think I have ever seen anything so beautiful in my life.'

'But will you wear them?'

'Immediately,' she said, standing up. 'If you will excuse me.'

The powder room was empty. From each gleaming mirror, she saw herself reflected back a

393

dozen times, her fingers shaking as she fastened first the necklace, then the bracelet. Finally she clipped on the earrings. No wonder he'd been pleased at her choice of dress. She would always have to have an emerald-green evening dress. It made the perfect foil for the brilliant sparkle and pale gleam of the first jewellery she'd ever possessed.

'Wonderful,' he said, 'wonderful,' as she slipped back into her seat. 'Some day you will wear them for my friend. He is nearly blind now, but his hands are so practised. Shall I tell him you are pleased?'

'That, Robert, would be an understatement such as only the English use,' she said firmly. 'I shall treasure them all my life,' she went on, much less steadily, as his worn face blurred with the mist of her welling tears.

CHAPTER TWENTY-TWO

The visit to the Gironde was a delight. The warm autumn sunshine glanced off the fading vine leaves, making their shades of bronze and gold more vivid; the waysides were fresh with new growth, the sky a rain-washed blue with small, white clouds moving rapidly in the breeze. Their tour of the vineyards was far more like a pleasurable outing than a necessary part of the job.

Clare enjoyed this new countryside, but what pleased her most as she stood again on the fringes of a vineyard, long harvested and now being pruned, was that the sadness of giving up Christian had faded away. She'd even been able to use all she'd learnt from Charles Moreau on that morning at Chirey without thinking yet once again about the events of the following day.

Among the proposed investors in this particular project were a number of Americans, quite unlike the slow-speaking and good-natured mid-Westerners she'd encountered so far. At times, she could almost imagine that this strangely assorted group with their briefcases and clipboards were deliberately trying to unnerve the château staff with their sharply aggressive questions. They didn't seem to appreciate that those who made the wine knew perfectly well what they did and how they did it, but found great difficulty in explaining *why* they did it.

Clare worked hard to smooth over some of the difficulties and take the edge out of the hostile questions, but she made sure never to look at Robert while she was doing it. She knew he was enjoying himself hugely. Only when they were left to themselves did she berate him for trying to catch her eye when he knew she was taking considerable liberties with the translation.

'At least now I can answer Keith Harvey's question,' she said, as they relaxed over coffee in their hotel.

'Which particular question was that?'

'He asked me if I always translated exactly and what I did if someone was rude or unpleasant.'

'You may tell him from me that you always defend the less articulate. At the same time, you impose a considerable control over those who should know better. I quite enjoyed hearing everything twice this time round.'

'Why do you think these Americans were so unfriendly? Particularly the tall one with the sharp face. Surely one can tell when people are competent by the quality of what they produce rather than by asking awkward technical questions.'

Robert poured himself more coffee and grunted.

'I can't answer that. Something about *amour propre* perhaps. If the Americans were trying to maintain face in an area where they're not very knowledgeable, hostile questioning might be their way of doing it. Don't forget you have a gift they certainly do not have. You know who you can trust. I think I've said that to you more than once before. Certainly I've had no cause to change my mind.'

'What about Christian Moreau?' she said, wryly.

'Including Christian Moreau,' he replied firmly. 'That young man was perfectly trustworthy as far as your relationship went. Beyond that, you did not go. Your intuitions warned you something was wrong. So it does with these edgy Americans. Alternatively, it guides you with diffident Englishmen.'

'Charles Langley?'

'Yes. I told you at the time I was confused by him. You saw through his difficulty to the man himself.'

Clare smiled. 'He's a dear man, quite incapable of deceit, but he hasn't begun to understand himself.'

'So that is why you rejected him?'

'Oh, no. I couldn't possibly *reject* Charles Langley. He's had too much of that already. No, I explained I wasn't the right person for him. He wasn't very happy about it, but at least it means we can be friends. We keep in touch and I shall certainly see him if he comes to Paris.'

Robert raised an eyebrow in a very Gallic manner.

'Perhaps it's a little early to speak of this, but our conversation makes it relevant. You have been a great success as a translator. But I think you might consider going beyond translation and moving to the financial side. Another year or so and you would be quite ready to take on some of the smaller accounts. I'd have to part with you, which would be a pity, but that has always been a possibility. You'd still be based in Paris, unless you wanted to move elsewhere.'

'Robert!'

He stood up and smiled down at her.

'There's no need to make any sort of decision. Just think about it. And perhaps you ought also to think about going to bed. You want to be on form for the gentleman of the sharp face and sharp questions tomorrow morning, don't you?'

When Clare arrived back in Paris, two days later, she was so glad to be home, weary after the intensity of the work and the long train journey, but buoyed up by the lovely autumn weather, the success of the negotiations and Robert's unexpected suggestions about her future.

Sitting in the Metro with only a few stops to go, she closed her book, put it in her handbag and sat back in her seat with her eyes closed. 'Could I be anywhere else in the world but Paris?' she asked herself, with that glow of pleasure that came to her so often when she was in the city. She focused on the sounds all around her, the noise of the rackety doors as they closed, the chatter of students, the sharpness of children's voices, the unfamiliar tones of two young Algerian men sitting opposite.

She'd loved this city since she was a little girl, far away in another country, listening to the wireless her father had reconditioned for Granda Scott. Now it was her home. What Robert said about moving to the financial side reminded her once more that it was Paris that spoke to her. However much she enjoyed travelling round this huge and varied country, however exciting the possibilities might be were she to move to a regional branch, she'd no intention of doing so. Paris was where she wanted to be.

'It might be the right thing for me, it might not. What matters is that Robert thinks I have the option. I can make a life of my own,' she said to herself, as she came up the steps of the Metro, put down her case and studied Madame Givrey's flowers.

'How are you, mam'selle? Where was it this time?'

'Bordeaux and the Gironde.'

'Oh, la la, so far away.'

'Yes, Madame. I'm glad to be home. I have a few days' holiday, so I shall be able to look after my flowers properly,' she said, choosing a mixed bouquet of pink and mauve stocks with Shasta daisies and sprays of gypsophila and maidenhair fern.

'These are lovely, Madame. They will keep me company when I sit by my window and read. I intend to be very lazy.'

Madame laughed heartily. Being lazy was not something she associated with this young woman who appeared early in the morning, often to return only late at night.

There was no sign of Madame Dubois as Clare let herself in to her apartment. To her surprise, there was an envelope face down on the carpet as she opened the door.

'Good gracious,' she said, amused that anyone could have managed to by-pass Madame.

She took her suitcase to the bedroom, changed and left her bouquet to soak in the kitchen before she came back into the sitting room to study the envelope. The writing looked familiar but she couldn't place it. Clearly a late birthday card, but the postmark was London. With a sudden spurt of anxiety, she ripped it open, took out the pretty floral card and glanced at the signature. 'Love, Ginny,' it said, in large, bold handwriting.

A sheet of lined paper folded inside fell on the carpet. She picked it up, her fingers trembling as she tried to open it out.

'My dearest Clare,' she read aloud, still standing in the middle of the room.

I am ashamed of myself. You wrote me such a lovely letter when you got to Paris and you sent a Christmas card too, even though I hadn't had the decency to reply. I am sorry, sorry, sorry. I think I just couldn't cope when you and Andrew split up. I've always been a bit soft on him, as I'm sure you guessed, but after Teddy died I just couldn't bear to see him so sad and so hurt. He did all the right things and worked so hard to sort out all the miserable stuff about probate and so on, but I couldn't bear it and didn't know how to tell you. He seems better now, but what has helped me most is finding Daniel. I met him when I was in London to have the plastic surgery Andrew organised for me, and now we're engaged. Do you remember when I cried all over you, you said that my scars wouldn't matter at all to someone who loved me? You were right. I met Daniel before I went into the Clinic and that's just what he said.

There's so much I want to tell you about, it's all bubbling over and I have to go. All I want is for you to say you forgive me for being such a silly girl and making such a mess of things when you'd been so good to me and helped me so much when Teddy died. Then I'll be the happiest girl in the world again. I shall probably get married in London next year. Please, PLEASE, will you come?

'Love, Ginny,' Clare repeated, and promptly burst into tears.

In the days that followed, Clare read and reread Ginny's letter many times. She knew perfectly well she was searching for something that wasn't there. Only Ginny herself could answer the questions that came crowding into her mind.

She sat by her window, staring across the waters of the Seine, swollen after the autumn rains, and suddenly saw a deep, narrow river flowing alongside a narrow, overgrown track leading to the shores of Lough Neagh. She closed her eyes and went back to that lovely summer day. Four young people having a picnic. Ginny and Teddy. Clare and Andrew. She felt the tears spill out under her closed lids. Within the year Teddy was dead, Ginny's face was scarred across her cheeks and forehead, and Clare and Andrew had parted, all their bright hopes ending in disappointment and despair.

She wept, longer and more bitterly than she had wept at the time. She wept for Teddy, for the boy he had been when she first knew him, for the hours they'd spent sitting by the tennis court talking history. She saw that pale, unmarked figure, unmoving on the high hospital bed, felt again Helen cling to her, knowing she was about to lose her only son.

'Loss and more loss,' she said, sobbing. 'Is that all life is about?' Losing those you love? Losing them to disease, like her parents, to age, like Robert, to accident, like Teddy, to circumstance, like Andrew. How could she bear to live with such a catalogue of loss?

'All those hopes and dreams,' she wept, shaking her head, thinking of the evening the four of them went up to the obelisk on Cannon Hill and sat in the dusk talking about their future. Teddy hadn't even a year of future. She and Andrew only a few days more than he had.

'And Jessie, too,' she added, sniffing. 'She's never been the same since Andrew and I parted.'

She thought of the empty house on the Malone Road, the room where they kept the paint, the smell of ancient wallpaper when you soaked it before you scraped it off. She remembered the night they dined for the first time, the four of them, Jessie a few months' pregnant and still her lively self.

'All gone,' she said. 'All gone.'

She tried to distract herself. Went for long walks, hardly noticing where she was going. Twice she found herself in parts of the city quite unknown to her, tired out and hungry, and had to find the nearest Metro to take her home. She went to the Louvre, determined to revisit pictures she'd not had time to enjoy when she went with Christian, and found herself standing looking at some tiny detail, a flower, or a tree, or some tangled grass, quite oblivious to the subject of the picture itself.

It was some time before she owned up to herself that she'd been thinking particularly about Andrew. His life had been disrupted too, just as her own had been. He'd lost a beloved cousin, inherited massive financial problems that she'd only just begun to grasp. He too had lost someone he'd loved and, with her, his hope of making a new life.

'He's better now,' were the only words in Ginny's letter to give her any comfort. And comfort was what she badly needed, for on top of Edward's death there was now the unbearable heartache of knowing Andrew had been 'sad and hurt'.

Time and time again, she went through the events of their last weeks together. She tried to see how anything could have been different. Whichever way she looked at it, she could see no alternative. Even so, she could not stop her tears whenever she thought of him facing up to the legal mess he'd inherited, disillusioned with the law and utterly distressed by her loss.

Only after Clare telephoned Marie-Claude to invite her to a long-delayed lunch, did she ask herself why she hadn't rung her as soon as Ginny's letter arrived. If she'd had the sense to talk to her wise friend, she might have fared much better these last, sad days.

'You look wonderful, Marie-Claude. The academic life suits you,' she said, greeting her friend under the trees in the Luxembourg Gardens. 'Sometimes I'd just love to sit and read a book, not just search for the bits I need.'

Marie-Claude took a long look at her young friend. She seemed thinner and a little drawn, but her eyes were sparkling and she was beautifully dressed. She'd been a model pupil, but in learning to dress like a Frenchwoman she had brought to the enterprise something special of her own, a way of moving, a light and warmth in her eyes.

She was not beautiful, but there was a liveliness

about her, a mobility of face, figure and mood, that was more appealing than beauty itself, a liveliness that did not wholly disappear even when she was sad.

'Gerard sends you his love. He hasn't asked how the lovers are since you turned down one of the most eligible young men in France. But he'll get over it,' she said wryly. 'You seem to me to be quite content with your decision,' she added, hugging her.

Clare smiled as they began to walk together, the gentle motion encouraging their thought processes as they strolled along, side by side.

'My concierge despairs of me still,' she began. 'Not even the sign of a lover when she comes to collect my laundry. Christian never came to the apartment. Robert sometimes sends me flowers when we dine. I know she tries to see the card, but even when it shows, he never signs it,' she said, laughing.

She fell silent, and they walked on a few paces while she brought herself to the point.

'I need your advice, Marie-Claude. I need it badly.'

Clare then told her about Ginny's letter and about the sad, distressed days she'd spent since it arrived.

'I've thought and thought, Marie-Claude, and I don't know what to do. I'm so grateful that

Ginny's written and I do so want to see her, but I can't decide what to do about Andrew. I can't get him out of my mind.'

'Do I take it you still love him?'

'I certainly care what happens to him,' she said, resignedly. 'Sometimes I think I don't really know what loving someone is supposed to feel like. I know about desire, and that's easy enough,' she added lightly. 'But that's never been what I wanted.'

'What do you want, chérie?'

'To feel safe. To feel in command of my life and have a friend at my side,' she said simply.

'And with Andrew you did feel safe? A friend at your side?'

'Yes. Most of the time. There was a kind of unspoken understanding between us. Even when he couldn't explain himself, I often knew what he was feeling. And it worked the other way round as well . . . mostly.'

'But not always?'

'No, not always. Sometimes I felt a barrier come between us. I blamed it on his family and the way they'd treated him. That's why we planned to go to Canada.'

'You were going to run away?'

'No, we were going to marry and go out and make a new life,' Clare replied, seriously. 'Like so many have done before us.'

Marie-Claude smiled at her. 'You're taking me

very literally, Clare,' she said gently. 'Are you sure that making a life in Canada would have resolved the difficulties? Were you not perhaps hoping to leave behind problems that would have been waiting for you when you arrived?'

'You may well be right,' Clare agreed promptly. 'I knew I had to get away from Ulster. Andrew was so relieved, so excited, when we decided on Canada.'

She paused, aware of a sudden revealing thought. 'Perhaps, after all, Canada meant different things for each of us.'

Marie-Claude looked at her, saw the familiar knitted eyebrows, the preoccupied look in her eyes. She decided to say nothing and wait and see what emerged.

'You know, the very first time I flew, the weather was awful,' Clare began. 'We climbed very steeply and suddenly we came out above all the murk and it was magnificent, pure blue sky and great mountains of cloud towering up to the west of us, snowy white. It made me think of Canada and the Rockies, all that space and clear air. That was what kept me going, those last months before my Finals, the thought of Canada, and Andrew, and escaping.'

'Escaping?'

Clare looked at her friend, saw the warmth and concern in her eyes, and took her hand.

'You are so tactful. So wise. What you have just helped me see is that Canada was a country of the mind, not a reality. Neither Andrew nor anyone else could ever take me there,' she said, suddenly weary. 'So what do I do now?'

Marie-Claude squeezed her hand in reply. 'You take me to lunch, and we celebrate your hard work. Separating reality from illusion is very hard work indeed. So hard, I have many friends twice your age who've never had the wisdom to attempt it. We shall need a very good lunch indeed. In a little while, you will begin to feel the rewards of your achievement.'

Late that afternoon, after the two friends had enjoyed each other's company and parted in the best of spirits, Clare sat down and wrote to Ginny. It wasn't really difficult at all, even after this amount of time. Clare wrote just as she would have spoken had Ginny been sitting on the other side of the table. Warmly and directly, she told her there was absolutely nothing to forgive. That she too had had things she'd not been able to cope with any better than she had.

She responded enthusiastically to the idea of a meeting in London, saying she was over quite often on business, though usually at rather short notice. She would certainly come to her wedding, and was already looking forward to meeting Daniel.

She told Ginny a bit about her own life, picking out what would entertain or interest her, describing the marvellous collection of horse pictures in her boss's office, her first attempts at skiing back in March, and some of the funny things that happened when translation broke down. It was only as she came towards the end of a second large sheet that she realised she had a decision to make. To mention or not to mention Andrew.

She sat quite still for a long minute, staring at the bright eyes of the daisies in Madame Givrey's bouquet. Yes, that was what they reminded her of. The ox-eye daisies outside the forge, growing up around the old reaping machine that no one ever came to collect, the one she'd driven across the Canadian prairies. She took up her pen again and finished the letter quickly.

'I'm glad things are better for Andrew now,' she wrote. 'I think of him and would like to know how he is. I've been told that winding up estates can be a rotten job. I hope the worst is over and that all is well at The Lodge. Do let me know when you get a chance to write. With love and all the good wishes in the world for your engagement. Clare.'

She read it through once and changed nothing, folded it, and wrote the address on the envelope. The breeze had got up and was blowing little spatters of rain across her window. She pulled on a jacket and took the letter to the post box, a sense of excitement rising as she turned to come back and felt the wind begin to buffet her, blowing rain in her face and whirling leaves around her feet.

'Life will always bring change, and unhappy change at that, but there will also be joy,' she said to the empty quayside. 'Like Aunt Sarah said, "All things pass, good and bad." Perhaps what is really important is learning to make the best you can of the good bits and accept as well as you can the bad. That was what Emile used to say when he was looking at the state of a company.

'It's going to be a wild old night,' she said to herself, as she stepped under the archway and climbed the steps to her own entrance. 'A good night to be at home by the fire,' she went on, 'with the lamp lit and a book.'

She was pleased at the idea of Emile's 'dictum', which had suddenly come to her. She could see him now, sitting so quietly at the boardroom table, his papers neatly lined up in front of him, suggesting to the prospective borrowers that perhaps they had resources that were not visible in their balance sheet, the resources that came from the experience they'd gained.

As she opened the door of her apartment and saw her writing materials where she'd left them, spread out on the table in a pool of light from the lamp, suddenly and unexpectedly her spirits soared. She felt just as if the sun had come out again from behind a cloud. Some darkness of spirit had passed away. Wouldn't Emile say she had gained precious experience from the pain of all her sadness and loss?

CHAPTER TWENTY-THREE

Refreshed by her few days' holiday and delighted by the prospect of seeing Ginny again, Clare shared her good news with Robert as soon as she went back to work.

'But this is splendid. Of course you must see her when next we go to London. I shall keep an afternoon free and you must ask her to lunch. Perhaps I shall go and look at some pictures,' he added, as if the thought had only just struck him.

'Like the morning you packed me off with Charles Langley?' she replied, laughing, and nodding towards his newest acquisition.

'I have few vices,' he said, with a slight twinkle. 'At least this one hurts nothing but my wallet.'

He stood up and handed her a sheaf of papers.

'You will find almost everything there is in French, but I should like you to assist me nevertheless. Regrettably it's Avignon and not London, but that's only a matter of time. Tell Ginny we shall certainly be over before Christmas.'

She looked down at the sheaf of papers in her hand, hesitated, and made up her mind.

'Robert, there's something I wanted to ask you, but I've never found quite the right moment. Perhaps there isn't a right one, so can I ask you now, or are you very pressed?'

By way of reply he lifted his phone.

'Paul, I do not wish to be interrupted. I shall tell you when I'm free.'

He put the phone down and waved her back to their armchairs.

'Last time we were in Avignon, I met some young people down by the river,' she began, taking a deep breath. 'It was the afternoon when you visited your sister. They were so nice, a boy and a girl and a spaniel called Conker. It was because of him we got talking. It emerged that the boy's mother ran away with him when the Germans advanced. She'd told them about the Stukers firing at them.'

She looked at Robert, anxious lest the memories should still be painful.

'The village she mentioned was Aiguilles.' He jerked his head upwards.

'That was where my sister-in-law lived,' he said flatly.

'So their mother might possibly have known your wife?'

'Inevitably,' he said abruptly. 'As likely as it

414

is for your grandfather to have known Charlie Running or Mosey Jackson.'

Clare looked at him sadly, wishing she hadn't spoken. Was it really worth upsetting him with the possibility that this chance meeting might somehow help to resolve the fate of his son, one way or another?

Robert leaned back in his chair as if he were suddenly very weary.

'What do you think we should do?' he asked.

Clare was taken aback. Often enough in the course of their work he asked her opinion. But never before had he put such a personal question to her. And never before had she seen such a strange, pained look on his face.

So what did she think? Was it better to let the past be the past? Or should she trust her intuitions. She thought again of the sturdy figure, so like Robert himself, walking along the river bank with Conker. Somewhere there might be another perfectly ordinary young man of the same age and the same sturdy shape who might turn out to be Robert's son.

'I know you tried to find out what happened to your son. You told me about it when first we met, but you haven't mentioned it since. Are you still in contact with any of the agencies?'

He shook his head sadly and said nothing, his whole manner suggesting he had no power to act. She had never seen him look so defeated before, not even when a major negotiation went wrong.

'Then I think we should look at the list together,' she said firmly, amazed at her own coolness. 'We can ask whichever one we choose to write to the children's mother and see if Madame Duchamps can help in any way. We've nothing to lose.'

'And everything to gain,' he said, gathering himself up and smiling, as if he'd been released from a disabling spell. 'A long time ago I set hope aside, but I have never turned my back upon it. I've often told you that banking is about risk. So is life. If you protect yourself all the time from hurt, there is little possibility of joy. But sometimes one needs to be encouraged. It is time to try again,' he said easily.

He stood up, crossed the room and took an envelope from his desk.

'I saw my old friend Hugo at the weekend, the jeweller who made your necklace. He is copying the Missus's brooch for you. Meantime, he has sent you this. I think you will find it interesting.'

He walked to the door with her.

'I'll bring my files of letters for you tomorrow and there'll be time in Avignon to answer your questions.'

Clare ran lightly downstairs, hardly aware of the familiar view over the banking hall or the still lingering smell of new paint and new carpet as she approached her office, her mind full of their conversation.

Expecting to see Louise, she smiled as she opened the door to their office, but the room was empty. On her desk a folded sheet of paper sat like a tent. She took it up and read:

Dentist and then couturier, by order of M.J. After the drill and the pins I shall expect lunch and sympathy. Rue Scribe 12.30. Your turn. All right?
Much love,
Louise

Clare smiled, amused by her note. She was pleased too, for Louise now left her notes in Italian and she'd managed all of it without having to fetch a dictionary.

She sat down and carefully opened the brown envelope Robert had given her. Inside, there was a letter written in a flowing hand on an elegant but yellowed sheet of paper, a note in biro in a firm, clear hand that sometimes ran below the lines designed to guide it and a sketch on a piece of invoice paper. Unambiguously, the sketch was the design for the emerald brooch the Missus had left her.

The letter was dated April 1895. The ink had

scarcely faded, but the loops and curlicues of the elaborate hand were difficult to disentangle. The French was not only old-fashioned, but slightly strange. The signature went some way to explain this. Despite the flourish with which it had been completed she was able to read quite clearly the word 'Voroshinsky'.

'Russian or Polish?' she whispered to herself.

'My dear Zimmerman,' she began, reading aloud.

I am returning the sketch at your hand. It is charming and I am sure will be to the pleasure of the lady in question. The Countess has been most indulgent and has contracted to me an emerald from The Great Necklace of which we have spoken. I shall have it in my keeping when I return to Paris next month. Please make ready the gold for the setting as I shall wish to take the brooch with me to Deauville with the greatest haste after my return.

There was some courteous expression which she couldn't decipher and then the flourishing signature. 'A signature fit for a Prince?'

She took up the note in biro. It was perfectly easy to read, despite the fact that the lines of words ran downhill.

Dear Mademoiselle Clare,

Thank you for your comments and good wishes. I hope your jewellery will bring you great pleasure, as it did for me in the making. I am most interested to hear from my good friend the story of the brooch the old lady gave to you. Now that I have examined it, I am sure my father fitted the emerald, but I remember I myself worked on the tracery. I also remember the young count when he came to the workshop so long ago and how pleased he was with the brooch. He was Polish and a very handsome young man. His family had large estates near Cracow. But he never came again.

Yours sincerely,
Hugo Zimmerman

'He never came again,' she repeated sadly, as she put the letters and sketch carefully back in their envelope.

It was Paul who'd suggested she have the emerald brooch copied because it was too valuable to wear, and Robert who'd expressed surprise at the similarity between the brooch she'd brought to him and the necklace he himself had given her for her birthday. She hadn't noticed herself until she'd seen them together. She was delighted. It seemed she'd made an important link with the Missus. They'd both had jewellery made by the Zimmermans in Paris.

'I hope you marry your Prince,' the Missus had written in the note Andrew had found and passed to her solicitors. Clare sighed. Well, she hadn't. So many puzzles, so many questions with no answers. She thought of the two gold rings in Harry's safe. She now knew the date they'd been made, but the story of those lovers she'd have to invent for herself.

She put the brown envelope in her top drawer, took up the first of the documents in front of her and gave her mind totally to the present.

It was some five weeks later that Clare and Robert once again had meetings in London.

'Clare, you look marvellous. I'm *so* pleased to see you,' said Ginny, as she threw her arms round Clare and hugged her vigorously, quite indifferent to the glances of the other women who sat in the foyer of the hotel in Park Lane.

'And I'm pleased to see you too, Ginny,' said Clare, kissing her. 'Any hope that Daniel will be able to come?'

'No,' she said, shaking her head vigorously. 'I told him he'd have to wait till the wedding; I wanted you all to myself. I want to hear *everything* about Paris and all these wonderful trips you do.

How was Italy? I loved your postcard . . .'

Clare could hardly believe the transformation. Admittedly, the last time they'd been together was the week of Edward's funeral, when at least one of them had been in tears at any time. But it was more than that. This was a quite new Ginny. She'd always been open and direct in manner and was often very amusing, but often enough in the past Clare had seen her withdraw quite suddenly, only happy when she was working alone with her horses.

'Louise sounds fun,' Ginny went on. 'Have you made a lot of new friends? Daniel seems to know *masses* of people. I've never been to so many parties in my life.'

As the two girls walked towards the dining room, she said shyly, 'Have you noticed, Clare?'

'Yes, I have,' said Clare honestly. 'It's quite wonderful. What about the other one?'

Ginny sat down and stroked back the shining auburn fringe that lay across her forehead. A fine white line ran above her left eye and disappeared into her hair on the right temple.

'I have special make-up I can wear if I want to put my hair up, but they say it will fade further. And if it doesn't, I can have it done like the ones on my cheeks. I can't believe it, Clare, I really can't. I thought it was the end of the world. Though I suppose it might have been but for Andrew.'

She stopped, put her hand to her mouth and gasped.

'Oh Clare, I'm sorry. I didn't mean to mention Andrew. It just slipped out. Anyway, we mustn't talk about my silly old scars. They're nearly gone. It's time I forgot them.

Clare shook her head. 'Don't be silly, Ginny. I want to know what's been happening to you. And you don't have to avoid mentioning Andrew. I want to hear about him too,' she said, reassuringly. 'And you mustn't "forget" your scars,' she went on, looking closely at Ginny's face, 'even if I can't see them any more. I have a lovely friend in Paris; she's a good deal older than we are. She says you must never forget what's happened to you. "How can you learn from your experience if you forget it?" she says. "Look back to learn, look forward to live," that's Marie-Claude's philosophy. I think she has a point, don't you?'

Ginny grinned sheepishly. 'You think more than I do, Clare. I don't believe I really thought about anything very much till Teddy died. Then I thought so much, I got in an awful mess. I had to have tablets for depression. I couldn't face seeing anyone. I didn't go out for weeks. I got Barney to sell Conker for me because I couldn't look after her properly. Andrew was the only one I could talk to. He said all things pass, however awful. That you have to see if you can make anything of them, so that, when you come out on the other side, you're further on than you were.'

Ginny broke off as the waiter came to take their order.

'Go on, Ginny. What happened then?' Clare said, as soon as he had retreated.

'Well, Andrew made me go out, and then he took me to this nice man in Belfast. He made me talk about Teddy and how I felt about him. It was awful, Clare. I used to just sit and cry and he'd pass me tissues and wait till I stopped. I went to him for weeks. It must have cost a fortune.'

When the food arrived they both admitted how hungry they were.

'Mm, this is marvellous,' said Ginny, as she munched her pasta.

Clare ate more slowly and listened as Ginny talked in short bursts, mostly about Daniel but also about Caledon and Drumsollen. A hazy picture of what had been happening to the Richardson estate began to emerge. By the time coffee appeared, Clare had quite a number of questions to ask, but she wasn't sure how accurately Ginny could answer them.

'So The Lodge will end up as a hotel, will it?'

'Probably. It was going to have to go anyway, because of the death duties and the upkeep costs. Mum and I have some money from Grandad Barbour, but dear old Barney hasn't a bean. His first wife was rolling in money and he helped her spend it. They had a wonderful time and were terribly happy, but when she died, hers was all gone and he was broke as well. I wondered why Mum ever got involved with him. Actually, I was rather horrible about it to begin with,' she confessed. 'If it hadn't been for Teddy I'd have gone on being a pain about him. But Teddy told me off. Barney is just so kind, and being kind is worth a ton of money, he said.'

She picked up her cup and drained it. 'Is there any more in that pot, Clare?'

'Yes, lots and lots,' Clare replied, reaching for her empty cup.

She remembered so clearly a tear-sodden morning when she herself had wept all over Barney's rough tweed jacket, and he'd lent her a silk handkerchief with racehorses on the border.

'Well, Andrew got stuck in,' Ginny went on. 'He took advice and sold off the Caledon farmland to the people it had been let to, except for some fields close to the house and the paddocks. Then he got a something on the death duties. Can't remember the word. It means they don't throw you in jail for debt provided you cough up what you can and pay the rest within a certain period. And he raised a loan, so Mum and Barney could find a house. Oh Clare, it's the loveliest house, quite small, only four bedrooms, down at Rostrevor, looking out over Carlingford Lough. It has wonderful gardens. You'd love them.'

Clare listened, delighted by Ginny's liveliness. She went on to talk about going to London to stay with friends of her mother when Andrew was able to find the money for her plastic surgery, but finding out something about Andrew himself was proving much more difficult than Clare had expected. She waited patiently. When Ginny paused to drink her coffee, she took her opportunity.

'So is Andrew farming at Drumsollen?'

'Goodness no,' she said laughing. 'What made you think of that? He's working as a solicitor in Armagh. Drumsollen's been shut up since the Missus died back in May. I expect he'll have to sell it. He probably needs the money for the death duties, like with The Lodge. The Lodge isn't on the market yet. He says it's not fit to sell till it's had a facelift. It's had nothing done to it for years. Good old Harry just fixed things and kept them going. You remember Teddy tackling the sitting room, don't you? No, there's no chance he can keep it. Drumsollen will have to go.'

'Charles, how lovely you could come,' she said, putting down her book and walking up to him, as he strode into the foyer and looked around. She kissed his cold cheek and brushed flakes of melting snow from his shoulders. 'Sorry about the short notice. And the weather,' she said lightly.

'Not a bit, I'm just so pleased to see you. What's Robert up to?'

'He hasn't told me,' she said, laughing. 'But if he appears with a parcel under his arm, don't be surprised. He went off yesterday afternoon and came back asking if I'd mind staying a few hours longer. There was some business he had to complete after this morning's meeting. So we're on the evening flight, not the afternoon one. Now, have you time for a drink first, or have you only got an hour?'

Charles Langley threw out his hands.

'I am yours to command,' he said cheerfully. 'I've run away, absconded. Absent without leave. Till about four o'clock anyway,' he added, with a wry smile.

'Oh that's lovely. I want to hear *all* your news.'

They settled comfortably and began to talk, moving easily between business and more personal matters. The Covent Garden project which had first brought them together was going from strength to strength, even better than anyone had expected.

'Do you still get fed up with the importing business, Charles?'

'Yes, I do,' he said honestly, leaning back in his armchair and twirling the stem of his sherry glass. 'But there are compensations. I fly at weekends. And I didn't have to come in a taxi,' he said laughing. 'I've got a new car. An actual new car, not off the second-hand lot.'

'Oh that's great news. I know how much you enjoy driving. You had the odd bad moment that day you took me on a Langley's Tour. On the steep hills.'

'And how. Wish I could whiz you round in the new one.'

'Ah, but there were advantages to the old one. I could take in the countryside. All those lovely patches of woodland and green fields. I sometimes think of your bit of England when we're doing vine-yards in the south of France. "England's green and pleasant land", as my school hymn would have it.'

'But your school was in Ireland. How come you sang 'Jerusalem'?'

Clare laughed and shook her head.

'I haven't the remotest idea, Charles, but I always sang it with passion. I think I miss *my* green and pleasant land.'

'Do you?' He looked at her in amazement.

'Wouldn't you miss yours?'

'Well, yes. I suppose I would. Never thought of it before.'

She smiled to herself, amused by the directness and the honesty of the man, who had always told her the truth, even when it was to his own disadvantage.

'Say you inherited a nice French château,' she began cheerfully. 'Lots of lovely vineyards running nicely. Guaranteed income, very large. Oh, and an airfield nearby for your private plane,' she added, as the thought struck her. 'But you had to go and *live* there. What would you do?' she said, looking him straight in the eye.

'You do ask them, don't you?'

She giggled.

'Well . . .' he said, opening the menu the waiter had just brought. 'If you like pasta, it was great yesterday,' she said, helpfully.

'Mm . . . yes, good idea.'

'Can I choose the wine, or will you?'

'You choose. I'm too busy walking round the vineyard I've inherited to see if I like its wine.'

'Well?' she asked, after she'd chosen a Châteauneuf-du-Pape she'd tasted in the vineyard near Avignon.

'Perhaps I could commute,' he suggested. 'Château in France and cottage on the Downs? How about that?'

'No, it has to be a real choice. No sneaky compromises.'

'Oh well, sad as it is, all that lovely wine and lolly, I'd choose the Downs.'

She laughed happily. 'Oh Charles, I'm so glad. I thought it was only me that got homesick when I'd everything I could ever wish for.'

'You?' he said, amazed. 'But I thought you loved France.'

'No, I like France; I do like it very much. I find it interesting and often very beautiful. It's Paris that I love, not France. But sometimes, even in Paris, I long for my little green hills. That day you took me out, I think it was homesickness that suddenly came upon me when we got back to your nice house.'

He smiled wryly. 'To my advantage.'

'To *our* advantage, Charles,' she said gently. 'I won't ever forget how loving you were.'

The wine waiter arrived, poured a taster into Charles's glass and stood back. Charles sipped it, looked severe and nodded.

'He should have let you taste it, given you chose it,' he said, as soon as the waiter was out of earshot.

She shook her head and smiled.

'Still a man's world, Charles, for all the talk of equality and women's rights. But it's coming on a bit. At least I can ring you up and ask you to lunch. My treat. What do you think of the pasta?'

'Great, just great. I've had worse in Italian restaurants. And I like this wine too, now that I'm not being asked to taste it.'

Clare was pleased that Charles could be so relaxed and easy with her. It hurt her still to remember how downcast he was when she told him she wasn't the right woman for him, however easy it would be to love him. It wasn't that they wouldn't get on well together – they would. But after the first joy of having someone to be with, someone to love, she knew they'd end up feeling lonely all over again. What Charles needed was someone like Ginny, someone far more outgoing than she was.

She watched him as he ate, enjoying his pasta, as he enjoyed so many things.

She knew she'd made him sad, and yet, by the time he'd taken her back to her hotel, he'd been able to take the friendship she'd offered. He'd hugged her and kissed her cheeks like a Frenchman.

'You are a funny one, Clare Hamilton,' he'd said. 'Here I am ready to die for you and you turn me round and point me in a different direction. At the bottom of it, I know you're right, damn it, yet I can't think how I know. Don't desert me, will you?'

She had promised willingly. 'Of course I won't. I'll come and dance at your wedding. And you can come to mine, should I ever marry.'

'Thank you,' she now said, as the waiter set down a tray of coffee and presented a document for her to sign.

She wrote her name and wondered if she would ever change it. Marriage had looked so easy when she and Andrew got engaged, but it had somehow become a much more problematic thing. Threatening, as well as promising. She would never forget how much she loved Christian Moreau, nor the frightening prospect which had opened up at the thought of being married to him.

'I haven't asked you about John and Jane Coleman,' she said, suddenly remembering the anxieties of that visit.

'Oh, they're fine. Absolutely besotted with son and heir. They've asked us to be godparents at his christening next month.'

She looked at him sharply, and laughed when he suddenly looked sheepish.

'All right. Confession,' he said, cheerfully. 'I *was* going to tell you. Her name's Lindy. She says it's short for Lindbergh. We met at the flying club. We went climbing in Scotland in October and things took off rather. She's been rather badly let down herself, so we're not rushing it, but when we do name the day you'll be the first to know.'

'Oh Charles, what lovely, lovely news. That's the second piece in two days. I saw an old friend from home yesterday and she's getting married here in June. Perhaps we could meet up when I'm over for that.'

'Great, I'd like you to meet Lindy. They say good news goes in threes. That leaves you,' he said, looking at her meaningfully.

She smiled, offered him more coffee and refilled their cups.

'Oh, I've had my good news,' she said quickly. 'Do you remember I told you about Robert Lafarge losing his wife and daughter in 1940 when the Germans invaded?'

'Yes, yes I do. There was a son as well, but he'd never been able to trace him.'

'It looks as if he's found him,' she said, beaming. 'It's an extraordinary story, one way and another. Robert had no sooner signed on with the agency than they contacted him about a young man who'd approached them several months earlier. He'd been trying to find his father and he'd seen Robert's picture in a newspaper. The details fitted perfectly. The photographs the agency sent were so like Robert it was incredible. If he arrives back with half a dozen pictures for his collection, I wouldn't be surprised, he's so excited about it all,' she ended up, laughing.

'That really *is* splendid. I always felt rather sorry for old Lafarge. He's fond of you, but he must know darn well he'll lose you one of these fine days.'

'Yes, he does, but maybe not just yet. He's offered me a job on the financial side from next October.'

'Whee . . .' Charles shook his head and put down his coffee cup. 'My goodness, Clare, you *are* going it. Will you take it? Will I have to come and grovel if I need new lorries?'

She shook her head. 'I honestly don't know. It's a big vote of confidence, but I actually enjoy being

Robert's assistant, whether it involves translation or not. I certainly wouldn't leave Paris for one of the regional branches.'

She glanced out of the window and saw the snow had begun to fall again, big, soft flakes out of a grey sky. The trees in Park Lane were already lightly covered, the traffic throwing up wet spray where the feathery flakes had turned to slush.

'I'll think about it in the springtime, Charles. I always think better in the spring.'

CHAPTER TWENTY-FOUR

The spring of 1960 came for Clare, neither on the Champs Elysées with Louise, nor in the Bois de Boulogne with the St Clair family, but in the Dolomites, in a small skiing resort that turned itself into a conference centre as soon as the first of the snow began to melt. After three dull, cloudy days, well matched by the series of lectures Clare had endured, the sun suddenly appeared.

She could hardly believe it when she drew back her curtains and opened the shutters. Dazzling white, the mountains rose into a clear blue sky, but below their precipitous peaks, the upland meadows, still snow-covered the day she'd arrived, now emerged green and fresh, so close in the clear mountain air she felt she could lean out of her window and touch them.

She stood in her dressing gown, breathing in the sharpness of the air, feeling the warm touch of the sun on her face. A little way below her, between a pair of older wooden houses, she saw a narrow path leading up towards the high meadows. The cattle were still indoors, but a few days more and they would be moved up the path to their summer pastures.

She'd never been here in summer, but there'd been enticing pictures in the brochure advertising the financial management course that Robert had felt she should attend. It was the easiest thing in the world to imagine the meadows full of flowers, pink and yellow and blue, whose names she knew in English and French, German and Italian, but whose delicate blooms she'd never seen or touched.

Feeling a sadness she couldn't explain, she turned away reluctantly from the window, showered, dressed and collected up the folder of papers for the morning's seminar. It would no doubt be valuable. Like all the sessions she'd already sat through, it would focus on some aspect of the economic developments the Treaty of Rome had brought to Europe.

Given how quickly things were changing, it would be useful to know precisely what was going on in the other European countries. She would listen, make notes, ask pertinent questions, and wonder if she might hear the sound of cow bells before she flew back to Paris.

She breakfasted with an earnest young German who had a particular interest in iron and steel, escaped as soon as she decently could and walked down the road to the largest of the new hotels where those who skied by day danced at night. This week, however, its vast ballroom accommodated well-dressed students from every part of Europe. With the heavy curtains shutting out the sunlight, the only peaks in view were the projections of economists and financial experts.

As she came level with the little path, she glanced at her watch, crossed the road and walked a short way on its rough, frost-shattered surface. Despite her high heels and the slim skirt of her costume, only a few minutes away from the main street, she found she had stepped into a different world.

The tall gable of a shallow-roofed house cast a dark shadow on the path, so that she shivered in the crystalline air, but ahead of her, beyond its barns and outhouses and their sheltering trees, she could see the lowest of the meadows. A moment later, she moved out of the shadow, stepped off the path and stood on the edge of the soft, green grass, the sunlight pouring round her, its warmth like the comfort of an embrace.

The view was different than from her hotel bedroom, but the elements were the same, the high peaks soaring into the clear air, their swelling shoulders shining with melting snow, the lower slopes green, so strikingly green after the city streets and the lifeless, grey vistas of the last three days.

'I'll make up my mind in the springtime,' she said to herself, as she moved quickly back to join the last few hurrying figures on their way to begin work.

The first wisps of cloud floated past the cabin window. They were beginning to lose height already. This was the point when the brilliant, sunlit snowfields that still made her think of Canada were suddenly transformed into grey, enveloping murk. She hated this bit, trapped and enclosed, until land appeared and she heard the wheels come down.

'Ladies and gentlemen, we will shortly be arriving at Aldergrove Airport. Will you fasten your seatbelts and extinguish all cigarettes . . .'

She listened attentively to an unmistakably Ulster voice pronouncing the familiar words with as much care as if she were speaking a foreign language. At any other time, it would have made her smile. But not today.

As they sank through the cloud, she went over again the sequence of events that had brought her back to Ireland on an April morning when she should have been preparing for a visit to Lyons.

'Mam'selle, I regret there is a telegram. I hope it is not bad news.'

Perhaps it was the echo of that phrase 'mauvaises nouvelles', the sudden remembrance of her grandfather's death, or simply the look of distress on Madame's face as she put the envelope in her hand, but she felt a sudden wave of panic, an overwhelming sense that her life was about to fall to pieces.

All she remembered was ripping open the envelope and reading the short message.

'Jessie poorly. I need you badly. Please ring. Harry.'

Her hands had trembled so much, she'd dropped her address book on the floor when she went to find their home number. She'd phoned Harry when she'd been in London in February, but the last time she'd phoned Belfast from Paris was the morning her degree results came out. It still took an eternity of time to get through.

Jessie had been in bed for a week now. The gynaecologist had said there was no specific problem he could discover, but she was badly run down. Unless she built up her strength before her labour she might lose the child. That was bad enough, but what came over in waves as Clare listened to Harry was his real fear that he was going to lose Jessie herself.

The moment she put down the phone she unpacked her suitcase, sorted the contents and immediately repacked it. She'd thought of ringing Robert at home, but it was already late. There was nothing to be done before morning. She'd spent a long, restless night, short patches of dream-filled sleep alternating with hours of lying wide-eyed, going over and over every detail of her last visit to Belfast, all that had happened to Jessie since the evening when the four of them had dined together in the new home and Jessie had asked her and Andrew to be godparents to the coming baby.

She dressed for work as usual, but took her suitcase with her and went up to Robert's room as soon as Paul let her know he was in.

'You must go, of course,' he said, picking up his phone. 'Denise, book a flight to Belfast via London for Mam'selle 'Amilton, an open return for the first possible flight. Allow enough time for her to get to Orly by car.

'I think your dear Jessie may need you for some time, perhaps even until her child is born, which you say is maybe a month away. You must stay till then, if you feel it necessary. But keep me informed. I shall be concerned for you and for her. Write or telephone, whatever is convenient. Do you have any sterling?'

She admitted she hadn't even thought about money. Looking at him, as he stood by his desk, ready to do anything he could to help her, the tears sprang to her eyes. They dripped on the lapels of her moss-green costume, sitting on the surface of the close-textured fabric as if she'd been caught in a shower of rain.

'There now, my dear. It is hard for you. Take courage,' he said, as she took out a minute handkerchief from the equally minute pocket of her jacket. 'I have only a little knowledge of the problems of pregnancy, but there is one piece of advice I must give you. Keep up your spirits. Do not allow your own anxiety to take away your warmth, or your humour. These may be the medicines that Harry and Jessie have most need of,' he said, as he took her hand and held it for a moment.

'Bon voyage,' he continued, quietly. 'And a happy return. I shall miss you. I shall think of you. I may even light a candle for you. You will not mind that, will you?'

'I should like that, Robert,' she said, mopping her eyes again. 'I think I shall need all the help I can get. Thank you,' she said, leaning forward and kissing his cheek. 'I'll come back as soon as I can.'

By the time she'd walked down to reception, Paul was already waiting with a hundred pounds in sterling, an authorisation for setting up an English bank account for her to sign, and her suitcase. Denise had the number of the tickets awaiting her at the BEA desk at Orly.

While Robert's chauffeur brought the car to the front of the building, she ran back to her office, but Louise was already on the way to the banking hall to meet her. She'd spoken to Paul and had come to kiss her goodbye.

The plane's descent steepened. Only five hours ago, she'd been driving through Paris at the end of the morning rush hour. She saw below her now, in misting rain, a patchwork of tiny fields, the white shapes of cottages and farms slipping away under the wing. As the grey murk dissolved they made a wide sweep over Lough Neagh.

She stared out at the flat grey waters, calm in the light, drifting drizzle, and saw a cart track leading to a small beach, a framework of poles covered with nets hanging up to dry. It might be the place they had picnicked; it might be another beach just like it. After all the anxiety and distress, to her sudden surprise, she felt steadier than she'd felt at any time since yesterday's call to Harry.

The wheels touched the wet runway, the engines roared and they taxied towards the newly completed airport buildings. In the rich grass verges of the new runways, the hares scattered as the Vanguard moved past. A few minutes later, they resumed their interrupted feeding as if nothing whatever had happened.

In spite of all Harry had told her, Clare was still shocked when she saw Jessie propped up on her pillows. Earlier, Harry said, she'd tried to come downstairs to be there when she arrived, but the effort was too much for her. She'd had to go back to bed.

'Hallo, Jessie,' she said gently, as Harry pushed open the bedroom door. 'Harry said you weren't feeling great.'

Ginny's scars had been hard to bear, but she found the paleness of Jessie's face and the blue smudges under her eyes every bit as bad. She heard Harry slip out of the room behind her. She moved closer to the limp figure lying back on the pillows and saw tears streaming down her face.

'What is it, love? What's wrong? Tell me what's wrong,' she said, perching on the side of the bed and putting her arms round her.

'I think I'm goin' to die, an' what'll Harry do wi' wee Fiona?' she sobbed, clutching Clare as if she'd never let her go.

'Who said anything about dying, Jessie? Who told you that?'

'Oh, nobody says it, but they're all that nice to me, the doctors and the nurse that comes. An' I feel so awful. I'm sure I'm goin' to die.'

'And I'm absolutely certain you're not,' said Clare firmly. 'If you go and die on me, I'll never forgive you.'

Jessie stopped sobbing and looked up at her for the first time. 'What makes you think that?'

'Think what?'

'That I won't die.'

442

'Sure you know only the good die young,' she replied matter-of-factly. 'Unless you've got religion since I went away, I'd have said you were safe as houses.'

Jessie stopped crying. Her eyes were still wet, her face thin and peaky, her lovely, wavy brown hair, lank and unwashed, but a touch of the old Jessie suddenly broke through as she grinned and said, 'Yer lookin' great. Ye diden buy that suit at C&A's, did ye?'

Clare laughed and the moment she did, Jessie laughed too. Coming up stairs with a tray of tea, Harry couldn't believe his ears.

'What's the joke?' he asked.

'Go on, show him,' said Jessie, poking Clare with surprising vigour. 'Take it off an' show him.'

Clare stood up and slid off the jacket of her costume, turning it so that Harry could read the label.

'I thought they made perfume,' he said vaguely, as he looked round the room for somewhere to put down the tray.

'Would ye listen to him, Clare,' she said, raising her eyes heavenwards in a familiar gesture. 'That, Harry,' she said, pointing to the label, 'is a famous dress designer, and Madam here said in one of her letters he makes all the overalls for her firm. Could ye believe her?'

* * *

Clare slept well that night, whether from relief or sheer exhaustion, she couldn't tell, but she woke early next morning and tried to think through what she ought to do. Jessie was indeed in a bad way, but something had changed since her last visit. Then, she'd been physically well but abstracted, totally preoccupied with Fiona. She'd often been sharp with Clare, reluctant to sit down and talk. This time, she was very unwell, but in many ways she was much more the direct and affectionate Jessie she had once known.

'She told me the other day you were the only one who could help her,' said Harry, as they washed up together later that evening. 'Did she say why, Harry?'

'No, I couldn't get her to say another word. I don't think she knew herself, to tell you the truth.'

'And the gynaecologist and the doctor have no suggestions?'

'The doctor said it might be some personal matter. He suggested our minister of religion,' he said, raising an eyebrow.

'How did that go down?'

'Not well,' he said, shaking his head. 'But I tried. I've tried everything, Clare,' he said, a dangerous catch in his voice.

'I know you have, Harry,' she said reassuringly. 'Now look, if she says I can help her, then probably somehow or other I can, even if I'm just as in the dark as you are. But we've got to keep our spirits up. That's the advice my boss gave me before I left. Let's make up our minds it's going to be all right, and see what we can do. How about it?'

'Whatever you say, Clare. You're the boss this time. I'll do whatever you tell me.'

The week that followed was one of the grimmest Clare had ever spent. Each morning Jessie would wake up in despair and lie weeping till Clare came and sent Harry off to make his own breakfast. Each morning, she'd talk to her, encourage her, help her to do her hair, put on make-up. By afternoon, Jessie was in good spirits, able to get up, play with Fiona when her grandmother brought her to visit, eat a proper meal in the evening. But next morning, the despair had returned as if nothing were any different.

There was nausea and sickness, as there had been in the first pregnancy, but the medical problems paled beside Jessie's fears and anxieties. That was the heart of the problem. It was just so unlike Jessie to be fearful.

Clare spent many a quiet night hour trying to think what could have triggered such a change. She talked to Harry, who said all had gone well enough till after Fiona's birth. He'd asked the doctor about post-natal depression, but the doctor said he didn't think the symptoms fitted the pattern. That was when he'd suggested they consult their minister of religion. They both knew there was no way forward there. After enduring church every Sunday morning when she was in Armagh, a 'dog-collar' was the last person Jessie would ever talk to.

Try as she would, Clare couldn't see anything that Harry or the doctors had missed. She talked to him about Jessie's father's death. He assured her she spoke of her father quite naturally, though not very often. That was hardly surprising, for he'd been away for so long in the war, he'd played a very small part in her life.

Each day, Clare set out hopefully, trying to find something to fill up the bottomless well of despair. One day, Jessie confessed she was afraid she'd lost her looks and that Harry would go off with someone else, so Clare washed and set her hair, made up her face, insisted she wear a dress instead of a nightie. When her mother came up from Armagh to visit that afternoon, Clare took a bus into town and bought Jessie a bottle of perfume, a box of handmade chocolates and some peaches from Sawyers.

She was so preoccupied with thoughts of Jessie, it was only on the way back from the city centre she registered where she was. The bus had just stopped outside Queen's. She watched as crowds of students poured across the pedestrian crossing. A moment later, peering out of her window, down Elmwood Avenue, she just glimpsed the bay of her old room, still visible, because the trees here in Belfast were only just coming into leaf, unlike those she'd left behind on the quay by the Seine.

Suddenly and passionately, she wished she were back in Paris, having coffee under the trees in the Champs-Elysées with Louise, or in the Bois de Boulogne with Marie-Claude, or sitting by the window of Robert's office, under the watchful eye of the chestnut mare.

That was when the solution came to her at last. Jessie was lonely. She'd been lonely since she'd had to leave the gallery. She was sure that was what it was. Harry was Harry, the dearest of men, but beyond him, who had Jessie got to share her thoughts, or her life?

Then, a more chilling thought struck her. It was just when Jessie had to leave the gallery, that she and Andrew had parted. They had been Jessie and Harry's closest friends. A week later, she herself had gone off to Paris and shown no signs of ever coming back.

Pregnancy had taken Jessie out of the gallery, where she so enjoyed talking to customers. Later, illness shut her up at home and little Fiona had to be parked round the corner at her grandmother's. Who had Jessie to talk to? Who was her Louise? Her Marie-Claude? Her Robert? Who was there with whom Jessie could be the self she'd been before marriage, pregnancy, motherhood and illness had changed her life?

'What about Jessie's sketching and painting?' she asked herself.

It struck her that she'd not seen so much as a pad of paper about the house, never mind watercolours, or oils. She recalled how totally dismissive Jessie had been when she'd mentioned the subject the last time she was over.

Suddenly, the hills appeared beyond the end of Balmoral Avenue. What a joy it always was to look up and see them, the broad strip of ordinary fields and hedges still surviving, sandwiched between the housing estates on the lower slopes and the angular screes and fierce rock outcrops that marked the summit ridge. How often she'd gazed up at them, in sunshine and in rain, old friends and companions that always reminded her of the countryside not so very far away, even when her work kept her shut up in rooms and lecture theatres in the city.

She stood up quickly, laughed at herself, as she picked up her parcels and made her way to the back of the bus. She'd gone on three stops beyond the stop for Jessie's road.

It was no matter. Her parcels were light and her heels not very high. It would be a pleasure to stroll back under the trees. She felt such a longing for the countryside – Italian countryside, French countryside or Ulster countryside, it didn't seem to matter which, just so long as it was countryside, with wind, sun or rain. Firmly, she put the thought out of mind as she quickened her step. No thinking about that until Jessie was back on her feet again.

Two weeks after Clare's arrival, just as she was beginning to doubt the value of all her efforts, Jessie announced she'd love to go out to lunch if they could find somewhere with big holes cut out of the tables. It was the sign Clare had been waiting for. They had an excellent meal. Jessie tackled it like her old self, and by the time they got to coffee she'd even begun to tease Clare in her old way.

Clare sat up late that night, writing a long letter to Robert. She shared with him her feeling that it was the radical changes in Jessie's life that had almost overwhelmed her. Because everything had gone so well for her from the moment she met Harry, poor dear Jessie just hadn't been prepared for the unhappinesses and disappointments that had come upon her. 'Perhaps,' she wrote, 'it is easier to face adversity if you know that's what you're doing. I don't think Jessie could see she had a problem. So she couldn't begin to deal with it.'

The first week in May was the date given for the birth of Jessie's child. It was now the third week in April. Doctor and gynaecologist agreed that the longer Jessie could carry her child the better. She'd begun to put on weight and they expected the child to do likewise. Clare rifled through all the cookery books she could find, searching for recipes that would encourage her to eat more. She was actually thinking what she might cook for dinner the following evening, when Harry made a proposal that caught her completely unawares.

'How would you girls like a little outing tomorrow?' he said, as they were drinking coffee in the sitting room. 'I've got some calls to do up around Armagh. You could visit home territory, the scenes of your former conquests.'

'Fine, count me in,' said Jessie promptly. 'I'll produce Number Two tonight, leave it with Granny tomorrow, and be ready for the road by nine. That's if my lady-in-waiting can have my make-up and hair done by then.'

Harry looked at her blankly, hardly able to believe she could move back into her old self so completely. He laughed and looked sheepish.

'Sorry, love, I suppose that was silly. The car makes you feel sick, doesn't it?'

'Oh, no. I'm grand, but it doesn't like it. It wants to stay at home. But I'll be fine on my own. Mrs D's here anyway. You must take Clare. She hasn't been anywhere since she came. Are you for Drumsollen?'

Clare was so taken aback at the sudden question, she nearly spilled her coffee.

In the last week, they'd talked about everything

450

that had been part of their life together except Andrew, till suddenly, one morning, Jessie herself brought up his name.

'D'you think you did the right thing when you broke it off, Clare? He was desperate cut up, Harry says. I didn't see him meself at the time. He's not been up in Belfast much since ye went. Has he got anyone else d'ye think?'

'I really don't know, Jessie. He's working in Armagh now, but that's about all I do know.'

'I still think he's yer man. I always did,' she said, a look of such sadness on her face that Clare was immediately on the alert. 'Sure I never thought you'd go to Canada. Or if ye did, ye'd be back in no time and we'd wheel our prams down the road together.'

As the implications of what Jessie was saying dawned upon her, she had a very bad moment. Perhaps that was why Jessie had been so distant, so unwelcoming, a year ago. She blamed her for going away and breaking up that small circle of support she'd been relying on to see her through.

'Well, I'll tell you what, Jessie,' Clare had said, recovering herself and seeing an opportunity. 'If you do what you're told and eat up like a good girl and produce another lovely little Burrows, I'll contact Andrew before I go back and see if we can still be friends. Then we could be godparents to

Number Two. How about that? Don't say I don't try to meet you halfway.'

'You're on. Before witnesses. I'll tell Harry tonight.'

Harry was much more sympathetic than Jessie when Clare admitted she didn't want to run into Andrew without warning. She'd really had too much on her mind to think how she wanted to go about a first meeting. Driving up to Armagh, he reassured her that Andrew was never at Drumsollen during the week. Their arrangement was for Harry to call when June Wiley was there and she'd help him pack whatever he'd left out ready. Harry had told June he was hoping to bring Clare up and June had been delighted. It would be a pity to disappoint her.

Thus reassured, Clare sat back and enjoyed the gentle April morning. While she'd been so totally preoccupied with Jessie, spring had finally reached Ulster. The warmth of the last few days had sprayed the hedgerows with green, the chestnuts were fully dressed and even the oaks, always the slowest to wake from winter, were showing tender leaves on lightly-clothed branches in the pale morning sun.

Clare felt her spirits rise. It was such joy to be in her own beloved countryside again, driving along familiar roads, looking forward to seeing such a dear old friend as June Wiley. When Harry said he'd drop her at Drumsollen, come back to collect her and the pictures when he'd done his other calls, she was happy to agree. She wouldn't let him drive her up to the house, but insisted he drop her off by the gates.

She stood and waved to him as he drove off into Armagh, crossed the empty road and looked down into the stream, the tiny trickle of water in its deep ravine, where she and Jessie once talked secrets. The willows and alders had grown up too much to see their old sitting place, but the steep slope down to the water's edge was unchanged. The bustling flow of the brown water was as it had always been.

'When we're old we'll have a whole team of fellas to lower us down on ropes,' Jessie had once said.

Clare sat on the low wall of the bridge, thinking of her, watching the sunlight filter through the new leaves and reflect back from the rippling water. They may have been country children, but their life was not the idyll celebrated in glowing reminiscences. Growing up hadn't been easy either. Their paths appeared so totally different, yet in the end, they'd both had to face despair and anxiety and learn to accept that none of us manage very well on our own. As Robert Lafarge had once admitted, if we try, we become distant, withdrawn and closed in upon ourselves.

She sat for a little longer, grateful to be alone, the

sun warm on her face, her mind moving between past and present. She let it go where it wished, recalling memories, thoughts, images. The lane to the forge on a summer morning, beaded with dew, the russet of vine leaves on a hillside in France. The sound of cow bells in an alpine meadow. Feeling suddenly such a quiet sense of well being, she stood up and walked across the road to the gates of Drumsollen, standing open and lit up by the bright morning sun.

CHAPTER TWENTY-FIVE

Having always cycled or been driven along the sweeping curve that led to Drumsollen, the walk was further than she thought. But the morning was so still, the sunlight so beautiful, that when at last she reached the wide sweep of gravel before the front door, she was reluctant to go inside. She stood looking around her for a long time. She sensed something different about the house. It seemed less forbidding, more welcoming.

Without pausing to consider, she walked round the back of the house and stepped cautiously down the steep stone steps that led into the basement rooms. She opened the door, caught the smell of fresh paint, saw light reflecting from newly whitened walls. As her high heels echoed on the wooden floor, a door swung open and June Wiley came to meet her, arms outstretched.

'Ach dear, it's great to see you,' June said, hugging her tightly. 'I was listening for Mr Burrow's car an' then I heard this wee noise at the back, an'

I thinks to myself, "sure no one else wou'd come to the back but Clarey." Come an' sit down, I have the kettle on the boil.'

They sat at the scrubbed wooden table and talked as they'd so often done before. Clare thought of all the hours they had worked together, the hundreds of cakes June had baked, the sandwiches she herself had made, the two funeral gatherings they'd shared and would never forget.

'Was it a big do for the Missus, June?'

'Ach, no. It was kinda sad really. I think a lot o' them older ones must've died themselves in the last year or two before the Missus went. Mrs Richardson and the husband came – Mrs Moore she is now, I should say – but Virginia wasn't home. To be honest, there was only a handful. There's really no one left now but Andrew,' she said, looking away quickly.

'Harry says he's well,' said Clare easily, to reassure her. 'I'm going to get in touch with him next week. I've promised Jessie we'll meet up and see if we can be friends. She wants us to be godparents to the new baby. We let her down on the first one,' she said matter-of-factly.

'It was an awful shock,' June admitted, shaking her head. 'D'ye think it was the right thing? I suppose I shouldn't ask ye that.'

'Ask away, June. Haven't you known us both since we were children? But I'm not sure I can answer you. I think it had to be, but it was a pity it happened as it did.'

'Ye were that fond of each other, it was plain to see. Sure, when ye's come here to arrange for Uncle Edward's funeral, he coud hardly bear to let ye out of his sight. He couden a done it at all, if ye haden been there at his back.'

Clare nodded, but said nothing. She'd often thought about Andrew's vulnerability, his difficulty with thinking problems out and making up his mind when things were complicated. 'You think about everything, all the time,' he had once said to her. 'Sometimes I don't, when I should.'

'When did the kitchen get painted, June? Ginny thought the house was being sold.'

'Oh yes, it'll have to go all right, but Andrew's been working on it at weekends for a long time now. Since he got the job in Armagh. If he didn't have things to see to at Caledon, he'd be here, working away. Did ye see the front steps and the porch? Dangerous with all that green on them, he said, so he got stuff and cleaned it. Made a great job of it. Sometimes John gives him a hand, though of course he works for Robinson's now.'

Clare was just about to enquire about John and the three Wiley girls when they heard tyres crunch on the gravel. June looked up, saw it was only just after twelve.

'That's never Mr Burrows back so soon,' she

said disbelievingly. 'An' I haven't even started to make a bite of lunch yet.'

They heard the front door open and shut with its usual heavy thud and felt the old ceilings of the kitchen vibrate slightly as footsteps strode across the hall and into the big drawing room.

'Ach, it's him all right. He's away in to look at the pictures. Woud ye go an' tell him I was gossipin' so much I haven't even a sandwich ready yet. Away an' give him a hand to pack them,' she said, as she took a sliced loaf from the bin and opened the door of the fridge.

Clare went upstairs and paused for a moment in the big hall. There were pale spaces on the wall left by the pictures that had already gone, but the chandelier she'd always loved still hung in its usual place, sparkling in the sunlight which filtered through the fan-light over the door and tinkling slightly from the passage of air as the door opened and closed.

She heard the sound of movement from the drawing room and went towards the open door. A figure stood with his back to her, looking up at a portrait hung over the fireplace. As she stepped into the room, he turned and spoke her name, his voice tight with surprise.

'Hello, Andrew,' she managed to reply, coolly and steadily, amazed at how easily the words came out after all. 'I was planning to give you a ring next week. Harry thought you were in court today, so I came to see June.'

She watched as his look of pure amazement turned to recognition, then to uneasy pleasure.

'Are you home on holiday?'

'No. I *was* planning a holiday in the summer, but Jessie's been very poorly. Harry asked me to come,' she explained. 'She's much better now.'

She walked across to an armchair by the fireplace and sat down. The last time she'd sat in this room, she had been perched on that terribly low chair beside the Missus, holding court at Uncle Edward's funeral.

Andrew leaned against the mantelpiece. For a moment, they regarded each other silently. Andrew smiled a slight half smile.

'To meet here, of all places,' he said, shaking his head.

'Where better?' she replied quietly. 'Though I certainly didn't plan it,' she added more vigorously. 'Harry said you were never here during the week.'

'Harry's quite right,' he said, grinning. 'I should've been in Belfast today, but the plaintiff decided to settle out of court. I only heard when I went in to pick up the post. Then I got a message at five to twelve to be here at twelve for Mr Burrows,' he said, opening his hands in a gesture that reminded her of the Gallic shrug he could mimic so beautifully.

'I can think of one prime suspect,' she said, as he came and sat down in the chair opposite, the only other armchair in the large, sun-lit room that was not draped in dust covers.

She looked at him, taking in the familiar features, his way of stretching out in a chair, of putting his hand round to the back of his neck, of leaning his shoulders against the worn leather. She felt waves of relief flow over her. If it *was* Jessie who'd brought them together, perhaps she'd got it right after all. Here at Drumsollen, the place that had shaped so much of Andrew's life and so much of their relationship, they had to resolve what had begun at its very gates, in one way or another.

'How's life treating you, Andrew? Is the job going any better?' she asked, meeting his gaze.

The face seemed a little thinner, but the blue eyes had lost none of their candour. His hair was the same thick, wavy and undisciplined mass.

'It goes. It's not what I want, but it pays the rent and sometimes I can help someone who's had a raw deal,' he replied. 'I don't expect too much so I'm not disappointed.'

'And the farming?'

'Fairly unlikely at the moment. Perhaps one day. It's not a fantasy, but making it a reality is probably more than I can manage. I'm not good with money, though I seem to be more practical than I thought I was,' he said, matter-of-factly.

'You've certainly done a wonderful job on the kitchen,' she agreed.

After the first easy words between them, she was now aware of a growing tension. She had not the slightest idea how she might resolve it.

'And you, Clare? I hear great things from Ginny. I knew you'd be successful whatever you did. Are you having a wonderful time?'

'Yes, I suppose I am,' she said, surprised herself at the flatness of her tone. 'I think I sometimes get homesick,' she said honestly, 'though I'm not entirely sure what that means.'

'Longing,' he said, promptly. 'Nameless longing. At least that's how I see it now. I've come to realise I've been homesick for Drumsollen most of my life. Now it's mine, for however brief a time, I still feel the longing,' he admitted wryly. 'At least I know Drumsollen stands for a part of what I want. And knowing makes it easier to bear. It came as a surprise to me,' he said, looking at her very directly. 'Knowing what you want when you can't have it is easier to bear than just not knowing what you want. At least it stops you reaching out for things you think might help, but won't. Like Canada.'

'Why was Canada wrong for you, Andrew?'

'Because I hoped I'd be able to escape all my confusions and make up my mind about things. But when Uncle Edward died and everything was such an enormous effort for me, I was afraid I'd never be able to make the right decisions. I thought I'd only let you down. That's why I let you go,' he said, sadly. 'Was I right?'

'You were right to let me go,' she said, smiling bleakly, 'but not because you couldn't make decisions. If two people work together, decisions can always be made,' she said softly. 'But I had things I needed to find out about me and I didn't know that till I went. You'd been around, seen things, done things. I hadn't. I'd felt so limited, so enclosed. I thought I could do it the easy way too: go off to Canada with you and have all the new experiences I needed with the comfort of having you around at the same time. But it wasn't that simple. I found out I had to do it on my own. Perhaps you had to, as well?'

'Yes,' he said simply. 'I thought if I worked hard, it would all come right, but it's not like that. No amount of work will solve a problem if you've got the wrong problem,' he said wryly. 'There was more out against us than we could have guessed.'

He paused, looked around the room as if it would help him to know what to say next.

'But better things ahead, yes?' he went on, his tone and manner giving away the fact that he was making a tremendous effort to be positive.

So there is someone, Clare thought, as she saw him move uneasily in the large, straight-backed wing chair the Missus had always claimed as her own. She felt suddenly overcome with sadness. In the short time they'd sat together, it was perfectly clear they could be very good friends. Whatever bitterness he'd felt at their parting had quite gone. He'd made the best of a sorry situation. Like herself, he'd worked his way through to a better understanding of what had happened between them. Jessie would have her wish. They would be friends. But no more than friends.

'When are you getting married, Clare?'

'Married?' she repeated, utterly amazed 'Me? Who told you I was getting married?'

'Well, Ginny did say there was someone in London waiting to take you out to dinner in some frightfully posh place,' he confessed uneasily. 'She said he sent in a note to tell you when the car would collect you.'

Clare laughed and breathed a sigh of relief.

'That was my boss, Andrew. I'm his interpreter. Mostly, I never leave his side, but he'd given me the afternoon off to spend with Ginny. We had a big business dinner in the evening.'

'Oh.'

She had never before heard a single syllable in any language convey such a wealth of meaning.

'So you're not engaged to anyone?'

'No, I'm not.'

The last few minutes had told her everything

she needed to know about her own feelings, but this time there must be no misunderstandings.

'What about you, Andrew?'

'Me? Marrying someone, you mean?'

'Don't sound so outraged,' she said, unable to stop herself laughing. 'If I might have been about to marry someone, why shouldn't you?'

'Do you *really* want to know?'

There was no mistaking the look in his eyes. For one strange and disturbing moment, like a reminder of all the sad and lonely times she'd had since first she'd read Ginny's letter and thought of Andrew 'sad and hurt', she wondered if she really did want the answer she knew he was going to make.

'Yes, Andrew,' she said firmly, 'I *do* want to know.'

'I've never loved anyone but you, Clare. I've not much to offer, but I'd do my best not to make a mess of things, if you'd try to keep me straight. If that's any good to you, then I'm your man.'

Sunlight spilled into the small bedroom at the top of the house as it moved westwards across the weathered stone facade of Drumsollen. It made bright patches on the worn carpet, illuminated the titles on a pile of boys' annuals stacked on the floor, and spilled over a battered armchair draped with discarded underwear and two business suits, one moss green, one grey. Beneath a shiny pink eiderdown, one of two sleeping figures stirred.

'Clare, are you awake?'

'No, I'm fast asleep. I'm having a lovely dream.'

He leaned over and kissed her. When she still didn't open her eyes, he protested. 'You're supposed to wake up when your Prince fights his way through the briar hedge and kisses you.'

She giggled and opened her eyes.

'Have you fought your way through briar hedges, then?'

'Yes, I think you could say I have. Very dense they were, too. I thought you might like to see what I'd been up to on the property of which you are presently mistress, if only for a little while.'

She rolled over and propped herself on one elbow.

'Andrew, why do you want to sell Drumsollen?'

He laughed shortly.

'Oh, I thought I'd prefer a nice three-bed semi.'

She looked at him severely, then relented and kissed him.

'Come on, tell me properly. I tried to find out from Ginny, but she's not exactly the most accurate informant, especially not when she's in love.'

He smiled and stroked her shoulder.

'I don't have much choice, Clare. In fact, when I tell you how bad things are, you may not want to accept my offer for your hand,' he said, trying to be light. 'Until The Lodge is sold, I'm up to my ears in debt. Unless I can hang on long enough and get the necessary work done, it's not going to fetch enough to clear the mortgages on top of the death duties. My partner in Armagh has been a real friend. If it hadn't been for him, I'd have let it go for what I could get and landed myself in real trouble. I just can't keep up the work on The Lodge and cope with this place as well.'

'Is there a mortgage on Drumsollen?'

'No, I tried to raise one for Ginny, but they wouldn't have it, given my erratic income. It was Ginny who lent Teddy the money for the roof here when it had to be done, so she'd no money of her own when she most needed it,' he said matter-of-factly. 'Apart from the said roof, there are other bits of Drumsollen ready to fall down and I've got nothing to prop them up with, except a pile of bills for The Lodge.'

'Sounds like you need some short-term capital input and a longer term loan,' she said thoughtfully. 'Shouldn't be difficult, given the available collateral and the general economic upswing.'

He looked at her blankly, not sure he knew what she was talking about.

'But, Clare, no bank here would touch me with a barge pole,' he said flatly. 'I'm certain of that. I've tried.'

'I wasn't thinking of you,' she said. 'I was

466

thinking of me. And it would be a French bank, probably the one where I have my investments.'

'Investments? Clare, you're joking. You have to be joking.'

'I'm not.'

Andrew laughed, and then looked at her seriously.

'No, my love, I can see that you're not. And it doesn't really surprise me. Do you remember Jessie once telling you that if you ever worked for a bank you'd make their fortune?'

'I'd forgotten all about that,' she said, amazed he should have remembered.

'But Clare, my love, doesn't your having investments make things worse? Here am I with nothing to offer you except myself and a load of debts. How can I possibly ask you to give up the life you have?'

He propped himself on one elbow. 'Come and share my encumbered estate, my often boring job, my fish and chips and baked beans,' he said soberly. 'Clare, it just wouldn't be fair,' he ended sadly.

'But life isn't fair, Andrew. Not in the way we expect it to be. You inherit an estate and for all your hard work, you're short of money. I hadn't a bean, except what Harry lent me, and I end up with more money than I ever dreamed of and some collateral I haven't even told you about yet. But if we put the two together we could make something good.'

'Do you really think so?'

'I know so.'

'How do you know?'

'Because I know I can trust you to do your best and to let me do mine. You've always done your best, Andrew, ever since I've known you, but you weren't given many options. I worked hard too, but no one got in my way. I may have been badly off, but at least I was able to make my own decisions. You just had to get stuck in with a mess you'd inherited. Where would Ginny be without what you did for her? And Barney and Helen? Neither of them would ever have coped with The Lodge having to go. It's time *you* had some choices.'

He grinned sheepishly.

'Poor old Ginny, she did have a bad time. Don't know how I'd have coped without that psychiatrist chappie.'

'Yes, but you found him and you found the money for his bills,' she said vigorously.

'Yes, I did. But I still don't see how I can ask you to give up all you have and come and marry me.'

'But you don't have to ask me to give anything up. I've done what I needed to do. It's given me so much. I've made some dear friends. But it's time for me to move on. I want to make a life here, with you, and the little green hills.'

'You really mean that, don't you,' he said, surprised.

She nodded vigorously, clear at last about the meaning of all the images that had come to her in the years she'd been away. From those daisies on the edge of the vineyard near Nimes, to the alpine pastures of the Dolomites, she'd been prompted time and time again. But the most potent prompt of all had been given to her on the turret of the château at Chirey. No wonder the words had come so easily, though she didn't know then that they were true.

'And for my next problem?' he said, teasingly.

'Right,' she replied.

'Have you kept up with the radical changes in the social and economic structure of your beloved province?'

'Yes, I have. Armagh Rural Council plans to replace its condemned houses within thirty years.'

'You didn't read that in *Le Monde*, did you?'

'No. Charlie Running told me when I was over last year. But Ronnie still keeps me posted. I've no illusions, Andrew. We may yet have to go on our travels. But at least we could try. What d'you think?'

'There is nothing in the world I would like more than you and me making a life together, wherever that might be. But I'd love if we could start at Drumsollen. Do you really think we could?'

'Yes, we can. I'll show you how when I've got a sheet of paper. But not just yet. We don't have to do sums in bed, do we?'

He lay down and shut his eyes.

'Don't wake me up. I'm having a lovely dream. You *and* Drumsollen. Could I bear so much happiness?' he said, opening his eyes and looking up at her.

'We could try. I think you'll survive the strain.'

'I don't know about you, but I'm starving,' Andrew said, as he came back from the bathroom and began to put on his socks.

'They say making love burns up an awful lot of calories,' she said, sitting up and laughing. 'That sandwich disappeared hours ago.'

'We could see what there is. Should be eggs at least.'

'And there's some sliced loaf,' she added, as he pulled on the rest of his clothes and left his dressing gown on the bed for her.

They had scrambled eggs on toast at the kitchen table and then made coffee.

'When do I have to part with you?' he asked, as he filled up her cup.

'Depends a bit on Jessie,' she said thoughtfully. 'If she's as pleased to see you tonight as I think she's going to be, it's probably safe to leave her. We could have the weekend together before I go.'

'That would be wonderful.'

She sipped her coffee and thought about Paris, about Robert and Louise and her life there. Of course it would be hard. Anything of any value is hard to part with.

'I could give a month's notice, but I think I need a bit longer. If I came back in August, we could be married in September. Would you still like a country wedding?'

'Grange Church?' he said, smiling.

'Yes, please. And only our nearest and dearest.'

He nodded vigorously.

'If I stay in Paris till August, you could come over for a holiday in June or July,' she went on, thinking how delighted Madame Dubois would be that she had at last produced a lover. 'I want you to meet Robert Lafarge. He'll love your Breton accent. Actually, I'd like him to give me away, if that's all right with you. Who will you have as best man?'

'Oh, my partner, John Creaney. He's been such a good friend. Heaven knows what would have happened if he hadn't known the ropes for keeping me out of jail.'

Clare laughed, leaned over and kissed him.

'Now it's my turn for the lovely dream. I can't believe it. This morning I was sitting here talking to June. Now we're planning our wedding. Can it really all happen so quickly?'

'Well, we did work on it for a long time,' he said thoughtfully.

'And then we worked on ourselves.'

'Yes, I suppose that's what makes it all so easy. We know what we want and what we can't have and what to do about it.'

'Speaking of which, have you got a sheet of paper?'

They finished their coffee and sat side by side at the scrubbed wooden table while Clare sketched out a financial plan for The Lodge and Drumsollen.

'Well, that's quite incredible,' he said, when she finished. 'Jessie was right. But you did say there'd have to be collateral for the development loan.'

She nodded.

'Do you remember the small gift the Missus promised me?'

'Yes, a brooch wasn't it? I never saw it. I just passed on her note to the solicitors so you'd know it was meant for you and not as a wedding present if you married me. I think they had it in a safe deposit.'

Clare suddenly thought of the night in Paris when Madame had brought the small packet to her door, the sheet of paper with the solicitor's letter folded and creased to fit round the small box. That strange moment when she thought it was her engagement ring.

'It was an emerald brooch, Andrew. There's a story to tell about her and about the emerald itself and where it came from, but the main thing is I had it valued a few weeks ago.'

472

She told him the amount and he whistled.

'So the Missus has given us back Drumsollen. That's our collateral,' she said quietly, as she saw the look of relief and joy spread across his face.

For a moment he sat so still, his face so immobile, his eyes downcast, that she thought he might cry. She hugged him and kissed his cheeks, feeling tears come to her own eyes. No one could give him back the home he had lost when his parents died, but having Drumsollen returned to him, with someone to help him make a new life there, would do much to heal the old hurt. The thought came to her that in healing his hurt she would probably heal her own.

'Why don't I take you on a tour of works in hand,' he said. 'I've had a go at grandfather's conservatory. June has some fuchsias in there. And I've done up the morning room,' he began, as he collected up their plates and took them to the sink.

'Actually, on second thoughts, why don't we go outside first while the sun is still shining. We can do inside any time.'

They went out through the front door, and followed the sweeping curve of the drive to the point where a gravel path led off under a wrought-iron arch and began to climb steeply to the highest point of the low, rounded hill that hid all but the chimneys of Drumsollen from the Loughgall Road.

The slope was steeper than Clare had imagined, and even at the end of the April afternoon the sun had real warmth in its rays. They climbed slowly, hand in hand, pausing every so often to look back at the changing perspective on the house and the surrounding landscape.

Nearest to the house, the lower slopes of the hill were planted with clumps of daffodils, now in full bloom. As they climbed higher, Clare's eye caught the pale, green-grey buds of honeysuckle, just beginning to unfold, on a trellis by the path. All around, in the still air, binds fluttered and scuffled. A large jackdaw passed over-head, a stick in its mouth, heading for the trees beyond the house.

'I don't think you've ever been up here before, have you?'

'No, I haven't.'

At the top of the climb, a wooden summer house looked out across the Drumsollen farmland to the north and west, its roof recently repaired, the elegant wrought-iron weather vane newly cleaned and painted.

'Andrew, I had no idea,' she said, as she ran her eye around the full sweep of the horizon, her voice breathless from the climb and the excitement of seeing her world suddenly opened up and spread out all round her.

Beyond the fields and meadows, the wooded hollows and the winding lanes of the adjoining townlands, she could just see the silver-blue acres of Lough Neagh, its unruffled surface sparkling in the low, late afternoon sunlight. Away to the west, the hills of Tyrone and Derry swelled up, layer beyond layer, higher and higher, till the eyes could no longer resolve the difference between the misty tones of the farthest ridges and the infinitely more distant bands of low grey-blue cloud.

Clare scanned every inch of the horizon. For a moment, her eyes rested on the little parish church of Grange, its spire a thin pencil in the arc of the sky. Suddenly, she remembered a morning, aeons ago, when she had climbed a ladder and stood steadying herself against the roof of the forge and saw Drumsollen alight with the morning sun.

Tears sprang to her eyes. Her beloved forge was gone, but its memory was hers to cherish for ever. In its place, Drumsollen itself. Perhaps 'the hill in the sun' was what the name really meant. No one could be sure. Her life had been full of puzzles and mysteries she couldn't resolve, but what was no longer a puzzle was the love they had for each other. Nor was her immediate future any mystery.

She glanced again at the spire of Grange Church, in whose lengthening shadow Robert and five generations of Scotts lay buried. It would be a happy wedding, a meeting of friends old and new. And afterwards they would drive back to Drumsollen to celebrate, and chase the old sad ghosts out of the house and launch it and them into a new life.

'Would you like a wedding ring?' she asked, as a thought came to her.

'If you'd like to give me one,' he replied, turning towards her.

'We've got two wedding rings in Harry's safe,' she said, smiling.

'And your engagement ring,' he added. 'Unless you'd like something different.'

She shook her head vigorously. 'Perhaps those rings were meant for us after all.'

He put his arm round her shoulders and they watched the shadows lengthen over the fields laid out below them. She moved closer to him and felt the comforting warmth of his body as the air began to chill.

With someone to love who loved her, she'd always be able to make a life, no matter how hard things were. And this was the place she needed to be.

'Look, Clare, you can even see the mountains of Donegal,' he said, gazing into the far distance. 'Beyond your beloved green hills.'

ACKNOWLEDGEMENTS

I am grateful, as always, to my agent Judith Murdoch for help and encouragement. It was she who suggested I continue Clare's story from *On A Clear Day* before I set out on the historical journey which took me back to 1861 and *The Woman from Kerry*, the story of Clare's great-grandmother which leads on into the twentieth century and returns to Clare and Andrew in the 1960.

My friends at the Irish Studies Centre, Armagh, have helped me once again and my husband, sister and closest friends have done some of the research I would have done myself had I been able to use my own legs.

Those who wrote to me and commented so generously on my earlier novels encouraged me greatly when writing proved to be very difficult, but my greatest debt, this time, must certainly be to the lovely people at Musgrave Park Hospital, Belfast, who gave me a second new hip so that I can once again walk my beloved green hills.